SMILING
FACELESS
WOMAN

SMILING FACELESS WOMAN

The following novel is a work of fiction. All characters depicted as well as names, places and events mentioned are created from the author's imagination for story purposes. Any resemblance to persons living or dead, or to places or events past or present, is entirely coincidental.

This 1st edition has been catalogued with the Library of Congress.

Library of Congress Control Number: 2025907049

ISBN:
979-8-9857160-4-7 E-Book
979-8-9857160-5-4 Paperback

Publisher Ghoti
Honolulu, Hawaii, United States of America

Cover design by Damonza
Logo design by M. Takajiro Tobita

www.tjgiii.com

Dedicated to Aunt Kathy

Thank you for fighting (literally) for my Game Boy

That little gray brick set the course for my entire life

SMILING FACELESS WOMAN

THOMAS J. GEBHARDT III

PART ONE

KINDRED

1

THE HEADLIGHTS ILLUMINATED the dark and winding road then shone over the grass to the unseeming house. Its horizontal wood panels were painted a dull yellow-beige that contrasted the pitch black. Its angled roof aligned with the darkened clouds and the sliver of moon overhead. When the preacher next to him put the car in park then yanked the e-brake up, an ominous dread set in. He remained in the passenger seat, waited, slouched, leaning back, swallowing a hard dry swallow. He had heard the stories before, a few times in fact, of the second to last house on the corner of 28th and Hartley. Never would he have dared to even walk on the patches of fluffy grass, let alone prepare to go inside of it.

After the preacher got out and went around to the trunk, he unbuckled his seat belt, scanned the house through the windshield once more. There was a smaller tree off to one side, a few thick bushes, stylish stones lined to make a little walkway, a big tree in back, and a paved half-circle that was well kept. A light gray picket fence lined the perimeter.

It was ice cold as he stepped out, joined the preacher who held the hood of the trunk open. They both peered down into it. A long black case was set against the inside wall, a short black case next to it, with two boxes closer to the front.

"Nervous?" The preacher took two flashlights, handed one of them to him.

"O-oh, uh, no." He turned, glanced at the house. "I . . . I'm good."

He watched as the preacher grabbed packets of salt, a small container of water, a copy of the bible. The others were already parked and grabbed various audiovisual equipment through the side door of the van.

"This is everything?"

"Yeah, c'mon. What else you need?" The preacher clapped him on the arm, started making his way toward the others. "I mean, what are you expecting, some big shoot-out?"

"I guess you're right, Pastor."

Aw, man. I don't know about this one . . .

He and the preacher walked towards the other three, two guys and a girl. They awaited with suitcases in hand, bundles of wiring and cables under arm, one of them carrying a tripod over their right shoulder.

When they all stood together, they formed an upside down pentagon. It was the van, the five of them huddled, the muscle car, then the house—a gate, a doorway, a portal.

"Okay, gang. 'Fore we head in there, let's go over a few last things. Cover our friggin' rear ends here." The preacher's voice was just a bit raspy. "This one's gonna be a little different than the other ones. More dangerous."

Everyone stepped closer, listened.

"Does anybody have any medical conditions we should be aware of? Anything to do with breathing, blood pressure, or heart-related."

The preacher paused, peering into each of their faces.

"Is anybody on any medications of any kind?" Again, the preacher paused. "Sleep medications? Supplements? Anti-anxiety, anti-psychotic, anti-depressant?"

"Um, no."

"Nope."

While he peeked at a couple of the others then the preacher, he crossed his arms, fidgeting on the ball of his foot.

The preacher nodded, breathed in. "Has anybody here ever contemplated suicide, attempted suicide or had a near-death experience?"

"Not me."

"Fuck no."

The girl shook her head.

"And, does anybody harbor any resentment or ill will? Hung up on an ex? Unresolved issues with a family member who's passed?"

Two of the others raised their hands up dismissively.

"Or perhaps troubled relationship with a parent? Not get along with their mother or father, maybe?"

As the preacher stared him straight in his eye, he couldn't help but blink then face away to the ground.

"Uh-huh. Bingo." The preacher turned to the others. "Keep an eye on Alexander. Note any change in his demeanor, mood, mannerisms. And Alexander, you stay close. Don't go wandering off. Seriously."

He nodded, bit at his bottom lip.

"All right then. Let's go."

While the three started to the front steps, he waited a second longer with his hands at his sides, head hanging down.

"You sure you're up for this?"

"Ah, I don't know. I . . ."

"So many other things you could be doing on a Friday night. Better things. Prob'ly should go hang with your girly-friend, make out and fondle each other and all that crap."

He smirked, relaxed his shoulders.

"I guess I'm ready. Thank you, Pastor Art."

He let the preacher take the lead then followed along, glancing up once again. Before them all was the allegedly haunted location, the so-called Demon House of Lower Bloom Hill. It would be a gateway, a door, a vortex, from which he could not escape.

2

Two Years Ago

THE ROUNDED DIRT path from the dormitories led behind some tall pine trees to a wide open field. It was just one week into the new semester, and he struggled to get acclimated and adjusted still. Alex was exhausted but determined at the same time. After all, this was his last semester before graduating—all night study sessions, early morning cramming, and balancing eighteen credits a semester would soon pay off. His first class was at seven-thirty but he always went to the Holden Library to study before, right when they opened. As the dirt transitioned to grass beneath his feet, Alex walked with both hands in his pockets, listening to the songs blasting on his generic MP3 player.

It was cool out, with the sun partway hidden behind the buildings and the tree line. He started to see the outline of the recreation center ahead. The campus was sprawling, and Alex blended in with the migration of students making their way from the roundabout. This scattered herd passed between the administrative offices and a ramp to the parking lot alongside a row of bulletin boards. There were stapled and thumbtacked flyers for upcoming concerts and parties, paid surveys, information about study abroad opportunities, tutoring available and used textbooks for sale.

One girl in front of him wore tight yoga pants and carried a water bottle covered in various stickers. Another wore a loose sweater top set at an angle revealing one shoulder with her bra strap showing. The two guys next to him wore sarcastic t-shirts that matched their sarcastic glasses, both in flip flops.

He walked up the back stairs of the rec center along with the crowd. Some of them forked left to the study area with tables and chairs lined. Some of them forked right to the food court and snack shop. Alex peeked to the right, catching one last glimpse of the yoga pants and bra strap before veering left.

Most of the square tables were empty. There were high counters against the back walls with backless stools where a few students took advantage of the wall outlets, plugging in their laptops and charging their phones.

Alex passed through the space back down to the ground level, through the art exhibits and to a long lane between all the main buildings. Beneath the canopy of thick branches and leaves overhead, it was almost like a large tunnel. At the foot of each trunk was a mini-garden with a circle of decorative bricks around it.

The automatic doors slid open as he entered, and a chill washed over his skin. It was always freezing inside there. He took the elevator to the fourth floor, found a quiet cubicle. Alex took off his sling backpack which was triangular in shape and had one thick strap that went across the chest. He set it on the carpet then scooted forward, reaching in for his folder. When he placed it down on the tabletop, the official foil logo flashed from the fluorescent lights: EMERALD CITY TECHNICAL INSTITUTE.

He flipped it open, took out the chapter questions, then reached down again for the textbook. As he read the assigned pages, he scribbled the notes regarding the answer. First, it was handwritten like this in his tiny messy chicken-scratch then later typed up.

Ugh. God damn it.

I don't know why, but this just ain't happening today . . .

Although he intended to get more done, the process was moving far too slow as perhaps he didn't get that much sleep. With enough failed attempts, Alex instead took out his Nintendo DS Lite. He flicked the little power switch on then popped the stylus out while waiting for the two screens to load up. The main gameplay used the directional pad and buttons, but it was good to have the stylus sticking out at the ready for when he needed the spare power-ups and also for mini-games.

There was this one specific coin he was trying to collect in this particular level, but he had to nail the jump just right. It was all in the timing, whether it was the triple jump or consecutive wall jumps.

Even playing, he found himself rubbing at his eyes, yawning. It was long blinks and unintentional head nods until he checked the time on his phone.

Huh?

Oh, shit!

Alex scrambled to his feet, put away the sheet, folder, textbook and DS, maneuvered the sling backpack over his head and shoulder, and jogged to the elevators. Most of his classes were pretty close to the Holden Library, over in the Morrison Center for International Studies, convenient for a situation like this.

He continued his light jog back out through the automatic doors around the open air seating in front of the Pine Branch Café. Some students headed inside, lined up to get their everything bagel and their blueberry scones.

When he got to the room with desks set around the interior in a U-shape, he sat down on the nearest empty chair, took out a piece of folder paper and began to take notes. The next assignment was scribbled on the whiteboard with the projected due date, which he took notice of. It was hectic taking six classes a semester, three credits each, but at the same time it was also exhilarating and fascinating to him. To immerse one's mind deep into the world of academia . . . Peer reviewed studies in published scholarly journals. Theories and principles set by historic figures and free thinkers of the time. All courses in the upper division, within his field of interest. Ah, nothing like morphology in the morning.

First, it was Morphology then Phonological Analysis, and then Sociolinguistics followed by Linguistic Structure. Tuesdays and Thursdays were the busier day. Between the last two classes, Alex had a nice long break where he and his friend (and also dorm mate) would hang out with some of the other classmates at Pine Branch. This group varied in size from about four or five to as much as eight or nine, even ten, depending. Sometimes a couple of the girls joined in, but it was a sausage fest majority of the time. In the upper division courses specific to the program major, it was often the same familiar faces. But there were some other courses that were kind of a blend. His third class was a mix of students who studied other fields, like second language teaching or sociology.

"Thanks for tagging along, dude."

"Sure. Not like the girls are there. I'll happily take my time, haha."

"I know, right?" The automatic doors slid open. "Just gonna make some copies real quick, for next class."

Alex followed along as they entered the library. To the right was a large computer area, the left a checkout and returns area, and straight ahead was a row of scanners and printers along with various office supplies available: a stapler, three-hole punch, tape dispenser. The elevators were next to that.

"Hey, Lex."

He watched some of the other students as his friend bent down and stuck the point card in the slot, entered his login info. "What's up?"

"Are you still, uh, recovering from your trip?"

"Glad you brought that up 'cause I am fuckin' dying a little inside."

They both laughed.

"Seriously. I am running on fumes here. Gotta go get an energy drink."

"I can tell, my dude. You look like you just been exhumed."

"Thanks." Alex shook his head, smirked. "It was an early graduation gift, to get to go see where I grew up as a young kid. But man, maybe it wasn't such a good idea . . ."

"Eh, it's all good. You'll get back in the swing of things. The semester just started. Quit being so emo."

"Brad, you know me. All emo, all the time." Alex flinched his head to one side, sweeping the bangs off his brow with the movement. "I'm one step away from a noose."

"You coming later? What's-her-face wanted to go to Bottom of the Barrel for happy hour. I need my wingman."

The two waited as the machine warmed up, the light swishing side to side with loud mechanical noises, stacking the copies in the slanted tray.

"Ah, I can't today. Got work, remember?"

"Dude. You don't need to work. Still broke-ass anyway."

It was just a short walk back to Pine Branch from Holden. There was a big tree and a couple more bulletin boards that they walked past. Some students sat in the shade playing acoustic guitar. Other students sat along a rock wall practicing sign language. Another student laid on the lawn.

"Um, are you ready?" Alex glanced over.

"What? To graduate? Hells yeah. I am done with all this. It's our last semester, and it has pretty much sucked balls the entire way."

"Our new motto . . . 'Wake Me Up When *Semester* Ends,' right?"

"Yup. Exactly."

The others waved to them from the long table by the side windows. Both raised a hand in acknowledgement then turned. There was a small coffee shop, a burger joint, a pizza place, plate lunches, Chinese food, as well as sandwiches, sushi, fruit cups.

"I guess I'm counting on it, too. Just kind of weird to think that we'll finally be out there in the real world."

"Lex. We're gonna change the world, my dude."

After his last class, Alex made his way to the roundabout in front of the campus. Public buses parked and waited for the scheduled departure time. Boyfriends pulled up to pick up their girlfriends, their friends. Frat guys were ready to get plastered, play beer pong and do keg stands. He kept walking towards the back area for pickup by the college shuttle. This would run a circuit around the main campus and the other campus, also select locations that were frequent hotspots, one of them being the Westgate Shopping Center where he worked. It was complimentary as long as a student had their college ID.

Several foreign girls talked amongst themselves in their native language, huddled in the shade. Alex squeezed past them and sat on the bench between a hippie chick with frizzy hair, dark sunglasses and an oversized tie-dye shirt, and a lanky guy with a man bun who wore an Emerald Tech jacket with the archer mascot across the back.

He cycled through the artists and songs on his MP3 player. First, he played "Are You Gonna Be My Girl" by Jet, "Here We Go Again" by OK Go, then "Take Me Out" by Franz Ferdinand. This fit his mood well, and helped to wake him up for his shift. Five hours in retail might as well be five hours in hell. Five and a half hours, to be exact.

Nodding to the rhythm of the guitar riffs and the drum beat blaring from his cheap earphones, Alex faced down and waited, fidgeting his feet.

When the shuttle arrived, he lined up with the rest then boarded. As he climbed in and walked down the aisle, there was a warm presence. It was a girl he hadn't seen in a long time, from his early semesters before he transferred. Their eyes met and they both kind of pointed and did a double take.

"Uh . . ." Alex tilted his head, crinkled his brow and scrunched his lips. "What are you doing here?"

"Hey, buddy!" She scooted over, patted the seat.

"Long time no see. So random." He plopped down next to her, adjusted his sling backpack and set it on his lap. "How you been?"

They both raised one arm and hugged.

"Wow. Weird." She smiled, faced forward with widened eyes. "Well, this is awkward. What the shit."

Both of them laughed.

"You look . . . different."

"Same to you. Lost some weight, huh?" She waved her hand as she talked. "Uhh, I don't know if I like it."

He smirked. "I like your hair. Very cool."

"Oh yeah? Got rid of that lame ponytail I used to do. Kind of a Rihanna thing going now, or Victoria Beckham."

Alex scanned her up and down. Her hair was shorter, hung at an angle past her earlobe along the line of her jaw. It was sleek black and had a light shine to it. She had full lips that stretched thin whenever she smiled or laughed. She wore skinny jeans which were faded at the knee with a slight tear, a fitted t-shirt, and had Chucks on. He was wearing a button-up over a long sleeve tee with black and gray stripes. His hair covered his ears, and ran down into his eyes, which he brushed out of the way with his fingers.

"You've got, like, a Beatles look there, huh." She shifted, squirmed in her seat.

"Damn it. I would prefer to think more Bruce Lee but sure."

"No. It's definitely Beatles, with an emo touch."

Behind her, through the windowpane, droves of students made their way between buildings. Some were headed off campus. Some were headed back towards the dorms. There were groups of friends standing together, and there were couples walking hand in hand.

"W-where'd you come from, April?"

Alex watched as she blinked, shuffled her feet.

"Oh. I was just at east campus, had to meet my lab partner for a project."

"Ah, the 'east' campus which is actually west."

"It is???"

"Yeah. You didn't know that? It's called EAST campus, but it isn't even east. It stands for Expanded Annex of Science and Technology."

The bus took a sharp left causing him to lean with the motion, the slightest touch of his upper arm to the slender of her shoulder.

"And, uh, where you going?"

"Headed to work, over at the mall."

"No . . ." He was taken aback, flinched. "Me, too. How come I never seen you?"

"I'm in the food court. Been slave there a couple of years now."

"Really? I work at the toy store, about the same. I do Thursday and Saturday nights, mid-day on Sunday."

"Hmm. I did recently change from Friday to Thursday. That could be it. And I guess the weekends are just busier?"

"Gotta be. What a coincidence."

Her eyebrows raised up with curiosity. "Hey. What were you listening to? Can I listen?"

"Nothing, just . . ." He gazed at her, paused. "You wanna pick next? Help us kill a little time?"

Taking the MP3 player from his pocket, Alex handed it over. He observed as she clicked the buttons, perusing the song selection. In his fingers, he held the earphones, waited.

"Oh. Nice, nice. Let's see. What else?"

Passing from Campus Heights through the different neigh-borhoods, they had one earphone each and nodded along to the music, making small comments and side jokes. The bus stopped in the Global District at Koreatown, then in the Capitol District at Uptown and at Midtown. First, she played "Great DJ" by The Ting Tings, "Nothing Better" by Postal Service, and then "Maps" by Yeah Yeah Yeahs.

⸙

As they got closer to the shopping center, Alex took the MP3 player back, wrapped the earphone wiring around then stuffed it in his pocket. The area near Westgate in comparison to the dreary pine trees and grunge vibe of the city streets was very upscale. It was a large mall, so it was no wonder the two never ran into each other. They pulled alongside the parking lot, rode parallel to the south wing where they could see the flagship department store with all glass windows and fancy displays showing. Faceless and headless mannequins posed in fancy ensembles, in sexy lingerie. Alex pulled the cord then stood by the door. When April joined him, he let her pass and exit the vehicle first.

She hopped from the last step onto the curb, the soles of her Chucks smacking the sidewalk. He plodded with casual and deliberate footing through the doors, using the pole of the bus stop to turn in her direction. They walked together down the path to the front entrance.

"I was thinking . . ." Alex shifted towards her. "We haven't seen each other since, uh, back at North Emerald Community College."

"Riiight. Our tenure at ol' NECC."

"Taking the prereqs and general ed and shit. Used to hang out at the cafeteria, all day, all of us. Just being dumb, silly. It was fun."

April chuckled, nodded. "Good times."

"What're you majoring in now?"

"Eh, just there 'cause my mom makes me, basically. Same as then. Going through the motions. I'll probably have to pick at some point but whatevs for now."

"So you just did the AA, Liberal Arts?"

"Yep. You?"

"I got mine, too. It was Pre-Ed since I thought about teaching, then switched programs when I switched schools. I'm majoring in Linguistics now, in my last semester. And did a minor in Southeast Asian Studies."

"Oh, wow. Look at you all grown up."

"Hehe, yeah. Know how they make you take a language as a requirement? All kind of stemmed from there. So interesting to me. It just clicked."

"You're a cunning linguist."

Both laughed out loud.

"It would shock you how often that term is used in our circles. That phrase, funny enough, goes back to the 1800s . . ."

As they entered inside, it switched from being nice and quiet to a light blend of noise and motion. There was a big fancy carpet with the design of the mall logo, one escalator going up, one escalator going down. A long counter with fresh crepes had a growing line. April leaned on the rail of the escalator, turned and faced him as they went up to the second floor.

"What time do you start work, Alex?"

"Uh, I start at four. You?"

"Three-thirty."

"Okay, just a few more minutes then. Shall I leave you to it?"

"No, no. It's cool. We can hang a little bit longer. Don't wanna be too early." She led them to a bench in front of the movie theater. "Here good?"

"Perfect."

There was a large clock on the wall in front of the box office. From where they sat, they could smell the fresh buttered popcorn. Alex peered at the movie posters lining the wall to the front entrance.

"See any good movies lately?"

April rested one elbow across the top of the bench. "Here and there. I kinda love doing nothing as my main priority."

"Yeah, true. That's always nice. I'm a big movie guy. Some pretty good ones last year, from like *3:10 to Yuma* to like *Across the Universe,* even the new *National Treasure.*"

"I liked *Superbad.* Freaking hilarious."

"Ooh, I loved that. Wanna see more from them. For sure." He smirked, slouched down. "Did you see *Saw?*"

"Did I . . . seesaw?"

"No, did you see *Saw?* As in *Saw IV,* that is."

She laughed, leaned in then crossed her legs. "Oh, hehe. Nah, but I did see *The Mist.* Now that one had a spectacular ending, god damn. Brutal. Harsh."

"Yeah, that was a real gut-wrencher. Hey, know what movie you should see?" Alex shifted in place.

"What?"

"It has the guy from *Superbad* in it, too. Maybe *Juno?* Totally you."

"Oh yeah. Right. I did see the trailer for that."

He pointed to the clock with his chin. "Guess you better get going then. Maybe I'll run into you again sometime."

"Yeah, maybe. See you around."

They both raised an arm and hugged again.

"See ya. Take it easy."

As the afternoon transitioned to evening, customers came and went. There was a family of four and a half: two parents, a boy, a girl and a toddler. There were couples expecting, and there were aunts and uncles searching for gifts for their nieces and nephews. Others had grandchildren and godchildren in mind. Teens often liked to stop by after school, with their little clique of friends. Closer to the end of the shift, Alex started straightening items on the shelves, then counted the total cash and credit card slips in the register drawer, while his co-worker restocked then vacuumed. When they dimmed the lights, the last few customers wrapped up and left. The two set the security alarm, locked the front doors.

"Um, I'll take the deposit today . . ."

"You sure?"

"Yeah, I got it."

"Cool. See you Saturday."

Alex almost never dropped off the bank deposit after work, but thought it was a good excuse to swing by the food court which was near the drop box. One security guard stood in front of the sliding doors, waiting for the workers inside to finish closing, finish cleaning. Alex peered through the glass but couldn't see anything nor anybody. He wasn't sure what he was even searching for, as there were two other food courts and April didn't say which restaurant or space she worked in, not to mention which wing.

Hmm.

Oh well.

Making his way to the shuttle pickup area, he thought he might run into her there but it was the same thing. Alex took out his MP3 player again, put in the earphones, lost himself in thought to the sound of My Chemical Romance.

He wondered why he tried to find her, maybe a mix of boredom and curiosity. He stared out the window as the shuttle went around the outside of the mall to a few other neighborhoods before heading back to the main campus. Alex knew he had some studying to do still, a couple unfinished assignments, but he was way too tired and would get to it in the morning instead. He made his way from the roundabout to the wide open field, behind the tall pine trees, along the rounded dirt path back to the dorms.

His mind was half-empty as he tidied up the room, put things away. It was all automatic movement. At the same time, his mind was somehow half-full as he continued to ponder. Alex reflected on his recent trip, thought about his new course schedule, thought about this being his last semester. He also thought about the "real world" out there, waiting.

This continued until he got ready for bed then belly flopped onto the mattress with his head sideways on the pillow. Alex closed his eyes, took a deep breath in and out. He tossed and turned in place, positioning on his side then on his back. First, he tried stuffing one hand behind his head but it didn't feel right, tried crossing his arms over his chest but that didn't feel right either. He tucked both arms beneath the blanket and pulled it up to his chin.

It was the closest to comfortable Alex would get, so he settled, remaining in that position as his brainwaves slowed towards deep sleep. His breathing and thinking synced until he began to drift off, little by little. Just when he was about to slip into the cozy, comfy subconscious dream world, he snapped his eyelids open.

The room was an abyss, darker than dark, blacker than black. At once, it drew him in but also repulsed him. On the one hand, it was so eerie quiet that it was downright strange. On the other hand, it was as if every sound had been amplified. There was a noise. Then there were noises. It seemed like a crinkling, a rustling, a little clink or a tick, like something moving in the closet. Perhaps a rodent crawling or an insect fluttering. He had never listened to anything with such intensity. He tilted his head to position his ear.

The noise, the noises, continued and appeared to warp and change almost with a certain level of intelligence. Like a voice, a whisper or a mumble, a footstep. Perhaps something dropping or moving.

What . . .

No, no.

I'm just being paranoid.

Alex shook his head, searched for logic, for reason. The rational part of his brain knew there was nothing. But the other part of his brain—the ancient, animalistic part—couldn't shake this nagging itch.

He threw the blanket off, rolled to the edge of the bed, touched his bare feet to the laminate floor. As he stood and tip-toed closer, he tilted his head again, repositioned his ear. It now sounded like faint music so he stopped in place.

With a slight shift, the music disappeared. But when he returned to that same spot, there it was again. He tested this out. If he took a step forward, it was gone. If he took a step back, there it was.

Huh?

Alex concluded it had to be some kind of wave interference, radio or television frequency, something. It creeped him out but it was more weird than anything, and more annoying than weird. He had enough going on. He ignored it and went back to bed.

3

THE NEXT MORNING, Alex felt like absolute garbage. He was haggard, drained. It was already a few days straight of not sleeping well, but it became even worse after that strange occurrence. At least it was the end of the week so he just had to get through one more day, then he would get the chance to hopefully reset and refresh over the weekend. Plus, compared to Tuesday/Thursday, his Monday/Wednesday/Friday was mellower. His first class was in a big lecture hall, Early Modern Asian Civilizations, and his second class was a pretty easy one to him, considering: Semantics & Pragmatics. Alex could proceed through the day like a zombie and it should be okay, at least in theory, although this was not sustainable for long.

What was that though?

He pondered the events from last night.

I mean, it could be anything, I suppose. Really.

Perhaps he caught a kind of signal somehow. The right alignment of a passing satellite, or the exact triangulation between cell phone users and cell phone towers. Perhaps it was a combination of something like that and cross-wiring between the hubs in the walls or cables in the ceiling.

Alex pushed in the handles of the double doors, adjusting the sunglasses set on the bridge of his nose. Most of the other students were already seated. He walked down the stairs, the textbook in the crook of his arm, and chose the emptiest row towards the lower middle. He switched to a side step along the linoleum, picked a chair closer to the right side. It was cold white plastic that had an ergonomic curve with a half-desktop that he flipped down into place, big enough for his binder to fit.

Or perhaps he was just tired. It could have been jet lag. It could have been sleep deprivation. Could be a type of hysteria starting to kick in from not getting the adequate rest intervals for his brain to function properly. Not to mention being overcaffeinated.

The associate professor pinched the clip of the lavalier microphone, did a subtle sound check while the sleep mode animation switched to an introductory presentation slide on the projector screen.

He opened his binder, sorted through the tabs to the proper section, waiting for the professor to start. His sunglasses now were hanging from the collar of his graphic tee. The mechanical pencil waved and twirled in his hand as he tried to stay awake.

One of the first things the professor mentioned was the assignment due, which Alex had forgotten about.

Ah, crap . . .

You gotta be freakin' kidding me.

Damn it.

It was hard enough getting up, getting ready, let alone getting anything done. Waking up before classes to squeeze in an assignment was something he did often, but it slipped his mind that day. Unlike his Tuesday/Thursday schedule which was back to back to back, he had a little breathing room so he could talk to the professor after. They had a decent rapport as Alex complimented his lecture style and presentation skills via e-mail the first day.

When the lecture wrapped up, Alex walked down the stairs to the floor, waited for a chance to talk to the professor. There was one other student who did the same. It was a quiet girl who sat in the front row, with her electronic translation dictionary open. She was skinny and had glasses and fair skin. As she left, the professor nodded then turned to Alex.

"Hey, what's up?" It was almost disarming how casual he was. He stood at about the same height as Alex, with longer hair parted in the middle. "Thank you for your last message, by the way."

Alex stepped close, one hand in his pocket and one hand holding the textbook. "No. Thank you."

Most of the other students already left through the upper and lower level exits.

"Listen. I, uh, don't have the assignment with me . . ."

"Oh, that's okay. Just drop it to the box on my office door by the end of the day, and it will still count as on time. I'll be coming in tomorrow to catch up on paperwork."

"Perfect. Cool. I appreciate that." Alex positioned the book under his arm to touch his palms together in gratitude, with a slight bow. "And it's on the syllabus?"

"Yeah, building and room number, all that, should be on there."

"Sweet. Thanks again."

"No problem. Have a good weekend."

Alex bowed again with a wave as he turned away, headed for the double doors. When he stepped out into the bright sunlight, there was a vibration in his left pocket.

It was a text from Bradley. He responded back.

They would meet at Pine Branch during that time so he confirmed this and headed down. He cut through a parking lot behind the lecture hall, then in between buildings back to the main lane. Under the canopy of branches and leaves like a tunnel, Alex continued ruminating as the wrinkles of light and shadow danced beneath his feet and intermittent haloes of lens flares gleamed above him.

Man.

I can't believe I forgot . . .

Still, despite having been given a chance to make it up, this bothered him. He had been working very hard to maintain his honor roll status and get on the Dean's List. He did all of the extracurricular activities to enhance his future application packets, both for grad school and for job opportunities, and developed relationships with professors so that he had references and letters of recommendation. Alex had big plans for the future, plans laid out in a meticulous and thorough manner.

Get it together here.

Oh. Or maybe that's *it, huh?*

Perhaps he was just burnt out. Perhaps burnout, routine stress, lack of adequate rest, combined with some kind of interference or something.

Whatever the case may have been, there was too much on the line for him to slack off or slow down now. This was it— everything he had been working towards, had been aiming for and hoping for, his whole future on a silver plate.

On top of his six classes, there was one other course in which he was also enrolled, perhaps auditing, either knowingly or unknowingly. Alex liked to call this LIFE101 in the back of his mind, or rather, LIFE101L. It was more hands-on, more practical, hence the "L" designation, as in lab. It was learning how the real world works, and learning one's place in this world. Learning the meaning of life.

He pondered this for a second then grabbed a large energy drink, got in line to pay. When he peeked to the open space, he spotted Bradley raising one hand up.

"Ah. The tall boy today."

"Yup, you?" Alex set his textbook down, his sling backpack.

"Double espresso shot." Bradley swilled the tiny aluminum can then chugged it.

The college staple diet included sugar, caffeine, junk food, and at least some amount of alcohol. It was caffeine high followed by sugar rush, and periodic carbo loading while splitting pitchers of cheap beer.

"We still on for study group tonight?"

"For sure." Alex popped open the tab, took a sip. "Although, I will be a little bit late. There's a thing I gotta go to first."

"Cool. At least it's Friday, right?"

"Totally."

"Mondays, Wednesday, Fridays are so much easier."

"It's rough 'cause there's only so many choices as we get closer and closer to graduating. Shit. On Tuesday, Thursday, I gotta run all the way from the sixth floor of Kettlethorpe Hall to the damn Clinical Psychology Building . . ."

Bradley snickered at this. "Dude. That dang elevator takes so long, too. Easier to use the stairs in Kettlethorpe."

"Right!? And you got like ten, fifteen minutes to do all this. Ugh."

"Luckily, most our classes are in Morrison. That helps. But hey, it's all gonna pay off, my dude. We are almost there."

"Yeah. Yeah, you're right."

"About to graduate. Live the good life. Make the big bucks. The future is lookin' up. We might even have a black president soon."

"I think we could all use a little break from Dick, Colin and Bush."

~§~

When he stepped inside the large conference room, it was already almost full. This was a surprise to Alex as he wasn't sure how many people would be in attendance. He learned of this information session from a flyer posted on one of the bulletin boards, and not all students checked those. Perhaps there were mass e-mails sent out, memo to faculty and staff, or some of the professors had announced it in their classes. Either way, a few last open seats remained and Alex was quick to spot one and snag it, squeeze in and sit down. He was elbow to elbow with other eager attendees, and had to be careful setting his textbook and backpack down on the tile floor.

"Thank you all for coming today. We're from the US Department of State, and we would like to go over the process of applying to be a Foreign Service Officer. You guys are all the perfect candidates. Experts in language, in culture, in communication, history, geography, economics, and psychology and political science."

It became quiet then. Ears perked up. Backs straightened. Alex folded his arms, rubbed his fingers over his chin with intrigue.

One member of the staff went row by row and handed pamphlets and brochures. Each attendee took one of each then handed the rest down.

"We have offices in twenty-two states, as well as DC. We

have assignments all over the world. It ranges from Central and South America to Canada, to Europe, Africa, Asia, Australia, and throughout the Pacific."

Alex flipped open the brochure, leafed through the pamphlet.

The same staff member went row by row again, this time with folders filled with data sheets and other materials.

"Some of you might be good in consular work. And some of you might be good in public diplomacy. Some might be better in management. The duties can vary, from adoption and evacuation, protecting borders, negotiating peace, resolving crises, working between governments on issues of trade, technology, environment, energy. We are at times influence and support and peace, at times a think tank."

In his lap, the thick packet seemed to radiate. There was a field of gravity around it that beckoned him. Alex held the business card in his hand, gazed at the official seal and the embossed lettering.

"Many of you believe in making the world a better place, in creating peace, sustainability, literacy, in doing overall good. . . . Well, you can do that all here."

And, with that, Alex was hooked. Those words had struck a chord. He already figured out so much of the master plan for his future, his life, from getting his BA, working overseas, getting his MA, and now this being the final endgame. It was all there before him, the last missing piece of the puzzle.

The rest of the info session went by pretty quick. While leaving the conference room, his mind continued to dissect and analyze. He considered the different steps in the process: the initial application including a personal narrative, exam, evaluation panel, an oral assessment, medical and security clearance, and then a review panel. They considered personality traits such as composure, adaptability, motivation, leadership, resourcefulness, integrity. His background in foreign languages would also lend extra points to his candidacy, as they used a literal points system to make their determination.

Before heading to the Holden Library to meet the others, Alex walked to the nearest building, leaned against the wall and slid down to the ground, sat there in place.

Okay. So, there.

I got it all figured it out now . . .

However, before I can do any of that, I have to get through this last semester. I got to get it together here. No more screwing around.

Alex leaned forward, rested his arms on his knees, taking a deep breath.

The campus was dead quiet, dead still. It was quite the opposite from the wave of geek bro energy that reeked of illegal bit torrents, pseudointellect and questionable hygiene back in the study room. After the others left, the two stayed behind to hang out a little longer, wrapping up their last assignments. With the death of brain cells from overwork and the inevitable sugar crash, they relaxed for a bit. Alex took out his Nintendo DS. He swayed in place as he dodged turtle shells and banana peels, crashing through colorful item boxes with the turn. Bradley opened up the side project he had been working on for fun, a lengthy guidebook on the notable similarities and differences between Grey-eleven and High-elven. Then, at last, they called it a day. Both were quiet as they exited, went around to the back of the library.

"So, you still thinking about trying for the GET Initiative?

Before your master's?" His friend knelt down, started to unlock his moped.

"Yeah. I think so." Alex nodded. "Pretty sure. All part of the master plan."

"And, where in your master plan are you ever gonna get laid, huh." Bradley glanced up with a wide and crooked grin.

"Dude. I ain't got time for no girls."

He lifted one hand up, fingers outstretched. "I got my chick right here. You ever meet her? Palmela Handerson."

Alex laughed, shook his head.

Bradley rolled the moped, threw one leg over then lowered onto the seat. "You sure you don't wanna piggyback?"

"Ah, I'm good. No worries. Had enough bromance for one night."

He turned on the ignition, adjusted the side mirror. "Gonna go be emo, huh?"

"Of course. My modus operandi."

Alex held out a hand, ready to either fist bump or clap palms. Bradley instead raised both arms out, waiting for a bro hug. The two embraced then let go.

He watched his friend ride away in the dark, the brake light flashing on before he made the turn. Taking his MP3 player out, he cycled through the selection. He played "This Night" by Black Lab, "Disarm" by Smashing Pumpkins, then "Hurt" by Johnny Cash. This was the perfect music for solitude and contemplation.

With his hands in his pockets, he kicked at the ground then headed back towards the dorms. He listened to the lyrics of the songs, the plucking of the slow notes, the strumming of the soft chords, the background orchestrals that accompanied the verses and choruses.

Along the side road which cut through campus, Alex could see the night sky above. It was a blend of a thin veil of clouds and faint stars.

Instead of the usual wide open field and tall pine trees, he came from around the athletic complex and the tennis courts along the other side of the rounded dirt path. His mind was again half-empty as he put things away, brushed his teeth. At the same time, his mind was half-full as the thoughts continued to pour out. Before he settled in, Alex stopped in front of the closet, rifled through the clothes on hangers, items on top of the plastic drawers, peeked in the laundry basket on the floor. Nothing seemed amiss.

It must have been a one time thing . . .
Meh.

4

ALTHOUGH HIS SLEEP wasn't disrupted, his mind not perturbed, it still was far from deep enough rest. When Alex awoke, the sun peeked through the window over his head sideways on the pillow and his hand under his cheek. He rolled from off his stomach to the edge of the bed, faced ahead, blinked, rubbing at his eyes with the long yawn. He was never the type to sleep in late, even under normal circumstances. So much to do, so much to enjoy, so much to take advantage of—there was plenty of time to sleep in the afterlife. Alex stood then went to his desk, started sorting through the different syllabi and schedules, being systematic as usual, setting a list of priorities in his head.

When Alex had a mini-plan for the day, he picked out dirty clothes from the basket and stuffed it into a mesh bag, grabbed a drawstring pouch filled with quarters, a box of detergent, a dryer sheet, and made his way to the laundry room. He also took his laptop and the chapter questions with the tiny messy chicken-scratch. It was smart to beat out the others before it got too busy down there, and it was even smarter to stay on guard. This gave him a chance to catch up on his weekly anime, too.

After laundry and anime, he returned to his room. He went

to his desk and sorted through the different portfolios. There were three, holding two classes each, one per pocket. He leafed between the sheets, took the one for his coming essay then went to sit on his bed. It was the usual instructions: one-sided, double spaced, Times New Roman font, size 12, MLA format, list of references. Alex put the sheet down, rubbed his fingers over his chin while brainstorming a topic, stood back up to start folding.

Hmm.

What would be a good subject?

Lemme check the sheet again.

When Alex turned to the bed, it wasn't there. He darted his eyes to the pillow, to the table by the side, then went over and lifted the blanket up. Nothing.

Huh? What in the fuck?

It was just *here.*

Alex shook out the blanket, searched beneath the pillow. He scanned the bed up and down, side to side, then went to the desk and sorted through the portfolios.

Did I put it back?

No.

No, I don't think so . . .

He searched the laundry basket, even the drawers with the clothes he just put away. Alex pulled the bed out, in case it slipped between the mattress and the wall, then he peeked under it. He stood back up, scratching his head.

This doesn't make any sense.

Only so many places it could be.

He retraced his steps, rechecked the pillows, the blankets, drawers, desk, panned the interior of the room until his eyes locked on the closet.

No, no.

It can't be.

Alex took a timid step forward, one hand raised, as the open closet taunted him. The sliding doors almost always remained on the left side for easy access. He peeped to the shelf above, slid the hangers one way then the other, rifled through items on the generic plastic drawers then the drawers themselves. When he turned back around, that's when he saw it.

Whaaat?

On top of the pillow, dead center at a perfect angle, like it had been placed with delicate care and thought in a meticulous fashion, was the pesky little piece of paper.

∾

All throughout the shuttle ride from campus to the mall, the strange happening replayed in his mind. Tiny prisms of raindrops on the windowpane twisted and warped the reflections of the different neighborhoods in a blur like a dream within a dream. Overcast skies behind the roofs of the houses, housing complexes and apartment buildings flashed blue-gray with splotches of thin white clouds. Alex reached in his pocket, felt for the button to increase the volume on the MP3 player. It was "Stop Crying Your Heart Out" by Oasis. The piano blended into the strings, with a slow build. Then the instrumental break kicked in with harmonized vocals as a flock of birds swept upward in a diagonal.

He plodded down the steps through the doors, using the pole of the bus stop to make a sharp turn. As he entered inside, there was the big fancy carpet with the mall logo, the two escalators, and the long counter with fresh crepes. Alex had some time to kill so he started one of his emo walks that Bradley often teased him for.

He dangled the earphones down, untangling them,

readjusted the buds in his ear, then stuck his hands in both pockets. It had been a while since he did this kind of meandering and window shopping.

First stop, the candy shop where the young female staff wore muted maroon aprons and scooped gummy bears and gummy worms, jelly beans, marshmallow puffs and dried fruit from jars into clear baggies. There was a slushie machine whirring behind the cash register. Second, the pet store where birds chirped and squeaked, flapped their wings and clung onto the cage with their talons and beaks. Groups of fish floated in aquariums while algae eaters sucked on multicolored pebbles. Turtles crawled in their tanks, and hamsters jogged on their wheels. Third stop, an electronics place where customizable radio control cars zoomed across the carpet and robot dogs hopped in place with a digital arf, arf.

So much to see, so much to enjoy—but there was just one thing on his mind while he continued to peruse.

His eyes and ears saw the sights, heard the sounds, but none of it registered. There was no connection from his body to his brain as it was just automatic movement. Alex instead was preoccupied with thought, to the point the fourth stop wasn't a conscious choice but an accident which happened to unfold all on its own.

Seriously, though. Shit . . .

What happened?

What was that?

Perhaps it was static electricity and the paper clung to the pillowcase. Perhaps he couldn't see it because the white of the paper matched the white of the pillowcase. Or maybe it just happened to slip down from the lampshade when he wasn't looking. Perhaps he put it up on there and didn't even notice.

Alex moved past the crowds on either side of him. Workers in front of kiosks tried to get his attention but he paid them no mind. A gang of little kids ran from one store to the next, mischievous and rambunctious. There was a couple with their baby in a stroller. Through the door, he could see a row of large massage chairs with occupants who had no intention of buying. On the other side, a male model posed in front of the clothing store topless.

"Hey, buddy!"

He flinched as he was snapped out of deep thought. April stood behind the glass with her smile spread wide.

"Oh, h-hey. What . . . What are you doing here?"

"Hellooo, silly. I work here. 'Member?" She fidgeted in place. "I start at three-thirty."

"Right." Alex brushed the bangs out of his eyes, took a step forward. "But you didn't mention where you worked exactly."

She laughed. "Ah, okay. I'll give you a pass then."

"So this is where you work." He glanced up at the sign, FRESH TAKE DELI.

"Yep. Indie sandwich artist. Slinging coleslaw and mashed potatoes, and tossin' salads."

He smirked, faced away.

"Probably thought I worked at Beijing BBQ or something, huh. Just kidding. I actually did work there for a little while."

April leaned on the counter with her elbow. Alex could see the baggy plastic gloves on her hands and her slanted white paper hat.

"You want anything? We got a pretty mean baked potato. We got paninis, Chicago style hot dogs."

"Uh, I'm about to start work too. I just came a li'l early today."

"Gotcha. How 'bout a sample? Mac salad? Pasta salad?"

"Hmm . . . Sure." Alex peeked through the glass. "Is that the pasta salad there?"

She nodded, scooped some into a paper cup then stuck in a small spoon.

"Awesome, thanks." He took a bite of it. "That's really good, actually. Damn. I might have to come back during my break."

"Yeah! You should! Stop on by."

⚜

The shift seemed to glide by pretty quick. It was busy since it was the weekend, but not so super busy that he was stressed out. Alex rang up the customers in the short line, scanning the barcodes on the back or on the bottom in the corner while his co-worker bagged for him. He printed extra gift receipts as requested, counted the bills and coins back in an efficient manner, thanking them for their patronage. Meanwhile, their other co-worker went around and offered to help customers on the floor, tidying up as they circled. The wooden train set on the floor by the stockroom had been ransacked. In the back of his mind, Alex kept thinking about the pesky little sheet of paper, and about the noises from the other night.

I just don't get it . . .

It doesn't make sense.

He forced himself to try to forget about it, to move on. Sometimes sheer coincidence can be perceived as strange or even downright shocking, he concluded. It must be a matter of statistics. Not like the chances of a mixed radio signal and a misplaced item were far outside the realm of possibility.

"Alex. You still never took lunch, er, dinner."

"Oh, right."

"Go for it. It's died down now. We got it from here."

"Thanks."

Although he wasn't hungry, Alex did go to the food court. This time, he knew which wing and which counter. The crowds had thinned out so he had room to move, to breathe, to think.

Yeah. Let it go.

It bothers me, but let it go.

Who cares.

"Back for more, huh?" She raised her eyebrows up. "What can I get ya?"

"Hey, April." He smirked, glanced at the menu overhead. "Earlier, the corn chowder in a bread bowl caught my eye."

"Ah, all the carb-y goodness. I'll even give you extra crackers."

While she grabbed a round loaf and started to cut, he watched her do so. Then she poured the ladle and packed it all up.

"You put some extra love in there, huh."

"Sure did." She smiled as she pushed the drawer back in with a ding, handed him back his change.

He dropped it all into the tip jar.

"Aww, you're so sweet."

While the other staff started to sweep and refill condiments, and there weren't customers around, Alex took the moment to talk some more. If it was the dinner rush still, he would have been on his way already.

"You know, I never got to say . . ."

She tilted her neck, perked her ears up.

"That was an awesome little playlist the other day. Pretty good taste."

"Yeah, I'm cool like that. Try to keep a wide range on my radar. One of those songs I first heard as a B-side on another single, from the UK."

"Wow. What else do you listen to?"

"I mean, so many good bands and good artists. Hard to think. Uh, off the top of my head, maybe Akon? Haha, or OneRepublic. This Amy Winehouse chick has a lot of potential, I think. How 'bout you?"

"Same, I listen to it all. It could be Gorillaz. It could be Black Eyed Peas. I can rock out to Muse just as hard as MGMT."

"Ooh, I fuckin' love Muse."

"For sure. Prob'ly my favorite band."

She smiled and he smirked, both facing away for a second then back towards one another. He licked his lips, starting to step back.

"Well, it was fun bothering you. I better get going, though."

"Hey. Us mall rats gotta stick together, right?"

"Right." He laughed. "Um . . ."

She tilted her neck again, perked her ears.

"I'll be at the bookstore after work for a little while, in that coffee area thing. If you find yourself bored later on."

"Oh, okay. Yeah. Maybe."

∾

Lingering on that last string of words, Alex finished the rest of his shift. He sprayed all the glass surfaces with Windex then wiped it down until it had a nice crisp squeak to it. He wondered why he had even said such a thing. He went to the bookstore, sure, of course, but not ever after work. There were still so many assignments to get through. The weekend was a critical period to set the tone for the week ahead. He waved goodbye to his two co-workers who took the deposit with them. One wore a baggy sweater with long sleeves that hung past the wrists, her mismatched accessories contrasting the color of her contacts. And the other had bleached bangs, and a small fanny pack strapped across his vintage jacket.

Ah, I said it . . .

Too late now.

I'll just head down there, hang out for a bit, cover my ass. And once enough time has passed and she doesn't show, I go home and forget this whole thing ever happened.

Compared to the rest of the stores in the mall, the bookstore was open a couple of hours later. He passed by locked up kiosks, darkened display windows, and janitorial staff taping off the hall to the restrooms. Some of the stores had metal gates down over them.

Alex pulled open the first door then pulled open the second door. He felt the cool rush of the air conditioning. In the small pass-through between entry doors, he glanced at the scattered bargain books as he walked inside. To the left was the line to the registers, with rotating displays of bookmarks and book bags. To the right was the small coffee shop with an area with tables and chairs.

He stopped by the new releases across the front shelves, debating which novel to check out. Alex ended up taking a copy of *Thirteen Reasons Why* then walked through the magazine section to the tables and chairs. There was just one spot left in the back corner, so he hurried and sat down. He could smell the fresh coffee brewing.

First, he admired the cover and this mysterious girl who sat on the swing, holding onto the two chains. She wore a beanie set just above her eyebrow as she stared off. Alex had almost finished Cassette 1, Side A by the time April arrived.

"Now what?"

"Uh, I-I have no idea." He let out a nervous laugh. "Did not think this through."

"I guess, let's hang out here?"

"Sure."

The two stood together and made their rounds. Alex snuck the copy back in the new releases as they entered the interior of the store on the non-fiction side. First, there was the cookbooks, then self-help, travel, history, some astrology books, then they ended up in front of a promotional table full of humor books. The kind one might find in a waiting room at a doctor's office or a dentist's office.

On the surface, it was the most unseeming and mundane encounter. However, deep down, in the passage of time, tiny seeds were being planted—circumstance intersecting with happenstance. He was about to learn another one of his first crucial lessons, LIFE101L, and that is plans never go to plan.

"You know, why *do* men have nipples?" She picked up the innocuous title, blinking as she leafed through it.

"Life's greater questions." Alex tapped his fingertips along, touching the covers on the other side. "Check this out. *The Zombie Survival Guide* and *The Action Hero's Handbook* right next to each other. Whoever put this little stash together deserves a raise."

"Haha. Cool. Now, this . . . This is the obvious winner . . ." April held up a book with Chuck Norris on the cover. "So freakin' ridonkulous. I love these."

"Oh, hell yeah." He snickered. "Me, too. Go and read us some."

"Let's see. 'Chuck Norris can strangle you with a cordless phone.' Nice, nice. Or how 'bout this. 'Chuck Norris can kill two stones with one bird.' Yes." She flipped through the pages, searching for a special one. "I got it . . ."

She had difficulty maintaining her composure as she tried

to read it. Her laughter was contagious, so much so he found himself laughing along just as hard.

"Dude. This is sooo good. 'The quickest way to a man's heart is Chuck Norris' fist.' Ah, hahaha!"

They both bawled out loud, almost howling. April borderline snorted while Alex hunched over and slapped his knee.

"Yeah, that was good." He gazed at her across the table. "Lemme see."

She wiped a happy tear from the corner of her eye, held the book out for him.

"Damn, I can't find it but . . . I always did like 'Chuck Norris can divide by zero.' Just, so absurd, you know?"

"That's fantastic."

"Very smart to bottle these up and sell it. Not like this guy created these jokes, it was created by the internet."

"I love memes. Numa Numa iei and fat *Star Wars* kid? Classic."

"Right. 'All your base are belong to us' and 'I can has cheezburger.' Good stuff."

They continued to linger on that table then migrated to a few last sections, but that was by far the highlight. Alex held open the first door, let her pass, then April held open the second door, let him pass.

"How are you getting home, April? Bus? Shuttle?"

"I just walk most of the time."

"Really?"

"It's not too far. Burn off some calories."

"Hmm." Alex thinned his lips, crinkled his brow. "I did have that bread bowl. Maybe I'll walk with you?"

"Hey, wait. You're not trying to pick me up, are you???"

"W-what?" He was caught off guard. "No, uh, I—"

"I'm just fuckin' with ya! Let's go."

The air was icy cold when they exited the shopping center. She zipped up her hoodie. He stuck his hands in both pockets. They made their way through the parking lot from the north-west wing, the flagship store still visible behind them.

"Nah, if you remember, I had a boyfriend before. He used to drop me off and pick me up. But not anymore."

"I actually forgot about that. Hell. I was in a relationship, too, back then. Wow, that takes me back."

"How long ago d'you guys break up?"

"Been a couple years. Like, two years. I kind of swore off girls after that. So, no worries, you're safe." Alex turned to her, raised one eyebrow. "I'm single mode right now. Got a lot going on. Lot on the line. I can't date anyone."

"It's only been a few months for me, about four months. So I'm not ready for anything like that, either."

"You . . . okay?"

"I'm all right. It kinda sucked at first. You get so used to a person, to your life together. Now that it's starting to settle in, though, not like we were perfect." April scrunched the corner of her lips, kicked at a pebble on the ground. "I mean, of course *I* was, nah, haha, but he could be not so great sometimes."

"Any guy who would hurt a girl like you has gotta be a real jerk."

She turned to him with a half-smile. There was a tiny spar-kle in her eye which matched her earrings that dazzled.

He never noticed before since her hair often covered it, but those dazzly ears of hers were sort of mesmerizing to him. Across the top, through the cartilage was a thin industrial bar. Near that, just below, along the outer edge were three helix rings. The tragus and side of the lobe had matching jewels, the size of a sesame seed. In the tender lobe of her ear was a small spacer, like a jet black Smarties tablet. The sterling silver metal gleamed and the cubic zirconia pieces shimmered like magic.

Alex stuck his hands deeper in his pockets. There was the slightest pause as they continued along the sidewalk.

"So, uh, where are most of your classes?" He swallowed, cleared his throat.

"I have to say, almost all in Keene Hall. Like the band. Prolly there and like Kettlethorpe."

"Different spelling, but yeah."

"What? The band?"

"Yeah. It's got two Es instead of an E-A."

"Maybe someone should tell them they spelled their name wrong."

Both laughed as the streetlights shined down on them, distorting their shadows like little streetlight people.

"They do have that one good song, though."

"Oh yeah. I like that song." He switched to the other side of her, closer to the passing traffic. "I got a couple classes in Kettlethorpe."

"You know where I like to go?"

Alex shifted. "Where?"

"Second floor of the rec center, with all those couchy sofa things. Oh, man." She motioned with her hands. "Just lay there, relax, doze off a bit. I even whip out my DS sometimes."

"You play DS?"

"Of course. Who doesn't? It's only the greatest thing ever."

"No way. Like, what games?"

"Right now, I'm playing this one, the sequel actually, where you're a lawyer. You gotta scream at the screen into the mic. Objection! Objection! Pretty fun, interactive. I like those kind of games for some reason. Taking care of dogs, pretending to cook. Stuff like that."

"Popular right now, for sure. I was playing this other one, similar, where you're doing surgery. Kind of cool to hold the scalpel, make the cut, do all the stitches."

"I got the DS Lite. How 'bout you?"

"C'mon, who doesn't have the DS Lite these days? Regular DS . . . Might as well be the gray brick."

The pavement beneath their feet was flat, then a slight incline, but soon became a steep incline without them noticing at first.

"Okay, wait. Where the hell do you live?" Alex was a touch out of breath. "Don't tell me it's like Midtown or Uptown . . . God damn."

"C'mon, tough it out. Good to get out of Campus Heights once in a while, away from Westgate. I'm just over in Bloom Hill. Not like it's Lower Bloom Hill."

"I hate you."

"No, you don't." She smiled wide, faced him. "I'm awesome."

"You know . . ." Alex stared straight ahead, blinked. "It's been a while since I did anything like this. Kind of a happy accident."

April inclined her head, listened.

"I just been so busy with school and stuff. Been grinding, eighteen credits. I even been doing summer school. Last summer, I took thirteen credits."

"Thirteen!? Damn. I thought six in the summer was plenty."

"Four classes and a lab. And I go to academic clubs, events, and even took a national language proficiency test on top of everything else."

"You're kind of a nerd."

Alex nodded, let out a quiet laugh. "And, guess what I'm saying is, this was nice."

"Do you have a MySpace?"

"Of course."

"I don't think I have you on there. I'll send you a friend request."

"Great, 'cause I only have Tom. And him looking back at me over his shoulder at the number one spot on my Top 8 is getting pretty sad."

"Me and Tom then." She shot her hand out, pointed. "Ooh, look!"

Alex lifted his head up, peered ahead.

"That building. See? We're almost there."

"Is it the one above Do-Re-Mi Pho?" He saw the apartment building about twelve stories high, with two small restaurants and a parking lot at the bottom.

"Yep, that's me. Well, me and my roommate."

"I love those kind of pun names, like Twenty Pho Seven. Or like What the Pho or like Pho Real."

"Pho Shizzle."

"Pho Q."

April chuckled, almost snorted. "If they open a second location, Pho Q II."

❧

As he tidied up and got ready to call it a night, Alex somehow felt lighter and more at peace. Perhaps he needed a chill hang-out like that, to relax, laugh, have fun. He was already falling asleep on the bus ride home. The rocky motion with each turn and each stop. The monotonous drone of the engine. Crossing his arms, closing his eyes, Alex could feel himself begin to drift, his head hanging down, nodding off. When he plopped backward on the bed, his mind and body quieted and slowed right away, cozy and comfy from the perfect fluff of the pillow and the soothing fuzz of the blanket.

His nervous system was in an anabolic state at last, meaning his circadian rhythm would soon be restored. While he transitioned from non-REM sleep to REM sleep, Alex floated off the periphery of the world of the dreaming. He was in a peaceful slumber like a bear in hibernation or a newborn baby in a swaddle. There may have been floating Zs and counting sheep and the chime of Brahms' lullaby.

That was when he was violently startled awake out of nowhere. He couldn't move. He could not open his eyelids. He tried to speak, tried yelling, tried shouting, but no sounds formed. He was paralyzed. It felt as if someone jumped on him, pressed him down into the bed with incredible force. Alex tried to roll but he was pinned. He struggled to breathe. There was a pressure on his chest and the sensation of being choked. He squirmed in place, clenching his teeth, squeezing his fingers together into balled fists, his knuckles white and red. Hot tears formed in the corner of his eyes wide shut.

Let . . . !

Let go a me . . . !

The terrifying ordeal lasted for a solid couple of minutes, slow passing, excruciating. He feared he might be choked to death but then it stopped. When he was able to move again, to breathe, to think, he sat bolt upright. However, there was nothing there. Nobody was in that room. It was just darkness and emptiness which taunted him.

5

IT WAS IMPOSSIBLE to sleep after that. Alex had been attacked, not by someone but by something. Some invisible entity. Some malicious being. He felt violated. His space had been invaded. His body had been snatched. He was so fearful and discombobulated and afflicted that he remained frozen in that same position for a long while—the hairs raised on his forearm, hard bumps formed on the skin, a tingling in his teeth down to the core. There was water in his eyes that he held back by a thin veneer of willpower. When enough time passed, he swiveled to the edge of the bed, lowered his feet to the floor. Alex sat there, staring, blinking, shaking his head, then he glanced around the room.

Could it be?

He stood, stepped to the interior between his desk, his bed, the closet.

No. No way.

What the hell was that?

Flashes of the prior strange occurrences replayed: the sounds, the noises, the one missing item. He touched his fingers to his lips and chin in thought, trying to make sense of it.

I had a funky nightmare, that's all. Maybe it's just a coincidence.

However, despite forcing such a conclusion, his instincts and the feeling in his gut still checked the closet, still searched under the bed, and still slept (or tried to sleep) with the light on. The soft yellow glow from the lamp was like a big night light.

Alex slipped back into bed, pulled the blanket to his chin, closed his eyes, swallowing a lump of air. His mind continued to wander back and forth, trying to understand and also dismissing it.

When the sun started to break through the window, he felt some semblance of safety, of sanity. A return to normality. Fear of the dark was something ingrained in children, embraced in ancient cultures. Perhaps, as advanced as science and technology had become, as civilized as society can pretend to be, there were still things that go bump in the night that are mysterious and unknown. Alex pondered this. On the one hand, he believed there had to be some kind of explanation. But, on the other hand, maybe it was real, plain and simple. Real as electricity. Real as the sunrise.

He moved to the desk, opened up his laptop, waited for it to load. Though he was flustered and distressed, there was still work to do. Alex concluded it was best to take his mind off of it and try to keep busy. Between essays and reports, projects and presentations, there was always the reading. When he rechecked the schedules, he noticed an upcoming small quiz as well. He could gather together all his notes, compile them, highlight, underline.

Yeah. It had to be a nightmare . . .

Nothing more.

He read some manga and watched some more anime after studying to prepare for his shift. Despite being tempted to call out, he decided it might be best to have a distraction and get a break from his room and his bed.

Before he took a shower and got ready, he checked out his MySpace and there she was in his notifications. She made a funny face in which her eyes were squinty, her lips half-pouted like the bill of a duckling. He could see just a glimpse of her dazzly ears beneath the layered angle of her hair. The warmth from the sun across his skin grew stronger in that moment, the brightness intensifying as he lingered on that picture. Alex slid his finger on the touchpad then clicked accept.

Rolling the paper down from the horizontal spool then pulling it upwards against the flat metal piece, Alex tore it in a perfect straight line. He placed the rectangular box upside down along the inside of the pastel colored paper designed with polka dots and little candles and cupcakes. After ripping off the price sticker, he folded the paper in, taped the ends, then turned it upright. He wrapped a thick ribbon around it in a plus-sign with extra ribbon that he curled into a poofy bow with fancy threads. He handed the customer their gift in a bag and thanked them, then placed his hand on the countertop, drummed his fingers.

"You're a real dope wrapper."

He didn't notice but she snuck up next to him.

"How long you been standing there?"

"Long enough to see the tape cutting and that little twirly move in the end. Very nicely done."

"Thanks. I've gotten a lot better. I used to only do box shapes, but I can do anything now. You just make a big candy. Kinda like a cough drop thing with two twists."

April started walking to the shelves. "Some interesting stuff . . . I never been in here before, Brainiac Toys."

"Yeah, lemme show you a few things." Alex followed her then took the lead.

First, he showed some metal and wooden puzzles. The kind one either had to figure out how to piece together or how to pull apart. There was a game called Bananagrams with an open sample that they tinkered with. There were various sizes and styles of Rubik's Cubes hanging up. The wall transitioned from Legos and K'Nex to arts and crafts like beads and jewelry, to window art, to science kits. There were fuzzy hand puppets and finger puppets on a spinning rack next to a bin with different kites. Across that was an impulse section with magnets, marbles, yo-yos, gyroscopes, wind-up toys, die-cast cars and putty.

He played with a kendama. She jiggled a cylindrical gel toy in her hand with a lecherous smile. Alex viewed her in the corner of his eye, smirked.

Last, they circled to the back, past a display of educational workbooks and an assortment of animal figurines, on the other side of the baby toys and bath toys, with construction trucks, with jigsaw puzzles and board games.

Alex crossed his arms, leaned on a small pillar between the two shelves. "Thanks for stoppin' by."

"Yeah, I wasn't hungry but still had to take my lunch break. I might be hungry later on, if you're up for it."

"Uh, I don't know . . . I should probably do some studying for once."

"Come on, live a little. It's Sunday so the mall closes early. Plus it is a holiday tomorrow. Three-day weekend."

"Hmm . . ."

With enough peer pressure, they agreed to meet in front of the center stage which was about halfway between the two. Alex got there first, tapped his foot, stood in place, then took out his MP3 player. He scrolled through and ended up playing "Existentialism on Prom Night" by Straylight Run. Closing his eyes for moment, he moved his head to the music, first side to side then a light bop to the beat. The light piano notes and soft guitar strumming hit the spot. In the middle of the song, after the second chorus, it blended with violins and harmonized background vocals. Almost as if on cue, April turned from around the corner and stepped towards him. He smirked, following her with his eyes as the rest of the song finished up.

He took off the earbuds, wrapped the wire then put it in his pocket. "There you are. I was about to bail on you."

"Pssh. You wouldn't dare." She smiled, placed her hands on the back of her hips. "What were you listening to?"

"Ah, just this one song. Emo band."

"You're kind of emo, huh? Like a mopey suicidal Eeyore."

"I kind of resent that." Alex shook his head, laughed. "Don't deny it, just resent it."

April bit her bottom lip. "You mind if I stop home first? I need to change . . ."

"Sure. But why?"

"Just somebody wanted extra butter on their panini, and it turned into extra butter down the side of my leg as well."

Alex glanced down at her thighs.

"We can take the bus this time, to save time. Since you're trying to be a good boy and study and all that."

"Oh. Maybe we better get going then. I think there's one coming, like, right now."

They went through the interior of the mall to the other side, a main bus terminal. There was a terminal on both sides, but the east side was less crowded and closer to where they met up. There was a scattered huddle of people so it appeared they made it in time.

He took out his phone, checked. "Just a few more minutes, maybe. If they're running late. Supposed to be here any minute now."

"Nice phone. What kinda phone is that?"

Alex handed it to her. "It's a Sony Ericsson. What do you got?"

"Check it out." She handed hers. "Mine is one of those Motorola Razr phones."

His was a slide phone and hers was a flip phone. The exterior of his was a smooth silver-gray. April turned it over in her hand, slid the screen up, revealing the QWERTY keyboard which was a brighter turquoise. Hers was a shiny metallic purple. Alex tilted it then flicked it with his thumb, opening it.

"S-should I put in my number?"

April chuckled. "Smooth."

"Hey, shut up. It's not like that." He entered his number into her phone.

She also entered hers into his phone. "Sure. Uh-huh."

"Um. Maybe don't scroll through my pics . . ."

"Now I wanna see."

"Hey! Give it back—"

The bus rolled in and they lined up with the others, found two open seats towards the back. She sat by the window and he sat by the aisle.

"I saw your wallpaper."

"Hmm?"

"Who was that?"

"Oh, that's my sister. Not sure if I ever mentioned."

Alex nodded. "Yeah. I didn't know you had a sister."

"Two, actually."

"I got a little brother."

"Names are May and June."

He laughed. "Are you serious???"

"The bane of my existence. My older sis was born May, so my parental units named her May. I was born in April. And then the littlest was born in June. April-May-June."

"I kind of like that name, June."

"What's wrong with April?"

"Guess I like April, too. Kinda reminds me of *Ninja Turtles,* which I love."

She smiled, shifted in place.

It was a short ride in comparison to their longer stroll the night before. When they got to her apartment building, they passed through the lobby between the two restaurants, took the elevator to the ninth floor.

"You wanna wait out here, or inside? It'll just be a sec."

"I can wait here."

There was no need for him to get used to her place. Not like this was going to become a habit or a routine, he concluded. He rested his shoulder blades on the wall, leaned his head back against it.

Gotta try keep this short. I still have to study.

Next to him, the door flew back open.

"Whoa. That was fast."

"Told ya."

April pulled in front of him, started to waddle then slow down. From behind, he noticed her jeggings wrapped tight, hugging every line and curve of her legs, her knees, her calves. It accentuated her hips and buttocks. He couldn't help but stare.

"So, where we going?"

"I . . ." He inclined his head, still gazing at her from behind. "I don't know."

"Okay, wait. Hold on. Nope. These are a bit tight. Haven't worn 'em in a while. Lemme go change again real quick. My bad."

April went back inside, to which he laughed.

He never thought of her in a provocative way before that. She was always kind of a tomboy, one of the boys. Alex still thought so, but now he also realized she had a nice butt.

Much to his internal dismay, he did end up staying out a little too late. He ate too much food and spent too much money. And all for a girl that was just friends. Alex lay on the pillow, closed his eyes, took a deep breath in and out, still thinking about it while beginning to drift. A part of him did think maybe it was okay. He was under a lot of stress after all, and two years of serious hardcore grinding may have caught up with him. Alex didn't even realize he made it back home, tidied up, got ready for bed, and was on the brink of falling asleep. Perhaps that was just what he needed—a good distraction, a quiet night out. His mind slipped away into the swirling haze of darkness where squiggly colored lines and shapes floated and warped.

Although he was able to rest for perhaps a good hour or so, that was when it happened again. Alex was awake, alert all of a sudden. Yet he could not move. Yet he could not see. He was mute. He was trapped. Then that pressing sensation over him as if he was being choked, choked to certain death.

Holy fuck!

Beads of sweat gathered on his forehead. Alex gasped, gagged, as the oxygen remained lodged in his throat, in his lungs, not circulating. He struggled and squirmed against the invisible force enough to lift his arms off the bed. His fingers outstretched and curled upwards, trembling. His eyelids remained closed, both from fear and from the inability to move or even twitch.

The horror lasted this time for about one minute, every single second like grains of sand in an overturned hourglass. When he was free, he rolled to the side, leaned on one elbow, glancing around the room, to nothing, to no one. His eyes darted from the table to the lamp to the desk to the closet. He turned his head from left to right, scanning the room in one long sweep. That same darkness and emptiness from before, quiet, still, stared right back at him like hollows from rotted eye sockets.

6

WITH THE LIGHTS on, it was difficult sleeping. Alex had experienced something unexplainable, inexplicable, twice now. Not to mention the strange noises, the strange sounds, and the one missing item which appeared like it had been deliberately placed. His immediate visceral reaction was fear, was dread. He could not dismiss this, at least not right away. What happened to him was so out of the ordinary, it shook him to his core, almost shattering his worldview, his understanding of the very laws of nature. Still, despite that nagging itch from his own intuition, Alex tried to rationalize it. He wanted to be logical, to be objective, and tried to find some kind of rhyme or reason.

Perhaps it was just stress, simple as that. Stress in combination with a major ongoing disruption to his sleep cycle. It could have been another nightmare. Not like it's unheard of to have recurrent dreams or dreams that are similar or related. Or, perhaps—and he hated to even entertain this preposterous concept but—maybe there was something else going on, something more sinister at large. An entity lurking in the shadows, beyond the veil, from the further, the depths of the abyss, that nether void.

No, it can't be . . .

It can't be . . .

Alex rubbed his eyes with a fatigued and frustrated yawn, pivoting to the edge of the bed. He buried his face in his palms then arched his neck back, staring at the ceiling. He shook his head to himself. Was there something to fear in the dark? Were there actual things that go bump in the night?

His hand squeezed the bed sheet then formed a light fist that he pounded onto the mattress. Alex hopped up and walked to the desk, flipped his laptop open, waiting for it to load. He scrolled over the touchpad, clicked, opened the browser, noticing the blinking cursor before entering the search terms: attacked in sleep.

Amongst the scattered results were a few possibilities including demon, sleep paralysis, nocturnal panic attack and night terrors. He hovered link to link regarding demon but could not bring himself to open it. Then he hovered over one of the links for sleep paralysis, about to open it. It had to be between one of those two as they appeared to be the most prevalent.

Sleep paralysis is a temporary state of consciousness upon falling asleep or waking in which one is not able to move, he read on the website. An episode might include auditory, tactile or visual hallucinations that often result in fear. Risk factors range from narcolepsy, sleep apnea and alcohol usage to sleep deprivation, and triggers may be psychological stress or abnormal sleep.

"Pretty spot-on there." He stared at the screen, leaning his chin into his palm. "Sleep paralysis, huh . . ."

Alex decided to check his e-mail before moving on to other things, trying to be somewhat productive. It was a lot of junk and spam as per usual. But there was also one other e-mail that stood out, pretty recent, notifying of the last day to withdraw from classes. He skimmed it over, lingering on the words. He thinned his lips, leaned back.

Damn.

How crazy would that be.

With a quick rifle through the different schedules and syllabi, he took his textbook and DS then went to the common area. Alex just needed a break from that room, and at the same time, to tackle an easy simpler task.

He plopped down on the soft recliner, throwing one leg over the armrest, laying there in a half-diagonal position with his back to the window. There were two coffee tables, a wooden case with a large TV, a loveseat, another matching recliner, and then a long sectional on one side. Sometimes the others in the dorm would hang in this area, watch a movie or watch the game perhaps. When he opened up to the assigned chapter, Alex found himself scanning it rather than reading it. It wasn't clicking. He reread the same sentence, same paragraph over and over and over again.

Closing the textbook, setting it aside, he instead took out his DS. Maybe something more active would hold his attention. He slid down a hill then hopped up, bouncing from one flying turtle to the next, almost getting the 1-Up. Then he went down the green pipe to the underworld where little spiky creatures crawled along the ceiling and over the question mark blocks. When he went back into the pipe, jumped up over the brick pyramid to the flagpole, it was an empty victory.

Alex turned off the DS, pressing the stylus back in, placed it on top of the closed textbook then peered out the window. He sighed then took his phone out from his pocket, scrolling through the contacts list. He gazed at her name, at her number, and peered out the window again.

⨁

Though it began as a simple text, out of boredom, out of curiosity, it turned into a conversation back and forth. There was slight trepidation before agreeing to get together and meet up, hang out. Alex found himself putting a little extra effort into his application of body spray, the styling of his hair with fiber gum putty. He glimpsed in the mirror once more before reaching for a t-shirt to wear. He threw on a pair of faded slim fit jeans, pushed his feet into his skater shoes then put on a hoodie. It had a beige skull design across the front with fur lining along the hood. On the ride to her building, he played "M+M's" by Blink-182 and then "Movies" by Alien Ant Farm on his MP3 player.

He texted her from downstairs, waited in the hall by the elevator in between the two restaurants. Again, he checked his hair and clothing but this time in the faint reflection of the glass window.

"Relax. You look good." April stepped towards him.

She was also wearing a hoodie. Her skinny jeans had light speckles of glitter and paint, and there were tears in which the skin of her knees poked through.

"Thanks for coming out. I could've suffered alone, but this is way better."

"Don't mention it. What're friends for?"

Alex smirked then moved his head, sweeping the bangs out of his eyes.

"Hey, we're matching hoodies." She jutted her elbow out as they walked side by side. "Do yours got these thingies?"

"No." He laughed. "What's the point of those?"

"I don't know. They're just extra thumb holes for when you're feeling extra cold or extra awesome, I guess."

"Which one are you feeling?"

"A li'l of both."

They laughed, shifted towards one another then faced ahead.

"Shall we take the long way, get some exercise?"

"Yeah, why not."

"It was a good idea to check this thing out." Alex fidgeted with his fingers in the pockets of the hoodie. "Nice suggestion."

"Right. I always heard of it, heard it wasn't half-bad. And since today is a special one, I threw it out there. Thanks for falling for it, er, I mean, taking the bait."

He shook his head, kicked at the pavement. "Hope you're hungry."

"With a name like Munchies Strike, it better be frickin' great."

They walked through the city streets, past designer boutiques and hipster coffee shops with roped off sitting areas with tables and chairs. There were potted plants in front of some establishments, credit unions and barber shops and repair services. The painted hydrants matched the painted utility poles. Bike paths lined each side of the street and a string of leafy green trees lined up over the median. A pair of shoes hung up on the cables before the intersection as they transitioned from Bloom Hill to Lower Bloom Hill.

This area was quieter, more of a residential neighborhood as they continued their trek over to Midtown in the Capitol District. There was one house with patches of fluffy grass, a small tree to the side, a big tree in the back, a few thick bushes, stones lined and a paved circle. It was painted a dull yellow-beige and had a light gray fence around the outside.

"You ever heard about this place?" April motioned with her head.

"A haunted house is supposed to be in this area, right? This the one?"

"People say it's a demon house . . ."

"That doesn't look very scary." Alex squinted his eyes, thinned his lips.

"Or, shit, maybe it's that house over there." She let out a chuckle, gesturing with her hand. "Anyway, one of these."

He stared again at the unseeming house as he followed along. There was one side window that stood out to him, had a hollow feeling to it. The gears and pulleys began to turn in his cerebral cortex.

∾

Several city blocks were sectioned off along the main street, branching to the regional community park. It was food trucks, food wagons and various vendors scattered across the asphalt and concrete, while local farmers and other merchants with natural and organic items were sprawled through the open grounds. Banners stretched over the entrance and along the main path, flashy signs waving as volunteer staff in bright shirts handed out pamphlets with event times and custom maps. Alex touched the small of her back then took the lead. April followed as they squeezed through the friends, families and couples passing. There was a ragtag band out front, with an acoustic guitar, a bass, a fiddle and a wooden box drum.

"I heart this kinda music."

"Me, too. Like folk songs. Indie, Celtic."

"Yeah. Got a Flogging Molly or Dropkick Murphys sound."

"Love those bands . . ."

He noticed her dazzly ears from the side, blinked, inclined his head, then turned away. As they observed the mismatched group continue on, Alex bopped along to the rhythm and April clapped with a wide smile.

"One more?"

She nodded with excitement, a tiny sparkle forming in the corner of her eye. They inched forward while others also joined in, growing the huddle to a mass. He held up an imaginary lighter and waved it overhead, to which she giggled.

Alex touched the small of her back again, pointed with his chin to follow. April held onto the hem of his hoodie while he guided them to where they were free to move about. He smirked, leaned in. She smiled, kept pace.

On either side of them, down the main path were booths that ran parallel, some with tents, some with tarps, some with multiple tables in various layouts displaying their items for sale. Almost all of them had select free samples to try. They perused at a slow pace, taking their time, taking it all in: the mood, the magic, the atmosphere, the ambience.

There were bins of assorted fruits and vegetables of yellow, orange, red, a gradient scale of green. Some vendors had bags of snacks hanging up and big boxes of desserts laid out. Alex grabbed a piece of peppered beef jerky while April grabbed a piece of pumpernickel bread. There were jars of spices, jams, pesto, salsa, salad dressing and dipping sauces. She reached for two multigrain crackers with a dollop of honey on it, handed one to him. They touched the edge of their crackers together before nibbling away. He licked his fingers while she smacked her lips.

"God. So much to choose from."

"We still got all that to get through, too."

April grabbed his sleeve and tugged him along. There was a machine with fresh popcorn raining down behind the oily, salty pane of glass. Open cartons of colored caramel popcorn were stacked up and the smell hit their nostrils at the same time. Another machine whirred from the next spot over, mixing different nuts with either brown sugar or cinnamon. These were on display in a cardboard cone in a holder tray like an ice cream cone.

She lifted a brow and pointed. "You know you want that in your mouth . . ."

There was a smoked meat place specializing in grass-fed beef that had plate lunches, sandwiches, and a sausage on a stick that April was referring to.

He shook his head but nodded.

One of their last stops was an area with succulents, potted plants, single flowers and whole arrangements of bouquets.

"This is pretty romantical, right?" Alex darted his eyes over the petals and stems.

"It is pretty, and it is romantical. But if I can't eat it then it's not necessary."

"Hey, here."

As he knelt, Alex lifted up a flower that had fallen off and flew away. He blew on it with a gentle puff, wiped it with his sleeve then placed it on her dazzly ear.

"Not weird 'cause, A, I didn't pay for it. And, B, well, you're helping this little guy out. It got lost and would not fulfill its floral destiny otherwise."

"Smooth."

"Hahaha, shut up."

They settled on splitting a combo plate, the sausage on a stick, roasted corn glazed with garlic butter and paprika, and two fresh squeezed ice tea lemonades.

All the benches and chairs were taken, even the standing

tables, so the two settled on sitting on the curb side by side. Their hands were full so they were careful in their movements, placing the cups down to make space. Alex let April have the first bite then he took a big bite himself. They tried each food with an enthusiastic nom, nom, nom.

He pointed out the savory touch of fennel seed as he chewed, and April commented on the subtle flavor of mint as she sipped through the straw. They started slowing down about halfway through, when they realized they may have gotten too much.

". . . I don't think this is quite what Dr. King had in mind."

"Basically, I *had* a dream, but then I poured gravy on it and ate it."

She had a glazed look in her eyes as she leaned further back, found a comfortable position. In front of them, the crowds continued to enjoy the festivities. Back by the entrance, the sound of the guitar, bass and fiddle were still audible but faint.

"Admit it."

He turned, shifted in her direction, listening.

"This is waay better than studying your ass off, right?"

Alex smirked. "Yeah. You're right. Hell, I'm starting to think maybe I am burnt out on scholarly life. At least a little bit."

"Nothing wrong with taking a break. Relax, enjoy things, and just . . ." April waved her hand in a circular motion as she tried coming up with the right words. "Just . . . Just be."

"Hmm. 'Just be.' Nice ring to that. I like it." He hung his head down then stared off. "Kind of got a Zen, almost Buddhist vibe. A new proverb."

She chuckled. "I be droppin' some wisdom. By accident."

Unbeknownst to him, he was about to learn another critical lesson, LIFE101L, and that was that people come into your life for a reason. Alex had the detailed steps of the next five years all planned out: work abroad, go to grad school, land a federal job. Perhaps he was so preoccupied with the future he somewhat neglected the present. And, at the present, it was a beautiful day unfolding, a beautiful moment, with a beautiful girl.

April readjusted the flower on her ear. Alex gazed at her while she did this.

"Um, how 'bout you? Glad you came along?"

"I mean, it was my idea." She nudged at him with her elbow. "But I am glad all this happened, yes. Great excuse to go outside, get out of my own head."

He paused, stared off again.

"Like, I know you been single for a while, and on purpose, which is cool. Respectable. But this is kinda weird for me. I got all this . . . all this time now."

"Funny. I feel like I never have enough time. I could use that little thing that Hermione used." Alex played with a crumpled napkin between his fingers.

"A time-turner."

"Right, that. I could use two of those."

She sat up, folded her arms, rested them on her knees. "You wanna listen to some music? Digest our food a bit?"

"Yeah, sure." He took out his MP3 player and held it out for her.

April untangled the wire, placing one earbud in her ear, giving him the other. She scrolled through the list of artists, settled on Motion City Soundtrack. They listened to the first three tracks then skipped to the eighth and ninth tracks of the album.

The upbeat guitar riffs and drums, the nonchalant vocals matched everything going on around them. Alex ran his fingers across his bangs, stole a quick glance. She stretched her legs out, crossed her feet, jittering her Chucks.

"Okay." April wrapped the earphones around again, stood, returned the MP3 player. "Shall we get going?"

He also stood, tossed their rubbish in the nearest garbage can. "I think so. Looks like there's other craft kinda stuff we didn't get to check out yet, in those sections in back."

"Uh, B-R-B. I gotta go to the restroom."

When she turned and half-jogged away, he couldn't help but check her out from behind again until he caught himself. He blinked, faced down.

Oh, man. Gotta stop doing that.

Can't make that a habit.

Dangerous . . .

He put his hands in pockets, leaned against the trunk of a slanted tree. Alex took a breath in and out.

As she made her way back, he observed her walk towards him with a smile across her face so wide it turned his smirk into a smile as well.

Seriously. Watch it.

This is not good.

No room in my life for a new friend, or an old friend renewed or whatever. And definitely no room for anything more than a friend.

Both were quieter this time, from the large meal but also from so much walking. These tents had handmade bracelets and necklaces on display, wallets, keychains, carved figurines, other knickknacks. April felt the material of one of the handkerchiefs then grabbed a scarf and wrapped it around herself.

First, she draped it from the sides of her neck, then tossed one side over herself down her back. She pulled it in front of her again, did a simple tie. She did a quick pose, put one hand on her hip with a slight pout of her lips. Then she looped it around her neck so that it hung down shorter. She opened it up, wrapped it around herself like a cape then like a shawl, with a sway back and forth.

While he viewed all this, Alex licked his lips and inclined his head, feeling the tiniest flutter in his chest. It was something he hadn't felt in a long time. For how many consecutive semesters, he had turned his heart off, locked it away in a box and hid the key. Now, though, it thumped, it pulsed, it rushed.

PART TWO

LIVING DEAD

1

AFTER THAT WEEKEND, Alex fought a constant battle. His life became a delicate tightrope of balancing the unstoppable forces around him against the immovable objects in front of him—a perfect thunderstorm in which he was trapped. It started to take a major toll on his mental and emotional state. Flashes of her lingered in his mind throughout the coming days. He found himself thinking about her eyelashes, her full lips, the bridge of her nose, her dazzly ears and the way her hair hung over them at a slight angle. The rounded dirt path from the dorms, the tall pine trees, the wide open field, it all passed by without his even realizing. Alex walked with his hands in his pockets through the rec center to the library, staring down at his feet.

Sleep paralysis . . .

That is so weird. So annoying.

Oh well.

It would happen late at night or early in the morning, sometimes straight in a row, sometimes skipping a night or two. Alex would be in bed, sound asleep, but also ready and waiting. He started to will himself to sit up, to resist. This shortened the duration of the attack. From just a few inches off the bed at first to a good several inches, until he was able to make it about a third of the way. Perhaps, if he could make it the whole way, he will have conquered this thing at last.

He was tempted to go right back to his dorm and pass out, but instead, forced himself up the elevator to the fourth floor at a quiet cubicle, dragging his feet, running on fumes. The day prior was productive enough that he could get through on minimal sleep with minimal effort. At some point, a coffee and a fifteen-minute power nap would be needed but he had to time it, make it count.

For a brief moment, he remembered the e-mail warning of the last day to withdraw from classes, but shook the thought away.

On one hand, it was enjoyable being out and about with his new partner in crime. It did take his mind off things, like school, like goals, the future, like whatever had been happening the past how many nights. On the other hand, he admitted it was not something he wanted or needed right now. It was not of importance, not a priority.

This is what he needed to focus on, not sleep disorders, not girls, not hanging out. His routine. His academia.

Okay. This is it.

If I'm gonna get caught up, it has to happen now.

Everything is on the line.

Somehow, he was able to plug away at the assignments one by one, even glimpse ahead to the next chapters of reading before heading home.

Alex shut his eyes, grit his teeth, clenched his fists then let out an agonized groan, falling down onto the bed. Breaking the train of thought, he felt the fabric of the blanket, took notice of the dark room around him. He was at risk once again. The difference this time was he had an idea of what it might be now, and had started to try to fight back.

If this is just so-called sleep paralysis . . .

He peeped down to the foot of the bed then glanced into the open closet.

Then, well, there's nothing to worry about. At all.

Right? Makes sense.

He remembered walking with April from Bloom Hill to Lower Bloom Hill, thought about that one specific house. For a brief moment, the closet appeared like the side window from earlier. Same shape. Same hollow feeling. Same empty stillness.

Alex couldn't stop from thinking. He thought about the present, thought about the future. Thought about spooky houses. He wondered what could be lurking in the shadows, invisible to the naked eye, unseen, unheard, unacknowledged. He pondered whether or not there was something more to life, there was an actual afterlife. And also, he kept seeing *her* as well. Her eyes that sparkled when she laughed. The way she crossed her legs over and jittered her feet. Her sense of humor. Her sense of style. Her taste in music.

It was a light blend of noise and motion inside the shopping center. Alex stared at his feet on the carpet of the second floor, walked towards the bench in front of the movie theater where she was already waiting. April leaned back with an elbow across the top of the bench, a soft smile on her face, waving him over with her fingertips. He saw the clock on the wall by the box office, glanced at the posters lining the wall to the entrance, then joined her. He plopped down as she inclined her head, eager. Her dazzly ears were visible beneath the angle of her hair, and he felt some comfort and relief at the sight of them. She scooted closer to him while he shifted over to face her.

"What's going on, Alex?"

"Sorry, I . . . Thanks for coming to hang. Had a rough few days, and wanted to kinda take my mind off it."

"You're definitely a little emo-er than usual." She smiled, blinked. "It might be T-M-I, but feel free to vent. I might not have advice but I can always listen. I'm a helluva listener."

Alex smirked, licked his lips. "First off, I ditched my last class to be here. I never do that, least not in a long time. I'm all over the place, it feels like. Behind on my shit. I got one of my quizzes back which I totally bombed. That hurt."

She nodded, kept her eyes locked.

He took a deep breath, leaned forward.

"I missed a big essay, half-assed a presentation. I've been staying up later, sleeping in longer. Not paying attention. I don't even know."

". . . Did anything happen?"

The tiny flutter in his chest returned in that instant as he gazed into her eyes, through her and at the entirety of her being. His lower lip hung open as he paused, mesmerized. Her eyes, her full lips. Her voice, her smooth skin. Her graphic tee that hugged her chest and midriff.

"Uh, n-no, not really."

In the end, there were just some things he could not tell her. The truth that possible supernatural, paranormal phenomena tortured him, tormented him every night. The truth that he was on the brink of a collapse. And also the truth that each time he and she talked like this, spent time together, his eyes tended to wander, tended to linger and stare.

"Eh, we all get behind sometimes. I mean, it sucks but it

does happen." April shook her head, gestured with her hands. "It's only a big deal if you make it a big deal. Y'know?"

"I guess, maybe you're right."

"Of course I'm right." She straightened with a quick and swift motion then hopped to her feet. "Here, come on."

Alex narrowed his eyes. "What?"

"Come. Here." April raised her arms out to the side.

He staggered up, took a single step towards her. Then they wrapped their arms around one another as they embraced.

His eyes closed, he breathed in the subtle scent of her hair and her perfume. It was pleasant, somehow perfect. Alex began to feel a warmth, not just from their bodies touching but from their energies overlapping and intertwining in a delicate mesh.

"April . . . Not gonna lie, this is like the best damn hug ever . . ."

She laughed. "I read this article about human contact and about hugging. That if you hold onto someone for, I forget, ten, twenty, thirty seconds or something, it releases happy chemicals in your brain."

"Oh. Wow, really."

"Better make it one minute to be safe. At least forty-five seconds."

They squeezed together closer, even tighter.

"I'm okay with that . . ."

Alex could feel said chemicals flood his skull as they swayed. She leaned the side of her head against the line of his jaw. He leaned his cheek against the top of her head first one way then the other. His palms tingled, feeling the small of her back and then the back of her shoulders through the fabric. The blood rushed as his crotch stiffened.

He had to remind himself they're friends, just friends. Nothing more.

This is just a girl.

She's a girl, and she's a friend. Not a girlfriend.

"Let's go cruise around before our shifts start."

April pulled away but kept her hands on his hips while motioning with her head.

"What're we doing?" Alex followed her lead, but with trepidation. "W-where are we going?"

"Dude. We're broke college kids that work at the mall. Of course our primary activity is to window shop and to people watch."

They walked along a shelf of lava lamps in the first store. She touched her fingers to a clear orb that set off charges of static electricity like mini-bolts of lightning. He pressed the button of an alarm clock with soothing ocean and rainforest sounds then flicked the switch of an oscillating air purifier fan.

In the next store, they searched bins of rocks and minerals and geodes. He played with two pieces of magnetic hematite, felt the force as they attracted and repelled. She tossed rose quartz between her hands then rotated the spinning display case. There were shark teeth, obsidian arrowheads and petrified wood on the other side.

"Used to love this kinda stuff as a kid." Alex dropped the pieces back in.

"Oh yeah?"

"For sure."

He led them back outside to the main walkway.

"You know, we're kinda all kids still inside, huh? Like, even if you grow up, there is a part of you that remains, like, frozen in that time."

Alex shifted, glanced at her with the corner of his eye. "That's true, huh."

"For instance, check this out."

She hurried to the front of another store where there was a large gumball machine with blinking lights and dinging sounds. It had a large glass pane which displayed all the winding tracks and little contraptions.

He joined her then loaded the quarters in the slot, gazing over at her with a raised brow.

April let out a squee of excitement, balled her hands into upturned fists that she held by her cheeks. She nibbled her bottom lip as the gumball dropped down, shot up and across, circled around the machine, looped, spiraled, fell into a scoop, rotated onto a lever, bounced off a spinning disc to a colored pinwheel then one last roller coaster ride to the bottom with a loud clicka clacka.

When she bent to get the gumball, a sliver of her lower back showed between the hem of her shirt and the top of the skinny jeans. Alex stared, swallowed then faced away.

"Do you wanna get some real food?"

"Yes!"

She bit into the gumball, gave him the other half.

He popped it in his mouth.

"Cool. We got a little time left. So, where shall we go?"

"There is this thing I wanted to try . . ."

Both made their way down the wing past a frozen yogurt shop, an upscale bakery and a store with fragrant lotions and foaming hand soaps, to a place with shakes and smoothies.

"I want that!" April pointed to the menu up top.

"How the hell do you even say that?"

"Just go for it." She laughed, gave him some cash and a nudge.

The cashier had thick glasses and purple hair, stared at him like he was an insect while he teetered to the counter.

"Can I get a, uh . . . An acchai? A-akai . . . ?"

"An açaí bowl?"

"Yes, yes. That. Can I get that. Please."

April cupped one hand over her mouth, held back a wave of laughter.

"Granola and honey okay?"

"Yes?"

"Name?"

"Lex."

With a raised brow and a jutted lip, the cashier scribbled on the styrofoam.

"That's a weird name. Nex, interesting."

"No. *Lex.* As in Alex."

"Oh . . ." The cashier held the Sharpie in mid-air. "Well, you're Nex now."

April blurted out, bawled in laughter behind him. She keeled over, slapping a hand to her knee and held at her side. He turned around, watched her in faux annoyance.

"Dude. That's totally your new name."

He thinned his lips, drooped his eyelids. "I'll have to come up with one for you too then. Like, I don't know, Avril instead of April or something. With a V."

"Or just V?"

"Yeah, maybe."

They waited for their bowl then walked to a nearby table. She held the bowl with both hands while he took two long plastic spoons and a wad of napkins.

April scooped the fruity paste with a slice of banana then brought it to his mouth. Alex obliged, let her feed him, nodded as it turned out quite good.

"Whoa. That ain't half-bad. Delish."

He scooped a chunk with an extra glaze of honey and extra granola flakes, instinctively brought it to her mouth without realizing. She opened her mouth, bit into it, licked her lips. As she chewed, for a moment, her inhibited smile caused her cheeks to curve and round like a chipmunk or a squirrel.

That tiny flutter kicked back in with this innocent and unintended scene, him watching her genuine enjoyment, noticing her dazzly ears again. Her face tilted downward, poking around with the spoon. He paused, blinked to himself, hung his shoulders low.

Ah, shit . . . Crap.

Do I have a thing for her?

All of the stress from overwork and from burnout in addition to the repetitive disturbance of sleep was turning into borderline insomnia. Plus, not to mention, although it started as an innocent harmless crush, it continued to grow stronger and deeper until it was now the pure agony of being infatuated, being smitten. Alex remained on the pillow tossing and turning with his eyes closed until, at last, he floated away into slumber. In that dream world, they were together, and it was peaceful and wonderful, whimsical and marvelous until he was viciously ripped from that imagined limbo to yet another pitch black nightmare.

He lay on the bed, unable to move, unable to make a sound, unable to open his eyes. Hard goosebumps formed on the skin of his forearms, on the sides of his shins and calves, all the way to the base of his neck. It was such an enormous pressure that it felt impossible to fight against. Above his head, he could feel a sort of tension in the air. This seemed to float in place, expand and then shrink, expand and then shrink—as if it were a regulated breath, a steady heartbeat, a poisonous jellyfish drifting in the high tide.

In the corners of his shut eyes, tears gathered. The goosebumps hardened even more, raising the hairs up straight and firm from each pore.

Between his arm and the wall, the surface of the mattress began to move up and down as if something stepped on it, jumped on it. He felt this bouncing glide from up by his head along his side to his arm, his leg, his foot, like a small child playing. For a moment, he may have heard a faint giggle.

Alex tried turning his head to better hear but had trouble doing so. He outstretched his fingers, started to raise his hands, lift his shoulder blades from the surface of the mattress, about halfway, then gasped for air as everything happening ceased all at once.

What the fuck *was that!?*

He hyperventilated while his eyes darted around the empty room. His eyes were wide, his mouth was agape, and a teardrop rolled down his cheek as he gulped. Alex buried his face in both palms then rocked in place.

No, no, no, no.

Please. Please. This can't be happening.

Even though the encounter was finished, the terror seemed to continue. He felt something watch him, a vicious sneer with derision and ridicule. It grimaced with utter malice, salivating in an insatiable bloodlust.

Fuuuck.

This ain't no bullshit sleep paralysis. God damn it.

2

WITH THE KNUCKLES on the back of his hand, he knocked on the door. Knocking again, this time a little bit harder, Alex listened inside to the slight squeak of a desk chair spring, the sound of rolling wheels and some rustling papers, the shutting of a drawer. He stood back as the locks were undone and the door pulled open. The associate professor lifted a hand up then waved him inside, gesturing to a stool on the wall by the side of a cabinet. It was a crowded space, stacked high with files, folders, binders, books. There was a corkboard stuck with thumbtacks next to the air conditioner. It had a calendar up next to mismatched sticky notes.

"Sorry. This place is sorta a dump."

"Nah, it's fine. Thank you for seeing me on such short notice."

The professor sat down, scooted in, drank from a plastic tumbler.

"What can I do for you? I might get an e-mail, an occasional word or two after class, but this is unexpected."

"You're right. The drop box is usually as far as I go."

Alex gazed down at his feet as the professor slouched in an open and casual manner.

"Well, professor—"

"Just call me Martin."

"Oh, okay. Martin . . ." Alex gulped. "I been having some trouble this semester. You may have noticed."

"Hmm. Other than the occasional late work, you're doing all right to me. You mentioned graduating soon so I figured that must be it. Let's go and check, though."

The click of the mouse was soft, the sound of the scroll wheel muted.

"Ah. You're right. You did miss one paper, but it was a fairly large one. And it appears you missed an exam as well?"

"Exactly. It has been a little difficult, to say the least. I didn't even get to e-mail you ahead of time for that."

"I know you had that trip, right? And you were jet lagged."

"Right. But that was a few weeks ago already."

"You're taking six classes? Eighteen credits?"

Alex nodded, thinned his lips.

"Things okay? Do you need to talk?"

"No, not really. I just want to know if there's anything that could be done to make those up. Or am I screwed here?"

"I can let you turn in the paper late, with a slight penalty. That's no problem. But I'm afraid the test score will have to stand as is. It wouldn't be fair to the other students."

"Understood."

"However, in the overall big picture, you're still doing fine in my opinion. It will make a ding on honor roll status, but you'll pass. You get to graduate. Just have to fly straight going forward, by the coming mid-terms."

Alex let out a sigh.

"You mentioned the master's program and the GET Initiative. Global Exchange Training, right? I myself did something similar."

"That's right. I think I'll work for a bit before, travel abroad, get some experience."

"Let me say this. You come off as a very ambitious, determined and capable individual. There have been many promising students I've met but just a select few stand out, put in that little extra effort to go above and beyond."

He waited, listening as the professor paused to drink.

"I think you can go far in the fields of linguistics and international studies. Whatever this is that is going on, getting in the way, figure it out and work through it. Because this is a tremendous opportunity."

Alex stood, smirked. "Thank you, prof—"

The professor also stood, extended his hand out.

"Thank you, Martin."

"Don't mention it. See you in class."

❧

The next time that it happened, he was extra determined. Alex felt the immense pressure over him, the invisible force holding him down. He willed himself through the paralysis, wiggled each of his fingers, wiggled his big toe, lifted his hands then his arms in slow and steady bursts of movement. He was able to raise his back up off the bed a few inches then about halfway. With enough effort, he did make it all of the way, full upright. This was it. This was his chance. Somehow, resisting over the last frightful and sleepless nights was about to pay off. There was no going back now. It was time to come face to face with whatever this thing was that continued to torment him and throw his life upside down. Despite his own good sense, he snapped his eyelids open.

Before him, wafting like smoke, was a translucent white that appeared like a mist or a haze, formless. It hovered for a moment then lifted away and vanished, blurry, as his vision adjusted to the darkness.

Holy shit . . .

I just saw the thing.

Alex took a slow breath in and out. The room was freezing cold, and there was a light touch of static in the air.

Though it was just for one second, maybe two, two and a half, that image haunted him to his very core.

From section to section, aisle to aisle, the two of them perused the interior of the superstore. April had suggested it as they began their evening galivanting after the long shift. It was a sidewalk sale that whole weekend so it was busier than usual during work. Plus, it was one of the few places still open, and free for the most part. He followed close behind as she grabbed packet after packet of different snacks: taffy, rice crackers, strawberry belts, chocolate covered peanuts, wavy garden salsa flavor chips. She held them all in her hands like an ecstatic child out on Halloween night, loaded them into an abandoned cart by the end of the shelf then began to climb in herself.

"W-whoa, watch out—"

Alex hurried over, held her hand tight for balance as the cart wobbled beneath her feet. April sat down, kicked her Chucks up on the front end of the cart.

"Thanks, Nex."

"Don't mention it, V."

Her nickname became a regular term of endearment for him but his nickname for her wouldn't stick. It did come up on occasion then faded again.

"Okay. Soon-to-be diabetic coma, check. Anything else?"

He didn't respond. There was a shiny foil candy wrapper that caught his eye. Its special white mystery flavor listed on the label reminded him of the other night—that puff of smoke, that poof of steam, obscure, ivory. What began as noises, sounds, missing items, turned into ongoing attacks in his sleep, and now a kind of matter materializing.

"Nex? Nex, you okay?" She touched at his forearm. "You . . . You look like you just seen a ghost . . ."

That innocent idiom hit him on a deeper level, to which he almost flinched. He stared back at her for a second, not saying a word.

"Sorry. Remembering some of the school work I should be doing." It was the first thing he could think of. "Maybe I should actually be responsi-ma-ble and head home."

April gave him a puppy dog face with scrunched brows and a curled lower lip. "What? I thought we were Taking Back Sunday?"

His half-smirk grew to a whole smirk. He nodded then pushed the cart in a zigzag, making a sudden sharp right. They continued their joyride past the office supplies then through the clothing and baby sections.

Random passersby stared at them like they were insane— her with her feet up, obnoxious, and him across the handles, hovering above her—but they didn't care. They wandered off in their own plane of existence, carefree and without consequence, like a little emo prince and a little punk princess.

Alex drove them over to the household items. The shelves

transitioned from storage containers to rubbish cans to laundry baskets, ironing boards, vacuum cleaners, and then to home decor.

"Now *that* is fucking cool."

She pointed to large decorative clock.

"Oh, wait. Now *that* is fucking cool."

Then she pointed to a piece of wall art.

Candles, picture frames and artificial flowers and plants lined the middle of the shelves in varied sizes, shapes and colors.

Alex rotated the cart at the end of the aisle so they both could see themselves in front of a body length mirror. He leaned lower against the handle on back of the cart while she still kept her Chucks kicked up high on the front end of it. April took out her Motorola Razr and snapped a quick picture.

"Yesss! Definitely a keeper."

Their joyride continued, bringing them to the outdoor section which had tents set up, grills out, tanks of propane, and a whole array of gardening tools. Above them was a hammock hanging across the top of the shelves.

April leaned her head back to glance up. "I wish we could lay in that thing. Gotta be super comfy."

He shook his head. "Don't think I ever tried that before. Don't think I ever will."

"You're right. I can see that becoming disastrous real quick."

Alex glanced around, noticed a foldable canvas camping chair as part of the showcase. "But we could maybe try this."

"That'll work. Hurry, help me out." April brought her feet down, waved her hands in front of her. "Careful, I'm fragile."

He held her hand and put his other hand on her hip as she hopped out of the cart to the floor. The cart slid out from under her and shot away.

"Whew, damn. That was close. I am very surprised security hasn't busted our asses yet."

"Been pretty lucky here thus far."

April plopped down on the seat, leaving just enough room for him to fit as well. Alex scooted in the tight squeeze.

"Little close. Trying to cop a feel, huh."

He smirked. "Hey. I'll take what I can get."

She nudged at him, then leaned against his side. "I'm just fuckin' with ya."

Everything was quiet and peaceful. No homework. No quizzes. No phenomena. His classes during the day were so hectic and chaotic, and the attempts at sleep during the night were so tainted. Yet here, now, like this, these random sporadic and spontaneous times with this girl had become a source of solace for him.

There was no one around as she shifted in place, touched her cheek to his arm. He leaned in close, thinned his lips.

"You ever . . . ever think about . . . us?"

"Oh, no. Don't. Please. You're gonna ruin it, Nex."

Alex swallowed, took a breath. "I know. But I've been feeling this for a while—"

"Listen. I just got out of a long relationship. I'm not looking for anything. I'm still messed up inside. I am not ready."

"I know that. I wasn't looking for anything either—"

"Then why? What?"

"Don't know what to tell you." Alex shook his head. "It just sort of happened. I'm sorry. It snuck up on me. But that's life, right?"

"I . . ." April stared ahead, leaning back. "I don't think of you like that. We're just friends, nothing else."

There were the dreaded words. It stabbed straight through

his chest, piercing the tissue of his heart like an arrow laced with poison.

"You really don't feel what I feel? That there's something here, between us? T-t-that we would be kinda great together."

"No, I don't."

"Oh. Okay then." Alex blinked, turned away. "So what should we do? Is this over?"

"It doesn't have to be. Can we like rewind to five minutes ago when we were still having a blast? Forgetting the world. Forgetting life."

He nibbled his bottom lip, didn't respond.

&

Now that he had all the information laid out before him, put everything on the line in terms of both personal and professional, the challenges and the stakes were clear. Alex had zero chance with this girl, not to mention there was not much room for friends in general, let alone just friends and being trapped in the friend zone. Which meant he either had to pull back or pull away altogether. In contrast, there was still a strong chance to graduate with decent grades and to achieve all of the goals he had been working towards, just so long as he could pull it together and make things work. So, the only real obstacle was whatever kept happening in that room late at night. The noises, the events, that pressing force, if he could overcome it, he will have made it.

Damn.

It kinda sucks that she doesn't like me back.

All about timing, I guess.

Maybe it's for the best somehow.

Alex rolled from on his side to on his back, closed his

eyes and laced his fingers, resting them between his chest and abdomen.

It was another key LIFE101L lesson creeping in, that there are tests in life, obstacles and forks in the road, and a limited number of second chances. This bed, this blanket, this pillow was the rock between hard places.

He took a slow and deep breath, relaxed enough that his head sank into the pillow, beginning the process of falling asleep.

Smack!

This time, before his mind even drifted, before any slowing of brainwaves, an invisible hand slapped him across his left cheek. It was with enough force that his whole head jerked to the side. He could feel the tingling sting on his skin, sat upright with a gasp, hovered a hand over his face, darted his eyes across the room.

What in the fuck???

Goosebumps broke out across his elbows to his wrists, his knees to his ankles, and on his back between the shoulder blades. His eyes watered as his mouth hung agape.

Now, it was beyond the rotating sleep cycles. Whatever this was just happened while he was still awake and conscious, too. It hurt him, hard and fast. It terrified him.

Alex grabbed the blanket and the pillow, left to go to the common area to lay down in the recliner instead. He approached from the dim lit hallway and noticed Bradley sitting at the end of the sectional.

"Brad?"

"Oh, hey. What you doin' up?"

He faced down, blinked. "I couldn't sleep."

"Gotcha. I'm on standby for a raid. My new guild is kind of strict."

From that angle, he could see the avatar doing an exaggerated dance emote and other characters joining in doing the same.

Alex still felt the tingling and the sting on his cheek, still felt frightened.

"Um. You okay, my dude? You look . . . like, pale. Sickly."

He gave in, his psyche cracking in that moment and giving way like a fresh nest toppled from a high branch. Alex shook his head, joined him on the sectional.

Bradley moved closer. "What is it?"

"Y-you're not gonna believe me . . ."

With a slow nod from Bradley, Alex proceeded to tell him everything. From the noises, the missing item, the ongoing attacks, the bed bouncing, the laugh, the misty haze, and now a cold hard smack.

"So, that's what's up." His friend leaned back, exhaled. "Me and the guys were getting a little worried about you. You're late, missing. You seem so distracted all the time, like worlds away. Graduation is right around the corner . . ."

"Thought I was gonna drop out, move to New York and start that grunge cover band like I always joked about, huh."

Bradley snickered, relaxed.

"Hey. I might be emo. Like slit my wrists and go hide in the corner level emo. But that's a little too emo, even for me."

"Uh, about all you just told me, no, you're not crazy."

Alex perked his ears, listened.

"I believe in God and I believe in heaven. And, well, if you believe in that, then you gotta believe the other side too. The devil, and hell. There is good and evil forces at work we cannot comprehend with our human mind."

He shifted, turned.

"When I was a teenager, like right before entering into college, I remember my mom had this co-worker. She was always super cool. And she started encountering some things, too."

"Like what?"

Bradley breathed out through pursed lips.

"I overheard her talk to my mom about it a few times. Something about seeing demons in her relative's eyes. The look on her face. The sound in her voice. It's burned into my memories. Just, the way she talked about seeing, hearing, also *feeling* like . . . An evil. A hatred there. Darkness."

"What'd she end up doing?"

"I never told anybody about that before. It was something strange, weird. But there was a group who you can call. She did and it worked. It helped."

"Yeah. I mean, I have to. Can't keep going on like this." Alex stared ahead in the darkness, at the wooden case and at the TV, at the empty fireplace behind it.

"Text you the number in the morning. I'll ask my mom."

He nodded to himself, felt some relief.

"For now, there is something else. You gonna sleep here tonight?"

"I think so. At least for one night."

"Hold on then."

Bradley walked to his room then came back. In his hand, he held a bible.

"You can borrow this. Keep it by your bed."

"I'm not . . . exactly a believer."

"That's okay. I can believe enough for the both of us."

Alex held it in one hand, drummed his fingers on the armrest with the other.

"So there you go. I heard you out. I believe you. You got

God on your side. And this'll all be over before you know. It's gonna be fine."

"Appreciate it. I owe you, dude."

"Go ahead and sleep if you want. But you'll be hearing me lay the smackdown on some blood elves."

He smirked as his friend turned back to the laptop. Pulling the blanket to his chin, Alex rolled over on his side, fluffing the pillow.

When he first reached out to SPIRAL, which stood for the Supernatural and Paranormal Investigations, Research and Assessment League, he almost hung up the phone. Alex listened to the slow ring, ring, ring with trepidation and ambivalence. His hand moved the Sony Ericsson from his ear to the top of the desk. He stared at the screen, hovering his thumb over the button ready to cancel the whole thing which felt so awkward. If a voicemail message came on, he would hang up for sure and find another way. Although he was grateful to get it off his chest and to have a possible solution, it still was overbearing. This was no normal ordinary matter. He rubbed his thumb over the button, just about to press it. But then a kind female voice came through that would change the course of his entire life.

"SPIRAL. How can I help?"

"Hi. H-hello, uh, I . . ."

Alex paused, closed his eyes as he forced the words out.

"I . . . I could use some help with something."

The voice was professional, courteous, also efficient as he could hear her take out a pen and paper to start jotting down.

"Strange things are happening to me in the middle of the night. For a few weeks straight now. Like, these kind of attacks in my sleep. Where I can't move and I can't talk, can't yell. I've heard sounds, noises. Things have gone missing. I felt the bed bounce up and down, weird tensions and pressures in the air, this feeling of almost dread."

"Go on."

"I think I heard a laugh, too. Not too sure. I-I saw a white mist the other night after I willed myself upright and opened my eyes. And, one of the last things that happened was that this thing, whatever it is, slapped me in the face."

"Anyone close to you pass recently? Loved one? Friend? Has there been any recent renovations in your home?"

"I go to Emerald Tech, and room in the dorms. I'm in college. So no new renovations, I don't think. And no, nobody's died."

"There any history of mental illness in your family? Schizophrenia?"

"Not that I know of."

Alex could hear her jotting, scribbling then turning the page over.

"I'll need your full name and address, before I forget. Sorry, my husband usually does this phone part but he is out of town."

"Sure, that's no problem."

He provided her the information.

"Alexander Jacobsen. Emerald City Technical Institute, in Maquilla Tower. Got it. And my name is Deidre. Deidre Callahan."

"Nice to meet you. I am grateful for your help. It feels good even to talk to somebody about everything. It's such a difficult matter."

"Right. It's hard enough to ask for help, admit you need help. Especially if it's something like this. And that adds to it. You feel even more isolated, more confused, helpless."

Alex nodded as if she could see him through the phone.

"This entity seems to be progressing, intensifying. Crossing the line over to the waking and to the physical, which is not good since it compromises your safety. I still need to get to the root of it. What could be a possible cause? Have you been under any particular stress, or maybe going through some life changing event perhaps?"

"I mean, it's been stressful at school. Often is but never this bad."

"Yeah, maybe. Hmm. That could be. But that still doesn't seem like enough." In the background, there was the sound of a pen clicking, almost like a nervous tic. "Did you do any kind of recent travel?"

"Oh, shit . . . Wait a second . . . I did go on a trip over winter break, now that you mention it. An early graduation present, to visit where I grew up as a kid."

More scribbling. "And we may have found the culprit."

"See, I was born in Mexico. I'm half. Lived there 'til I was about six or so, then moved over here to the states. I grew up here."

"Tell me more."

3

Olas de Oro, Mexico

DESPITE IT BEING the winter time, it didn't feel like it since it was so bright out, and sunny and hot and humid. Alex pressed the sunglasses to the crook of his nose, swept the bangs out of his eyes as he pulled along his rolling suitcase. He had his sling back-pack on and a small bottle of water that he got from the plane. The airport around him was bustling as he continued forward, a little discombobulated. It was a whole different time zone. It was a whole different language. Over the semesters and years, he spent the majority of his time burying his face in textbooks, listening to lectures, and staring at whiteboards and at PowerPoint presentations on a projector screen. This was a nice change of pace, change of scenery. If he planned to live and work abroad, he would have to become used to this sort of culture shock.

"Alejandro! Alejandro, sobrino joven!"

He stood on tippy toes, peeking over the crowd in front of the airport. "Aunty Divina!"

The two walked closer together then hugged.

"Woow, you're so big now. You are no longer a little boy but a handsome young man."

She grabbed his suitcase, started leading the way.

"How is everything? How's your mom and dad?"

"You know, I don't see them as much since I go to school. I'm in a different state. The usual, though."

The memories of his early childhood were fragmented, just bits and pieces. Little things like playing by the guava tree, almost getting run over by a tricycle, and having a slew of animals: dogs, chickens, pigs. There was a garden in back, and he remembered star fruit and banana peppers hanging that he would pick and pop into his mouth. He remembered having to use a water pump, or bomba, to fill a bucket before taking a bath. Flying to another time zone felt like flying through a time warp.

His aunty drove them from the airport through an area in the slums then onto the busy freeway. Alex stared out the window at the farms and mountains and forests as the inner city transitioned to the countryside. They dropped off his suitcase, stopped by a nearby market for some ingredients for dinner then came back.

"Do you still eat sopa de pollo y arroz?"

"No, aunty. Never." He laughed. "Thank you. That'll be great. My favorite."

"Of course. I remembered."

Alex watched from the living room as she shred the chicken then sliced up green onion and ginger.

"You thirsty, Alejandro?"

"Little bit, yes."

"Oh, okay. Let me boil some water first, to be safe. You wouldn't be used to the water here. Might get sick."

"Ah, I see. That makes—"

He didn't finish his sentence as he noticed a face floating in the doorway. Two wide eyes, a button nose, and thin lips stared right at him from the bedroom.

"Finally, he is awake. Come. Aquí. Say hi to your cousin." Divina washed her hands then joined the child in the hall. "I don't think you've ever met."

"I seen pictures." Alex waved. "Hey there, little guy."

Then the bedroom door closed.

"Sorry, he's shy. Plus it has been rough week for him."

"What happened?"

Divina walked back to the kitchen, motioned with her head to follow. Alex stood and joined her in a hushed manner, sat down on a stool.

"It was the year anniversary of his mother's death."

"I knew she died, but I don't know too much more. Sorry. I just been kinda busy with school and stuff."

"Too busy with your classes and partying and girls, right?"

"Not so much partying and girls. The occasional cerveza, sure. But no girls. No time and no money for that."

She smiled, shook her head. "Anyway, your poor Aunt Sonsoles. Aunty Sol. Do you remember her?"

"How could I forget?" Alex stared off. "She was beautiful, and had a voice sent straight from heaven. My mom used to let me watch her sing with the band at practice in the city."

"Well, her husband . . . I won't even utter the name of that piece of garbage . . . He was always so mean to her, abusive. They would yell and argue and fight all of the time. We knew what was happening, but she was so patient and forgiving and kind."

"He pushed her or something, right? My mom told me that much."

Divina sighed.

Images of it played in his mind as if he was there.

The angry yelling. The arms flailing. Fingers pointing and

fists shaking. Things being thrown. Her shoving him. Him slapping her. Again. Again. Then one last shove across the room, all the way to the back, shattering the glass and tearing the side paneling. Her hands reaching out in desperation—for something, anything. Her body toppling backwards over the balcony ledge, in mid-rotation in an oblong arch, almost like a ballerina in her flowing white dress. The slow decent, the echoed scream, the dull thudded splat, then silence. The cold dead silence.

"Poor kid. Losing his mom like that." Alex cleared his throat.

"Lucio was better when his sister was still around. But everybody is moving now to Puerto Rico or to Cuba or across the border, for work, for school."

"Did they catch him?"

"No, he's been on the run. In hiding. God knows what he did, though. He has a special place in the depths of hell waiting. Bastardo."

After dinner, his aunty boiled more water, this time for bathing. Alex was patient, understood to follow along with the different customs. This municipality in this sovereign state was far different than the country he was from, with not the same luxuries. It was a luxury to have running water. It was a luxury to have clean water, hot water. Divina offered for Alex to take a bath first, but he insisted that she and Lucio go first since there was school the next morning. While waiting, Alex perused the living room, the kitchen and the hall, glancing at the family heirlooms and the decor. There were paintings hanging up, an array of various plates on display. There were candles, figurines, a wooden crucifix.

He stared at each of the family pictures one by one. Divina

and Sonsoles as young girls, playing on the beach in the sand, then later as teens and as young women. Sonsoles kneeling down and holding Lucio and his sister, Merced.

The bathroom door opened then the bedroom door. Alex peeked down the hall, watched as Lucio stared back at him, raised a hand up with a half-wave good night. Maybe the little one was starting to open up.

While she tucked Lucio in, Alex brushed his teeth, rinsed his face and washed up. Divina offered to sleep on the couch while he take the bedroom. He tried to object but she insisted on it. With the door closed, in that isolated neighborhood, he slept sound. Not a passing car. No accidents. Nobody having a party. Nobody out on the town. He wasn't used to it so quiet but it was nice. He rested in peace except for one instance where he heard Lucio crying in the middle of the night and Divina consoling him.

In the morning, he awoke to the sound of roosters crowing. He set an alarm on his phone but the roosters beat that out. Alex had never heard that cock-a-doodle-doo sound before, not in real life anyway, maybe in cartoons.

He walked outside to the living room where his aunty was just waking up, acknowledged him then yawned, still lying supine. He sat down by the kitchen table.

"Buenos dias, Alejandro. Did you sleep well?"

"I knocked out like a baby last night. It's so quiet here. Back home, I'm used to the noises of city life, you know? Always an ambulance, a fire truck, cars honking, loud tourists, some crazy homeless person roaming around."

She laughed. "That's how it is in Mexico City, or one of the popular vacation spots. We can maybe visit sometime this week."

Alex noticed all the pictures again. "Aunty Di. You and Aunty Sol were real close, huh?"

"Oh, yes. She was and still is my bestest friend in the whole world." She sat up, glanced at the pictures herself. "I miss her. Dearly."

"She and Lucio, Merced, they were all close?"

"Your Aunty Sol was the most loving mother and doted on those two."

He nodded then faced down to the floor.

"Let me cook breakfast, then I will drop Lucio off to school."

Divina made hard-boiled eggs, fried sausage and rice. But Alex said he would save it for later like around brunch since he wasn't that hungry. Instead, he sipped black tea and took slow bites of a piece of toasted bolillo.

"I'll be right back. Say hasta luego, Lucio."

The child smiled with more enthusiasm. Perhaps he was growing used to the idea of his foreign cousin staying with them. Alex raised a hand and smirked as they walked out the door and down the street.

He went to the bedroom, took out his MP3 player and played music while taking a walk around the kitchen, the hall-way, the two bedrooms, the one bathroom, then along the exterior of the house.

First, he played "Hands Down" and "Vindicated" by Dashboard Confessional, and then he played "Your Guardian Angel" by Red Jumpsuit Apparatus. Last, he played "Only One" by Yellowcard.

There were flowers in the backyard, potted plants along the front porch which had a small bench on it and a table off to the side. A toppled wagon and scattered action-figures and water guns were strewn on the dirt and in the grass. The dog next door barked to himself on the other side of the chain-link fence.

Alex sat down on the couch, leaned back, was able to

squeeze in "My World" by SR-71 then "Let It Enfold You" by Senses Fail before his aunty returned.

"Sorry . . . I went to the store on the way home. Got some more of your favorite foods as a kid."

"Oh, wow. Thank you, Aunty Di."

"Try this. Here. It's rice pudding and caramel flan."

He took a plastic cup and a plastic spoon, scooped it and took a bite. "This is reeally good. Gracias."

She did the same. This time, she sat at the table while he sat on the couch.

"Lucio doing good in school?"

"He is okay, considering all he has been through. His grades could be better but he is mostly a good boy and stays out of trouble."

Alex stood up to grab a napkin. "I heard him crying last night. Bad dream? Sad?"

Divina was quiet, stared ahead.

He wiped his mouth then his fingers.

"I don't know how much your mom ever told you. About our family. But our bloodline is, well, strong. We have a sort of gift, you could say."

Alex was quiet, shifted towards her.

"Ever since Aunty Sol passed away, Lucio has been seeing a woman in the night. Not every night but often enough that it's difficult for him."

He scrunched his eyebrows, inclined his head, crossing his arms.

"Before going to bed, I like to peep in first, check on Lucio and his sister. She was still here back then. And so, one of the first nights this happened, he saw me do that as usual. Peep my head in, check, then walk back out." She blinked, paused then continued. "Little later, when he got up to either use the bath-room or get a drink of water, he noticed that I wasn't wearing the same dress. In fact, I wasn't wearing a dress. That wasn't me."

"Really?" He joined her, rested his elbows on the table.

"And last night, he saw that same woman. He said the top of her head was wet, like dripping down." She leaned in closer. "From what he described, it sounded like blood running from her head to her neck, her back. Like, as if she fell from some great height."

"Do you think it's her?"

"It has to be."

Alex adjusted in his seat, interlocking his fingers and resting his chin on them. "Maybe it's a form of trauma? Visions. Even memories."

"Is that what you think?"

"I, uh, don't believe in that kind of stuff, aunty."

"What? In ghosts?" Divina thinned her lips. "Maybe you lived in the states, the city for so long, but here, they are very real. They're real to us, our people. The dead are still alive in a way."

As she said all this, he was beside himself. This was not the kind of typical conversation he had from day to day. Alex blinked, almost flinched.

"You ever notice that your mom always leaves a light on at night? Or, you ever notice your mom always likes the TV on, as background noise?"

He was quiet. She was right, his mother did do those things.

"Ask her about it sometime. We have seen and felt some insane stuff. Fireballs. Fantasma."

"I must not have this . . . gift, as you call it."

"Some are stronger and some are not as strong. But, our familia, we seem to have a kind of sixth sense."

❧

Most of the trip went by without a single hitch. Every day, his aunty took him on some little outing, to the mall or to the beach or the mountains. Every night, his aunty made him delicious home cooked meals with fresh ingredients and had some kind of unique dessert. Alex would walk outside and gaze up at the starry night sky after dinner, watching the twinkling of the moon and the stars, listening to stray dogs howl and bark in the distance. There was often the smell of something burning in the air but it wasn't unpleasant. Somehow, it was nostalgic to him, reminded him of a long lost time—his childhood that had been locked away. Things he hadn't thought about, hadn't felt in forever, at least fifteen years.

On one of the outings, Alex bought Lucio some toy robots. Divina watched as he and the little one sat on the floor, playing together, making whooshing noises and pew-pew-pew sound effects with their mouths. When Lucio aimed the arm of the robot point blank at Alex, he flew backwards on the floor and started to convulse. He motioned with his hands as if spurts of blood squirted from his throat, then stuck his tongue out and pretend died.

"All right. Happy now, Lucio? Troublemaker." Divina bent down and scooped him up in her arms. "You killed your cousin."

He remained in that position, head turned and arms sprawled.

"We will go take a bath already. You too, Alejandro. Long day tomorrow so try to get an early sleep."

Alex waited until he heard the bathroom door close before opening one eye, peeking at his surroundings.

He cleaned up the toys, took all the spoons and plates,

bowls and glasses from the table, stacked them in the sink. Then he sat on the couch and waited, reflected on how nice it's been to be away from everything. Although he was tempted to get his MP3 player, instead he enjoyed the quiet.

The bathroom door opened then the bedroom door. When Alex peeked down the hallway, Lucio let out a wide smile, waved his hand up high and side to side. He smirked, gesturing back with finger guns.

It was that same great big smile the next morning, with another exaggerated wave. Alex knelt down and patted the child on the head while Divina stood at the door. When she finished dropping Lucio off at school, they drove along a winding road by the ocean.

"Aunty, how come you never got married? Never had kids of your own?"

"Life just didn't work out that way."

"So weird. Like, you're just as pretty as Aunty Sol was."

"Thank you, Alejandro. Aww. Very sweet." She rotated the wheel one way then the other. "You know, there was a man for a while. 'Round the same time your mom and dad got together. If I did have a child, he would've been half, like you."

Alex pulled down the sunshade.

"But, sometimes, things don't line up. It's the wrong time, the wrong place. Maybe, although it may hurt, it's not the right person."

There was an idea that started to creep into his mind from time to time, LIFE101L. He thought of this then, staring out the window at the reflection on the surface of the water.

"No, you're right. That makes sense."

"I was all alone, wondering what my purpose was. But then

I was able to be there when Lucio and Merced needed somebody. So, it all fell into place."

"Hmm. Good point. You're a nice person, aunty."

"Alejandro, do you remember the family house? We're almost there."

"Barely." He leaned into the cushion. "Like, there was a big guava tree, I think. Out back. My cousins used to climb up, all the way to top. We had three pigs. They weren't little pigs, though. They were fat pigs."

She laughed, turned up the off-ramp.

"I remember star fruit. It was kinda sour but I always picked it and ate it when it was low enough for me to reach. Oh, and we used a bomba."

Divina chimed in. "Right. Things have changed a lot since. No more bomba. We all have cell phones now, and even HBO."

"That it, Aunty Di?"

"Yup. We're here." She parked, took off her seatbelt. "Like I said, everybody moved away already. Nobody has lived here for a long time."

Alex stepped out, closed the door behind him and gazed at the house. It was dark and gray, with rust growing on the sheet metal roof that stained the aged cement and cement blocks.

"Wow. Seeing it up close, it's all coming back to me . . . We used to have these puppies in this enclosure thing. I remember I kept wanting to let the puppies out, and my grandpa kept putting the puppies back in."

She shook her head with a crooked smile.

"Aw, man. It's pretty pathetic, but I yelled at him over that. It was this big fight and we never did talk again. I guess I was just a dumb kid but still."

"He talked about you at the end, you know? He was think-ing about you on the day that he passed away."

"Really? That's so weird. I would've thought he forgot all about me."

"Yeah, he said, tell little Alejandro I'm sorry . . ."

Alex felt his eyes water but forced a smirk.

They walked to the front gate, stood there, peeking inside. It was metal, made of vertical bars which had sharp points at the top. Behind that was an area for livestock, a water pump, and one smaller house next to a bigger house. One was single-story and one had two floors. It didn't appear to have the big guava tree anymore.

"Oh, man. That's right. There were two houses. In that big one, there was a winding staircase. Always had little ants crawl-ing all over it."

He stepped to the side, reached for the handle.

"W-w-wait. I thought we just came to *see* the house. We don't actually own this property anymore. I don't want to get in trouble."

"Come on. Like, we came all this way. It's my last weekend."

"I don't know, Alejandro. Kind of creepy, don't you think? Run down, abandoned. I have this weird feeling."

"It'll be fine. Please, aunty."

She folded her arms and tapped her feet.

"Can I just make it quick?"

Divina sighed. "Okay, okay. But no going in the actual house, and you have one minute. No more. And be careful."

"You're not coming in?"

"No, I'll wait here. In case somebody comes. Hurry."

Alex turned the handle, pushed the gate open and entered into another realm. It was just one minute, maybe two or three, but it seemed to last much longer than that. He dragged his fingers across the brick wall in front of the small house. There was a space between the wall and the house where his dog would sleep. In the mornings, he would wake up early then wake the dog up early as well so he had someone to play with. Alex peered through the window but couldn't see anything. He wondered if there were still mosquito nets hanging up over the beds, and coils of incense burning.

The dirt was covered with weeds. The walls were covered in soot. Yet somehow, all throughout, there were these beautiful flowers sprouting from beautiful plants. It was almost eerie how each petal and each leaf was so full and so vibrant compared to the worn fixtures and foundations, dilapidated and unkept. In the space between the two houses, there used to be the make-shift enclosure he mentioned, the one with the puppies. He wandered through there then around to the back in kind of a figure-eight, touching the flowers and branches hanging. Alex tugged on one, inhaled the fresh scent with one deep breath.

"Everything went okay?"

"Yes, aunty." He nodded as he followed her back to the car. "Thank you for that. It was kind of beautiful, and peaceful."

She turned the ignition.

"Like you said, though. There is also sadness there, something off."

On his last day there, his last night, he chose to remain at home in order to spend as much of it as he could with his aunty and his cousin. Alex chased Lucio through the living room out the back door then around the side of the house. They threw a ball back and forth, and then played with the robot toys on the floor again. Divina finished cooking some carne guisada stew and sliced up fresh mango. For dessert, they all had a piece of tres leches cake. When he hugged Lucio good night, he knew he would miss the hell out of that kid. When he started to pack his belongings, glancing around at the items in the room, he knew he would miss the hell out of this place. It was just a couple weeks but it had been an amazing couple of weeks.

Alex walked outside to gaze up at the clear night sky once more. Each star and each planet, even the moon itself gleamed so bright onto him. He closed his eyes, took a slow breath in and out.

Later that night, as he lay down to sleep, he effortlessly slipped into a sound slumber. The pillow was soft. The blanket was smooth. The air was just the right temperature.

In the morning, he awoke to the sound of something fluttering, almost crawling. If he didn't know better, he felt like it was right there in the room with him. Alex opened his eyes, squinted in the early morning daylight, darted his eyes along the four corners of the popcorn ceiling. More fluttering, more crawling.

When he sat up, he tilted his head to listen. It was the sound of feathers and talons, he realized. Perhaps it was one of the morning roosters but somehow made its way to the roof. The sound intensified, turning the light fluttering to a heavy flapping as if there were not just one bird but an entire flock of birds encircling him.

4

THE PHONE FELT heavy, his shoulder sore from staying in that same position. Alex switched it to his other hand, adjusted in place, straightened up then swiveled in his chair from left to right. His feet bounced at the ankles beneath the desk over the rolling wheels. He blinked to himself, staring ahead at the blank wall. No other words came to mind. There was nothing else to say, to add. Deidre let him speak uninterrupted like he was undergoing hypnosis in a therapy session until it felt like they reached some major breakthrough in his progress, a revelation or a conclusion. Clearing his throat, he broke the moment of silence.

"I, uh . . ." He shut his eyes, shook his head. "I can't believe I forgot about that. I guess I blocked it from my mind. It didn't make sense."

"That's okay."

"Assumed it was just birds, you know? It was weird, but . . . I just thought roosters had got on the roof. Right? Why would it be anything else?"

He could hear the pen clicking again through the phone, her tic, her tell.

"Well, you mentioned an aunt of yours and a grandfather who passed. Is it possible this is one of them?"

"No. No way. I don't think so. Like, I can't explain it but my gut tells me no."

"And, I mean, this old family house might have been a place where any number of spirits dwelled. It could be another relative. Maybe it's somebody discriminating against you, since you're half-half as you said."

Touching a palm to his forehead, Alex exhaled.

"We hear that kind of stuff. It's not uncommon. Black families move into former homes of someone hateful, who despised their kind. White families staying in a certain area where they are unwelcome from Native American ancestors."

"For some reason, my mind's telling me it's not that. Now, still not sure how I feel about all this . . . I don't believe in this kinda stuff, even after everything . . ." He leaned forward, slid his palm down his face to his chin. "But, if there is something going on, I'm thinking there was something lurking in that place. Something dark, and evil, hiding, waiting. It must have attached itself to me. Don't know where that's coming from."

"If your family blood is special, more inclined to encounter the supernatural, then maybe your own subconscious intuition is nudging you. Maybe you do have this gift after all."

"Gift or curse?"

"Definitely can feel that way."

There was a slight pause, the heaviness a bit burdensome.

"I think you're right. It's either an evil spirit, or demonic in nature. When you mentioned hearing wings and talons . . . Either way, it is a powerful entity and we need to act soon as possible. You're in danger."

"H-hold on, wait. Again, I just—"

"Listen, I know this is a lot to take in. Repressed memories. Realizing you might be sensitive to the paranormal. But if it's demonic, and if it's already becoming physical, this is a grave situation."

Alex arched his head back, slumped his shoulders.

"Okay, what do we do now then?"

❧

Although it was imperative that he focus and concentrate on his studies, it was near impossible at this point. There was too much new information affecting his current priorities and affecting his faculties. Alex paced back and forth in the room, stared at the screen of his phone in his hand. He was so tempted to reach out to April, to laugh, joke, flirt, get his mind off of things but it wasn't a good idea. Instead, he sat at the desk and opened up his laptop, wrote e-mails to each professor. Lucky for him, it wasn't the one professor he had a recent conversation with, not that day. It was painful and shameful to type those words and to lie to them. However, he didn't have a choice. He wasn't in the right state of mind, plain and simple.

I'll get back on it when this is all said and done.

After this is over with . . .

He would have missed the last afternoon class anyway since it was the soonest Deidre could meet with him. Taking the other three classes off was because his entire life view was beginning to crumble. He wondered about life and death, about the living and the dead. He wondered if people, his family and himself, did have certain abilities.

The questions bombarded him throughout the day, even on his way to the train station where they decided to meet. He waited in the main terminal in front of the large clock. Behind him, he could hear a light bell which meant it was the top of the hour.

Deidre made her way down from the revolving doors. He saw her picture on the website but she was even more beautiful in person, a woman of elegance.

Alex shook her hand as she approached.

"It's nice to see you versus just hear you. Thanks for coming all this way."

"No, it's fine. You mentioned taking the bus so I didn't mind picking a spot closer to you but still about halfway. At least for this first meeting." Her smile was bright. "Usually I ride with the others in the van but since I'm flying solo here . . ."

"I'm just glad to get things going."

"You hungry or anything? Need a coffee?"

"Uh, I think I'm okay. Haven't had much appetite."

She nodded. "Understandable. Go pick a seat, maybe that one over there. With not too much people around so we have a little space to ourselves. I'll just get a bottle of juice and a donut or something."

Alex walked down the row of benches to the side of the terminal where there were tables and chairs. He picked one away from the exits or entrances, away from the vending machines.

When she came back out of the snack shop with a can of iced tea and a bag of crackers, Deidre panned the terminal until she saw him waving her over.

"Okay. Sorry about that."

Deidre placed down her tote bag which had a binder, folders and notebooks.

"Let's get started. I know our main theory is that this is an entity that was lurking, and not a relative who passed."

He nodded, swallowed.

"I've done some research, to cover all angles. There hasn't been anything major regarding a death on campus except something I found in an old paper, and that was like a hundred years ago. Before the campus was even fully built."

"Plus, I been dorming a couple years already. I doubt it's the place itself."

"Agreed. And so, I went in another direction . . ."

She laid out some printed papers on the table.

"I think it's this." Deidre tapped her finger, pointed. "Maybe it's not very common in these areas, but it does occur all throughout the world. In English and American folklore, they refer to it as a hag. In some African cultures, they refer to it as a boo hag. Across many different countries, from Germanic to Slavic to Scandinavian, the term is mare or mara."

Alex felt his eyes widen and his jaw drop.

"The Japanese refer to it as kanashibari. The Filipinos call it bangungot or batibat. In Thailand, the people often say lai tai. In China and in Taiwan, it is known as either gui ya shen or gui ya chuáng, meaning ghost oppression."

He leaned forward, tilted his head to better see.

"Stories of a 'choking ghost' or 'pressing ghost' are very prevalent, and go as far as the Hawaiian Islands even."

Flipping through the pages, he leafed through the illustrations and blocks of text. "Choking ghost . . ."

"We usually start by doing a formal investigation. Bring in cameras and recorders, do readings with various equipment. However, I know you said you're unsure about all this, and that you are having trouble accepting it."

On the table was a simple brochure for SPIRAL. Alex opened this, saw the names of each team member.

"I mean, I also can't quite bring in a whole investigative team into the dorms without drawing huge attention."

"It could just be me, me alone."

He bit his lip, turned away. "Can we get right to a solution? Is that possible?"

"Of course. How sure do you think it's this choking ghost?"

"Pretty sure you hit it dead on. This seems like it."

"Right. And it's not about pinpointing who or what, for sure, but to have a general idea or explanation. Once we can make some sense of it, we can proceed. I think if we do a blessing or cleansing of your room, that should do it."

"Yeah, okay. Sure."

Deidre took a slow sip of tea. "The tricky part will be the timing. It would be most effective if we do two blessings. I have a specialist in mind who does great work, but he is in high demand so we will have to wait for his availability. Do the first then have him do the second shortly after."

Alex crossed his arms.

"Now, I know you're not a believer, but I would also like to pray with you at some point. So that's three levels of reversal, and three layers of protection."

He slouched in place, scooted forward. "About how long do we have to wait?"

"I will be in touch. But I'm thinking two weeks total. In ten days, we can do the first blessing, two weeks the second blessing."

"What should I do for now?"

"Perhaps you can stay with someone. It doesn't seem to happen other than in your room, so I think this choking ghost attached itself to you but could be residing there. Waiting for the opportune moment."

"Guess I can figure it out. I'll deal."

Maybe call April? Nah.

"Sorry, Alex. These things take time, if you wanna do it right. If we do it wrong, rush, things could get a whole lot worse. We anger the entity. We escalate the attacks."

"Guess so. Oh, hey, I also wanted to ask . . . I read about this thing called sleep paralysis. And also night terrors. How sure are we this isn't scientific? I mean, should I see a doctor or something?"

"You know, it is that, technically. If they hooked you up to machines and ran tests, it would read as sleep paralysis or night terrors, I'm sure. The difference is in the origin. A doctor or scientist would explain this as all mundane coincidence, factors affecting sleep, anxiety, stress. Whereas someone like me, I would say this was caused by a dark entity."

He placed one elbow on the table, rested his cheek in his palm.

"Like, the term, kanashibari, for instance. There have been many studies in Japan about this, common in college students. I came across it when I was preparing your case. But there are kind of three meanings to kanashibari. One, it simply means sleep paralysis, the researched and accepted phenomenon. Two, it can be a side effect of a spiritual attack like from a creature or a witch. And three, it can also be the type of ghost causing this."

Alex blinked, leaned in, rubbed his fingers over his jaw.

"So, it's a little bit of a po-tay-to, po-tah-to, chicken-before-the-egg type thing. Know what I mean? Different sides of the same coin."

"Right. Semantics."

"But I suppose, like anything else, it's up to the individual to make up their own mind on the matter. Looking at the goosebumps on your arm and those circles around your eyes, you know very well what's going on."

He shook his head, thinned his lips. "I'm still working through it. A lot to take, like you mentioned. I don't know, though. You may be right. I can admit that much."

"Which brings me to one last thing I wanna talk to you about . . ."

"Hmm?"

"I think this ability, this gift, made you susceptible to attack in the first place. You were vulnerable."

"Can I tell you something?"

She nodded.

"Ever since talking to you on the phone, recalling what happened, a lot of things have been coming back to me that I must have chosen to forget. Things that I seen and I heard throughout my life."

Deidre motioned with her head as if to say, go on, continue, let it out.

"Me and my brother, we saw something in the hallway one night. Like, a shadow, a shape moving back and forth. We were little kids then. And, uh, we also once saw a cart roll across a room and crash into a wall once. That was back when we were teens."

"I see."

"Now, maybe as a kid or a teen, I did believe. As many of us do. But these days, I try to be logical, rational, make sense of things. But there is one instance I'm having trouble denying now that it's come to mind."

". . . Your grandfather?"

Alex felt his eyes water. "H-how did you know?"

She stared him straight in the eye, waited.

"One time, playing behind the apartment building we used to live in, I heard an old man's voice calling my name. It was distinct and clear, right in my ear. It scared the living crap right out of me. I ran to my mom and told her what happened."

Deidre placed her hands on the table, laced her fingers.

"And, well, less than two hours later, we got the call from Aunty Di that my grandpa had passed away."

"That is a powerful account. Wow. Thank you for sharing with me." She twiddled her thumbs. "See. Like I was saying, this gift, this ability, you need to know more about it. It would be in your best interest to accept it."

"Oh, man. I don't know."

"Let me just explain in general then we can discuss you specifically. There are some people born with a certain brain chemistry, certain bloodlines. And there are some people that change after, say, a near-death experience. They grow up sensitive or they become sensitive, sensitive as in they can see and feel things that others can't."

He gulped as he listened.

"Sensitive is a very broad term. A person can learn to hone this ability. That is a psychic. There are all kinds of psychics. Some can read minds. Some can speak through the mind. And others can see in dreams. Some can see into the future, like precognition. They have hunches, predictions. A clairvoyant has flashes or visions, but more physical items or objects. An empath absorbs emotions or a state of mind, either from the living or deceased, or from the location itself. And there are also mediums who can communicate with the dead."

Alex opened his mouth to say something, to ask something, but no words formed.

"For most people, it's the littlest things. You think of

somebody, and boom, the phone rings. It's them. What a coincidence. Or you have a dream about them. Or a glass might chip or a plate might crack, like an omen. That feeling when someone is looking at you, coming towards you, and when you lift your head up or turn around, boom, there they are. Perhaps this is based on a deeper connection, like the mother-child relationship, like twins. Perhaps it's an evolved sense for survival, like an animal instinct. A heightened fight-or-flight response."

He blinked, licked his lips.

"My point is not everyone has this gift, or curse as you put it. You're unique, Alex. You're special. And, as such, well, you will have to do some soul searching and hard thinking about where all of this falls into your life and who you are. What it means to you. What you choose to do with it, or not. And it is only when you do that, make peace with it, truly accept it, that you will be strong, that you will be free."

Now that he had these conversations, one over the phone and one in person, the whole world around him appeared so different. This world had a world behind the world, an underworld. It was more than just college transcripts and punching a time clock, but way way more. There was a whole invisible layer. Alex could see that now, feel it. Every time a little smudge of something, a faint blur popped into the corner of his eye, he questioned it. Every time a vague noise echoed in the background. To him, these occurrences were no longer obscure or inconsequential but signs of the otherworldly, the extraordinary. It passed through the veil. It slipped between planes and dimensions. It crossed the streams.

He forced himself to get ready, get to class, but as he sat

there in the lecture hall with the auditorium seating, Alex was preoccupied. Towards the middle of class, he stood up and walked out. Some of the other students glanced as he scooted down the row. He shifted back, peeked down at the professor on the floor, somber, sullen.

I feel terrible about this . . .

But I just can't do it, Martin. Not today.

Making his way through the parking lot then in between buildings, Alex walked with his hands in his pockets, staring down at his feet. First, he found a nice quiet spot in the library to try to get something done, anything, but it wasn't happening. Next, he picked out a quiet spot at Pine Branch but nothing. Last, he tried another spot at the rec center, the same. No matter where, none of these places were working so he decided to leave campus.

He wouldn't be productive, not even if it was simple or passive. And, if he was going to clear his head, perhaps this was not the place.

Alex wandered to the roundabout, hopped on the shuttle which arrived just as he got there. Through the window, he watched as the world passed him by. A married couple unloaded groceries from their minivan. Two girls walked together, both between their first or second trimester. One guy rode his bicycle while another guy jogged in the opposite direction. All of these people proceeding as if things were normal, fine and dandy, as if they weren't suffering from ghosts terrorizing them at night or grappling with learning the fact that they may be "sensitive."

Though he considered getting off at the Global District or at Midtown, both had sights and sounds to check out while he sorted through his internal conflicted thoughts, Alex ended up heading to Westgate as per usual. It was comfortable there. It was familiar.

Right when he was about to hop off, he noticed April through the glass getting on. He stopped, hovered by the exit as he watched her. He considering leaving, not having any interaction with her, but went back to his seat and waited.

God damn it.

What am I doing?

I suppose I'm already in a funk, so why not add to that.

Fuck it.

"Oh, hey . . ." She pointed with her head inclined, an awkward smile.

He scooted to the window, let her sit by the aisle.

"Been avoiding me, huh?"

"Shut up." Alex smirked. "I mean, you did shut me down."

"We can be friends. Right?"

He shook his head, still smirking. "Not really my style. But sure, fine."

"You okay? You look . . . stressed or something. Then again, you kinda always do carry on in constant emo vibe."

She placed her hands on either side of her legs in her skinny jeans, her feet kicking backward and forward, carefree, aloof.

"I'm fine. And you? What you doing out and about? Didn't think I'd run into you. Like, you're not working."

"Eh, I was bored."

"Hmm. I felt bored, too. Kinda."

"Let's hang out then. We can be bored together."

"Where should we go?"

April tilted her head, shrugged her shoulders. "You wanna check out Yellow Leaf?"

"Not really. That place is kinda snooty."

"True, true." She giggled. "We'll make fun of them. Snob these snobs. Call it a, uh, Simple Plan. Get it?"

"Funny. Maybe we'll come across A New Found Glory, like The All-American Rejects that we are."

Getting off in the middle of Yellow Leaf, they walked alongside a wide lake with calm blue-green water. The reflection on the surface of the water was crystal clear. A flock of birds circled above them high in the skies. With the shade of the trees providing cover from the afternoon sun, a cool breeze swept through.

"You know, this is kind of a beautiful. And I hate the sun. I hate fresh air."

He laughed. "The same. But you're right. It's really nice out. Here we are, cruising around. You in jeans and a dark t-shirt. I'm wearing this hoodie. You got Chucks and I got Vans. So out of place."

"That kind of adds to it, though, huh. We're being, like, introverted extroverts."

Alex gazed at April from the side, saw the contour of her cheek and her dazzly ears. His eyes traced the slender of her jaw down to the nape of her neck above her collar bone. He bit his lip then faced away.

"Ooh, over here." She led them down a wooden dock to a pier hovering over the water.

Both sat on the edge, dangled their feet. They could see fish floating in and out of view from the shallow depths.

"You got your MP3 player?"

"Of course." He smirked. "I couldn't be emo without my emo music. Or screamo."

"Pick a song. Usually I pick."

"Me? Hmm."

As he handed her one earbud, put the other one in his ear, he thought about what to choose. Two cover songs came to mind. First, he played "Time After Time" by Quietdrive and then he played "Every Little Thing She Does Is Magic" by Ra. Both listened and watched the light ripples on the water.

She leaned in, rested her head on his shoulder. He leaned back in towards her, touched his cheek to the top of her head.

"Hope this doesn't mess with you too bad, Nex." April nuzzled her cheek, scooted closer. "This is nice. I always enjoy our time together, especially the accidental ones."

"You know, I'll take you any way I can."

"Like, when you're single, this is the kind of the stuff you miss, right? Having someone to talk to. Someone to go places with, hold hands with."

"That's true. Even hugging, right? All the happy chemicals."

She laughed. "Yeah, let's not forget that later."

". . . Doing a little better these days? Adjusting?"

"I guess so. Been spending time with my sisters and my mom. Funny, we don't quite get along but hey, they're family."

Alex thought about his own family for a moment, stayed quiet.

"Tell me something, anything."

"Huh?"

"Whatever you want. You can tell me what kind of kid you were in high school, or talk about your previous relationships."

"I do have a random story, since we're sitting here over the lake like this." He put away the MP3 player, which he almost forgot about.

"This sounds promising."

"Me and my friends were hanging out one time, about to watch a movie. Most of us got there way before, already deciding which movie. But our other friend got there kinda late, like last second. So he didn't get to look at the posters or talk about them. Just had to go along with whatever."

April nodded in anticipation. "Uh-huh. And?"

"Well, we kinda tricked him into thinking *The Lake House* was a horror movie."

"Oh, you guys are dicks." She let out a loud chuckle, squirmed in place from the laughter. "Isn't that like a romance, a drama? Epic."

He laughed. "Our friend looked at the marquee and was all, 'Rated PG? Gotta be lame.' After it was over, ninety minutes of mopey, lovey-dovey Keanu Reeves and Sandra Bullock, he was pretty pissed. But it was worth it."

She regained her composure, wiped a happy tear from her eye. "That's awesome sauce. Good job."

"Never thought about that 'til now. Been doing that a lot lately, it seems." He gazed out over the water. "What else did you ask about, high school?"

"Yeah. Always fascinating to hear who somebody was back in the day. Like, me, I was a bit of an outcast. Just did my own thing. All by lonesome."

Alex squinted his eyes. "Really?"

"My mom would drop me and my sisters off real early, since her work schedule. So I liked to take naps at lunch. I didn't have any friends."

"I was kinda the artsy type, I guess. I did a lot of drama and theater and acting and all that. Got the award for best actor once. I was in a couple talent shows, did some singing. It was like alternative rock."

"You can sing???"

He shook his head, felt a slight flush in his cheeks. "I mean, I ain't no James Blunt or Josh Groban or some shit."

April nibbled her bottom lip, turned to face him.

"No way, haha. I am *not* singing. Hell no. Maybe if we were at karaoke or something."

"Aww, come on!"

∽

They didn't even realize that one conversation blended into another, seamless and fluid, and that whole afternoon had flew by. When the gradual sunset was over, they migrated from on the pier over the water to a wide grassy area with concrete picnic tables and empty barbecue pits. Alex stepped all the way up, sat on the tabletop with his feet on the chair. April copied him and did the same, both moving in an innocent yet rebellious manner. Between the trees, they could see up into the sky turning dusk. It was a mix of thin layers of cloud with faint stars starting to show. The curve of the half-moon partway hidden from their view, the two scooted closer to one another, their chill vibe matching the chill of the air.

"Getting cold?"

She rubbed at her arms. "A little. I wasn't expecting to be out late. Usually, I wear layers but nope, not today."

"Here." He unzipped his hoodie, took it off and wrapped it around her like a cape, over her shoulders. "That should help."

"You're not cold?"

"Nah, c'mon. Look at me." Alex straightened up, raised his chin and puffed out his chest. "I'm tough."

April smiled, stared down into the blades of grass.

She hunched forward. "Like I was saying, kind of weird having a stepdad. He's not a jerk or anything, but he's just there."

"Right. I mean, I don't even get along with my own dad.

Can't imagine some douchey stranger in the background. Where's your real dad?"

"He lives up in Vancouver."

"Oh, that's not too far."

"It's far from where we all grew up, in Macau. Me and my sisters." She pulled the hoodie tighter around her, shifted in place.

"How old were you when you moved here?"

"Like, nine."

"Really? I was about six when my fam flew down."

"We're both transplants then." April nodded to herself then inclined her head. "That explains it."

He turned to face her, waited for her to continue.

"Like, we don't belong. Kinda like right here, now in this upscale neighborhood of yoga moms and soccer moms, their hubbies all coaching softball."

Alex watched her as she spoke, her eyes, her lips, her nose. His hoodie around her petite frame was a bit oversized but also somehow felt right. He adjusted in place then cleared his throat.

Damn it.

Why?

No, no, no.

"I been having a lot of fun with you, April. I think you're awesome, you're amazing. But it might not be enough anymore, to just do . . ." He pointed between them. "I think I need . . . I-I want . . ."

She wore a thin smile on her face.

"I want more, April. I wanna be with you. Like, together. The whole shebang."

"Nex . . ." She reached over, touched his knee. "You're a cool guy, but I'm not looking for a relationship. Sorry. I only recently got out of one, and I don't need that right now. Please don't be mad."

"But what we have . . . We would be so good together. I like you. Don't you like me?"

"No. I'm sorry, I don't. I don't feel that way."

Alex faced away, contradictory feelings washing over him. He fought back the urge to get up and leave, never speak to her again.

"D-don't you know we'd be perfect together?"

She didn't say anything, kept her thin smile, pulled her hand back, crossed her arms, rocked back and forth.

There was silence as they both stared ahead, out into the growing dark.

"Damn it, April."

"I'm sorry . . ."

"No, it's okay." He softened, put his hand on her knee now. "I'm the one who's sorry. I wish I didn't say anything, again. But I couldn't hold it in anymore, again."

She took his hand in hers, squeezed it.

"You know what? I *am* cold." Alex let out a nervous laugh. "God, I really messed this all up, huh. Of course. My bad."

"It's okay. It's not that . . . bad."

"Know what really sucks?"

"What?"

"I just . . . I just kinda wanted to kiss you."

April gazed into his eyes, touched, then smiled. She pulled him in closer by the hand, tilted her head towards his, began to pout her full lips.

"No, no. T-that's okay. I don't need your pity kiss." Alex smirked, arched his neck. "Come on, maybe we better get outta here."

He led them through the grassy field lined with pine trees. Each was quiet. His mind ran rampant with second guesses, ruminating, dwelling. Should he have kissed her? Was it for the best? What would even be the point?

Somewhere along the way, the two acquaintances from NECC started to share earphones, started to hug long enough to release oxytocin, dopamine and serotonin in their brains. They were mall rats window shopping and people watching, exchanging Chuck Norris jokes. From checking her out from behind to placing a flower upon her dazzly ear, his feelings transitioned from a subtle platonic spark to a blazing inferno of unrequited love. He was inside out and upside down, a perpetual looping spiral like the gumball machine they happened across during their outing.

All at once, in one quick motion, he spun around, held her at the waist and drew her in, dipping her back and pausing.

"Okay, fuck it."

He began to kiss her, and she began to kiss him back. Their hands slid over one another. Up and down her back. Over his shoulders, through his hair, dangling in his arms. The two twisted, wrapped, entangled and intertwined, their lips and tongues in perfect rhythm and harmony while the stars above them twinkled.

<h1 style="text-align:center">5</h1>

FIRST, THEY WERE just friends. Then when he realized he had feelings for her, he was trapped in the friend zone. Mayor of the zone. Now, he found himself in whole new territory. Alex reached over and held her hand in her lap, interlocking his fingers between. April reciprocated, rubbing her fingertips over the skin of his knuckles. When they first met up in the mall, for some reason, they acted as if nothing had happened. After getting on the bus, sitting down towards the middle back en route to their destination, they felt safe enough to cross that line once more. Perhaps it was being away from prying eyes. Perhaps it was keeping whatever this was hidden. No questions, no answers. No labels and boxes, and no checkmarks.

"We should've been doing this from the beginning, huh."

She laughed, smiled.

"It was a really good kiss."

"I'll say, O-M-G, it was like a movie kiss. Never felt that before. Like, whoosh."

He smirked, raised one brow. "Try again later?"

"Maybe. See where the night takes us. You might get lucky."

April shrugged her shoulders in a playful tease. "Uh, where are we going?"

"There is this one place I always meant to see. So I thought why not."

"Cool. It can be 'Somewhere Only We Know' or something."

"Exactly."

Alex switched hands, reached across and rubbed his palm over her thigh, wrapping his other arm around her shoulders. She leaned on his collar bone, touching a hand to his chest. As they got off at their destination, they continued to walk in a similar manner: his arm around her shoulder blades, her arm around his waist, and both their hands linked in front of them. It appeared to be a perfect fit.

"What is this place?"

"It's called Serling Park."

"Oh, cool."

There was an area with water fountains and restrooms. They walked in front of this, past its stone walls to a large gazebo with wooden rails and a high ceiling. Both sat down on one side of the semi-circle.

"Hey. I wanted to play you something, too. I came across it on MySpace."

"Sure. What is it?"

As usual, they shared the MP3 player with one earbud each. The light piano notes rang in their ears on a repeated loop, then the chords and vocals kicked in. All of the lines seemed to match their moment. It built up with light strumming then with violin in the background.

"That is a really good song. Heart that."

"It's called 'These Are the Nights' by Making April." He

wrapped the wire, put it back in his pocket. "Reminded me of you, obviously."

April let a smile spread across her face.

"Sorry if that's kinda corny. I haven't held a girl, kissed a girl in, like, two years. I'm rusty as hell. Probably can't even unhook a bra with one hand anymore."

"No way, you couldn't even do that before." She hit him with a soft touch. "Could you?"

"What? It's not that hard."

"Prove it."

He smirked, leaned in, touched his lips to hers. April parted her mouth, let their tongues writhe and slither together.

Alex reached behind, ran his hand up the back of her shirt. Her skin was warm and smooth. He could feel the slender curve of her back which was pleasant to the touch. He fiddled with the clasp of her bra, their movement of their mouths increasing in intensity. With his free hand, he cupped one of her breasts over the fabric.

It took a minute but it came undone and he could feel the bra come loose, almost slipped straight off beneath her shirt.

"Had me worried for a sec there. But I got it."

"Um. Can you hook it back?"

"Well, I . . . I only know how to undo it."

They both laughed as they let go and composed themselves. He stood, helped her up while she fixed her clothing. The two followed the main walking path into the interior. It had rounded bushes on either side. When they got to an open field, they stepped off the pavement into the grass.

"Here. This." Alex held her at the waist, gazed upward. "It's what I wanted to see. Wanted you, us to see."

"It's all so vivid and clear. Woow."

"Guess we're far enough away from the city, the city lights."

April pulled away, found a soft section of grass and laid down. She waved him over, gestured for him to come join her.

The cosmos above them was scattered in a splash of bright dots, some steady and some blinking. Layers of nebulous indigo were smeared in light baby blue.

"Hey, look at that one." She shot her arm up, pointed.

"Interesting. Kind of like a T."

"To me, more a mushroom shape." April rolled on her side, placed her hand on his arm. "It can be our shroom."

Alex smirked, let out a slow breath.

"I just kissed a girl. I just touched a boob. Now I'm laying down, watching the stars in the sky, forgetting anything and everything else going on in life."

She slid her hand from his arm to his torso, rubbing his sternum.

"Like, I could die right now, April. I'm completely at peace."

"Just be, right?"

"Right. I'm so not used to this . . . I am right where I belong, magically somehow."

It was an interesting blend of events in his life. During the day, Alex continued to miss classes and fall behind on assignments. At night, he would meet up with April and have these grand misadventures that were intimate and passionate, weaving in and out of deep existential conversations. His school life crumbled and his love life flourished. While all that was going on, the odd occurrences and occasional attacks also still happened, though not as frequent and not as intense as before. He waited at the front of the main campus past the roundabout with both hands in his pockets, staring away into nothingness. There was a lot on his mind as it was the day of the first blessing.

There she was, pulling up in the Yaris as she described. He waved, pointed ahead to the entrance of the parking lot. Alex started heading that way as Deidre parked. In front of him, as he got closer, he could see Deidre gather her belongings. She again carried a tote bag, this time filled with smaller items.

"How has everything been here?"

"It's still happening, but just every now and then. Seems to be pretty stable now. I can fight through it and get up each time."

"Good. Maybe its hold on you is finally starting to weaken. Could there be anything new in your life?"

Alex was quiet, didn't answer.

"I see. There's a girl then."

He flinched, almost did a double take.

"That makes sense. Very often an entity will go after someone that's isolated versus happy, whole, surrounded by loved ones. She gonna be okay with you bringing a woman into your dorm room all alone?"

Alex shook his head, smirked.

"No, but seriously. If you haven't already, don't bring her to that room until after the second blessing is through. For safety."

"Got it."

They transitioned from the parking lot down a zigzagged ramp, and then down a paved walkway alongside a courtyard between office buildings.

"Is that Maquilla Tower up there?"

"Yup."

"Me and my husband, Miles, we developed an all-inclusive and holistic approach to blessings. A little bit Hindu. A little bit

Buddhist. Based on Christian and Catholic ideas, with a little bit of new age feng shui kind of concepts."

"Oh, God . . ."

Deidre came to a sudden halt, dropped her arms at her sides. "C'mon, Alex. You gotta be open to this stuff in order for it to work."

"Sorry, I know. It is all j-just weird to me."

He hung his head, blinked, then took out his keys and walked up the steps. She opened her mouth to say something but followed without a word.

"Again, no rules or anything about bringing a woman in here?"

"No. In fact, it'll probably make me more popular with the other boys." Alex let out a crooked smirk, allowing her in first.

He closed the door behind them. For a quick second, he realized he hadn't had a girl in his room, let alone a beautiful woman. Pausing, he gulped then stepped closer.

"What is this energy? So strange."

The minute she entered inside, her face changed.

"I've never felt . . . Interesting . . . Is this a choking ghost?" She raised a hand, panned from right to left in a slow scan. "You don't feel that?"

"Uh, I don't."

"I see you have lots of shirts with skull designs and skeletons on them and such. All black and gray, brown, dark blue. An insect. A dark tree. You, like, a goth?"

He raised his eyebrows, exhaled. "I mean, guess I'm kinda emo."

"Those black roses there?"

"Yeah, but plastic, fake. I forget where I got them. On sale at a pop-up Halloween store or something."

"Hmm. Now, all seemingly little and insignificant things but they do add up. Our lives, our being, it's composed of energy. And these are negative energy. You are walking around with a cloak around you, a cloud hanging over your head."

Alex folded his arms over his chest.

"I see it now. I can feel it. Yes. You act so strong, so smart around other people. You might even smile, joke, laugh, flirt. But deep down, inside, when no one is looking, you're sad and alone and you feel—"

She jerked, darted her eyes across the far wall to the corner of the ceiling.

"Whoa, it just moved. I think it's onto me. Better get started." Deidre reached in her tote, took out a bible. "Here, I put a sticky note on each of the pages, highlighted them for you. They are numbered."

"Here?"

She nodded, knelt down to go through her bag.

Alex cleared his throat, followed the line with his finger. "Uh . . . 'As for me and my household, we will serve the Lord.' Joshua 24:15."

Deidre motioned to continue. He found the next one.

"Let's see. 'Unless the Lord builds the house, the builders labor in vain.' Psalm 127:1."

Deidre motioned again.

"Right. Hmm. 'Be alert and of sober mind. Your enemy the devil prowls around like a roaring lion looking for someone to devour. Resist him, standing firm in the faith, because you know that the family of believers through the world is undergoing the same kind of sufferings. Peter 5:8 to 5:9."

She moved her pointer finger in a circular motion.

"And lastly . . . 'Put on the full armor of God, so that you can take your stand against the devil's schemes. For our struggle is not against flesh and blood, but against the rulers, against the authorities, against the powers of this dark world and against the spiritual forces of evil in this heavenly realm.' Ephesians 6:11 to 6:12."

"Hey, not too bad."

"I've never quoted scripture before."

"We usually get an ordained priest to do this, with actual holy water and anointing oil and all that. He marks little crosses on the windows and doors. But you made your feelings clear on the matter."

Alex rolled his eyes, clicked his tongue.

She held back a smile as he forced himself to go along with it.

"Okay. Now, this is the part where we go door to door and room to room, from the front entrance to the back entrance, the living room, the kitchen, each bedroom and each bathroom. But since it's just one room . . ."

He held the bible tight in his right hand, walked around her. Deidre sprinkled salt along the walls, placed little cloves of garlic in each corner, on either side of the door frame and the frame around the window.

"In the name of Jesus Christ, I ask for peace and joy to inhabit this dorm room. I ask for prosperity, purity, serenity."

Deidre reached into the tote, took out a white string and a pink candle. She chanted as she held the ends of the white string. It was thicker than yarn but thinner than rope. Alex could almost feel the vibrations from the prayers.

"This pink candle represents love and kindness. We are inviting these energies in by letting this burn for one hour. Let's place it on the most eastern facing window or door, towards the energy of the sun that is life giving."

"Uh, the window, probably."

She placed it on the windowsill, wrapped the string around it and let it dangle.

"Leave the window open and the door for one hour while the candle burns."

"Okay. Can I leave the door ajar?"

Deidre nodded, moved in a side step. "It is time to address the entity directly now. But we will use Spanish as it's stronger. This thing attached itself to you in Mexico, so there is a possibility it uses that native language."

"I . . . I don't really speak."

"It's fine. I asked around beforehand." She took out some notes from her pocket, unfolded them.

He watched as she straightened up, breathed from her diaphragm.

"Vete. Sal de aquí. Lárgate. You are not welcome here. Say it, Alex."

"Uh . . . Um . . ." He took the notes, paced. "Vete. Sal de aquí. Lárgate. You are not welcome here."

"Say it again, with conviction. And spray this salt while doing so."

Alex threw some salt. "Vete."

More salt. "Sal de aquí."

More salt. "Lárgate."

"You are not welcome!" He threw some more salt, and then again. "You're not welcome here!"

"Good, Alex. Stand in front of me." She waved him over.

He hesitated then stepped close.

Deidre took both of his hands, held them. "Close your eyes. Here."

The warmth from her palms spread from his fingers through

his arms to his torso, until Alex felt lighter and the room felt brighter. As she continued to pray aloud, Deidre pulled him in close and hugged him, touching a hand to the back of his head.

"It just left. Not far, though, so still be on guard." She held him at the shoulders. "Couple more days and we do the second blessing."

He sighed. "Thank you."

"While touching you, I felt your energies. Your passion and your hard work with your studies. Your ambitions."

Alex blinked as he reopened his eyes.

"In fact, let me see your palms." Deidre turned his hands over. "Hmm, interesting. See how you have all these crosses and wrinkles. You got lots of them. That's supposed to mean you're an old soul. Wise."

He shifted, glanced up at her.

Deidre touched her fingertips, slid it along the inside of his palm. "You have a very strong heart line. You're all heart. Your life line seems uncommon, unique. It's strong as well but there's this kind of gap or shift about midway through. Perhaps something drastic will change the trajectory, or you will go off in this totally different direction later on down the road. Go against the grain, opposite of the crowd."

"You think?"

"Alex, there is this whole life ahead of you. Follow your heart. Let it be your guide. Trust your instincts."

❧

The two sat together side by side on the park bench. Compared to their earlier misadventures, it was less verbal and more physical. More hand holding. More holding one another. First, he put his arm around her as she leaned on his shoulder and collar bone. A soft peck became a deep passionate kiss and then heavy making out, an unofficial public display of affection. April maneuvered on top of him, wrapped her legs around his torso. She touched her hands to his back then his shoulders, put one hand on each of his cheeks. Alex rubbed his palms over the fabric of her shirt, touching her chest then slid them up her thighs to her buttocks, squeezing them. She let out a subdued moan, purred like a kitten.

He leaned back, smirked. ". . . 'Lips of an Angel.' I can barely contain myself."

She caught her breath. "Mmm, and the tongue of a demigod."

April leaned her head on his shoulder again. He felt between her shoulder blades, cradled her on his lap.

"W-what are we doing? What is this?"

"I don't know, Nex."

He was quiet, kissed her on the top of her head.

"Guess maybe I want the best parts of a relationship, but not a relationship."

Alex scrunched his lips, crinkled his brow. "Is that like FTF?"

"What is FTF?"

"Isn't that what people say? Like, friends that flirt. Friends that fool around. Friends that fuck. Either that or like friends with benefits."

She laughed. "Fuck buddies?"

"These terms get worse and worse, huh." Alex touched a finger to her chin. "You know what? Let's not try to define it, put this label. Let's just . . . Let's just be."

"Becoming our little slogan."

"Just be together. Just be happy. Just be in the moment. Just be. I like you. I like whatever this is."

She pecked him on each cheek, hovered in front of his face with a smile. He pressed his lips to hers, parted them, entwined their mouths and their tongues.

"Wanna lay in the grass again?"

Alex stood with her legs still wrapped around him, carried her like that to which she let out an excited squee. He found a smooth area on the ground, lowered her, placing her head down with his hand behind it. Joining her at her side, they stared up at the sky.

"I can't find it."

He narrowed his eyes, pointed. "Over there. Like an itty-bitty swoop and cross."

"Ah, I see. Our shroom."

She rolled over, placed her hand on his chest.

"This is perfect. No other way to put it." Alex let out a content sigh, turned and kissed her on the forehead. "Whatever might happen tomorrow or for the rest of my life, I'm happy right here and right now."

April leaned in, hugged him tight from the side.

"Wish I could stay like this all night."

"You used to always worry about heading home. And now, seems like you don't ever wanna go back, huh."

Her hand worked its way skillfully around his zipper, undid his belt. She reached in and touched his crotch, rubbing it, feeling it harden.

"I wonder why that is."

Alex kept his eyes closed while April did her magic, sliding one palm from his navel to his chest beneath his shirt. A light suckle on the side of his neck became a light nibble on the edge of his earlobe.

6

THEIR ENCOUNTERS ACCELERATED, with all of the happy chemicals heightened and turning into a lustful ricochet. It was to the point they could no longer keep their hands off one another, even in a quiet corner of a store. What started as a gentle caress became this uncontrollable pressing together and rubbing together, their mouths open, their tongues slipping in. Both escaped away from the aisle to the nearest park as soon as nightfall hit. On the empty playground equipment, it was far from child's play. Alex hovered over her, an intense gaze, a cocky smirk. April nibbled her bottom lip, waiting, a seductive luster. Then, at once, they were all over each other again.

"You're kind of a freak, huh?" She caught her breath in between kissing and touching. "Like, insatiable . . ."

He lay down next to her as they took a break.

"I was never like this before. It was either all repressed or bottled up or . . ." Alex wiped the bangs out of his eyes. "Or maybe it's just you, April. You bring this outta me."

"At this rate, we might have to migrate to your dorm or my place."

She rolled onto her side, and he did the same. They brought their hands together and interlocked their fingers.

"My roommate's not home."

Alex swallowed. "I have a feeling part of the reason we tried keeping it this way is we know we're about to cross a line, huh."

"Let's take it slow, though to the next level. What's the term? Like, go from second to third base?"

"We definitely flew past first, reached second, and now rounding to third. Funny, maybe we can call it shortstop." He shook his head, glanced over. "Still way better than striking out altogether, I suppose."

April draped her leg over his, nuzzled into him.

"Third base sounds good. That's foreplay kinda stuff, right?"

It was light with soft pecks along the way, holding hands and hands on hips. Right when the door flew open, the two pounced, unabashed and uninhibited.

Over the bra, under the hoodie, Chucks off. Then over the panties, no bra, hoodie unzipped, Levi's in a ball. From the living room sofa to the hallway wall then the balcony until they were covered in hickeys. A streak of orange broke across the horizon.

He lay on his back while she straddled him, her expression saucy, deviant.

"What do you want?"

Alex placed his hand on top her head while she licked from spot to spot down his torso, the sun beginning to peer in through the curtains.

Right then and there, a new class started in his mind, LOVE102. No introductory course, straight into it, learning about relationships and the differences between men and women. Were they still just friends? Were they more than friends now? Did she still not like him back, after everything? It was this gray area. It was playing with fire, dancing on the line. It didn't make any sense but it also didn't matter. Henceforth, the very first lesson—women, in all their multifaceted allure and complicated splendor, are a labyrinth.

～

It was bustling and rowdy, almost every seat taken in the beer garden. The middle rows of long tables were lined with entire groups of friends celebrating and commiserating, some of them strangers elbow to elbow. Around the outside were smaller tables, for singles or for couples. Alex waited with a cheek in his palm, taking in the cacophony of movement and noise and inebriation. He could see Bradley carry the foamy pitcher and two empty mugs back, careful when placing them down. He sat down across from Alex, tilted and poured one mug then the other. Together, in unison, they each raised them up and clinked them together in a quiet mellow cheers compared to their surroundings.

"Been a little while, huh?"

"Feels like forever."

Alex wiped his mouth, slouched.

"Things get any better?"

"It's not fully resolved yet but it has been, in general. Lot going on. Which is why I do have some news to report."

"What is it, my dude?" Bradley chugged then slammed the glass down. "Damn, that hits the spot."

"It was a tough conclusion to come to, but I've decided to withdraw from classes."

His friend faced downward, scrunched his lips.

"It really, really sucks. Like, a lot. But I just can't seem to bounce back."

"Ah, geez. What's gonna happen then?"

"I did e-mail the counselor, meet up and talk. I'll take the summer off then return next semester and finish everything." Alex sipped from the mug. "I get to stay in the dorm still. But I did miss the cutoff date so I'm on track to get all Fs unless I apply for this special waiver thing which is this huge pain in the ass."

"Damn, dude. That's so crazy. You all right, though?"

"Yeah. I'm okay, at least with the logic of it. This is not the way I wanted things to go, but not sure what else to do."

"Eff it. No shame in that. Gotta do what you gotta do." Bradley raised his mug, waited. "Hey. Remember? 'Wake Me Up When *Semester* Ends,' right?"

Alex smirked, lifted up for another soft cheers.

"Can't pretend it doesn't sting, Brad. All I can say is, I think, eighteen credits a semester the past few years finally caught up to me. Then add in these noises, these attacks. Plus I learned something about myself recently, about my family. And that's been . . ."

"Look on the bright side."

He lifted his brows up. "What?"

"No, that's it. Look on the bright side." Brad leaned back, let out a howling laugh.

Alex chuckled, shook his head. "You ass."

"It'll all be fine, dude. No worries."

He refilled the two mugs from the pitcher which was already down by half.

"Why do I get this feeling I'm not gonna see you for a while, Lex?"

⌁

The air was cool as they waited past the roundabout, above

them the sky a mixture of royal blue and eggshell white. Alex stood with his hands behind his back. Next to him, Deidre held the strap of her tote bag. When they exchanged niceties and then updates, they waited in mutual silence. As the pickup truck pulled up, they waved and pointed to the parking lot. Both went in that direction where the man parked, got out, went around and lowered the tailgate to gather his items: a duffel bag, a suitcase. He was an older man, bulky with broad shoulders. He had a receding hairline and thinning hair, a thick gray mustache and beard. He wore a full suit, matching jacket and slacks but no tie.

"Okay, now that we're all together, proper introductions." She turned, stood between the two of them. "Alex, this is Liwanu. Liwanu, this is Alex."

"Nice to meet you." He had a firm handshake, a very stoic look on his face.

"Thank you for coming down." Alex nodded.

"Deidre informed me on the situation. I am a traditional elder of the Suquamish tribe, and I will be conducting the indigenous cleansing ceremony."

"Let's get started."

All three walked from the parking lot down the ramp, alongside a courtyard then to the steps of Maquilla Tower.

They let Alex walk in first. He unlocked the doors, leading the way to the room.

Deidre let the elder pass and enter before her. He panned from left to right, slow strides as he paced, placing the duffel bag and the suitcase down.

"What we're doing today is called smudging. It is for healing, not just of the place but of the people within that place.

It is a purification, blessing, restoring balance and warmth and peace."

Alex watched as the elder removed his jacket, put on a few pieces of regalia. First, he donned a thick animal hide with distinct tribal symbols then an ivory breastplate with colored stones over that. Next, he put on a large headdress with painted feathers sticking out.

"Everything I'm doing here today is done with the utmost respect to the ancient customs of my people, passed down verbally, generation to generation."

Deidre stood by the wall behind Alex.

"Now, this is a handmade whisk broom. It is to wipe clean any bad memories or negative thoughts, all grudges, hostilities, sadness and sorrow."

The two watched the careful flicking across the floor surface, the intentional sweeping motion and deliberate sound that it made.

"We give humble and gracious thanks, first and foremost. Thank you, Giver of Life. Thank you to our dear Grandfather Sun, for giving us all light as well as shadow, which are fundamental. Thank you, Mother Earth."

Next, the elder knelt down, rang a string of bells laced together on a leather strap.

"These are essential oils of mugwort, birch, fir oil, juniper berry, peppermint and wormwood. Breathe in each of the pure fragrances mixed together. Let them fill the air, fill our lungs, and our bodies and hearts and souls."

Again, he rang the string of bells, twice this time, then flicked the broom.

"Here is an assortment of beans and rice. Let this serve as a symbol of abundance and fruitfulness, of health, of happiness and well-being."

This was placed on either side of the window where the pink candle once was.

"And, onto the most important part, the actual smudging. White sage is for healing, ridding pain and freeing from concern. Red cedar is for restoration, to sanctify. Sweetgrass is for goodness and attracting in loving power."

He struck a wooden match, lit the bundle, held it up.

In his left hand was a hollowed abalone shell which acted as the bowl. It had a metallic sheen to it. In his right hand was a splayed fan with a beaded handle.

"Thank you, Liwanu." Deidre stepped forward, demonstrated.

She cupped and wafted through the smoke, spreading it over her face, her hair, her chest, shoulders and abdomen. Then she breathed it in.

"Now, as our Deidre just showed, wash this cleansing smoke over your skin and your body. Inhale deep and slow. Take your time. Close your eyes. Meditate."

Alex inched forward, leaning into the rising plume. He waved his hand in a light circular motion, rippling the twisting tendrils. First, he splashed the smoke towards his forehead and his cheeks then the top of his head. He did his neck, each shoulder, then down his arms to the forearm. There was a calming sensation settling in that relaxed the tension in his chest and slowed his heart rate. Alex closed his eyes, let his mind go blank.

"Very good."

The elder did the same and washed the smoke over himself, over the entirety of the room. Along the east, west, north and south facing walls. Along the window, the door. In front of the closet and inside the closet. Over the bed, the desk, the lamp. Then he stood before Alex, placed both hands on his shoulders and bowed his head.

"Let this young man know peace. May all that Alex says and thinks and does be in harmony. Fill him with light, with hope. Ancestral spirits, please help him hold onto what is good and all that he must do."

When the man began to chant in his Native American tongue, Alex felt a strange aura emanate and fill the room, the whole building. To him, it was as if a bear stood on its hind legs, perhaps the statue of a bear or a tree trunk carved with a bear's image.

"It is done."

As he turned and removed the regalia, put each item away in his bag and suitcase, Deidre stood next to Alex. The air was lighter, clean. It was calm, silent.

"T-thank you, Liwanu. I don't know what else to say. You are obviously a wise man, with great inner strength. Can't quite describe it but . . . I felt that just now. I see why you come highly recommended."

"You are welcome, friend. Everything will be okay from here. Deidre, feel free to reach out if you need me again but I am certain whatever inhabited this dwelling is no more."

"He's right. It's gone, for good."

The two shook his hand once again as he let himself out.

"Wow." Alex blinked, let out a breath. "I'm kinda speechless. That was, like, majestic or something. Holy crap."

"Ain't he something? My husband, Miles, he is the one that connected with him when we were first getting started."

"Incredible presence."

"Let me pray with you again as well."

She pulled him in for a tight embrace with a slight sway. Deidre held him as she proceeded to pray in a low whisper.

"You feel good, huh?"

"I do. It's so weird."

"Like this, again, I can feel all your drive and ambition. Don't ever let that flame extinguish. It may be flickering, wavering, but rekindle it. And stoke it."

Alex nodded.

"I could also sense . . . your connection with this girl. That is a pure love, raw, deep like a river. It appears you were to meant cross paths and to coincide. She is going to have a major impact on your life."

"H-how do you know this?"

Deidre smiled, let go and stepped backward. "Which brings me to the last thing I been meaning to say. As we already established, you have a gift, Alex. Same as myself. Same as how many others. If the time should ever come, please reach out and maybe we can explore this ability."

The scent of sage, cedar and sweetgrass still lingered as he stared at her with narrowed eyes and a crinkled brow.

"In fact, it's quite possible that I will be the one who contacts you. I might need your help one day. Not for certain, but something tells me we will meet again."

PART THREE

THE LONG EASTER

1

One Year Later

WHAT STARTED AS fun, flirty friendship soon turned into more than friends. Then "more than friends" eventually went on to become official In a Relationship status on their MySpace accounts. In the happy honeymoon phase, hot and heavy making out escalated to crossing the line into the intimate, the sensual, then of course consummating. From first base to second base, lingering at shortstop, then through third all the way down to home plate. Their lives together as boyfriend and girlfriend were full and joyous and passionate, with never a dull moment. Both now knew what it was to be lovers, and to be two separate halves of a whole interconnected and superimposed.

April moved on from food service to sales, working at a popular jewelry store. Alex had some trouble finding a new job amidst the economic climate but settled in customer service at a call center for a credit union. This would be enough for them to move on from walking and shuttle hopping and bus rides to getting their own rundown sedan.

He glanced over at her with a smirk. She leaned into the

cushion, smiling. The road before them through the quiet neighborhood was winding, the asphalt in good condition, the grass on the median well maintained.

Oh, wow. Yeah.

Pretty sure we made the right choice.

The couple considered multiple areas but ultimately were torn between a final top three, two being North Emerald and Rainward. A gated community by their old community college where they first met was tempting, but the management seemed a bit uptight. A modern duplex at the foot of the valley over in Rainward was a close match, but they got beat out by the gaggle of other applicants with better credit scores and actual rental history. In the end, they ended up taking a one-bedroom in Tuscarora.

It was the last building on the left at the corner before the stop sign. He pulled into the near empty lot, parking in their new assigned stall.

"Hey. Never too late to go back and crap out."

"Of course, just lose our security deposit." He laughed. "And I'm sure that they would loove to keep me at the dorms even though I already graduated."

His last semester wasn't the usual eighteen credits. There was only three classes left to finish up the degree program. Being the overachiever, Alex still gunned for overtime the semester prior, which of course ended in disaster. For the hell of it, he did do a fourth with April, retaking a psych course to help boost his GPA after that string of Fs.

"Can't wait to grad. Dropping to part-time helps, but I wanna be done. Like, done-done. Kaput. Finie. Dunzo."

"Getting close. You're almost there."

Alex reached in the glove box, took out their signed paperwork.

"Think you can drop this off? I wanna head in there first before we start unloading, take care of something."

April flipped through the pages.

"Your name is so pompous. Alexander Clark Jacobsen."

"I suppose April Wen is much better, huh."

"Okay. You go do whatever then, and I'll stop by and hand them this. I gotta pick up the extra set of keys anyway."

She unbuckled then leaned over the center console for a quick peck but he pulled her in for a deeper kiss, parting her lips. He could feel her body melt and swoon in turn as their tongues danced.

Alex touched her chin with a half-fist. "My precious . . ."

The way he gazed at her was always obsessive, enamored and mesmerized like he was under some sort of spell, thus the new term of endearment.

His eyes tracked her from behind, savoring the curve of her buttocks and the sway of her hips. Then he got out and walked up the side stairs.

It was clean and empty inside, the carpet a fluffy salmon. The living room had large windows overlooking a wide field then forest beyond that. Alex stared out at this as he stepped through the kitchen, tapping the countertop. He peeked down the hall to the bedroom then reached into his back pocket.

One by one, he sprinkled salt along the walls. Being thorough, it was each wall in each room, then in the center of each room. Next, he placed cloves of garlic in all the corners and on both sides of every window.

"That . . . garlic?"

Alex was caught off guard. "H-hey. Sorry, I was hoping to be done before you got in."

"What are you up to? What is that?"

"Let's just say, it's kind of a Mexican blessing thingy. For protection."

"Oh. Okay then." April laughed it off and moved on. "I don't wanna know."

She lowered the cardboard box, shoved it over with the ball of her foot. Then she dropped two pillows and a blanket down. He joined her and wrapped his arms around her waist, pecked her on the side of her head above her dazzly ear.

"You know, I was thinking of a different way we can *bless* this house." April lifted a brow with a sultry smile. "Come on, we gotta do each room."

Alex let her pull him by the hand into the kitchen where they kissed and touched, a delicate pace at first. She pressed him against the wall, rubbing his back beneath his shirt, unbuckling his belt, unzipping. He began to take off her shirt, bringing his mouth back to hers before the fabric was even off her eyes and nose. Then he scooped her up and lifted her onto the counter as April squeezed her legs into his sides, the light kissing turning into heavy pawing and fondling. With a pass through the living room and a pause in the hallway, the kitchen counter became the bathroom sink. Still kissing, still touching, their clothes still half-on, they ended up on the carpet in the bedroom next to the blanket and two pillows.

The two took their time licking, rubbing, moaning and grunting and breathing. There was no roommate to worry about. There was no paper thin walls between dorms where zero sounds were muted. April held his face, stroked his hair back, then ran her hand down his neck and chest where he began to sweat. She bit into the corner of the pillowcase then covered her face with the pillow to try to contain herself while her thighs shivered. Alex shut his eyes, writhed and convulsed. He then gazed down at her, saw that all the energy had left her body. As she lay there limp, letting out light gasps, she was like a doll or a plaything in his arms. It was a familiar scene then, with the sun beginning to peer in through the vertical blinds.

"Thank you." April caught her breath, paused. "I needed that."

Alex smirked, lowered and kissed her on the forehead.

"You just . . ." She blinked, nibbled her bottom lip. "You just fucked me like an animal."

"I love that fuckin' song."

"Speaking of, I'll put together a playlist for us. Make unpacking fly by a li'l quicker. Come on. Let's get to work."

"That was work."

Both laughed as they got dressed. She reached in, took out her laptop and plug while he went to the car to get the next box. When Alex returned, the music already started. The first song was "Welcome Home" by Coheed and Cambria.

"Ha, very fitting. I get it." He banged his head to the rhythm, jammed on an imaginary air guitar to the heavy riff.

Alternating, they walked down and unloaded, brought it all up then unpacked. It was cookery and silverware, toiletries, commodities, clothing and shoes. Then it was furniture and small appliances, the rest of the bedding and the TV. While working, the playlist continued on with "Collide" by Howie Day and "Fall for You" by Secondhand Serenade. In between songs, they exchanged content glances.

She passed by as he was about to hang a framed poster, then shuddered and flinched in place. "Whoa. Whoa. Wait, wait, wait."

"Huh?"

"Don't put that there. I don't want *Scarface* watching over me while I sleep."

Alex instead flipped through the different posters. "It's either that, big boob anime girl, Heath Ledger's Joker or Iron Man."

"Jesus."

She threaded the clips of the *Psycho* shower curtain they came across in a variety store clearance section. Then she placed a fluffy Yoshi doll next to a poofy Kirby doll in the middle of the bed. He placed a Gryffindor sword letter opener next to the microwave on the counter then set up their Nintendo Wii.

The playlist wrapped up with "Teenage Dirtbag" by Wheatus then culminated in an extended version of "Kernkraft 400" by Zombie Nation. April and Alex bopped to the beat on that last one as it built up from a metronome and snare to heavy hi-hats and funky synth notes. Each stopped what they were doing, came together in a matching nerdy dance. The kind without judgment or shame, letting loose and being silly.

"Okay, let's take a break there."

Unopened boxes and plastic bins remained scattered and strewn but the space was coming together, now appeared livable to some degree.

"I think I'm done unpacking for today. My brain is fried."

"Same. You wanna go catch a movie, celebrate?" April put her hands on her hips.

"Ah, I don't know. We been on a pretty good roll with our movies but this year is sorta lackluster so far."

"Last year was pretty great for movies."

"It really was. From like *21* to *The Dark Knight* to like *Valkyrie.* It was a winning streak, nonstop."

He circled the living room, scooped up some stray papers and envelopes, mixed in was the brochure and printouts from a year ago. Alex almost didn't notice but the corner sticking out caught his eye.

"I liked *Wall-E* a lot. And *Pineapple Express* was fun-ny."

Although his mind started to wander, he forced himself to snap out of it. "Not to mention, *Forgetting Sarah Marshall* and *Tropic Thunder* and *Yes Man.* We got to see *Saw* even."

"Seesaw?"

"You know what I mean. *Saw V,* come on." This joke was ongoing the night that they watched it. "The last one."

He lingered then stashed everything away, including the brochure.

"Do you think?"

"I'm sure. Not just gonna keep going and going and going." Alex scratched his head, folded his arms.

"Oh, oh. And then *Marley & Me* of course. Despite still recovering from that trauma."

She leaned back, tapped a finger to her chin in thought.

"Better idea?"

"Maybe do early dinner then relax. There's some pretty good restaurants in the area. Spotted 'em as we drove in."

❧

The three cornerstones of a stable relationship are conversation, intercourse and consumption. It was essential to have chemistry, both in the bedroom and out. From witty banter to inside jokes to monogamous ravaging. Before getting their own place, it was the park in broad daylight, the back of the movie theater, the passenger seat, the public bathroom at the mall, the second floor of the library—they were quite adventurous and impetuous, borderline reckless. Each could equally stay up all night talking and joking or making out and making love, in and out of topics, in and out of positions. As the two settled in and simmered down, it was more shopping and going to the movies and dining out.

Alex was a little less emo and more metro. April was a little less punk and more club. He often wore long sleeve collar shirts, sometimes a vest or a tie. On this outing, he wore a light beige blazer over a casual polo with a graphic design. She wore a sleek dress that showed off her smooth legs and a sliver of cleavage. He traded his Vans for stylish slip-ons while she traded her Chucks in for flats.

If it wasn't an early dinner or a late lunch, then it was mid-morning brunch. Always tended to flow smoother when it wasn't too crowded. Going out for dinner the night prior bled into going out for brunch the next morning, naturally.

Both enjoyed the food and enjoyed the view, in no apparent rush. The lake behind them was pristine through the window while the waitress refilled their drinks. It was a shared appetizer to start, their own entrees which they sampled from as planned, and of course, unnecessary but delectable sweets afterward.

"So, this everything you imagined?"

"Hmm?" April finished chewing her dessert.

"Getting together, I mean. Us." He scooted his chair forward, wiped his hands with the cloth napkin. "It took some doing but I finally did wear you down and win you over."

She blushed a faint pink while he let out an I-told-you-so smirk.

"That you did, Nex." April placed one elbow on the table, touching her jawline with her fingertips. "We're in this together now. If you jump, then I jump."

He was about to say more but felt a vibration in his pocket. Alex took out his phone, glanced at the screen. It was an unknown number. Though it was the newer updated versions, they both still had their Sony Ericsson and Motorola Razr.

"Is that Brad?"

"No, uh . . . I actually haven't talked to him in a while."

Something wasn't right. There was a nagging itch at the base of his skull, a kind of twisting in his chest, a sinking sensation in the pit of his stomach.

"Hold on. Lemme take this . . ."

"Go ahead."

Alex slid the screen up in a light click, revealing the QWERTY keyboard.

"H-hello?"

"May I please speak to Alex?" The voice was polite albeit choppy and garbled, with a touch of static.

"Yes, this is him."

"I'm sorry to bother you. My name is Ned Berenson, I'm a friend of Deidre. She told me to call you. There's been an incident."

2

BEFORE THAT BRIEF exchange, Alex never knew of anybody who suffered a violent and serious crime. What happened to Deidre was heinous and despicable. It was downright evil and downright shocking. However, by some fortunate cosmic miracle, against all astronomical odds, she managed to survive the horrific ordeal and now rested in stable condition in a recovery room hooked up to life support. Alex raced there, ready to meet the rest of the team at her bedside. The steep incline of the hill carried him from within the city to a suburban neighborhood just along the rural outskirts. Up ahead, he could see the sign at the front of the driveway: SAINT FLORIAN HEALTHCARE SYSTEM.

Alex pulled in behind the other cars waiting to take the ticket from the attendant. While not moving, he shifted toward the passenger seat where the brochure lay. He snuck it out after dropping off April. It had been a long time since he last thought about SPIRAL or about spooks, specters or ghosts, or anything close.

It began as a simple passion project for Miles and Deidre. The husband-wife duo first formed the group under the name,

Emerald Studies of the Paranormal or ESP for short. Miles grew up in a devout household and held strong ties to the church while Deidre always seemed to have budding psychic abilities. Together, they handled some very famous cases throughout the northwest and became well-known paranormal investigators and demonologists. One case was a murder house. One case was an asylum, a coven. There were a couple possessions they assisted in that made national headlines, having to testify in court. There were even claims of a raggedy doll in a sailor outfit they encountered that moved, changed facial expressions and made giggling noises.

When they expanded, they changed the group name and took on other experts to assist in conducting investigations, interviews and historical research, as well as handling all of the audiovisual equipment and business operations.

He stared down at his feet as he approached the lobby, ready to make his way toward the elevators.

"Uh, Alex?"

On one of the cushioned chairs, a guy popped up with a single hand raised.

"Thanks for coming. I was the one earlier, that spoke on the phone."

Alex reached forward, shook his hand.

"Edward Berenson, right?"

The guy nodded. "My friends call me Ned."

He appeared almost the exact same as his photograph in the brochure, with a thick hipster beard and wearing flannel.

"I did wanna get you up to date before introducing you."

Both stood together in the middle of the rows.

"There's no nice way to say this . . ." He swallowed, faced away. "Apparently, it was an attempted murder-suicide."

Jaw agape, a blank stare, Alex was stunned, speechless.

"Not sure what happened. I know her husband was working overtime for a high profile client, off the record. Over a year of that. It's possible his involvement compromised him. There were concerns about anger and violence escalating, verbal threats."

"Did he . . . Did he actually ever mention wanting to hit her, hurt her . . . kill her?"

Without a word, the guy narrowed his eyes.

"God damn."

"Such a shame. He was the nicest man you'd ever meet. Did so much good. Believed in good. And he loved her more than anything, I'm telling you."

Exhaling, Alex shuffled on his feet.

"Obviously, this is a huge blow to the group. Without our founders, one gone, and the other recovering, we could sure use some help. She recommended you."

"W-why?"

"You'll have to ask her yourself. The doctors are in there now, routine questions. But then you can go in and talk."

Although it was just a short walk from the lobby to the elevator then to the hallway by the waiting room, it felt longer. Each step across the squeaky floor seemed to linger and drag, as if time itself slowed down. While staff talked amongst themselves at the nursing station, typing away on the computers and answering phones, there were various alarms blaring and machines bleeping steadily. One pushed along large x-ray equipment. One removed a fresh needle from sterile packaging. Alex followed Edward who led them over, hanging both arms at his sides in a lurched posture. From behind, Alex could tell how tall the guy was and how pale. His heavy boots gave a muted thud on the ceramic tile.

"Guys, it's Alex. The one that D talked about." Edward motioned with his hand, palm up, turning his body between them. "This is Cameron and this is Erin."

"Cam."

His handshake was firm. He must have grown since his photo, where he was once lanky and gangly. Now, his arm was muscular and bulged from beneath his button-up.

"Erin. Nice to meet you, though under terrible circumstances."

She was thin with clear rimmed glasses and had parted wavy bleached hair. As he took her hand, he noticed her appearance was similar to her photo but that she was prettier now, with light makeup on and hair styled.

It was kind of a mismatched group when they all huddled. A hipster who better fit in at a craft beer tasting event. A gym rat who probably frequented the hotel pools on spring break. A girl who could have passed for a barista at an obscure hole-in-the-wall. And an emo, metro kid who chased them all down the rabbit hole against his better judgment.

"You, uh, see dead people?"

Edward smacked him on his bulky upper arm. The girl shook her head, brought an open palm to her face.

"What?"

"Looks like they're finishing up. After the docs leave, just go right in."

Alex did as he was asked, carefully turned the handle and pushed the door panel while the three waited outside to give them some privacy.

The minute he saw Deidre lying there on that hospital bed in that hospital gown, it all came rushing back. It was him, her, and the ghosts of his past: the choking ghost, his aunty, his grandpa, the old eerie family house.

"You look . . . different."

She let out a wide smile, despite dried blood on her face and cuts around her lips and all over her chin.

He slid into the chair, reached forward and held her hand. "Deidre, I am so so sorry this happened to you."

"Ned told you everything?"

He shook his head, let go and leaned back. "Can't believe it."

"That wasn't my husband. Usually, a case is a pretty standard. Ask questions. Do some tests, some checking. Do a blessing." Her head adjusted on the pillow as she stared him straight in the eye. "But, from time to time, you come across something altogether sinister, insidious, conjuring up pure evil. It's also very dangerous."

Alex rubbed his palms together, listened.

"Now, I wouldn't ask. But we are already backlogged as it is. People are frightened out there, restless, overwhelmed. You remember what it was like. One of the core principles that we are firm on is that we have to help everybody that we can and as soon as possible. You're not obligated. Know that. But out of all people, for some reason, it is you and only you that my intuition is really nudging me towards."

"Why do you think that is?"

"I don't know. Maybe there's something you're supposed to do, see, feel. Maybe there's somebody you're supposed to meet. Or, maybe, only you can help with whatever might occur."

"Your husband . . . What do you think happened . . . ?"

"Not sure. I wasn't involved with that case. But I can say, whether it's a demon or an apparition, that negativity and that darkness can infect you like a plague. You may start to hallucinate or experience changes in your personality."

"Like, possession?"

"It could be full-on, spirit attaching and trying to take control. Sure. It could also just be affecting you too, mentally, emotionally."

"Hmm. I see."

"Should you choose to join, a couple of things. I think, for safety, maybe keep a little distance between yourself and your significant other when it comes to this. I might recommend not telling her, at least not right away. This is only temporary after all. You don't want to risk anything like what happened to me."

Breathing out a long sigh, he slouched in the chair.

"And, the other thing. The first step would be to convince a certain someone. He will be quite resistant to getting involved. He's a preacher that me and my husband worked with first starting out. Good man, but a bit quirky."

He crinkled his brow.

"Anyway, he'll be the one to take charge until I'm back on my feet. Something tells me it won't be Ned, or Cam or Erin. It's going to be you he'll listen to."

"Me?"

Deidre nodded, smiled.

"One last note. There is good out there as well, not just evil. Look. I'm talking with you, ain't I? I'm alive. I'm breathing. Must have an angel with me right now."

"That's one helluva angel then. Funny thing to say, but yeah."

"You're right." She laughed then coughed. "I-I'm happy to see you again, Alex. That girl and you are pretty happy, huh."

Alex held back a half-smirk.

"See. There's good and bad, angels and demons. Be patient. Be kind. The forces of good will help guide you. And also Pastor Art."

The sun started to go down behind the buildings and the trees, causing the overcast skies to turn canary and golden. Streaks of gray combined into blobby fluffs of red and smeared patches of purple as Alex rotated the wheel, turning into the quiet neighborhood. It was a lot of take in. It was a lot to think about. But deep down, without overthinking, somehow he did already know the answer. He parked, got out, remained in place with a hand on the frame of the door. Then he closed it, stepped to the side of the fender, leaned on it. Alex put both hands in his pockets, staring away as murky thoughts formed into a concrete decision.

Okay. Fine. I'll do this.

I owe you her that much at least.

From the parking lot up the stairs down the hall to their new apartment, it was as if Alex were a robot. He glided on his feet, quiet. As he opened the door and entered inside, he relaxed a little to the sound of her voice.

"That you, Nex?"

"Yeah." He kicked off his shoes. "Yeah, it's me."

When he stepped into the bedroom, he could see her from behind in the prone position with her laptop glowing. She wore a comfy shirt, no bra, and cutesy girly panties that showed off the lower butt cheeks, like a peach or an apple bottom. This angle immediately had a calming effect, also turned him on.

Hovering over, he gave her buttocks a light smack then a light squeeze.

"'Ello, love." Alex had the swagger of a drunken pirate.

April glanced up from the bed, pouted her lips, waiting. Without makeup on and wearing glasses, she was just as beautiful if not more so.

"Heart you."

"I heart you, too."

Leaning down, he pressed his lips to hers. First, just a quick peck. Then, once more, soft, open mouthed.

"Fan fiction put you in a good mood, huh."

"Been really hooked on his one, hehe." She lifted herself up on her elbows. "So, how'd everything go? With your friend? He okay?"

Alex nodded. "It was weird. You know, seeing him like that. He, uh, is pretty beat up from the accident."

"Oh, God. Poor thing."

He swallowed, conscious that he didn't tell her the whole truth, far from it. Then he licked his lips, blinked and went on.

"Listen, I . . . I'll be helping out with the business 'til he recovers, if that's cool. It would mean some late nights and some weekends."

"Of course. Whatever he needs."

It was a very strict rule of LOVE102 that he bent and broke right then—trust and communication are the primary ingredients of every relationship.

3

Plainsdock, OR

A LITTLE LESS than three hours down the I-5 brought them to their destination. However, it took another hour and a half to track the preacher. The group hobbled out of the van at the first stop, the actual residence, but no luck despite loud and repeated knock, knock, knocks. Next was his church but the assistant preacher redirected them to a different church. It turned out a local tragedy occurred that required his full and immediate attention. For some reason, there seemed to be this cornucopia of misfortune spreading out in a vicious cycle, like the high tide, like the full moon, surreal like an impending natural disaster ready to strike.

Before anybody said a word, Alex already knew—it was Pastor Art.

"Yo. That's him, dude." Cameron pointed.

"Nah, I don't think so."

"Did you even look at the picture!?"

The preacher walked with a gloomy facial expression, his lips thinned. His coat flapping in the wind matched the flickering of the police tape as he went up the sidewalk to the front steps of the historic chapel. One of the officers shook his head, raised his arms up, but another officer vouched, reasoned then let the preacher through.

Alex followed along as the others got out and stood in the street.

"Can't even believe this . . ." Erin brought a hand to her mouth. "I hope to never endure such a sickening act . . ."

Four of them stood together on the curb next to a phone booth and two coin-operated newspaper racks.

Edward arched his neck without a word.

Cameron folded his arms. "What do we do?"

Squinting his eyes, Alex could see into the chapel. Pastor Art entered through the door frame, passed the first wooden pews then knelt down, presumably examining a chalk outline or an empty shell casing marked by little alphanumeric stands. He could see the preacher close his eyes and cover his face, remaining in that position.

Perhaps it was a muttered prayer. Perhaps it was a simple moment of silence. Mourning, sadness. A mix of all these things, even slight morbid curiosity.

After enough time passed, he circled around the interior then exited. He waved to the one officer, plodded down the steps, ducking beneath the police tape. Then in a brisk walk, he hurried across the street. In no less than a minute, Pastor Art was in the chapel one moment then the bar the next.

"Maybe we should fuck off . . . This is . . ."

Cameron wasn't wrong.

"But we came all this way." Erin swayed on her feet, shifted.

"Just one of us should go, I think. He obviously knows the

people here, knows this community. It would be smart to tread light."

Alex faced the ground to his feet then glanced up.

"Leave it to me."

Unsure where that confidence came from, Alex stepped forward then turned to them. With a slow nod, he headed towards the bar.

Hope Deidre was right.

Moment of truth.

Light music played from an old jukebox as he turned the handle and entered inside. It was empty except for a handful of patrons who sat on scattered tables, keeping to themselves. He spotted the preacher right away, at the end of the bar top, swilling a glass.

Alex walked over and sat down.

"Buddy. I'm already in a church, and not interested in insurance." He took a swig, slammed the glass on the counter. "Whatever you're selling, I'm not buying."

Swiveling on the stool, Alex took a moment before speaking, careful to choose his words and his actions.

"I can't get it exactly. Course not. But I kinda understand what you're going through."

Pastor Art hunched, sniffled. "You know, I haven't drank in a looong time. Takes something pretty dang horrible for me to fall off the wagon."

He watched him from the side, stayed quiet.

"I just don't understand what's going on in the world these days. Know what I mean? First, it was the massacre at Washington High. Like, that opened up this big wound and the wound got infected. It played on the news over and over for how long? Then it was that psycho at Emerald Tech, who was inspired, obsessed.

And then, even worse, it was friggin' little kids over at Rocky Point Elementary School. Helpless, innocent . . ."

Pastor Art pounded a fist, shuddered in place in anger and rage as a single tear rolled down his cheek.

Alex felt his own eyes water, glancing at the long mirror lining the wall.

"What the heck did those kids do? Huh??? It's so wrong."

He blinked, fighting back tears as the preacher spoke.

"And what did any of these churchgoers do? It was the middle of a friggin' bible study, in the middle of the friggin' week. This dang sick, sadistic son of a whore . . ."

On instinct, almost as a reflex, Alex reached out and put a hand on his shoulder, patted then rubbed it.

"This thing is spreading to churches now, too. Disgusting. What'll be next?"

"You're right, Pastor. The world is going to hell in a handbasket. Fast." He leaned closer. "I, uh . . ."

Pastor Art straightened up, perked his ears. He wiped his cheek with his sleeve.

"I came pretty close. Got lucky. My first year at Emerald Tech was when what you mentioned happened. It was close to the end of the semester, like around finals. One of the professors switched to this scantron thing for the weekly quiz and I couldn't for the life of me find that lab to sit down and even try to take it. That's when we got the text alerts, and so I never did make it that day into the right building. Could've easily been myself trying to outrun a bullet. Me, in my pumped up kicks I used to wear."

The preacher raised an arm, gestured with a lazy peace sign. "Two more, the same. One for me and one for this punk kid."

Alex drummed his fingers.

"I'm assuming you're twenty-one and that you like bourbon."

"Sure, sure. Game for anything."

"Put some hair on your balls." The preacher finished the rest, smacked his lips then let out a sharp sigh. "Listen, sorry for breaking down earlier."

"It's all good, Pastor."

"What's your name anyway?"

"Alex."

The bartender poured the bronze liquid in two glasses over two large ice blocks, then left to go wipe down the bar back.

"Well, Alexander, have a drink with me."

In the long mirror, he saw their reflection side by side. Each raised a glass, brought them together, the ice clinking.

"Here's to Cale. My good friend. A good fellow pastor and all-around good person."

"Cheers. To Cale." Alex nodded then took a slow sip.

Pastor Art slumped his shoulders. "Man. He always said he would run for senator one day, though not too sure how serious that might have been."

Alex took another sip, felt the burn.

"Well, him and the other eleven . . . Twelve of them all together . . . They're up there with Lord God now. In a much, much better place."

"Hmm." He turned to the preacher. "Kind of like the disciples, huh?"

"You're right. Twelve angels. Twelve saints." Pastor Art swilled the glass. "Caleb, Caleb. I miss you already, ol' pal."

For a moment, Alex thought of Bradley, and wondered what he was up to.

"All righty then. So what is it?"

"Uh . . ." Alex breathed out, leaned over on his elbows.

"Speaking of old friends, that is kinda why I'm here. Deidre wanted me to find you, talk to you."

"Deidre? Deidre Callahan? Phew." The preacher inclined his head. "Is she still foxy?"

He held back a smirk, half-nodded.

"Oh, wow. Deids. You know, Cale had a real thing for her. Could ya blame him? We all used to hang out back in the day. Her and her boyfriend back then, now husband."

"She's at Saint Florian, in the recovery unit. And her husband . . . he passed away."

"W-w-what?"

Alex took two quick and hard chugs. "That's the reason I'm here, Pastor. She needs your help. We all do."

"Jesus Christ."

&

By the time he went back outside to gather the rest of them, news reporters swarmed the area. Alex peeked over at vans pulling up in droves on both sides of the street. A single anchorwoman and a single cameraman were the first to start preparing their equipment, with a single producer planning their shot in front of the taped off chapel. The chief of police and other public officials appeared ready to make statements as well. Edward, Cameron and Erin stood in the very same spot. Alex updated them and led the three back to the bar and grill. Pastor Art had moved from the end of the counter to a wide booth on the side wall, was finishing up a phone call as he raised an arm up towards the others.

"Is that the new Blackberry?"

Pastor Art either didn't hear or didn't care to answer.

"Um. Cool story, bro." Cameron scooted in after Edward.

Although Alex offered to let her sit on the cushioned seat, Erin remained outside, grabbing a nearby chair that she spun around backwards. She rested both her arms across the top of it.

When he finished, Pastor Art put away his phone then stared each of them dead in the eye. This was the new interim leader and this was the new temporary roster. And this was their first impromptu meeting.

"Sorry for . . . Sorry for your loss." Erin interlocked her fingers.

"Thank you." He brought a closed fist over his mouth, fighting back emotion before continuing. "Alexander here, Mister Jacobsen, he informed me of the situation. I just got off the phone to start figuring out some logistics. How all this is gonna work. I'll be here a few more days to help some of the people, do outreach, offer support. The new assistant pastor has had enough training to take on new duties, hold down the fort. But I think I'll still need to drive back here once a week, every other week or so."

While they listened, the bartender placed down glasses of ice water then menus and utensils wrapped in napkins.

"I will visit Misses Callahan, catch up and touch base, make sure she's okay. Then, well, we can resume investigations by the following weekend. But wait, hold on, I'm getting a little ahead of myself. I am Arturo Selga. Please, just call me Pastor Art. Why don't you all introduce yourselves. Gimme your first and last names, and then position."

"Edward Berenson. I go by Ned. I'm lead researcher."

"Lead investigator, and also the muscle." He grinned but Pastor Art was not amused.

"C-Cameron Gallo. Or just Cam."

Shaking her head, Erin brought a palm to her face. "It's

pretty easy to remember him. He is the one that likes the 'camera on,' always likes to have the 'camera on' him."

"Funny. And you, miss?"

"I am the equipment expert. Erin Woodfeld."

"You already know, but Alexander Jacobsen. And still not sure what the hell I'm even doing here." Alex let out a half-smirk.

Erin chuckled, tapped him on his shoulder blade.

"Okay. Good. It's nice to meet you all, though we have a lot on our plates. Which, yeah, let's get some food and drink in us, yeah."

"Dude, never woulda thought I'd be in a bar with a pastor like this." Cameron grabbed the menu. "Can we do a shot?"

"Enjoy it while you can. Gonna get back on the straight and narrow in the morning. No selfies, though. No incriminating evidence. No *tagging* me. You dang millennials and your dang interwebs, social medias, blah blah blah. I dread whatever pathetic generation comes after you."

"Can we do a buttery nipple or maybe a masturbating butterfly?"

Pastor Art stared at him, speechless.

"Jager bomb?"

"Are you in a sorority or something. C'mon."

Everybody laughed except Cameron. The bartender returned and jotted their orders as more customers entered.

"I'm . . ." Alex cleared his throat. "Well, this is all still pretty new to me. In fact, I find it kinda weird, if I am being honest. Can I ask you guys, what is your general explanation of ghosts and of hauntings?"

"To put it simply, a ghost is the soul of a dead person." Edward crossed his arms, leaned back. "And a haunting kind of depends. There are three types of hauntings."

He crinkled his brow.

"Residual, intelligent, and projected."

Cameron slurped through the straw. Erin undid her napkin, placing the fork and knife aside.

"What's that?"

"If it's like repetitive sounds, for example, footsteps, or doors opening or closing, that could be residual. Residual can also be ghosts that always roam the grounds, always do the same sort of things. But there doesn't seem to be anything more to it than that, a constant loop, on replay. Like memories ingrained. Or perhaps the spirit energy almost left like this stain on the space-time continuum."

"I see." Alex nodded.

"And an intelligent haunting would be if the ghost reacts in real time, like answering your question or affecting the environment in different ways, based on where you are or what you might be doing. For instance, a drawer slamming or a painting falling in a particular room if you're perceived as invading their territory. Or perhaps they disapprove, as an old-fashioned spirit might not care for an unmarried couple sharing the same bed. In other words, it is expressing itself and making its presence known."

"Hmm. And what's projected?"

"Projected can be poltergeist activity."

"Oh, like the movie."

"No, no. Not quite. Poltergeist means 'noisy ghost,' we all get that. It is disturbances in a location, like physical objects rearranging or even levitating. It can be electrical disruptions, television sets turning off or on by themselves, light switches, faucets. Can seem hostile, dangerous, threatening."

Edward paused, rolled up his sleeves.

"There are different theories behind this. I interned for a famed parapsychologist, and we studied this quite extensively. One idea is that these are the doings of a young child in the household, joking around, playing tricks. Illusion, delusion, even hallucination might play a factor. Another idea is that this is unexplained natural occurrences. Perhaps water running deep in the soil, nearby power lines, various metal deposits might be impacting the location. Some have attributed it to friction of quartz in the ground from seismic activity causing a kind of ball lightning effect. Or maybe it's the intersecting of ley lines between ancient sacred sites."

Alex rubbed his chin, fascinated. Pastor Art stared into his water, taking a short break from the alcohol.

"But the number one theory, at least in my observation, is psychokinesis. Like, inhabitants going through mental-emotional stress is somehow creating this phenomenon. It could be a teenage girl going through changes in puberty. It could be young women going through pregnancy, older women going through menopause. This can be a 'projected' haunting as I mentioned. In fact, it's possible many people are unaware of their own ability to manipulate their surroundings. Sometimes a window might break in the middle of a heated argument between loved ones. A glass might slide right off of the table. Things like that."

"Now that Ned is finished with his lengthy dissertation, I'm about starving here. Way overdue for some protein."

"I think that's it right there, Mister Gallo." Pastor Art pointed with his chin.

"Aw, hell yeah. Finally."

The waitress seemed to have just started her shift. She tied her apron then brought their plates, setting them down in front of each of them with care.

"How 'bout you guys?"

Erin pressed her glasses to the bridge of her nose. "I been with these guys a couple of years now, and I'm still not sure."

Alex observed as she poked her salad with her fork.

"There's definitely something going on. Paranormal activity of some sort. You would have to be a fool to deny it. I handle the audiovisual stuff, and I'll say, EVPs alone can be so common and so compelling."

"EVPs?"

She shifted towards him. "Stands for electronic voice phenomena."

"I see."

"And also, some of the things we've caught on tape . . . Authentic reactions of family members. Fluctuations in temperature. Motion sensors going off. Light anomalies. Figures. It is kind of crazy how much can happen, and there's no way to debunk it all."

He stabbed at his poutine, chewed, swallowed. "Do you guys think it could be sleep paralysis or night terrors or something like that?"

Cameron cut into his sirloin. "I mean, could be. Or a combination of sorts. Paranoia, hysteria, mind tricks. A very real fear factor which can skew the data. We do always check for mental illness before an investigation, too."

Pastor Art took another bite of his sandwich, the saucy pulled pork about to spill out.

Alex waited for Cameron to elaborate further. He cut another piece, mixed it with the sauteed mushrooms and onions, held it up and waved it.

"We look into the historical records. The background of a building, a location, the truth is out there. Family history. If you take a map of Emerald City as it used to be and lay it over a map of Emerald City as it is now, you will see, the most haunted places directly correlate to old burial grounds, and places they used to do executions or even sacrifices. So, just like Erin said, there is something. For damned sure."

Cameron then took the lingering bite at last.

Edward placed his pizza crust down, picked up the next slice. "We need more science. Footage, imagery, the records, the recordings, personal accounts, all of it is available."

The four of them sensed the preacher preparing to speak. It was obvious that theories on parapsychology, technical aspects of audiovisual evidence and historical lore had been represented. But what about faith, spirituality and the divine?

"Science . . ."

Pastor Art wiped his mouth with the napkin, pressed the plate away.

"Eh, science can be an organized system of ignorance. A majority of the scientific community will easily dismiss all that we're talking about. It's this cycle of self-righteous snobbery and condescension, being small minded. Now me, I choose to be pretty open."

He lifted up the glass to himself in a soft cheers. Alex copied, albeit delayed.

"Where the hell's *my* drink?" Cameron shot a quick glance at the bar. "Motherfucker."

"Some of the most knowledgeable experts can agree that there is something more to all of this, to life. Doctors and surgeons understand the complexity of the human body, of the human brain, the mysterious link between body and mind. Research into near-death experiences have many of the same elements and characteristics. The chances of the required conditions for life to develop on earth, and for all the perfectly balanced ecosystems to have formed as coincidence is astronomical. In other words, there is so much we have no idea about, not even close, though we like to think we do. About life. About the afterlife. And it would be wise to conclude such."

Erin drizzled some more dressing. Edward finished his second piece of pizza, again leaving the bitten crust. Cameron lifted a finger up, trying to flag down the waitress, but was relieved to see the rest of the drinks on a tray.

"There we go."

"On the other side of the argument, bible scholars can be just as stubborn and ignorant, if not more so. They act almost like lawyers of the bible, studying and dissecting and twisting every word, every translation of a word. As an atheist or agnostic has reason to dismiss ghosts and hauntings, devout believers can do the exact same."

When their round of drinks was set up, they automatically brought them together over the middle of the table.

"A toast. To the ghosts, goblins and ghouls." Cameron grinned, mug in hand.

"Here, here." Erin shook her head with a smile.

Edward tapped the bottom of his glass on the table before drinking. "Bottom's up."

Alex slouched. "You were saying, Pastor?"

"I actually forgot where I was but uh . . . The word, ghost, it's mentioned over a hundred times in the bible. Jesus even acknowledged it when speaking to the apostles, on more than one occasion. Heck, everything is in there if you dig deep enough. Ghosts, spirits. Spiritual beings. Angels and demons. Cherubim. Seraphim. Nephilim. Giants and witches and prophets. The whole of Sheol."

"Sheol?"

"The Hebrew word for 'realm of the dead.' The boundary between heaven and earth is described as overlapping. Could it be possible Sheol is right here, overlapping, behind and beneath the world in the same way, invisible to our naked eyes? At least part of it. Death is sometimes referred to as sleep in scripture. And, in sleep, it's not that we cease to exist but rather are in this inactive, unconscious state. Maybe the dead can wander, like sleepwalkers, but in this other dimension, what they call Sheol."

Everyone fell silent then, let it all sink in.

Pastor Art lowered his drink after an extended sip, stared into it. "Truth is, whether believer or nonbeliever, a scientist or a theologian, we won't and can't know it all. No way. Not even in death probably when we've met God Himself. There will always be this level of unknown. Some things weren't meant for mere mortal man."

Cameron no longer grinned. Alex licked his lips while Erin's smile faded. Edward rubbed his chin then his beard.

"Now, how in the heck do you drink this dang thing, huh? You kids these days."

A round of laughter lightened the mood.

"So, drop the shot glass into it. That's the 'bomb.' Then you chug down the whole thing all at once."

※

When the group returned outside, most of the reporters and officers had already finished up and left. There was instead a crowd gathered praying and singing, hugging each other and crying together. Along the steps of the chapel, there were bouquets and wreaths and single flowers piling up, cards propped against them diagonally and ribbons tied onto the main and side handrails. Pastor Art was wracked with emotion, his eyes welling up, about to keel right over. One by one, they joined in and hugged the preacher. It was first bulky arms from Cameron then thin arms from Erin, then the beard of Edward pressed up against him. Alex was the last, and all five held this position for a long while.

"Good thing we had the chips and dip after. Helped the buzz wear off." Pastor Art proceeded to dab his eyes with the back of his sleeve. "I'll stay, check in on these guys. See you in a few days. I look forward to working with you all."

"Thank you, Pastor. And take care."

As they loaded into the van and pulled away, Alex stared out the window with a last open wave to which Pastor Art nodded.

"I like that dude. Most pastors are kinda stuck up or boring. Ya know?" Cameron signaled, rotating the wheel. "He keeps it real."

"He's obviously a great man." Edward chimed in from the passenger seat, swiveled and put back the sunshade.

"You guys know Liwanu?"

Erin was in the back seat next to Alex, peeked over at him. "Oh, yeah. We work with him now and then."

"He has a similar presence. Like, deep and wise or something."

"I'll say, being scientific, I try to keep the belief system out of it. But I have to admit, there seems to be a kind of connection to the spiritual, to religion, when it comes to ghosts. And whether it's somebody like Liwanu or Pastor Art or Deidre, well, some people are simply more attuned to these other realms. This . . . Sheol . . . or whatever it's called."

<h1 style="text-align:center">4</h1>

BEFORE HE OPENED his eyes, Alex let April have her fun a little longer. Alex could feel her palm on his chest, her finger tapping and touching his skin beneath his shirt in a playful and tender manner. She pressed her lips to his cheek then his ear and the right side of his neck, going slow. He gave in and kissed her back when she pecked him on the lips. Their fingers interlocked under the blankets while he rolled over on his side. The two gazed into each other's faces without one word. Alex enjoyed these kind of moments, always wondered what she was thinking. He felt like he could memorize every line and every curve of her naked face, before the contact lenses, still without makeup on.

"'Ello, love."

April let out a content smile. "'Ello, love. Heart you."

"I heart you, too."

"Heart you more."

He paused, stroked her hair. "I heart you times infinity."

She fluttered her eyelids then twitched her nose like a bunny. Alex sat upright, stretching one arm out overhead with a light yawn.

They reached and grabbed their laptops, scooting side by side, propping the pillows behind them against the wall. While some couples maybe did crossword puzzles in the morning on the weekend or read the newspaper, this is what they liked to do.

"The road trip go okay?"

"It was fine. Didn't wanna wake you, since it was pretty late already. And how was the work shift?"

Even in the form of omission, he was well aware he didn't tell her the whole truth. Again, violating that sacred rule of LOVE102.

"Meh, the usual. You remember all the dramas. This one biotch not getting along with the other biznotch. Pfft."

Alex shook his head, smirked. There was a touch of guilt settling in but he chose to ignore it.

"Okie dokie. Shall we kick the day off with some FAIL Blog?"

"How about I go to eBaum's World and you go to YouTube. I'm in the mood for, like, the double rainbow guy or something."

As the web page loaded up, a string of trollface images and basic text populated.

"Check these out. 'One does not simply eat one Pringle.' Haha." April leaned in as Alex scrolled further down. "Ooh. This one. 'One does not simply cowbell into Mordor.' Ah, hahaha!"

"Now, what about your own laptop, huh."

She laughed once more, a borderline snort, then regained her composure, facing forward and clicking the touchpad.

"Let's watch this again."

"Dude, you seen that like a hundred times." Alex scrunched

his lips in faux disapproval. "If that little boy bites the other little boy's finger one more time . . ."

The video started playing, the usual cute footage.

"Adorbs."

Before it got even a few seconds in, it immediately switched over to a retro music video intact with mediocre drumbeat and mundane dancing.

"Nooo! Shit! Again!?"

"Rickroll!!!" April fell over on her side, bawling out loud with happy tears in the corners of her eyes.

"You!" He pointed a stern finger at her screen. "Evil, despicable, low-down scumbags!"

His annoyance and aggravation seemed to amplify her joy.

"Since we rewatched *my* fave, we can rewatch your fave . . ."

April searched for then opened up the amateur animation which began with a simple generic polyphonic MIDI file. When an iconic giant reptilian monster fought an iconic caped superhero, it escalated to a battle between an athlete, a robot, a martial artist and a historical figure, culminating in a huge ongoing war between celebrities and various movie, television and comic book characters including yes, indeed, their beloved Chuck Norris, in a fun and epic Microsoft Paint-esque bloodbath.

"Dude. This always puts me in a good mood. 'The Ultimate Showdown of Ultimate Destiny.' Hell yeah."

They proceeded to watch clips from Charlie Murphy's True Hollywood Stories about Prince and Rick James on *Chapelle's Show*, and then the "I'm Fucking Ben Affleck" musical sketch from Jimmy Kimmel.

It was the perfect way to start the perfect day.

❧

After their dose of morning memes, and with enough relaxing and geeking out, Alex cooked them up a simple breakfast. There was nothing special planned, though they did bounce a few different ideas out there: a movie, the park, window shopping at some outlet mall. Both decided to continue brainstorming while they finished cleaning. He washed the dishes, stacked the coffee mugs and frying pans in the dish rack while April vacuumed, tossing the dirty clothes which were strewn about into the piled up hamper where they belonged. After he got done, he sat down and watched her from behind. She pushed and pulled the handle in a zigzag motion, adjusting the cord. Then she stopped in place all of a sudden.

"You . . . wanna go to Canada?"

"What? Just like that?" Alex lifted a brow, surprised, perplexed. "Random and out of nowhere? Out of the blue?"

"Why not."

"Hmm." He touched a hand to his chin, reasoned in his head then shrugged. "Yeah, fuck it. Let's go."

She giggled an excited squee.

A little less than three hours up the I-5 would bring them to their destination. For him, it was the opposite direction from the last road trip, in kind of an ironic symbolism of the momentum of his life. On the one hand, Alex enjoyed relationship mode, being serious and committed, satisfied and content. But, on the other hand, venturing through that elusive veil of the non-living in secret did pique his curiosities as well.

"Now that we have our own apartment, we can finally get that puppy we been talking about, huh. Maybe a kitten?"

"Of course, my precious." He drove with one hand firm on

the steering wheel, his other elbow resting along the window panel. "Whichever you want. Like the TI song that I probably just butchered."

"I don't know. What do you think is easier?"

"As long as the little critter doesn't turn out like our Venus flytrap or that cacti, either or should be fine, I'd say."

She inclined her head then stared out the window. When she turned back, he could see that familiar tantalizing gaze.

They weren't even far on the highway yet when April leaned over, undid his belt and the button, unzipped his pants. Alex tried to drive like normal, raising both hands on the wheel, but then had to pull over at the nearest rest stop, shifting to park and reclining the seat. He put his hand on top of her head, touching her hair as she rhythmically moved up and down, in and out with torrid fiery desire.

Each remained frozen as they caught their breath. Alex arched his neck back against the headrest and raised a forearm over his face. He slid down in the cushion, proceeded to readjust his clothing. She cleaned up the mess of scattered paper products with a hot flush of pink starting to radiate from her cheeks. They were always adventurous even from their early unofficial courtship, making out and fooling around, and things continued to be fresh and exciting still, even past the honeymoon phase. Back when they took psych class together, they often chuckled because they were working their way well through Freud's stages of development.

"Sorry . . ." April rested her head on his chest. "You know me. Oral fixation."

"No, no. That was . . ." He let out a slow breath, half-dazed. "What better way to kick off this latest escapade."

While composing themselves, the two noticed a large billboard just past the line of the pine trees.

"You see that? How crazy. What's the odds?"

"Like, we were only talking about that a moment ago. Hehe."

"Should we go check it out?"

"I mean, I'm down. But we do still got a long drive to Canada."

"We'll make it quick then."

The humane society was a short trip from the rest stop, a sharp right, a long stretch of road and then a sharp left. They walked up the steps into the reception area, signed in. It was obvious this adoption center must have had a good amount of funding since everything appeared modern and up to date, in tip-top shape.

A small eatery was on one side with snacks, beverages and light prepared foods. A gift shop was on the other side, a majority of the items necessities for when new fur mommies and daddies took home their new fur babies. Bundles of products for their bundles of joy.

Behind these was an isolation area for new admissions and a vet clinic. Alex peeked into the double doors, saw an x-ray room, two treatment rooms, even a surgery room. April scanned a large map posted on the pillar between the other three buildings. The feline ward had five holdings and the canine ward had six holdings. There was a single holding for various other lost or abandoned pets including birds, bunnies and guinea pigs.

He noticed the stylized sign. "Ooh, Cool Cats. I kinda like that."

"And I think the other side is the Hot Dogs."

"Oh. Okay. I kind of hate that."

They both laughed a hushed laugh.

Before the rows of cages and crates, there was an open room where a few of the kittens scratched at pillows and rugs, clawed at feathery strings hanging from makeshift fishing poles, and chased plastic balls and tiny bells through long cylindrical tubes and up layered shelves. An attendant waved then gestured for them to enter. It was one door first, a small space between, then a second door as a security measure in case the little hairballs tried to escape.

A round sphere of gray fuzz scurried from the door as both stepped inside. A plump whitish cat hissed from atop her throne, raising up a threatening paw.

"Damn, dawg . . . I mean, cat."

Three kittens started inching over with caution. One was big and black. One was brown, medium sized. And one was orange and tiny. Along the thin carpeted floor, their padded footfalls were silent. Each encircled them, nuzzling at their ankles.

"Awww." April cupped a hand over her mouth then knelt down.

She touched a finger to its pink nose then over the top of its head, in between the two pointy ears in a wriggling motion. He joined her, rubbing the other kitty along the neck and the back down to its tail. The two then let the litter lick at their upturned palms.

After playing a bit, they washed their hands at the wash station then perused down each row, peering through the panes of glass.

"C'mere, pussycat."

"That cat in the back looks hella grumpy."

He put both hands in his pockets, let out a half-smirk. "Oh, man. What if our child turned out like that, huh?"

April paused, shifted. "You know . . . I'm not too sure if I want to have kids."

"Hmm." Alex stopped in place. "We never did talk about that, did we."

"I guess we usually like to keep things pretty light and fun, mostly steamy. How 'bout you? Do you want kids?"

He turned towards her. "I never really thought about it, to be honest. I mean, that's what is expected, the norm. So I kind of just assumed."

She crossed her arms. "Same. Although, now that I think about it, I don't know if that's for me. Or if it's something I want. Like, I can't even take care of a houseplant."

"It was two houseplants." He raised his brow up, teasing. "Also, let's just say, the one bouquet turned into potpourri awfully fast . . ."

April chuckled. "See."

"Maybe let life take us where it takes us. I mean, remember what we used to always say? 'Just be,' right?"

Behind them, a single tabby tapped and touched at the glass in a pleading manner.

"I can see us having a little one, two. That might be cute, kind of fun." Alex touched the surface, his fingertip and the paw appearing like a reflection. "But I'm also not super attached to the idea."

"Could be cool to be an empty nester, too. Whatever people call it. Go on vacation all the time. Buy nice things. Sleep in. Have fun, relax."

"Yeah, maybe."

At some point, liking each other turns into dating. Then dating turns into a committed relationship. In much the same way, a committed relationship also has to turn into something. A couple gets engaged, gets married. They buy a house to grow old in. They raise a family. They build a life together.

Thus, another major rule of LOVE102—grow together and not apart. To live with one another for years, decades, all through the twenties into the thirties, the forties into the fifties consists of ongoing change and continual evolving.

He followed her to the next area, where she scooped up a squishy guinea pig and held it lovingly in her arms like a tiny newborn. In front of him, he watched as her face and her heart melted away in delightful affection.

Ah, just look at you. I'm sure you'll come around.

I am gonna marry this girl.

5

NEXT TO THE headquarters of SPIRAL was a small jewelry store and a pawn shop on either side of it. Alex parked, fed the meter, then went up the cracking and uneven pavement. He paused, peeked in through the display window. He could see it was messy inside, a trove of lost treasures. A few of the shelves were lined with old records, videocassettes, mismatched CDs and DVDs and video games of all types. There was a large television set and a few boomboxes piled up. In the back, there was a varied collection of multiple electric and acoustic guitars hanging, along with straps, amps, pedals and cords. He pulled away, began to walk once again, this time noticing the jewelry store.

Hmm.

Guess I am early.

It wasn't his intention to go in and check it out, but the pawn shop window must have opened him up to the idea.

The display cases were laid out in an alternating pattern, with a floating island in the middle. It transitioned from rows of wristwatches and cufflinks to a few chokers and charms, then necklaces, bracelets, anklets, to earrings then rings which is what he was somewhat interested in.

While Alex hovered and stared, no clue as to what he was searching for or even doing there, the sales clerk asked if he needed any help.

"I'm just looking right now."

The clerk was polite, nodded and smiled, began to turn.

"But, uh . . . could you maybe show me these?" Alex pointed. "They seem kinda cool."

She hunched down, proceeded to unlock the case, describing the kind of metal and the kind of gem, how they were a new growing trend. Alex placed both hands on the edge of the case, nibbling his lower lip.

The truth was a part of him had already known, even before their spontaneous road trip and subsequent detour. Maybe not from the very first shuttle ride, no, but from the bookstore, the fair, all the way to their star shroom and back, even the silly gumball machine they happened across—that she was the one. He only wanted a simple way of showing her, to him, she was flawless, and his withered heart would forever love her.

A slight chime sounded as he turned the handle and pushed the door open. When Alex went inside, he felt like he had entered a strange library. It was quiet, clean, relaxing. Behind the desk, he could see Erin sitting with the cordless phone in her left hand, pressed close to her cheek. She touched the rim of her glasses, realigning them on her face. He stepped forward, stood in front of her then waited, while she smiled and flittered her fingers in warm acknowledgement. After she finished jotting down her notes, explaining the next steps in the process to the client, the two went around the side of the desk and hugged.

"Welcome to our operations center. Ever been here before?"

"No, actually." Alex faced down to the floor. "Back at that time, I chose to opt out. Met up somewhere else."

"Ah. I get it." She stretched the corner of her lips in a crooked smile. "Lemme give you a little tour."

Erin first showed him around the front office. He noticed the same brochure he once was handed himself sticking out of a plastic holder next to a desk organizer tray, a calendar, sticky notes, notepads and a pencil cup. On the wall were framed official documents and a corkboard with notes and reminders posted. There was a large all-in-one printer, reams of paper stacked next to it, and a water dispenser along with cone cups.

In the next room, the back wall was lined with file cabinets, and the side wall had detailed maps of the city and the state, tiny colored pins dotted here and there. Behind an empty square table, off to one corner, a refrigerator hummed next to a generic microwave. In the other room, there were wire shelves and metal racks filled with boxes and bins. A long table that had monitors, headsets and fancy machinery with rows of buttons, knobs and dials was placed against the far wall. Alex could see the van through the back window, and Edward and Cameron loading and unloading.

"You 'member our ghost ride." She spun around, slid up onto a stool.

"I do. That was one helluva trip, plus dinner and drinks." Alex joined her, pulled a stool over and got on top. "You handle this stuff, right?"

"We all chip in. But yeah, I do know more AV than the others. Kinda my thang."

They heard Edward and Cameron squabble in the back. Both peeked then ignored it. He wondered if maybe they didn't get along or if there was any tension there.

"Sorry about that. Too much testosterone and dick measuring at times."

"Probably a better balance when Deidre is around, huh?"

Erin nodded with widened eyes. "Yesss. Exactly."

Cameron staggered in, boxes in hand, noticed Alex and Erin. "Well, you two look nice and chummy in here. I thought you weren't into dudes."

"I'm bi-curious, asshole."

"Sheesh. My bad."

"Don't mind this guy." Edward followed with a suitcase. "Hey there, Alex."

He reached over and shook his hand.

"Yeah, yeah. I'm just man-struating." Cameron placed the two boxes down. "It's not that Ned Flanders over here is a douchebag. No way."

They exchanged a quick glare.

"Okay, children." Erin hopped off the stool. "Lemme show you the equipment while these dudes cool off."

"Well, of course I know some of these." Alex followed her, scanned the rack. "It looks like a first aid kit, some flashlights, walkie-talkies."

"Those are basic. Can't work if you can't see. Can't plan if you can't talk. And hey, it's dark. It can get spooky. You might run, trip. Bump your head. Things happen."

He hung his arms at his sides. "You guys or any clients ever get . . . slapped?"

Brief memories of the old encounters flashed through his mind.

"Like, we've heard of all kinds of things. People being pushed. They can be scratched, pinched, get their hair pulled. And sure, even hit."

Edward chimed in from the middle of the room. "It can be positive or negative. Kissing, stroking hair. In an old brothel or something, it might be groping."

Cameron continued sorting through the boxes, ignoring them.

"Are these . . . toys and stuff?"

"It's called a trigger object." Erin stood next to him, placing her hands behind her. "If the spirit is of a child, they sometimes react to a ball or a stuffed animal, piece a candy. And a young woman, we might try a mirror or a brush. It could be anything. Power tools, musical instruments. A hat. Something familiar and of interest."

He let out a slow nod as she led them to the next section.

"Now, these are the bread and butter of all investigating. Audio recorders to track reactions and voiceover commentary. It is the highest quality crystal clear sound whether loud or quiet, near or far."

She handed one of them to him.

"That can capture from both sides. It can hear ninety degrees in front, a hundred and twenty degrees in back. There is also a mode using both mics at the same time that can cover a full three-sixty."

"And this is how we catch those EVPs?"

"Yep."

He stepped then pointed. "Cameras."

"First, digital still cams. We set them up to take photos in bursts. It can be up to a thousand in one night, over that. It's a pain to go through when reviewing evidence, but you never know."

Alex traded the recorder for a camera, turned it over in his hand.

"Second, handheld video cams. This is helpful when we go lights out, since it has night vision. It can also be used for thermal imaging. These are all full spectrum."

"Full spectrum?"

Edward chimed in again. "Light waves invisible to the naked eye. Shadow figures and apparitions tend to be seen on the infrared or ultraviolet spectrum."

"We can't see them and can't hear them. But with these, we can."

"It's tricky. 'Cause sometimes you can without all this. Or else there'd be no calls, no claims without proper equipment. It is all about being at the right place at the right time, under the right circumstances."

He glanced at her. "Makes sense."

"Oh. And these other cameras are stationary, for surveillance. Covers eight separate points throughout the location. We also have motion detectors and laser grids."

Alex inclined his head, blinked.

"Helpful to catch anything that passes through it, any kind of movement. The beams get interrupted."

"I see."

"Do you have a Nintendo Wii?"

"Of course."

"Well, building on that, Xbox is coming up with their own kind of interactive motion device. It will use something called SLS, or structured light sensor. Basically, it's designed to activate when there is an individual in the room. It can read your body's height and width, positioning, depth, where the face and limbs and torso are, tracking a person's figure. Experts say it may be able to catch *any* human form, again, even on different spectrums. It could be a game changer."

He smirked. "Heh, game changer."

Erin nudged at him with a smile. "Ah. Clever."

The two lingered, enjoying a moment of appreciation for bad puns.

"All righty. Up next is the spirit box. This rapidly scans through multiple stations. The idea is ghosts tend to communicate on different radio frequencies, or even through white noise and static. Not everyone's a fan, though."

"I kinda hate that piece of shit . . ."

Alex turned back to Edward, raised a brow.

"Trying to be scientific, there is so much that can taint the data. For instance, if you're using that and asking a question like, how old are you? How many radio stations have a number in them. How many times in an hour do they reference that, play a clip that says that same number."

"Huh. That's a good point. Very true."

"And if you ask something such as what's the letter of your first name? Same thing. How many radio stations have a damn letter. Not to mention, this is all based on interpretation, which is completely subjective. The mind will always try to make sense of whatever it sees or hears. Like, pareidolia."

Erin leaned in as she added to that. "Same as ink blot tests or something, right? People might see what they wanna see."

"Yeah. I think, even in psych, there's been studies about how the brain rearranges letters of jumbled words. It's our natural tendency."

Edward snapped his fingers. "Exactly. You get it, Alex."

"So, these last two. This is a thermometer, plain and simple, to measure changes or drops in temperature. Just point it and click it. But as I mentioned, video cam also has thermal imaging. And this other one is an EMF."

"Is that electromagnetic field . . . ?" Alex crossed his arms, unsure.

Erin shifted in place. "Correct. EMFs are actually all around us. Every object emits them, even our bodies. They're in appliances, in power lines. However, in an investigation, there are often spikes in EMF with paranormal activity. This helps to detect and record that."

"You guys about ready?"

Nobody realized Pastor Art was leaning in the doorway.

"Let's have our first official meeting."

The group moved into the first room with the file cabinets and the maps on the wall because it was less cluttered and more open. Pastor Art led the way, sat at the top side of the square table. Alex and Erin filed in after, taking up the side and the bottom, while Cameron grabbed a folding chair which was leaning on the wall and set it down behind them at a diagonal, motioned to Edward with a nudge of his chin. It appeared enough time had passed since their little spat and this act of kindness was a simple peace treaty. He then went around and plopped down on the last side next to Pastor Art.

"It's good to see you guys again. I wish we could always hang out at the pub, but this'll have to do."

Alex smirked. Erin cupped a hand over her mouth, hiding back a smile. With his elbows on the table, Cameron grinned away. Edward listened, blinked.

"First of all, I did get to talk to Deids. Or Deidre to you guys." Pastor Art breathed in sharp through his nostrils then paused. "I have to be frank. Things are not good."

The smirk, smile and grin faded into grim and dire expressions.

"Doctors first thought it was only a mild TBI, or traumatic brain injury, in addition to her other wounds. Her speech and memory appeared intact, close to normal. They initially predicted less than one month. But after further tests, her physical coordination including balance and walking have been impaired, so now they are starting to lean more towards it being a moderate to severe TBI that is not presenting in the typical way . . ."

Edward shook his head, leaned back and gazed up at the ceiling.

Cameron pounded a light fist on the tabletop.

"Everybody's injury, situation and recovery will be different. And there is no clear-cut answer on a timeline. But they are thinking it could take at least six months to gain full walking, or even up to a whole year."

"Is she going to be okay?"

"Yes. They say the neuroplasticity is strongest in the first six months, and given her age and good health, she will recover. It's just a matter of time."

"Aw, man. Poor D."

"This blows."

Pastor Art stared each of them in the eye with a somber nod. "I know. This arrangement of ours is extended until further notice and we will just have to play it by ear."

Erin clasped her hands in front of her as Alex slouched down. Cameron leaned with a cheek in his palm. Edward folded his arms over his chest, crinkling his brow.

"I'm game if you're game. She needs us. There's plenty of work to be done. Hunting things, saving people. As we speak, many are afraid of the dark. But we don't get to be. Lots of unspoken wickedness goes bump in the night. And we get the chance to stop that bump, and heck, every now and then bump right friggin' back."

PART FOUR

UNTIL DUSK

1

Case #001399

IT WAS A familiar scene after they loaded into the van and began to pull away. Cameron was once again in the driver's seat, and Edward again in the front passenger seat. Alex sat in the back seat next to Erin. He let her climb in first, holding onto the handle then the middle seat, crouching and squeezing in, scooching to the inside. She peeked over at him as he settled in, reached for the belt buckle. Pastor Art was the last to get in and took up that awkward lone middle seat, lowering the armrest and kicking his feet forward crisscrossed. Alex watched the buildings through the window blend from Midtown to Uptown.

"There's a lot of activity in these old buildings."

Before he adjusted and faced forward, he noticed the post office, the courthouse, the capitol building, and the state art museum.

"We don't get that many calls but we do hear the stories. Things falling off shelves. Lights turning off and on. Loud noises."

"Ya know what they say, right?"

Everybody was quiet, waited for Pastor Art to elaborate.

"All of the state workers, city and county, when they die, they don't go to heaven or hell. No, no, no. They go right back to work."

Cameron chuckled, slapped a hand on the wheel. "Well, no worries. That won't be us. I guarantee when our documentary airs, things are going to be clutch."

"Oh, here we go again with the damn documentary. I told you, we should instead focus all efforts on research and experimentation." Edward raised a hand up as he spoke. "If we isolate one of the senses, we can provide verified quantifiable data—"

"Stop. Stop. Unless you want me to crash this van right here and now, please. Your snoozefest is unbearable. And this is why I'm lead, 'kay? Jesus Christ."

"Knock it off."

The two responded right away to Pastor Art's words by holding their tongue and dropping it.

Alex turned to Erin. "Is this the call you were on yesterday?"

"Yes, it was."

"What was their names again?"

She leafed through the pages on the clipboard. "Let's see. Three roommates. Zoë, Olivia and Simone."

"I think I watched that video last night." Cameron spoke in a hushed whisper to which Edward let out a light snicker. "Twice."

Pastor Art shifted in his seat. "Miss Woodfeld, don't tell Alexander any more. The less he knows the better."

∾

When they first pulled in front of the cozy cottage, it felt as if they must have made an error. There was no way the address was correct. A small chimney stuck out of the roof tiles that were three varying shades of reddish brown like floating autumn leaves. That feeling continued up the two front steps into the arched doorway. Inside, the carpet and furniture was immaculate, spotless and modern, almost from out of a magazine. One of the girls had greeted them then led the group inside where the other two were already on the couch. Alex followed Pastor Art who sat on one of the recliners. He sat on the other one, and Erin plopped on the armrest next to him. Cameron and Edward pulled two chairs out from the dining table behind the living room arrangement.

"I am Arturo Selga. You can call me Pastor Art."

The young woman shook his hand, still standing. "My name is Zoë. I was the one on the phone."

She wore an olive green halter top and tight black jeans. As she also was the one that opened the front door and took them all in, maybe she acted as their unofficial leader.

"Ah, that was me. I'm Erin."

With a wave, she joined her two friends on the long couch.

"You're Simone?" Alex then shifted. "And you're Olivia?"

Both nodded in affirmation.

One girl had blond hair and blue eyes that matched her baby blue dress with a black sash across the middle. The other girl had long red hair which complemented her maroon sweater and beige capri pants. All three down the line was a subtle splash of blue, red and green.

Pastor Art noticed his correct guess, pulled the corner of his lips into a thin smile.

"Mister Gallo is in the back there and that's Mister Berenson next to him."

"Call me Cam."

"Ned."

"Alexander is the one who asked you your names."

"We are so happy that you came in on such short notice."

Erin squirmed, jutted an elbow out over the top of the recliner near Alex. "It was good timing on your end."

"So, tell us a little about yourselves. Only the basics. Then we will do a small sweep cold before hearing the details."

"Okay . . ." That same girl in green was first to speak up. "Well, the three of us work together down at Troy Manning's. You know guys know that place?"

"Heard of the name."

"I'm a server. Sims is a hostess, and Liv helps at the bar." She turned to the others with each reference to their nicknames. "We all kinda became fast friends."

"Like, it's easy to become close in food service. Some customers can get super nitpicky or impatient or needy. Some customers drink too much and get all wild."

Cameron grinned. "Oh, we know how that goes."

Edward shook his head.

"And, well, after work, that venting would sometimes turn to going out."

The others nodded.

"Zoë just moved here so she was renting a room somewhere. I had gotten tired of living at home, and Liv just broke up with her boyfriend at the time. It seemed natural to look for a place together."

"Okay. Good." Pastor Art brought his palms together in a light clap. "You can tell us more while we do the first sweep. Try to let the tech and other readings speak for itself."

From the living room, they splintered off into two groups. Alex and Pastor Art followed Olivia and Simone upstairs. The fluffy carpet muted their footsteps. Erin breathed out a soft sigh then joined Edward and Cameron who went down the hallway with Zoë. Cameron already began narrating their movements into a voice recorder while Edward took random snapshots of the living room and kitchen. In a similar fashion, Pastor Art waved the EMF detector up, down, left and right, which blinked and bleeped to a low crackle of static. Alex fumbled with the handheld thermometer which wouldn't turn on. He tapped at it, shook it.

"Huh. That's weird."

"What is it?"

"The battery just died. I swear, it was fully charged."

"Yep. Always bring extras." Pastor Art tossed him a spare.

Simone turned back. "D-does that happen often?"

In front of them, the hem of her baby blue dress swayed with her hips.

"Entities can zap electronics, drain the energy right out. We can't definitively prove anything. But it is interesting how these kind of things tend to happen often on investigations."

"Ah, I see." She stopped in the door frame, straightened her dress. "This is my room."

On the other side, Alex noticed Olivia had a pink cast on her wrist up to the forearm. It was partway hidden from the sleeve of her baggy maroon sweater, and she tended to keep this hidden from view. She walked in a careful manner, hanging it at her side or behind her back.

"Temp looks normal here."

"No spikes in EMF."

Both stepped back out, about to continue to the next room.

"Wait, wait."

He stopped in place, shifted to Pastor Art.

Everybody paused.

"Quiet your mind. Drown all the outside noise, Alexander. Listen."

Alex breathed. "I . . ."

Olivia hung her head down and skulked.

"I think I *feel* something here."

Pastor Art scanned the picture frames, the lamp, the closet, proceeded forward then glanced back. "It is a little higher as we get closer to the master bedroom."

He raised a hand out in front of his torso, continued to point the thermometer with his other hand.

"This is Liv's room." Simone stood behind the two as they walked in with their equipment. "I suggested Zoë take it but she liked the corner one better."

Alex narrowed his eyes, moved with a short side step.

The preacher waved the device over the mattress. "Whoa, this thing is shooting up."

Olivia hung her jaw open.

"Looks like the mattress is new, and the comforter, pillows. But the bed frame looks kinda old, huh."

"Actually . . ." Simone paused, crossing her arms. "Those were already in here. A lot of the furniture was. We're on tight budgets so, uh, it saved us a few bucks."

"So, the bed frames. What else?"

"Curtains. Bedside tables, mirrors."

"The recliners? The couch?"

"No, those are new. Mostly things in the bedrooms, I guess. It wasn't really the downstairs."

"Hmm. Got anything?"

"I'm not sure. But again, something about that hall."

"Okay. Tell me, was there any kind of occurrence in the hallway?"

Simone turned to Olivia, blinked.

"I-i-it didn't start until later on. When we first moved in, things were fine. Then I don't know what happened." The girl touched at her cast, fought back a watery sheen in her eyes.

Pastor Art placed one hand on the side of her good arm. "Hey, everything'll be all right."

"Did this thing . . . push you?" Alex felt goosebumps break out on his forearms then along his shins.

The girl began to whimper, which built up to a heavy sob. Simone leaned in and hugged her tight.

"It was sounds at night. Like, knocking on the walls, the doors. I mean, it was kind of funny at first. Playful. Trying to get attention. Or maybe just to interact."

She spoke over her friend's shoulder, rubbed at her back.

"Before long, an item would randomly be placed in the rooms or in a line down the hall. Like a shoe. A purse. Once, it was a row of various things down the stairs, one on each step. In the kitchen, canned goods would be stacked up."

With a soft sniffle, Olivia regained her composure enough to face Pastor Art and Alex, clearing her throat.

"Like Sims said, again, it was kinda lighthearted in the beginning. But then it became less so. It felt darker. We all started to feel like something was watching us. Whenever we got dressed. Whenever we took a shower."

Alex clenched a fist, gritted his teeth.

"Next thing we know, it's not just knocking, not just items here and there, not just a feeling of being watched but . . . whispers."

"Yeah. It was, like, calling out to us. Calling our names. It wanted us to go outside, follow it. Right, Liv?"

"One night, I heard a big thud and then a scratch so I woke up. I heard it again in the hall so I came out here to look and my wallet was on the floor." Olivia wiped at each cheek then continued. "When I w-walked down to try to get it, that's when I was shoved from behind down that top stair."

"My God. I'm so sorry."

He moved from one side of Pastor Art to the other, leaning on the dresser.

"Did you happen to see anything?"

Olivia cried out, buried her face in her forearm. Simone hugged her again.

"She mentioned seeing a little boy. Like, a boy was staring down at her from the top of the stairs."

The preacher swallowed a dry swallow, remaining stoic. "And that's when you called?"

Alex glanced at the two girls—one of them with bright blue eyes filled with worry and concern, and one of them with her face buried deep in the other's shoulder.

"I know Alexander was fixated on the hall, and that turned out to be pretty significant. I can't help but keep coming back to the beds myself. They look out of place to me."

Pastor Art walked into the middle of the room and lifted up the mattress.

"See. It's old, old iron. I wonder if there could be some kind of magnetism or something emanating from these. Neuroscientists have studied the effects of erratic magnetic fields to the temporal lobes of the brain, and it did result in altered perception and sensations."

The two girls peeked at the rusty antique metal.

"Let's finish the next room then go back downstairs, regroup, then we'll switch. Other than that, next step is do the overnight."

&

After all of the equipment was set up, Erin double checked the systems, the connections, each microphone and each monitor. She also checked the quality of both audio and visual recordings, made sure everything was clear and crisp. Alex observed as she adjusted the knobs and dials, pressed at the different buttons with the seriousness of a symphony conductor. Then she glanced over with a firm thumbs up. Meanwhile, inside, the others got ready to do their first round. They could see Cameron, Edward and Pastor Art on-screen making last minute adjustments for optimal placement. Zoë and Simone were about to leave to start their shifts, and went to say goodbye to Olivia who waited outside the van.

"Liv, you gonna be okay here?"

"I wish you didn't have to do this alone, without us . . ." Simone reached out and patted her roommate on the shoulder.

Olivia twirled at a fluff of her red hair. "No, it's fine. Could be a good chance to face my fears or something."

"Attagirl."

"Plus I couldn't work even if I tried." She lifted up her cast. "So yeah, Sims, Zo, you two go knock out those tips for me."

The three friends embraced in a long group hug.

Alex and Erin both peeked, exchanged a respective smile and smirk, then returned to facing forward.

Behind them, Olivia entered through the sliding door.

"Hey, guys. Sorry. I hope that wasn't too over-the-top sentimental."

"Nah. You guys are pretty tight, though, huh?"

"Yeah, we are. Like family."

The walkie-talkie bleeped then, followed by the preacher checking in.

"Ready to go here."

On the split monitors, in varying angles, Pastor Art signaled to Cameron who turned the handheld video camera towards himself.

"My name is Cam Gallo, and I've set out with the rest of the SPIRAL team to investigate reported activity at the Warner Cottage where three roommates have been experiencing various disturbing and dangerous phenomenas."

Edward hovered his own video camera, using infrared and thermal imaging.

Pastor Art stepped forward. "I go this way. You go that way."

They each took up one side of the living room.

"I heard you like stacking up canned foods. Why don't you open these cabinets up right now?" Cameron pointed the lens straight ahead, panning the interior of the kitchen. "We got plenty of choices. Spam. Nalley Jalapeño Hot Chili. Chef Boyardee."

"Anything up there, Erin?" Edward turned around, faced Pastor Art who turned his palms up with a shrug.

"Nothing yet."

"Doin' okay?" Alex leaned in toward Olivia.

"So far, so good. Thank you."

Edward checked the guest bathroom. The preacher waited for Cameron.

"We are moving now to the upstairs bedrooms where most of the activity is said to have taken place. Watch your step."

Cameron framed the shot of Pastor Art walking up step by step, hand on the rail. Edward followed, capturing the two making their way.

"Okay. Each of us take a room."

"At the top of this stairs, one of the roommates was lured out then pushed, which ended in an injury to the wrist." Cameron puffed his chest, raised his chin. "Well, you not-so-friendly ghost, try pushing *me* down these stairs."

Edward nudged at Cameron. "Hey. Be respectful."

"It's called provocation. And it works, every time."

They entered the bedrooms. Edward took the first, Cameron took the second, and then Pastor Art the third.

Cameron checked the master bathroom.

"I got an idea."

Alex, Erin and Olivia watched the monitors cover their movements, their faces lit in the dark. The sound of Edward on the walkie-talkie echoed through the speakers.

"Yeah, Neddy Krueger?"

"Mister Berenson, go on."

Edward raised the walkie-talkie, held it close. "Since Pastor Art pointed out the old bed frames, I say we all lay down in one. Just see what happens."

"That cool?" Erin lifted an eyebrow.

"I mean, I guess." Olivia scratched her head, breathing out. "Rude."

Pastor Art placed the handheld camera on the bedside table, pointed it at himself sitting on the edge of the bed, instead took out the voice recorder.

"If there is anybody here that wants to make contact, please do so now. We're not here to hurt you. In fact, we want to help."

He then stretched out and waited.

"Nothing yet, Erin?" Edward darted his head then right on the pillow.

"Nope. Nada."

"Still cams? Laser? Trigger?"

"Zip. Zilch."

"Ah, okay. Hmm."

For a good long while, about twenty minutes, the three remained in the beds, waiting for any signs. Cameron suggested they try the same but with everything out. Edward went downstairs, flicked the kitchen and living room switches. Pastor Art waited for him to return then hit the hallway light. They each turned off the bedroom lights then laid back down again for another half an hour or so.

"I'm not getting anything on cam or on mic. But I have been feeling strange, like I'm being watched. Like there's another person in the room with me."

Cameron let go of the button, breathed in then out.

"Someone here?"

He changed to night vision on the camera, showing off a fuzzy green and black image of his surroundings.

After enough time passed, the two teams uploaded their data and handed off their equipment. Cameron and Edward traded places with Erin and Olivia in the van. They asked if Olivia was sure she wanted to participate, to which she confirmed. Alex and Pastor Art stood in front of the house for a minute, touched base.

"I still don't know what I'm doing, Pastor."

"Best I can say is trust your intuition. Follow your gut." The preacher touched a finger below his sternum. "There is no instruction booklet for this sort of thing."

He lowered his head, began to turn away.

"Oh, wait. You know, Deids . . . She used to do this thing with her temples." Pastor Art gestured with his hands on the sides of his face, shrugged.

Alex smirked then went inside.

With the lights on, the activity was minimal like before. With the lights out, however, this time, it was not as uneventful as the last run.

"You guys okay in there?" Edward sounded a bit worried through the static.

Erin held her breath as she shined the flashlight. "Feels, like, eerie in here. All of a sudden. Weird."

"It does. She's right."

Alex shined a light on the two girls in the hall, was about to step towards them when there was an audible knock-knock-knock.

Holy shit!

"Guys, we just heard a knocking. Seems it was from the kitchen. And the laser grid in the living room went off." It was Cameron on the speaker this time. "Looks like a trigger object moved, too."

"Which one?" Erin brought the walkie-talkie to her mouth.

"The shiny red ball."

"It just moved again." Edward's voice was faint, speaking from beside Cameron.

"Yeah, we definitely got activity. Keep your guard—"

Before Cameron finished his sentence, Alex almost toppled from the top stair.

Shit. Shit.

Erin reached out and squeezed his forearm, pulled him in close. "Be careful, Alex."

There was another knock, to which Olivia let out a sharp gasp. It was at the bottom of the stairs.

"Um. Motion sensors are going off."

"Get back, get back!" Alex turned around, jutted his arm out to shield the girls.

"I-it's coming right at you."

Erin rushed to point the lens forward, pressed record. "Cams."

Alex changed from the sound recorder to the video camera, inching backward. Olivia held onto his shoulder with a slight tremble.

It was quiet. It was still. The trio stared in the darkness at the end of the hall, waited, afraid in the pitch black.

There was a pause before soft whispers sounded in all their ears at once.

What the . . .

And then there was a faint indigo blur that shot from left to right, causing them all to shout and scream. Erin was about to trip backward when Alex caught her, his body half-turned.

Olivia squeezed the back of his shirt in a balled fist. "Fuck!"

"I know. God damn it. Everyone okay?"

"Relax. Calm down." Pastor Art spoke through, his voice soothing to the three. "Take a nice deep breath. This is what we came here for. 'Member? To get to the bottom of this. So, stick together."

Alex licked his lips. "Erin? Olivia?"

He moved his body all the way around, facing the two girls.

Erin touched the bridge of her glasses, normalizing her breathing. Olivia appeared pale, like she would soon pass out.

"Let's take a break." Alex went to turn on the nearest light.

He then led Olivia over to a small bench in front of the wooden vanity.

"I'll get her some water." He pointed the flashlight, proceeded with caution towards the stairs.

The one bedroom light shined all the way down into the living room and kitchen, enough for him to see without having to turn on more lights.

When he came back, Erin had an arm around Olivia who shivered. She stood while he took her place next to Olivia, offering the glass.

Erin started reviewing the recent footage. "Interesting."

Olivia blinked to herself in between sips.

"Hey, Alex. Lemme see your cam."

He reached up and handed it to her.

"You guys doing okay?"

"Seems like things have calmed down now."

It was Edward then Cameron on the walkie-talkie, followed by sharp static.

"Uh, we're chillin' for now and then we shall see. But I do think Olivia may have had enough."

"As I review this footage, me and Alex may have caught something."

"Gonna be all right?" He glanced at Olivia.

She forced a brave nod in return.

"Just one second, okay?"

"Check this out."

Alex stood next to Erin who rewound then pushed play.

On the LED screen, panel flipped at an angle, the video showed the end of the hall from her point of view. He could see the outline of his own back along the edge. Then she alternated between play and pause, play and pause, slowing it down enough to point out a little sphere shooting from the top of the stairs across to the wall then disappearing.

"Crap. What was that?"

"It's an orb. Not uncommon." She turned to him. "But now here, from your cam."

Erin did the same: rewind, play, pause, play, pause, play. It created a kind of slow motion effect.

From his angle, it was a clear shot of the top of the stairs and instead an indigo figure glided from left to right.

"About the height of a little boy. Wouldn't you say?"

"That does make sense."

Olivia rocked forward and back, facing down. "I think I'm gonna be sick."

Pastor Art spoke through the speaker with authority. "Call it. We're comin' in. Lights on."

Alex stepped out into the hall, began to flip the switches back on.

"Uh . . . Erin . . . ?"

She went out and joined him then halted in place.

"No fucking way."

"I swear, that thing was not open earlier."

They both walked closer toward it.

"How did—"

"Was it the orb?"

Before them, at the end of the hall, across from the top stair, a window remained open at a diagonal. The branches of a tree swayed, leaves rustling.

Pastor Art and Cameron came in through the front door, turning on all the lights as they made their way up.

"Is she okay?"

The preacher went in and checked on Olivia.

Cameron stood with Alex and Erin. He brought the recorder to his lips.

"When we start an investigation, we always make sure all the windows are shut in order to not contaminate evidence. This window was closed, but after an orb and a figure was caught simultaneously from two different camera angles, it appears to have been opened."

He then took the lead, went up to the window. Erin stayed closer to Alex behind Cameron.

"Shit. Look at that."

"Oh, my God."

"Neden." Cameron spoke into the walkie-talkie. "Did you catch that there's a freaking treehouse in the back?"

Edward responded between a loud beep and crackling static. "Sorry. I must've missed it when I did perimeter check. That's my bad."

"No, it's okay. It's real discreet. Probably wouldn't have caught it myself either, bro."

Erin leapt back with both hands covering her mouth.

"What?"

Her voice cracked. "T-there was . . ."

"I saw it too. A bluish black thing, like a silhouette."

Cameron stared down into the treehouse which was empty. Parts of it were blocked from view by large branches, like a subtle camouflage. The perfect hiding spot.

The group moved from the house to the base of the single tree.

"Who wants to do the honors?"

"Uh, I'm a little OG for this, I think."

Pastor Art hung back while the rest turned to one another.

"I wouldn't mind but I'm kinda top heavy." Cameron flexed

both biceps to prove it. "Olivia has a broken wrist, and she is shaken up."

"Both go? Together?"

Alex feigned courage. "Sure."

Cameron boosted them up to the handholds. The planks of wood matched the trunk and the branches, very difficult to see.

Erin pressed on the square door, swiveling it then popping her head in.

"Wow."

She climbed up then held a hand out for Alex.

"Appreciate it."

He stood next to her as they panned the interior. Playing cards were placed on a square crate in an unfinished game of solitaire. Empty glass soda bottles lined the wall. There was a stack of comic books, a clunky radio on a barrel, and a bucket turned over that acted as a chair.

"Pretty . . ."

Their bodies grazed in the tight space, faces hovering close as they turned and pointed flashlights.

"Pretty cool actually."

Cameron shouted from below, pointing the lens. "You guys see anything?"

"Just normal kiddie stuff. But wait, hold on." Erin squeezed past Alex. "I think I . . . Help me take this off."

Alex reached around to a small metal locker off in the corner.

"What the . . ."

"It's jammed, huh."

"Rust?"

"No, maybe . . ." Alex glanced around. "Listen. I know this is your place. These are your things. We're just here to help. Okay?"

Then he pulled again but this time it swung open, the hinges squeaking.

Erin raised the walkie-talkie. "We're inside of the treehouse now. We found a piggy bank, some toy soldiers. A bunch of clay figurines."

"Nicely done." Pastor Art spoke up the tree. "I think we have enough. Good job, ladies and gents. Time to go over footage. Do a little more research."

❦

When they all gathered in the living room again, even Zoë and Simone, the team carried a confidence and a finality, and the girls had an air of peace and understanding. Olivia informed them of everything during the investigation which left them shaken, shocked. They had a chance at least to make some sense of the happenings in their dwelling. Pastor Art sat on the first recliner with a manila folder. Alex sat on the second recliner, waved to the three girls side by side on the long couch. Erin set up a laptop on the coffee table, turned it around. She placed a few printed stills next to it then sat on the armrest by Alex. In the back, Edward and Cameron pulled up chairs by the dining table.

"First of all, I want to give a special thanks to you, miss. You seem to have been key to this unsolved mystery."

Olivia touched her cast then straightened up.

"Really, you did pretty dang great. Now let's go over the findings."

Erin went to the coffee table, sorted through the photographs. "Okay, first we did have some anomalies. Before the actual investigation, during the sweep, Ned took snapshots of the place if you didn't notice. While there was nothing particularly noteworthy, there were two pics of interest. Both on the stairs as Simone and Olivia led Pastor Art and Alex up."

The three girls leaned in to better see.

"It's that blue blur I was telling you guys about."

Zoë brought a hand over her mouth, held her breath. "Dear God."

Simone crossed her arms and leaned back.

"Now, there was quite a bit of interesting footage. The first was a collective occurrence so let me break this down. All the surveillance cams caught the knocking, both times."

Erin pushed play. It was a compilation from multiple angles in the kitchen and in the very living room they were sitting in.

The repeated sound made the three wince and cringe.

"Next is an interesting one. If you look closely, we capture a few things one after the other. The laser grid goes off, the trigger object moves, and then the motion sensors on the stairs are activated, followed by what me and Alex caught."

She played the laser beams being interrupted by an unseen force and the red ball rolling about one inch. This replayed and zoomed in, demonstrating the clear yet unexplained movement.

"Almost like we got the whole flow of a spirit going from the living room up the stairs here. Pretty compelling."

The girls watched as the orb and the figure played before finding the open window.

"Our last piece is an enhanced sound recording. Me, Alex and Olivia all heard whispers. I wasn't able to catch all of it, but here's one . . ."

Erin minimized the last video files, opened a separate audio file.

"C o ome pl a a y wi i i i th me."

She clicked it again. The girls tilted their ears to better hear.

Pastor Art cleared his throat, interlocking his fingers. "All in all, a very successful investigation. There's plenty of good evidence here and we got a strong lead discovering the treehouse in the back."

"About that . . ." Zoë turned to Simone and Olivia. "I'm so sorry, you guys. This is my fault."

The preacher narrowed his eyes. Erin closed the laptop then moved back to the armrest. Cameron and Edward peeked from the dining table.

"I saw the treehouse when we first moved in. But, you know, we're so busy working, running errands, cleaning. If it's not that, then we're relaxing and having fun. You know? I never thought much of it."

Alex stared at Zoë, rubbing at his chin.

"But when I was cleaning up once, I did find some toys and stuff in the yard. I thought they were cute so I put one in each of our rooms as a good omen. I just told these guys about it before you came in."

Everybody waited, listening.

"I put a porcelain figure in Liv's room. It was so cute and had this little musical instrument. Since she used to play in band."

Zoë sniffled, licked her lips. Olivia rested her head on Simone's shoulder, and Simone touched a hand to Olivia's knee.

"Maybe I shoulda put a normal toy like me and Sims. Is that the reason this thing could have gravitated towards her?"

"Can't say for sure."

"Uh, me and Cam actually found out more about the cottage too. Turns there was a young boy who passed away while living here. Tragic accident."

Edward rested his hands in his lap. Cameron thinned his lips.

Pastor Art handed Olivia the manila folder. "Here."

"He played the flute?" She glanced up from the page then returned to reading. "He was decapitated?"

"Something called 'internal decapitation.' Or atlanto-occipital dislocation. Rare, but it's when the ligaments that attach the skull to the spine are severed. Can be from a vehicle collision or a train derailment . . . In his case, sadly, it was at the local water park."

The three stared at the papers with mouths agape.

"I'll lead us in prayer, directed towards this unfortunate child. And then we will do a blessing, right here and right now. Blessing is not just about the place but each person within that place. In other words, I'd like to pray for all of you."

2

Case #001408

THE LONG DRIVE was incredibly scenic, with the sun going down over the mountain range and hitting the treetops of the surrounding forests. It was a straight shot east along the interstate which gave Cameron and Edward enough free mental energy to bicker over something insignificant. Pastor Art took the opportunity to doze off for majority of the ride. Erin instead used that time to ask Alex a string of probing questions: where did he grow up, did he have any siblings, what was he like as a little kid, what did he study in college. Alex answered each of these then proceeded to ask her some of his own as well.

"Same. I have kind of a useless degree . . ." She leaned into the cushion. "It felt so right to follow our passion back then, but then this big recession hits and there are no jobs."

"True."

"Would've been better to do one of those 'practical' tracks. You know? Like business or computers, legal or healthcare. I might try to go back."

He inclined his head. "You'd do that?"

"I'll be a dental hygienist or a radiologic technician or some shit."

"Yeah, I would make a great paralegal."

Both laughed.

As they got closer to their destination, more inland and further from the ocean, the terrain became drier.

Cameron took a sharp turn onto a paved dirt road. The shift from smooth asphalt to rocky jerks and bumps startled Pastor Art awake, who rubbed his eyes and yawned. Edward pointed at a large sign stretching across the entrance, SCHWEIZ RANCH.

On either side of them were wooden fences. Behind these, they saw brown, white and black horses chewing away at hay. There was a large stable opposite the scattered pack with doors swung open. Cattle was separated off in an enclosed area in back, and a pair of dogs ran around near them.

They pulled up between the barn and the living quarters.

A windmill rotated in place as they exited the van. Two men walked together while the five of them waited.

It was a taller, thinner man and a shorter, stockier man. Both had facial hair and sideburns and jeans on. One wore a Chicago Cubs cap and the other wore an LA Dodgers cap.

"Good to see you. I'm Gareth." Up close, they could see his mustache had stubble along his chin and cheeks. "That's my younger brother."

"Merle." His facial hair was more clean shaven.

Pastor Art shook each of their hands.

"I would really like to get started, soon as possible. Like I mentioned the other day, things are pretty dire. The deaths are escalating."

There was a sudden silence.

"Yes." Pastor Art faced both men, fidgeted with his fingers at his side. "Actually, we all have been debriefed."

Alex shifted in place, blinked.

Erin leaned over, whispered in his ear. "Sorry. I would've told you but . . ."

"No. No, I get it."

"How 'bout I show you where to put your fancy gear. The pastor described to me the overall plan."

Cameron went to grab bundles of cables, more than usual. Edward already had a suitcase in hand.

"Oh. While we start setting up in the main building, can Merle show Alexander around? Maybe the stable first."

"No problem."

The taller man turned to Alex. "You can see ghosts?"

"Something like that."

Erin glanced over with a thin smile, joined the others as they followed along.

Alex smirked in return, watching as she walked away.

"Okey dokey." The man pointed. "Let's, uh, go."

∽

Overhead, there were sturdy planks and crossbeams. It appeared to be designed well, maintained well, and kept clean and up to date. Alongside each of the stalls was a bucket and a trough. The lower section of the sliding stall door was thick square wiring, a middle platform of varnished wood above that, and then vertical bars low enough for the horses to stick their heads through. Ropes hung from little hooks between the different quadrants of the stable. The floor was littered with dirt and grass and hay. Alex stayed close to Merle who walked at a slow pace, scanning the environment as if he himself did not know the place.

"Gareth's the oldest?"

"Correct." He was careful touching the snout. "I'm the kid brother."

His hair was more wavy, had a bounce to it that matched the bounce in his step. The brother had straight hair that seemed to match his rigid posture.

Alex moved to one side. "I got a little bro, too."

"Not sure where to begin . . ."

"How well do you know this farm?"

Merle was quiet, patted the head then ran a hand through the mane.

"I'll be honest with you. Me and my brother don't know jack about ranches and farms and animals, none of this shit."

Alex stood next to him, placed a hand on the gate.

The horse blew air out through its lips.

"Only reason we're here is our uncle passed away and we inherited this property. We are looking for someone to take over management here. Now, that's tricky when crazy things keep happening."

"What kinda things?"

"Things . . . Things that have haunted me to my core. There is darkness, and it seeps in every pillar and every wall. A resident evil. There is some type of evil within. An evil that hungers for fear, for pain and suffering."

As the man drew back, Alex moved to touch the horse.

"Does something spook these animals? I get the feeling she's scared."

"Yep. That's actually the first thing me and my brother noticed. At night, we'd hear the animals make noises as if something was attacking them. Some got so rattled they broke out, then we had to wrangle 'em all back in."

"How did your uncle pass? How was your relationship with your uncle?"

"I'll be honest with you. Whatever's going on here, it ain't our uncle. I know that for damned sure."

Alex swallowed, turned around and took a side step.

"Um, there's a lot of empty stalls, huh."

"Like my brother mentioned, there's been death. Something was bothering the animals, but the animals started dying off as well."

He listened to the man who appeared to search his memory banks.

"There's parakeets that died. My uncle had a pair and they both died one morning. It was strange but that does happen, right? Pets sometimes pass when their owner passes. Then there was a stray cat we came across that was mutilated. Its insides were spilling out and one eyeball had been smashed in. We thought maybe it was a predator or it had been hit by a car or something, and made it to this place with its last breaths."

Images of the dead cat popped into his mind, with its mangy fur matted with dried blood, limbs contorted, disemboweled.

"One of the dogs died. That's like the only thing I remember about this place as a kid, was the dogs. See, our uncle always loved dogs, trained them, bred them. We'd spend a week or two here in the summer, and the mutts would come along on the hiking trails out back."

Merle narrowed his eyes and thinned his lips.

"Ya know, the way he died was so bizarre. The three are usually chained up at night, behind. Not sure if he was chasing something or if he was running away, but poor guy must have jumped in a way that the leash got caught . . . Found him hanging by his neck the next morning. Soul crushing to see 'im like that."

Crossing his arms, Alex shook his head and nibbled his bottom lip. The dead dog flashed through his mind's eye, with a clink of a chain, a whimper, and its paws scurrying and scrambling then swinging lifelessly.

"And then the cows and horses started dying. I've lost count. Some are pretty sick now, and the veterinarian can't explain it. Can't explain any of it."

"Damn." With the ball of his foot, he kicked forward at a wad of straw. "I'm so sorry for all that's been—"

Just then, the hanging lights flickered above them.

"You seen the buildings. They're in pretty good condition for the most part. A few are pretty old, of course. Our uncle renovated this whole place a year and a half ago, not everything, but all of the wiring and the lighting fixtures. It doesn't make sense."

"The animals are scared. Some have died. Some are sick now." Alex started listing them off, counting with his thumb and fingers.

"Oh, plants are withering too. Like, the whole crop. We have a small orchard and it's not lookin' so good . . ."

"Plants are starting to die. The lights. Has there been anything else? Anything you've seen or felt?"

"I'll tell you." Merle swallowed, fought back water in the corner of his eye. "The scariest, most frightening thing I have *ever* seen or felt in my whole entire life."

Alex waited, inhaled then exhaled.

"Other than the lights like you just saw, and the animals making noise, getting sick, passing away . . . There was one thing out of the ordinary that's happened."

He watched as the man's lower lip began to quiver.

"I don't believe in the boogeyman. No. No way. And so,

I got it in my head that the next time I hear those horses, I'm gonna go and see for myself. Sure enough, the animals wail and groan so I come check it out. A couple had escaped so I'm tryna track 'em down. I'm walking through the orchard 'cause I swear I heard a growl and a sniff that way . . ."

The light tremble became full shivering and then breaking down.

"W-w-when I came up close to the water hole, the well, something wasn't right. Like, a static in the air. Then, before my eyes, this kind of shadow came out. I h-had to blink to double check if it was r-real." His cheeks were sopping wet now. "I saw one limb, another limb, another, then the torso of the thing, slow and steady, like its bones were shattered. And then, in one sudden burst, it came rushing at me . . . This big black mass . . ."

"You run?"

Merle wiped at one cheek then the other. "I got the hell outta there. I ran and I screamed and I cried."

He reached out and touched the man on the upper arm. "You know, I been in that kind of situation myself before. It's terrifying. And you feel helpless, and confused. Kind of shreds your reality into pieces."

"It does. It really does."

Alex patted him on the shoulder. "Leave it to us."

Spread out across a couple of picnic tables, the brothers and the team sat down together. Alexander and Merle had moved from the stable to the barn where the lights flickered on more than one occasion. The others moved from the living quarters then to the main enclosures and each contained shed. When all the equipment had been set up, they walked as one big tour group along the hiking trails and through the half-withered orchard. It was an arduous process but calm and peaceful returning to the main buildings, in particular this little grassy outdoor area in back. Gareth even had two pitchers of fresh squeezed lemonade ready, with heavy beads of condensation dripping down.

"Now that's some good-ass lemonade." Cameron smacked his lips. "God damn. Like an explosion in my mouth."

"Dollar per glass, plus tax."

There was a round of much needed laughter.

"Everything all right?" Alex noticed Erin shiver, rub at her arms.

"It's just I don't like ice. Makes my teeth cold."

Alex nodded to himself.

"Okay, before it gets dark, I wanted us all to talk." Pastor Art glanced left then right. "Mister Berenson, you wanna kick it off?"

"Yeah. Thanks." Edward straightened up. "One of the first things is this place is kind of huge compared to our usual investigation. We always try to conduct from as far as possible to not taint evidence."

Gareth touched the brim of his cap.

Erin bent down, let the dogs lick at her palms.

"So that's why Cam here brought extension cords. The van will be smack-dab in the middle of the pens and pastures, the house, and barn and stable. It's going to make for pure readings, pure recordings and thus pure findings. However, since we'll be so isolated and farther away from one another, there is an element of danger here."

"Also, Alexander said you mentioned all the electrical ports and lights in place are fairly new? Do you know about the plumbing or the foundations?"

Merle shrugged his shoulders. Gareth shook his head.

Pastor Art leaned on one elbow then continued. "The reason I ask is it's possible there could be some kind of toxicity occurring. In older buildings with inadequate ventilation and poor air quality, sometimes mold or fungal spores can cause hallucinogenic effects. It might be carbon monoxide leaking from a faulty furnace, for example. It might be formaldehyde or even pesticides in this case."

Edward cleared his throat. "You said you're not used to caring for livestock. Can it be a change in diet or routine? Perhaps improper hygienic protocols leading to some kind of infection?"

"I mean, could be any of those. The vet prolly would've caught if it was a germ or virus or anything. But mold or chemicals, maybe. We don't know." Gareth nodded. "Definitely in the realm of possibility."

Cameron drummed his fingers. "And it sounds like neither of you want to be involved in the actual investigation?"

"My brother encountered something pretty ominous. I'm gonna have to say on his behalf that he sits this one out." Gareth removed his cap, tousled his hair, then put it back on. "As for me, I can help keep eye on the screens at least, anything like that. Out of the line of fire, so to speak."

"There we go. Game plan all worked out. Enjoy that citrus. I have a feeling it's going to be a long friggin' night."

⁖

With the last few drops of lemonade came the last few rays of sunlight. They moved from the picnic tables to the van to get ready. Alex followed Edward and Cameron, the three of them making up the first group. Both handed him a video camera with a strap, a voice recorder and a walkie-talkie. The two took similar equipment but also an EMF detector and a handheld thermometer. Erin climbed into the van, sat down in front of the screens with one of the headsets wrapped around her neck like a DJ ready to open up a show. Gareth hugged Merle, clapped him on the shoulders. Pastor Art stood outside, staring up at the sky that changed from twilight to nightfall.

"Hey. You be careful here." Merle tugged on his cap, heading to the truck. "Really, everybody. Watch out. Watch your backs."

As the truck reversed then spun around, the headlights shone past.

Pastor Art waved over, watching the man drive off.

"Okay, so how do I help?" Gareth lingered.

"I guess grab a chair. You can be a set of extra eyes. See this?" Erin waved a hand towards the panel. "These are all the surveillance cams set up. Got one in the stable. Got one in the barn. In the living quarters on each floor. One in each pen. The orchard. The field. And outside the van. It's a lot to cover but it's the best that we could do."

"Ah, got it."

"Mister Gallo. Mister Berenson. Y'guys ready to go?"

They both nodded.

"Gimme a minute with the kid, will ya?"

"Sure."

"Cool, go ahead."

Alex joined the preacher who returned to staring at the sky. The two stood shoulder to shoulder.

"Nervous?"

"Oh. Always, Pastor."

"You been on a few of these now. You know what to do."

"I have a question."

Pastor Art didn't move but made a *hrmm* sound in response.

"Noticed you seem to have these scientific explanations when we get into these. Why is that? I would think, between your faith and what we do . . ."

"Wise to always be a skeptic first."

Alex shifted his gaze to the preacher then back to the sky.

"Before we start, Alexander, I did want to say that I think your abilities are generally 'sensitive' as in you have feelings, hunches. Not sure if this might include visions. But the main thing, and I wanted to make sure you're aware, is I have a feeling you're also a conduit. An antenna of sorts."

He scrunched his face, leaned over.

"Like, there might be a chance you're drawing these things out. They're attracted to you like winged insects to a bright fluorescent light."

"So what do I do?"

"Nothing. Continue as you have been." Pastor Art tapped him on the back. "I just wanted you to be aware. To be mindful."

Alex faced down to the grass.

"Testing. Testing." Erin broke through the speakers in unison.

"Read you loud and clear." Cameron pressed the button on the walkie-talkie. "Locked and loaded."

Edward raised a thumbs up towards Alex and Pastor Art.

"It's time."

The preacher went to the van, closed the sliding door behind him.

Cameron handed flashlights to Alex and Edward. "Let's do our first sweeps, lights on. Stick together building to building before we split up."

All three of them started to walk along the patches of dirt and grass towards the main house, its lit windows appearing like yellow eyes. Their flashlight beams waved, piercing through the darkness.

Edward breathed in deep through his nostrils. "Kinda nice to be out in the countryside."

"I'm a city kid . . ." Alex felt the grass crunch beneath the soles of his shoes. "Not used to this quiet. Home is car crashes and ambulances and crazy people."

"Same." Cameron chuckled. "I hate the smell."

"Eh, it's not so bad."

Pastor Art cut through the chatter. "Let's pull it in, gentlemen."

They made it to the front steps of the porch, their streams of light crossing over.

Cameron opened the screen door then the wooden door, let Alex and Edward pass through first. Both took out their video cameras and pointed them forward.

In back, he pointed his camera at himself. "I'm Cam Gallo, and I'm here with SPIRAL to investigate Schweiz Ranch. The brothers living here have reported animals being frightened at night. Some have gotten sick and some have even passed away. A mysterious shadow figure has been seen lurking as well."

"Got a lot to cover. Cam, you wanna get the upstairs?"

Alex nodded. "Sounds good. And I'll get this side."

The three went around the interior, spreading out and filming their separate movements.

From the living room to the dining room to the pantry, to the bedrooms and to the bathrooms, there was nothing. They came back together then walked out the back door. In the midst of the clear sky, all could see the slow revolving windmill.

Erin chimed in through the static. "I think I heard something. I'll review the recordings now. Proceed with caution."

"Let's head to the animals first."

They used a combination of their flashlights and night vision on their cameras. The blurry black and green images played on each screen like a low budget found footage flick.

Up ahead, they saw the outlines of the cows.

"Guys, wait . . ."

Cameron and Alex turned to Edward.

"The steaks are high."

Alex smirked while Cameron grinned. Both shook their heads then kept walking forward, closer to the enclosure.

"Have to enhance it later. I can't quite catch it. But definitely EVPs."

Perhaps from next to her, they heard Gareth still appreciate the silly pun.

With the lights on throughout the property, it was still creepy. The farm was so spread out and so far from civilization. The cattle turned to them as they approached, appearing on edge with uneasy breathing.

"Relax there, fella."

"I think that's a girl."

"Oh."

Back by the horses, in the distance, the sound of the dogs barking cut through the air, along to a dull echo.

Holy crap!

"Did you hear that?" Cameron darted his head back, peered into the dark. "Which way is that coming from?"

"Uh, the dogs stay near the thing, right? They chain them."

The barking intensified, deep guttural noises from their diaphragm into their throats, scraping at their vocal cords.

"Let's move it. Double time."

Alex turned to follow Edward and Cameron who raced to the back of the stables where the kennel was located. He stubbed his foot, was about to trip but caught himself, creating some distance between the others.

"Uh, surveillance cams don't cover the canines." The static cut in, followed by a sharp beep. "But we hear them from the other cams. For sure responding to something."

One of the barks now turned to a wail. It was a set of clear furious barking and a set of faint obscure whining.

"Go, go, go!"

Cameron sped up, rushing far ahead, displaying that he had the speed to match his bulk and strength.

"W-wait up, Cam—"

Alex almost tripped again, lagging even further behind.

"Guys!"

Right then and there, with the three spaced apart in the grass, all of the lights on the property shut off. The flood lights. The lights in the house. The barn, the stable. Everything. It was only the light from the crescent moon.

"Can you hear me? Alexander?"

"The power is out. I repeat, the power is out."

Gareth was audible in the background. "Mamma mia . . ."

Alex remained frozen in place, panning from right to left in the pitch black. He tried stepping forward but tripped and fell at last. He rolled onto the ground, hard.

Damn it! Fuck.

"Mister Berenson? Mister Gallo?"

"You okay, Alex? Alex?"

He sat upright, regained his bearings. His flashlight had gone out so he banged it with his palm until it came back on.

"Dang. I'm goin' out there . . . Hang on."

Erin's voice started to crack. "Pastor Art is on his way. Be careful, please."

"Ned? Cam?" Alex staggered to his feet, aiming the light.

While he crept forward, he heard unintelligible shouts and muffled barking. It was coming from all around him. He had no idea which direction the sound originated. His hand trembled as he raised the walkie-talkie.

"This is Alex, over." He let go then pressed the button again. "I . . . I got turned around. I lost the other two."

"Alex! Oh, thank God." There was relief in her voice, almost elation. "Maybe wave your flashlight around. I'll see if I can make you out."

He did like she said, moving it overhead and side to side.

"Okay, I see you. I see you." There was rolling static then a beep. "Actually, wait. Turn around. You're going the wrong way, looks like."

It felt like he was blindfolded and they did a trust building exercise.

"Keep turning, turning. There. And walk." She seemed to concentrate, calm her breathing. "Perfect. You should be able to see the stable now."

"I owe you one. Thanks, Erin."

"Don't mention it." Her voice was quiet. "Just glad you're all right."

He started jogging as he spotted a flashlight in the distance, although it was stationary and aimed at an odd angle. "I see a light. I can hear one of the dogs."

"Maybe wait there? Pastor Art is on his way."

As Alex approached, he spotted one of the chains swinging from a hook as well as a flashlight toppled in the grass. It shined over the field toward the orchard, almost as an ominous signpost. The other dog barked and whined, pacing in a circle around himself in the open kennel.

He stepped inside, knelt in place, patted the dog on the head then the neck and back to try to calm him down. It was obvious the dog was frantic, with heavy panting and keeping its tail down.

"You're gonna be all right, boy."

The echo of muffled shouts and barking came back, from in the distance.

"I'll go find your sister."

God, please . . .

Erin tried to interject, but the walkie-talkie cut in and out.

So sorry.

But I can't leave those guys hanging.

His heart thumped in his chest as he proceeded into the darkness. The light grind of the dirt beneath his shoes was so clear in the silence. No other sounds nearby, just his own breath and rustling from the wind.

Some of the trees were lush, the leaves thick and the fruit plump. Other trees appeared brittle, the branches near bare and ready to break apart.

Alex continued through the mix of seeded and stoned fruits. First, it was the lemons. The thin trunks were like spindly legs to his racing mind. He feared one of them would turn and walk away. Most of the looming fruit was vibrant splashes of yellow but there were a few that were spotted with a gray-brown.

"Um. Is that you?"

He darted sideways, shining the light to flannel, thick glasses and a thick beard.

"Oh. What in the fucking fuck, man."

The two hugged tight as if they were long lost twins. They stood between the rows.

"Where's Cam?"

"I-I-I don't know. I lost him, dude. I lost my walkie too." Edward shook his head, shrugged his shoulders. "Lost my way. Lost my mind a little out here."

"Jesus. Well, at least I found you. I'm glad."

"Sorry, I would've called out . . ." He put a finger to his lips and crouched down. "But there's something with us."

Alex inclined his head, also crouched. "Got your flashlight, Ned?"

"No. It died on me."

"Everything okay?" The walkie-talkie cut in with light static. "Alex?"

He handed it to Edward.

"I'm with Alex now, Erin. Can you read me?"

It sputtered mere sentence fragments.

"You're breaking up. This is Ned. I'm with Alex. My flashlight is dead. I lost my walkie. Cam is M-I-A. And our equipment is down except for still cam."

"Oh, of course." The signal was clear for a moment. "Down to a freaking potato camera. Pastor Art just found . . ."

From further away, deep in the orchard, they heard a long shout blending into a sharp high-pitched shriek. It was off-putting to hear Cameron vocalizing in that way. His usual cool, calm, cocky and carefree voice now turned desperate, deranged, disconcerted.

Alex and Edward glanced at one another for a split second, jaws agape, then sprinted through the trees.

Beyond the lemons were nectarines and apricots, followed by apples which had larger and thicker trunks. Both slowed as the shouting became louder and more clear.

"Cam? Caaam!"

He paced next to Edward, cupping his hands over his mouth. "Cameron!!!"

"This is no bueno."

What the . . .

Alex froze in place, staring past. Nothing was there that he could see with his naked eye but he sensed something—invisible, lurking, with fangs and claws, with malice.

"B-behind you, Ned."

Edward leapt in place, spinning around. He began to take picture after picture without thinking, lighting up the space with the bright flash. Like a slow flipbook, a slender figure manifested, hovering, teleporting closer and closer and closer, its long limbs and bony facial features more visible, distinct and prominent as it appeared and then reappeared.

Alex inched backward, arms out to his side.

"Get away!"

Both felt water splash on their faces. They wiped at their forehead and cheeks, opened their eyes to Pastor Art standing with a bible in hand.

"The heck was that?"

"Did you just throw . . . holy water?"

"It's blessed water. What am I, a friggin' Catholic?"

Cameron shouted again from somewhere close. "Ned!"

Pastor Art began leafing through the pages. "You guys go, I'll catch up. I'm gonna pray for some protection. This is a little beyond us."

"Ned!!!"

"Hold on, Cam."

Alex and Edward searched the next few rows of apple trees, with the one flashlight between them.

"Try using the light from your screen."

"Good idea. My phone's kinda junk, though." Edward unlocked it, held it up. "Still got that candy bar phone."

"Ned? Ned, is that you?"

"I think it's this way."

The two traced the faint voice down the lane, to where Cameron squatted on the ground holding the dog in his arms.

"What happened? Are you okay?"

"Bro. I've never been so happy to see your fugly face, Needlenose." Cameron shook his head. "I get to the kennel thing, and this little doggy is digging, clawing, scratching. Even broke the chain off . . . Look it . . ."

He pointed out the leash which still had the circular hoop and a few links dangling.

"I chased after her and finally caught up. Poor girl. But then something was following us, and passed right by me."

"If it's whatever the hell we just saw then holy damn."

Cameron remained in the same position, listening.

"Don't even know how to describe it. Like a big, black shadow. Tall and skinny."

"You could see its skull, I wanna say."

Pastor Art spoke up from behind. "To me, it appeared to have tendrils or tentacles. I mean, maybe it's demonic. I don't know. Never seen anything like that in my life."

"Oh my God." Alex stared into each of their faces. "W-what do we do?"

"First off, everybody just calm down. Relax. Catch your breaths. Let's do a quick status check here."

They each did as the preacher said, quieted, hushed.

"Now, the power went out. So it looks like we'll be lights

off by default. The laser grids and motion detectors, most of our video cams are gone."

"A lot of our equipment has died on us."

"I noticed. Except walkies, which have been spotty. Still got mine and Alexander's flashlights. Luckily, the surveillance cams we use are hooked up to the van."

Edward nudged and tilted in place, as if he was shoved at the shoulder. It caused him to stumble.

One by one, the others turned to him, confused.

"Uh . . ."

In front of their very eyes, some force yanked him backwards into the air and slammed him down onto the ground. Before they could even check to see if he was okay, he was dragged into the rows.

"Ned! Ned!"

"NED!!!"

Pastor Art sprinted after their colleague. Alex followed close behind. The leaves and branches scraped against the sides of their arms.

Edward was just out of their line of sight when he was pulled in a different direction and disappeared from their view.

Cameron lingered, still carrying the dog, unsure whether or not he should accompany the others. He followed but kept plenty of room in between.

"Ned!!!"

When the rows ended, Alex and Pastor Art found themselves in an open field.

They started searching the area but there was no sign of him. Cameron came out of the orchard, stepping over a single cinder block. A few other blocks littered the ground.

As the night air engulfed them, the beams from the flashlights emanated like a pair of fireflies hovering.

"Oh, crap. Is that the well?"

"No . . ."

The dog began to whine and whimper, wriggled and squirmed. Cameron tried holding on but lost his grip.

All watched as the dog scampered back into the rows.

"I get it, buddy."

When they faced the well once more, there was slight hesitation. Nobody moved. A dread crept over their feet up through their bodies, crawling in their skin.

Each took an apprehensive small step.

The ring from the opening of the well from that angle was an oval shape that grew larger like a pill then like an egg.

"Hey! There he is!" Cameron took the lead. "On the other side."

Like he was placed, Edward leaned against the rock wall. His eyes were closed and he wasn't moving.

Pastor Art bent down, tapped at his cheek.

"Mister Berenson. Mister Berenson. You gotta wake up."

The preacher kept tapping, both cheeks, then slapped him a good hard one.

He shot his eyes open, gasping with rapid blinks. ". . . W-what happened? I must've passed out."

"You're okay now. Everything's going to be fine."

Cameron motioned to Alex then went around. Alex got on one side and Cameron got on the other, about to help him to his feet.

"Watch out!"

A cinder block hurled through the air, dangerously close to hitting them.

Pastor Art inched away, holding a hand up to keep the rest back.

"Whoa, whoa, whoa!"

Another cinder block crashed onto the ground.

"Jesus Christ."

Alex stood back up, watched as Pastor Art rifled through his jacket pockets. He took out a cylindrical carton and started pouring it into his hands.

"Salt?"

"That's right." He tossed the particles on the ground around them and down into the well. "Heck, I wish I brought rock salt instead, and the pump-action."

"You mean a . . . shotgun?"

"I keep one in the trunk of my ride. A handgun too." Pastor Art arched his neck. "Haven't seen anything to this degree since back in the day with Deids. After that, I was strapped."

"Except we all rode in the van."

"Precisely."

Cameron neared his breaking point. "Fuck. My. Life."

On the walkie-talkie, they heard Erin scream. "Hurry! Hurry! Something—"

No, no, no, no.

"Something's attacking the van!!!"

"You two, stay here." Pastor Art turned to each of them. "We gotta pair up. It's way too easy to get lost if we're in a big group. Things are falling apart, fast. Less chance of anybody getting hurt along the way."

"Are you sure?"

"I'm sure. Alexander, you and me."

The preacher stepped past and jogged back into the orchard.

Alex handed Cameron the walkie-talkie then followed.

Some kind of adrenaline pumped this time as they rushed through. Neither was as nervous or afraid, more so dead set, dead serious, understanding the imminent threat.

They went through the apples, apricots and nectarines, the lemons, then between the barn and living quarters to where the van was parked.

As the two approached, both slowed down, staring in disbelief. The van moved as if it was being rammed into, leaning far over, about to topple. Except nothing was there. No stampeding beast. No riotous frenzy. No sign of an earthquake.

Pastor Art began to pray but the crashing continued. Metal twisted. Glass cracked then shattered. He continued praying with conviction, raising his voice.

Everything ceased all at once.

Alex hurried over, yanked the sliding door open. Erin ran out and hugged him tight, crying into his collar bone. Gareth hobbled out, his face gaunt and his skin pale.

The four were quiet, no one saying a word. It was the sound of sobbing and the sound of barking in the deafening silence.

Pastor Art reached into his pocket, took out the walkie-talkie.

"Okay. We're calling it a night. Bring it on in."

✧

Even though it was broad daylight, every light and lamp was turned on and every curtain drawn throughout the living quarters. The two brothers greeted them then led the group from the entrance into the common area, the hall and the kitchen. They sat on one end of the round dining table while Alex, Erin and Cameron took up the other side. Edward shook his head and held a hand up, preferring not to sit and leaning against the counter instead. Pastor Art appeared to drag his feet, took up an empty chair between the brothers and the group. Erin had the photos and laptop ready. Cameron had a manila folder with printed papers.

"How have things been?"

"I'll be honest with you, Pastor. We been staying at a motel a few miles away. Just come in to tend to the animals, then we take off again."

"That's probably for the best. The level of activity we experienced here is some of the highest we've ever seen or come across. Definitely malevolent forces at work. Now, let's review the findings."

"Usually, I'd be more involved." Edward hung his head low. "But I'm still pretty shook up. Sorry."

Merle gave a firm nod. Gareth folded his arms over with thinned lips.

"Hey, it's okay." Alex glanced over. "No need to apologize."

Cameron leaned across the top of the chair. "Hell. I screamed like a prepubescent girl that night. May have peed myself."

"First off, there were those EVPs that I had to enhance . . . Take a listen."

Erin flipped the laptop around, moved it more towards the center.

"I I I hh a t e N ed."

She pushed rewind, played it again.

"I I I hh a t e N ed."

Then she went through and clicked another file.

"K i lll N ed."

Edward cringed at the sound, shuddered in place and faced away.

"We didn't get too much this time due to power issues and

equipment failure. But still, there were a few. Before the dogs start to bark, you can hear a light growling noise. It was from, well, right here. In this building."

She opened the file then rubbed her fingers together.

Gareth shook his head. "Sounds like a damn grizzly bear."

"Or a mountain lion, something." Merle rubbed at his eyebrows.

Alex shifted towards Erin, adjusting in his seat then resting on both elbows.

"There is a blurry shot of one of the blocks flying."

Everybody leaned closer to view the clip which was slow motion and zoomed in. The boys huddled on the ground by the well, the preacher stood near, while the block lifted through the air in an oblong arc, with each of their synced reactions following.

"Now, the best footage . . . It's possibly one of the best we've ever gotten. Considered kind of a unicorn in our field. Right as the lights go out, this is something we were able to capture. Here."

A wide angle played on the screen. At first, there was nothing. Then, from one side of the stable to the other, a shadowy figure like a frozen pillar of smoke appeared to glide from one stall across the open space into the other stall.

It was the longest awkward moment of silence when Pastor Art scooted forward and cleared his throat.

"That's what we call a full-bodied apparition."

Both brothers stared with crinkled brows.

"Suffice to say, it's confirmed. This is an intelligent haunting, and a very powerful and dangerous one at that. Although not all of the activity is recorded on audio or video, we included everything in our written reports. It's five of us so multiple eyewitness accounts, from different places and different times."

Erin closed the laptop. "And with that, we hand it off to Cam."

"Uh, I tried my best, you guys. Ned is our main research guy but he was already on the fence. And after hearing those EVPs, understandably, he needed to step away."

He opened the manila folder and leafed through the pages.

"I'll be honest, I'm still not sure about this one. It's kind of a stretch in my opinion but I do have a theory . . ."

The group perked up, facing Cameron and listening.

"Before your uncle settled down at this ranch, he served in the military. When he and a few of his buddies got out of the service, they traveled through Europe. Since they had backgrounds in farming and breeding, that was the kind of work they picked up, mostly in rural areas. One common laborer's job to the next."

Alex licked his lips.

Erin arched her neck, inclined her head.

"I found a couple of articles. That brought me down an entire twisting maze. Again, I don't know if this is what's happening. But it sure is strange."

Edward crossed one leg over the other, tightened his crossed arms and faced down to the floor again.

"The first is, while they were helping out in the boonies, the sticks, he and his buddies came across a body floating in the bog. When the authorities were called in, it turned out this was a case of natural mummification. The corpse was from like the Iron Ages. I've never heard of this 'til now but this can occur in many places. Bodies have been found in bogs in England and Denmark. Sweden, Germany, Poland, the Netherlands. Hell, there were hundreds of skeletons preserved in a similar way out in Florida, that still had brain matter."

Cameron turned the page over, skimmed the next few paragraphs.

"Something about the conditions in a bog. The temperature's cold enough, stays cold enough year-round. The peat and the biomass. Moss that consumes oxygen in the water. So tissues tend to tan or leather versus decay."

Erin winced, leaned her head on Alex.

"It was a man believed to be a human sacrifice. He had fractured ribs, stab wounds in his chest, arrows lodged in his shoulder blade, and a noose around his neck."

"What a horrible way to go."

"For real."

"That's the first article. The second is from after. Many people who came into contact with this body were almost, like, cursed. Head of the forensic team died of a sudden brain aneurism. The archeologist on-site was struck by a falling boulder in a landslide. Each of his buddies also passed, all young, not long after going bankrupt from bad harvests and poor livestock production . . ."

Everybody listened, let it sink in. The air seemed thicker and heavier then.

Alex swallowed a hard dry swallow, felt Erin sigh from his collar bone.

"Near the end of the piece, they interviewed a medium who saw the body up close. According to her, the man felt angry and wanted his stolen stuff back. At that time, it was just your uncle left remaining. Rumor had it maybe he felt guilty or got scared, perhaps both, and returned whatever item to the body."

"Like Mister Gallo said, we don't know. But it's quite the coincidence." Pastor Art placed both hands in front of him. "I'll do a blessing of the property and each person here today one by one. We already contacted Liwanu, another expert, who will do a second blessing in about ten days. And I even reached out to the friggin' Catholics to try to get an exorcism performed."

"Is that all gonna work?" Merle's eyes softened.

"We won't know until we know, to be frank. That is way more than we usually do, I can tell you that."

Gareth sighed. "Let's try it. Sure. But, if this doesn't go our way and it continues on, we have no choice but to move the animals, move the plants. We will not hesitate to bulldoze this forsaken calamity to the ground. Close it off for good."

Pastor Art nodded with a slow blink.

"This evil has got to be stopped."

3

Case #001412

WHEN PASTOR ART knocked on the door then stood back and waited, there was no response. They all glanced at one another, shrugging their shoulders. He tried knocking again, this time louder and harder, more deliberate, also pressing the circular button to ring the doorbell. Alex leaned his ear to the door, heard some rummaging inside and light footsteps. He lifted a hand, motioned to the others to wait. Erin swayed in place. Cameron stretched his arms to the side with a big yawn. Edward turned away, covering up his own yawn. It took another long minute but the door opened a crack and a droopy eyeball peeked out at them.

"Are you guys SPIRAL?"

"Yes, I'm—"

The man closed the door, undid the chain and deadbolt.

"Come on in."

He had a receding hairline and a growing bald spot on the back of his head, which may have been early for his age. His eyes had dark circles and puffy bags. The deep wrinkles on his forehead matched the cut of his frown lines and laugh lines.

Each of them followed, taking up the cozy space.

"I'm Arturo Selga. Call me Pastor Art. And I believe you already met Miss Woodfeld at our office."

Erin waved as she sat on the recliner.

"Ned."

"Cam."

They both sat down on the folding chairs as the man placed them down.

"Uh . . ."

"It's okay. I'll sit here." Pastor Art pulled out a rolling chair by the desk.

"My name is Lewis Casey. Or Lew. I have . . ."

The preacher raised a finger up. "Hold on a sec. Let's wait before we talk actually, give Alexander some time to explore the area."

Passing by, Alex noticed the man was spotted with freckles all over his face and arms. A window was covered with newspaper and duct tape. The kitchen was littered with paper cups and paper plates, plastic forks and plastic spoons, old bags of takeout. Unopened envelopes overflowed in the tray. A garbage bin was filled to the brink.

Hmm.

In a similar fashion, the toilet and tub appeared to not have been cleaned in a while, with a layer of sludge spreading and water stains showing. Another window was covered with newspaper. The rubbish can was pretty full as well.

There was a random pleasant scent he caught, though just for a moment. It was out of place compared to the borderline filth.

Alex closed his eyes, took another whiff.

Floral? Fruity?

More windows in the other two bedrooms were covered, and had strips of duct tape in a big X pattern over them. By the last bedroom, he caught the aroma again and followed it. He closed his eyes, raised a hand with outstretched fingers.

Show me where you are.

He turned to the bed, stepping closer. On the mattress, the image of a beautiful woman entered his mind as if from a forgotten dream, a dream that was alluring and sensual. Her eyes drew him in. The nubile flesh of her bare midriff. The perky contour of her supple bosoms. He felt a potent rush within.

The iris and pupil had a profound magnetic pull, an electrical charge. He had the strong urge to rub his hands along her naked thighs, to part them. He was so tempted to squeeze and rub her breasts, kiss her, lick her, to penetrate her.

No, no. Wait.

He flinched, snapping out of it.

Alex walked backwards into the hallway.

"You saw her, didn't you?" The man spoke in a murmur. "That bitch."

∽

The others remained quiet as Alex plodded across the carpet then stood against the wall. He blinked to himself, shaking his head and crossing his arms over his chest. For a moment, he peeked at Erin, their eyes meeting from opposite sides of the living room. Her face showed slight concern. She feigned a half-smile then mouthed the words, it's all right. Edward nudged an elbow at Cameron who nodded, took the laptop out from the case and set it on his lap. Pastor Art rotated in the chair, adjusted in place, finding a comfortable position by lifting one foot and resting it on the opposite knee.

"What'd ya see? What'd ya hear?" The preacher narrowed his eyes. "Did you sense anything?"

"I . . ." Alex stared off. "I smelled, like, a strong fragrance. Perfume? There was a female presence."

"Uh huh. Anything else?"

"A little embarrassed to say but . . . This mystery woman was beautiful. Gorgeous, tantalizing. It kind of messed with my head."

"Like, it turned you on?" Cameron had a big grin.

"That's her. She is like a temptress, a seductress." Lewis slouched, with shoulders hunched. "Also, she hates the light, the sun. Which is why the windows are like that."

"I see." Pastor Art straightened up. "Now that our friend has dipped his toes, let's go back to the beginning."

"Me and my wife . . ." Lewis nodded, sniffled, not making eye contact. "Me and my ex, I should say . . ."

Alex glanced around the room, noticed several framed photos of the once happy couple in various poses, holding one another and hugging. He almost could not believe that cheery and jovial man was the same glum, gloomy person before them now.

"We moved here 'cause of my work. There was a lotta places we coulda picked, maybe shoulda picked. But this was the one . . . Nice and quiet. Near the woods. Not far from the water."

Edward tilted his head as he listened.

Cameron cracked his knuckles, leaned back.

"Things were pretty good for a while. But then I had this very, veery vivid dream one night. An erotic, passionate fantasy.

I don't know why. I don't know where that came from. But this woman came to me in my subconscious, lured me right in. I couldn't help myself."

Erin faced away, fidgeted her feet.

"I know it was in my mind but it was so real. Realer than real. The pleasures . . . It was one of the most mind-blowing experiences of my life."

Alex held up a half-fist by his chin.

"This happened for a week and a half, give or take. It felt like I was having an affair. And, to be completely honest, I was about head over heels. Weird, I know. But I was that enraptured."

Lewis closed his eyes and arched his neck.

"But then things took a bad turn. One of the last times . . ." He clenched his jaws, forcing out the mumbled words. "I was in absolute heaven one minute then I was in absolute hell the next. She changed from this flawless, luscious delight to a spiteful, abominable, disgusting shrew."

He blinked to himself, placing his hands on his knees.

"I'd wake up with these terrible bruises all over me. Like, around my throat or across my forehead, my cheek. Up and down my back. On the side of my leg."

He paused there, began to rock in place.

Pastor Art rolled the chair towards Lewis, put a firm hand on his shoulder. "Go on. It's okay."

"The worst, though, was these bruises started showing up on the missus. She would wake up covered in them like she had been mugged. No dreams. Just bruises. I can't help but feel so guilty. I'm a motherfucking asshole."

"You didn't know."

"It started happening not only at night in bed but during

the day at random. She'd be moving from the kitchen to the bedroom and, pow, she'd keel over in pain, holding at her side. A fresh dark bruise would already be swelling up."

Erin scooted forward. "Um. You mentioned pics of these?"

"Ah, yes." The man handed her a small stack.

"That's got both me and my wife's bruise marks. Until she left, anyway. Enough time, and she couldn't take it anymore. I don't blame her. Being afraid. Being attacked."

The bruises were undeniable—darkened black, blue and purple flesh starting to yellow along the edges.

Cameron scratched his head then opened the laptop.

"I went through the flash drive you dropped off when you stopped by. Usually one of these guys does the scanning." He pointed with his chin to Edward then to Erin. "But I been helping lately. Holdin' down the fort."

"Again, the nightmares and bruises were getting so intense. I felt I had to start taking video when I slept at night." Lewis shook his head. "But I haven't been able to bring myself to look through it, no."

"There's a few instances where you're muttering in your sleep. Flinching, jerking. Nothing super out of the ordinary. However, there is one that did stand out."

Cameron slid his finger on the touchpad.

"At this exact moment . . ."

He pointed then clicked the button.

Lewis stared into the screen, watching the recorded version of himself lie in bed. First, in a slurred mutter, he began to groan and moan. Then, he shivered and shuddered, until he darted both hands from underneath the blanket, flailing as if he was trying to get something off of him—like he was being attacked, being choked.

Alex recalled his own experiences that still crept in the back of his psyche. Goosebumps broke out over his skin, the hairs in each pore standing on end.

The recorded struggle continued until the open window behind the bed slammed shut and the drawers in the nightstand flung open on their hinges. Lewis sat upright on-screen, hyperventilating in a cold sweat, unaware of all that just happened.

"Dear God."

"Okay, let's get to work."

As Cameron and Edward went to the van to grab the cables and tripods, Erin planned where to place the surveillance cameras for optimal coverage. She stared up at the ceiling, scanning from left to right back to the left again, repeating this throughout each of the rooms and the hall. Alex helped her plan then helped the other two transfer equipment. Lewis crossed one arm over his torso and rubbed his far elbow. His raccoon eyes observed the commotion as they set up motion sensors and laser grids, almost cringing at the sight of it all. Pastor Art noticed this and walked over to him.

"Hey. It's going to be fine."

"Thank you."

"Don't mention it." Pastor Art faced the man then faced forward. "When was the last time you saw the entity?"

Lewis didn't answer right away, waited.

The preacher shifted on his feet.

"When we were talking in the living room. She was right behind you, this mean scowl on her resting bitch face. She is *not* happy you're here, any of you. But especially you."

"I guess I'll go first then." He forced a smile in an attempt to bring some levity. "Do you want to participate?"

"No, no. She's going to be even more pissed."

Alex heard the exchange as he plugged in the power cord, adjusted the wiring. He locked eyes with the preacher then returned to setting up.

"You know, when we begin an investigation, I sometimes point out any activity experienced kind of says more about the person than the place or the thing itself. Could be somebody is anxious, or paranoid. It could be somebody is sensitive."

Lewis thinned his lips, blinked.

"Have you ever had an affair? Did you ever want to cheat? I don't need to know, but it's something to consider." Pastor Art folded his arms. "Ever develop an emotional attachment? You ever been in an abusive or manipulative relationship? Were you perhaps unhappy in your marriage?"

The man sniffed then rubbed his chin.

"Spirits tend to seek out these vulnerabilities, these . . . cracks."

Both were quiet.

"Another thing is d'you hear that?"

"Hear w-what?" Lewis crinkled his brow. "I don't hear a thing."

"Me neither. It's pretty dang quiet for a tight neighborhood. All these fresh, new, uniformly matching, perfectly spaced houses in this little development. Which made me wonder if something about that could be occurring. There is sound below the range of human hearing. Less than twenty hertz, I believe. 'Infrasound,' it's called."

Alex continued to listen as he set up the still camera, narrowing his eyes.

"Studies have shown at nineteen hertz, the eyeball can start to vibrate and see optical illusions. This could be, for instance, from a fan or something that you may not notice. Reactions to infrasound might include bizarre sensations, uneasy feelings, nervousness, sorrow."

"I think we're all set, Pastor." Alex stood up.

"Got it. Thanks, Alexander. I'll be taking the first shift. Maybe me, Mister Gallo and Miss Woodfeld, if they're up for it."

He nodded, went to tell the others.

Behind him, Pastor Art and Lewis still talked, however, no longer in earshot.

With the van door open, Alex saw Edward face the controls, press a button and flick a switch. He held the headset sideways against his ear, listening then adjusting the dial.

"Ready?"

"Yeah. Cam and Erin are up first, with Pastor Art."

"Cool."

"Let's get this party started."

Cameron grabbed a video camera and a handheld thermometer, extras for Pastor Art. He took an EMF detector on the way out.

Erin did the same but Alex handed her the voice recorder.

"Thanks."

She turned to walk away but he touched her hip. "Listen. Be careful."

"Well, it seems this vengeful spirit is out for *your* kind, right? Men. So I think I might be safe." Erin let out a light giggle.

"You remember his ex."

Her smile faded.

"Now don't be nervous. I didn't mean for that."

"Thanks, Alex."

"But you saw those polaroids."

"No, you're right. Sometimes, all this is kind of fun, exhilarating. It's so interesting to chase after things beyond our understanding." Erin faced down, pouted. "Also frightening at times, though. And dangerous."

Alex gazed in her eyes, gulped.

She pressed the glasses to her face then stepped backward. "I'll be careful. Catch you on the flippity-flip."

He smirked then waited. He let Lewis climb in the van first, followed, then closed the sliding door behind them.

"And we are live, people." Edward spoke into the walkie-talkie. "We see you on the screens. Good placement."

Across the multiple screens, Cameron paced the living room with the EMF detector in front of him.

"I'm Cam Gallo . . ." He pointed the camera at himself, was about to do his usual announcement but stopped to fix the spikes in his hair.

Erin walked in, raised an eyebrow.

"What? This could be the one that lands us a big film festival. I'm the face of this operation."

Pastor Art aimed the handheld thermometer like a cowboy gun. "I got a cold spot."

The other two joined him.

"Yeah." The preacher waved his hand around in front of him. "I got a couple, one down there and one right here. Feel that."

Erin copied, swishing her hand through the air. "Ooh, it's freezing."

She then lifted the voice recorder up.

"Got another one here." Cameron poked an arm in the nearest room. "Has that happened before? Is that normal?"

Alex turned to Lewis who nodded.

"That's an affirmative."

"Listen up. I know what you been doing to this couple. I saw what you did to that poor woman. You pushed her away, drove her out. Ruined their marriage."

Pastor Art showed Erin the thermometer reading. She recorded it on video.

Cameron straightened. "Why don't you come try that with me? Huh?"

"Hey . . ." Edward pointed to the screen. "Catch that?"

Alex and Lewis leaned in.

"There it is again. I saw it earlier, too."

"Um. Pastor, we got a kinda glitch or blip thing happening. It keeps materializing near you. Not constantly but tends to come and go."

"I appreciate the heads up." He turned left then right. "Let's finish this sweep. Between cold spots and whatever those guys are seeing, I say we go lights off. The place is small enough we can cover it in time."

Cameron lifted the EMF detector, moved it sideways. "We did get kind of a late start."

"True."

Erin switched from video camera to still camera, began to take picture after picture. She paused, hesitated with her finger on the button.

Alex kept his eye on her through the screen.

"Don't be nervous. 'Member, Erin?"

She smiled, nodded, and took the shot.

Pastor Art glanced at the others then went to the main switches. "Good to go?"

"Just about."

With that last camera flash, Pastor Art started flicking the lights off. It was the porch, living room, kitchen, hallway. Cameron turned off the two bedrooms and the bathroom, leaving them all in darkness.

They each activated their flashlights, inadvertently distorting their faces as if they had scary stories to tell in the dark.

"Split up."

Cameron switched to night vision then navigated through the furniture in the living room. Pastor Art stepped into the kitchen, walked alongside the counter and cabinets. Erin went to the first bedroom, peeked inside, shining her flashlight.

"Just wanna point out, that fucking globe scared the shit out of me."

Alex and Edward held back a light chuckle. Lewis kept his flat affect, unamused.

"Happens to us all."

Despite multiple cold spots and the false alarm of the globe, nothing else occurred during the first shift. They were thorough, patient, checked then rechecked, but it was a dead end.

Cameron handed his equipment to Edward. Erin handed her equipment to Alex.

Pastor Art offered to do double duties but Lewis interjected at the last second.

"Wait, wait." The man fidgeted, shut his eyes. ". . . I'll try."

"Good on ya."

"You sure? You don't have to do this."

Lewis swallowed, hung his jaw. "No. I can do it."

"Also, gentlemen." Pastor Art peeked at the clock, then stared each of them straight in the eye. "It's witching hour."

Edward leaned in, explained. "Three o'clock in the morn."

"Is that . . . not good?"

"Supposed to be peak time for supernatural activity." Edward waved a hand. "But, I mean, that's word on the street, from folklore and stuff. It could be bull."

The second group went down and got started right away. No activity in their sweep with the lights on so they cut the lights for the next.

Alex panned the bedroom with the night vision on his camera. This time, there was no woman lying there in wait, in heat. He watched the still curtains in the small screen, the tall dresser, the open closet.

Lewis stayed near Edward by the kitchen then to the living room. Both shined a flashlight through the pitch black, illuminating each piece of furniture.

When Alex finished the last bedroom, he stepped in the hall, catching Edward at the end just about to turn.

All of a sudden, he shouted and leapt back.

"Oh, my God!"

Lewis shuddered, stumbling over himself from the movement and sound.

Without thinking, Alex rushed ahead. "What? What is it?"

"I just fucking saw her." Edward widened his eyes.

Alex waved the camera over his colleague, recording his short sharp gasps and mild perspiration.

"That was chilling."

Pastor Art broke through the walkie-talkie. "Can you describe what you saw?"

"I mean, like Alex said before, she was a total knockout.

Stunning. Sitting on the edge of the bathtub with not a thing on." Edward swallowed. "Like, waving her finger to me and licking her lips."

Lewis stood in the doorframe. "Kinda like Marilyn Monroe or something, right?"

"Was she blond?" Pastor Art was choppy with static.

"Uh . . ."

Lewis crossed his arms. "Actually, she's a redhead. Thin with fair skin. Her hair in a tight braid to one side."

"I did see a blonde. She had short wavy hair." Alex leaned against the wall, glanced into the surveillance camera lens.

Edward turned to Alex and Lewis. "Brunette. Voluptuous."

"That's interesting. Huh."

"Well, I suppose—"

Right then and there, they heard the cabinets and drawers in the kitchen shoot open and each door around them slammed one by one.

Edward bent forward in a half-squat, about to collapse. Lewis held a hand over his chest, grimacing, arching his neck.

Alex was crouched. "Jesus Christ. Is everyone okay?"

"Generally, yeah."

"One of the most terrifying moments of my life but sure."

They began to take video of the bedroom and bathroom doors. The kitchen appeared as if a tornado had blown through.

"Guys. I swear, there's . . ." Edward walked to the back door.

"What, Ned?"

As Alex followed, he could also hear it. He lifted the voice recorder up.

Lewis dragged behind.

There was a light squeak as Edward swung the door open to

the trees out back, where an ungodly inhuman scream continually echoed through the air.

Alex felt all the energy drain from his limbs then, both knees becoming wobbly. "Holy fuckin' shit . . ."

Edward took a timid step, was about to enter the trees when Lewis fell forward on all fours, grunting. His eyes were closed, teeth gritted. He trembled in place then jerked, jerked, jerked until he rolled on his side then onto his back.

The two were powerless, watched the poor man with their lower lips hanging.

By the time Pastor Art arrived with bible in hand, it had subsided. Erin hurried with the first aid kit and Cameron brought some ice.

&

When the group returned to do the blessing, Pastor Art knocked on the door once again but there was no response. He tried knocking even louder, even harder, ringing the doorbell, but it was more of the same. Alex tried listening inside but couldn't hear anything definitive. It was already a longer delay so they began to worry. Erin crossed her arms and tapped one of her feet. Alex stepped back, stood next to her, placing both hands on the back of his hips. Tilting his head, touching the lining of his coat, Pastor Art leaned and pushed the button again. Cameron went around the side of the house. Edward followed.

"Lewis! Lewis Casey!"

"Lew? You all right in there?"

There was a muffle back through the wall then rummaging. The front door opened but it was kept ajar, with the chain and deadbolt firm. That same droopy eyeball peeked out.

Alex could see his eye was blackened and his cheek bruised.

"Go away . . ."

"We're here to help put a stop to this, Lew. As planned."

"No. You'll just make things worse." There was a watery sheen in his bloodshot eye. "Please. Please go away."

Pastor Art placed a hand near the doorframe, leaned on it. "Of course you're scared. I understand. We all understand. But let us try to help you."

"No. No, no. There is only one way out." Lewis faced down and shook his head. "I see that now. I know exactly what to do."

The man blinked, sniffled, then closed the door.

"Lewis!!!"

"Lew!?"

"Don't do this. Don't turn us away."

Cameron was about to go to the side again but Pastor Art grabbed him by the arm, motioned to Erin and Alex. He led them all back to the van.

Edward lingered. "Lew! Lew! Lew!!!"

One by one, they got in. Cameron sat in the driver's seat, squeezed the steering wheel. Pastor Art opened the sliding door, let Alex and Erin climb into the back seat. He went to the middle seat. Edward took his time before entering into the passenger seat.

"Can we really let him do this?" Erin poked her head out. "Or not do this?"

"We don't have much choice. Can't force a blessing. It doesn't work that way, for one. But two, it's also a matter of legality, and ethics."

"You think he might do something stupid?"

Pastor Art buckled the seat belt. "I have a few friends in the police force. I'll ask one of them to do a wellness check, maybe keep an eye out."

Cameron tapped the steering wheel. "We didn't even get to go over this being a possible succubus. I did all that extra research on sirens, too."

"Succubi."

Alex turned to Erin. "You like that word, don't you?"

He then felt a vibration in his pocket, checked but ignored it.

Why the hell is he *calling . . . ?*

Edward glanced once more at the closed front door. "This sucks balls."

"I know. Couldn't have put it better myself, Mister Berenson."

4

FROM RACK TO rack, through the different bins and now at the end of the long aisle, he stayed close behind carrying the items of clothing on hangers. Alex held them across his forearm with a subtle smirk across his face. He locked eyes on her, tracing her every movement, catching a glimpse of her dazzly ears as she shifted from side to side and then a sliver of her lower back when she bent forward. April gave a lecherous smile in return, turning around and flashing the cutesy girly panties for his approval to which he nodded, nodded. This kind of fashion store and the task of shopping was never that big deal of a deal to him. He always remained patient, curious. She tended to make it light and fun and quick.

Alex waited outside by the wide mirror, tilted his head at an angle enough to peep beneath the dressing room door where he saw her ankles bounce, changing from one outfit to the next. When she had a nice one that she liked, she stepped out and pranced around with it draped over her. April would spin in a circle for him when he twirled his finger. He scanned her up and down, jutted out his lower lip and raised a brow as if to say, hey, not bad.

No matter how crazy things can get, at least I come back home to this . . .

"That looks great on you, my precious. I'm gonna have to fight dudes off constantly."

"Just for you, Nex."

She hopped over to him barefoot and pecked him on the cheek.

Both checked if the clerk paid any attention then kissed again, on the lips, open mouthed.

This was the first destination on their planned day of adventure. April kept busy with her sales job and part-time school work, and of course Alex kept busy with his customer service job as well as investigating nights and weekends. The hours between the store and the credit union didn't quite match either so they found their free time together was cut down, meaning they had to make it count.

Relaxing at home was easy enough, cuddling and making love, but they did take the extra effort to always try to go out too.

After the two dropped off the large shopping bags to the car, they went to go get their latest obsession and craving, a new trendy delectable treat: customizable caramel and choco- late covered apples.

He put his arm around her shoulders. She put her arm around his hip. With their free hands, they both reached and interlocked fingers in a funky joint walking yoga position that only the two of them could somehow manage to fit. They often joked they were the perfect match, like they were specifically made for one another.

Both peeked through the pane of glass, brainstorming their next concoction. The bright green apples on sticks were dipped in caramel then in a wide variety of chocolate and choices of toppings. There was milk chocolate, white chocolate, dark chocolate. There was different sizes of sprinkles, different kinds of candies, sliced and chopped pieces of nuts, crumbles of cookies, cake, cheesecake, graham crackers or pie crust, even small chunks of fudge.

"I heart these new kinda apple and yogurt places."

"Hell yeah. Part of the fun, getting to make it your own way."

"And plus, we can tell ourselves it's 'healthy,' right?"

They each snickered.

Walking from the parking lot to the community theater, the two held hands and swung their arms between them in a playful manner. It was a slight incline alongside a quiet walking path lined with bushes and plants. Both had dressed up for the occasion, him in a nice blazer and her in a new scarf and new boots. They could see the back of the building behind the pine trees. A flock of birds flew in formation in the vast skies past. April had heard from a co-worker about how the place ran this big fundraiser and was able to do major renovations, and now a slate of new plays was out for the season. Alex pulled her hand to his lips and kissed the back of it like from a classic black and white movie.

"This is pretty cool, huh." She hugged around his upper arm.

"Sophisti-ma-cated."

"Guess we're trying to be more extroverted introverts versus our usual introverted extrovert selves."

He glanced over at the crowd gathered. There were fine

gentlemen shaking hands as if they were at a ribbon cutting ceremony. A few middle-aged couples made their rounds, holding copies of the program and hovering over each informational display about the director and the actors. There was a line of women standing together in front of the velvet ropes, one of them handing their cell phone to an attendant to take their picture. They wore a mix of low cut, high slit, low back.

"Ooh, champaña." She gestured with her fingers like a little chef's kiss.

"I'll go grab us a couple."

Alex came back, joined April in back of the short will call line. The sun started to set.

"Here you are, love."

They clinked their glasses together. He lifted a pinky up as they took a sip, almost causing her to spit it up.

"Dude, O-M-G. You almost killed me."

"A bit much?" He laughed.

Beneath the flashy lights of the arched marquee, the air conditioning was steady and cool. On either side of the doors were framed posters of an upcoming musical production.

Inside, the slanted and curved rows were already almost full. They found their row and number in the appropriate section, sat down on the cushioned seats under the overhang of the balcony. The lights were dim. The curtains were pulled. A few props littered the stage, waiting to be utilized. It was quiet except for polite commentary.

Alex panned around at all the designs along the walls and on each pillar. It was grated in some areas, gold plated in other areas. The ceiling had a circular window in the middle, and large subtle murals that blended into the surroundings.

When the play started and each actor performed their

movements and read their lines, the magic and the glitz dissipated and they both found themselves a bit bored. April covered yawn after yawn with the back of her hand. Alex tried to keep his eyes open, his head up. His new schedule and sleep cycle didn't help matters. It was a struggle but they made it to intermission and migrated with the crowd back outside.

"You like it so far?" He put his arm around her waist.

They stood at the edge of the gathered mob.

"It's pretty cool. Being all artsy and stuff, getting dolled up."

"Agreed." He leaned in, whispered. "It's a bit slower than I thought it would be. Maybe we could be more careful which play we choose next time. Something funner, faster."

"Still, it is kinda the experience."

"You . . ." He cupped a hand to her dazzly ear. "You wanna ditch?"

"Oh, that's fucked up. But yeah, please."

Hand in hand, they snuck away with a side step then a brisk walk back down the hill to the parking lot. They had a matching smirk and smile. This turned into bawled laughter the minute they entered the car.

Alex clicked his seat belt, turned the ignition, shifted into reverse.

"We. Are. Assholes."

April wiped away a happy tear from the corner of her eye as they exited.

"Now what?"

"It's been a while since we went to our little secret spot. 'Somewhere Only We Know.' Let's go."

He rubbed up and down her thigh as the road unfolded before them.

She hopped out, led the way with an excited chortle. He

followed with his hands in his pockets, gazing at her from behind.

They each laid on the poofy grass then stared up at the sky.

"Do you see it?"

"Yup. It's right there." Alex scooted and pointed. "Between those two clouds."

"Our shroom . . ."

She took a deep breath in and out, leaned back, melting away.

"Never does get old."

For some reason, her words seemed to hit him then—deep in his sternum where his heartbeat slowed, almost stopped altogether. He found himself blinking, drifting off.

This is it.

What better time. What better place.

For a while, he kept the two promise rings hidden in their dresser but started carrying them around in case if there was a good opportunity.

"Hey. I got these a while back and been waiting for the perfect moment." He pulled them out and held them in front of her eyes.

"Oh, wow. Nex . . . I don't even know what to say . . ."

"Gimme your hand."

Alex took one of the rings and slid it onto the fourth finger of her left hand, then took the other ring and did the same on his.

"Shiny." April let out a wide smile.

Both had come a long way in their relationship, from just friends to the friend zone, to friends with benefits, In a Relationship status, and now this.

"These are great! Thank you oh, so much." She rolled over

and hugged him tight. "Yours is kind of plain silver with this simple curve and mines is more exaggerated with jewels all on it."

"Put 'em together and it's kind of a heart." He put his hand next to hers. "See?"

"I get it."

Each of their hands hovered side by side against the stars twinkling. It was like they were reaching for the very heavens.

April nibbled her bottom lip. "So, what does this mean?"

"Uh, I thought about that actually." He thinned his lips, fought back a smile. "I was thinking it means that we're 'engaged to be engaged.' In fact, maybe we could have a nice extended engagement."

"I like the sound of that."

Her peck on the cheek became a soft and slow kiss, and then passionate fondling and making out.

"You're not gonna hurt me, are you?"

"Never, love."

Alex rolled over, clasping fingers and squeezing her hands, pressed his body onto hers. April wrapped her legs around his lower torso, pulling him in tight. Their tongues slithered in sync as they writhed on the ground, tilting their heads one way then the other.

Back when they took psych class together, neither of them realized but they were also working their way well through Erikson's stages of development.

First, trust versus mistrust, then identity versus role confusion, and now, intimacy versus isolation.

✍

Around them, other couples clinked their glassware and

silverware, made quiet chitchat which was both meaningful and meaningless. The two of them sat against the far wall on the raised table, still waiting but enjoying the moment, taking in all of the ambience and decor. Each table had the flickering warm glow from short candles in small glass holders, almost like a fancy luminaria. Tasteful and elegant paintings with elaborate frames and subtle mats hung from the walls. April rested a cheek in her palm. Alex interlocked his fingers over the table. Both gazed into one another's eyes without a peep, their promise rings visible.

Then they reached across the table, slid together their left hands and squeezed them, rings touching.

"You know, that surprise message the other day was sooo cute." She smiled. "I should have known there was something up your sleeve, even before Serling Park."

Between them, they had several games for the DS Lite. However, there was only one that they both had a separate copy of and played together often. It was a simulation game where they lived in villages with anthropomorphic animals. He would collect seashells, dig up fossils and sell them to the museum. She would collect fruits, catch fish and sell them to the aquarium.

When he last visited in the game, Alex noticed the mailbox in front of her two-story house and thought to send her a short and sweet love letter.

"All this time and I just found that feature."

The server placed down a carafe of malbec and two pristine wine glasses, pouring a splash of the red liquid. She raised it up first, waited for him, and they both touched the rim of the edge together before a nice long sip.

"It's another fun filled time, as always. One of the best. But

I also can't help but feel, like, maybe something is on your mind or something too. Everything okay, Nex?"

"Yeah, I'm good. I . . ."

He crinkled his brow, faced down to the white of the tablecloth.

Should I tell her? Finally?

No, not that. But I probably have to soon.

I can tell her the other thing, though.

"After the last job, I got a call from my dad. It's been bothering me a little, but came on strong during the drive."

"Oh."

"You know how I told you we don't really get along, have kind of a rocky relationship? I'm not even sure what happened but one awkward thing led to another, and we had this pretty bad fight over the phone."

"What was it about?"

"Ah, I don't really wanna get into details. In a nutshell, he didn't get why I'm working customer service when I got my degree now. I told him it's a fucking recession. Have you seen the news??? There's mass layoffs. Unemployment rate is through the roof. Companies are going out of business. Government furloughs. And I'm this new grad with zero experience."

She stared with soft eyes and a soft smile, rubbing his fingertips.

"Whatever."

"It's okay, Nex."

Alex shrugged his shoulders, sighed.

Both paused as the server placed down two small empty plates and then a large plate of pear and gorgonzola salad with walnuts.

"Changing the subject a little, maybe we should go see *your* dad? I mean, it's not far to the border, over to Vancouver."

"Yeah, maybe. It's not like we're cool or anything either. I haven't seen that guy in a long-ass time. So weird."

The server came back with a pizza tray stand and put down their thin crust with spinach, garlic and mushrooms.

"Another way we go together perfectly, huh?"

"What? That we're all screwed up from disastrous parental units?"

"Pretty much."

5

IT STILL WEIGHED heavy on his mind as he walked down the ramp between levels. Alex passed by pillars and cars on either side of him through the parking garage. There were two young female nurses walking in the opposite direction, one in blue scrubs and one in black scrubs. There was a bulky security guard taking his time making rounds on the far end of the lane. When Alex got to the elevator, a woman with a walker was waiting with an older man in a power scooter so he decided to take the stairs instead. He turned the corner near the entrance as the barrier gate arm raised then went straight.

Sad to say, but that bastard does have a point.

Grr.

Just my luck with this recession . . .

Alex turned one way then the other, wondering which way to go. He had forgotten since the last time. There were four main buildings making a kind of E-shape, and another building and lot in back but it was still under construction. In the middle of the grounds was a long grassy median. Up ahead, he saw an area for drop off and pick up, and decided to head that way.

He entered the automatic sliding doors into the lobby. An

empty reception desk had a box of tissues, multiple pamphlets and a telephone and placard if anybody needed further assistance. Alex heard a light ding, was about to jog over to the open elevator but Pastor Art stepped out in front of him.

"Oh, hey."

They did a quick hug.

"Deids didn't mention you were coming. Good to see you."

"What you doin' here, Pastor?"

The preacher motioned with his head, led them to a line of fancy cushioned seats near a grand piano.

"Same as you, I suppose. Came to see 'er off before the switch back. I already took a bunch of her stuff to drop off, help out a bit."

"Nice. Probably a pain in the ass."

"A little. But I'm so dang proud of her. It's the least I can do."

"I mean, she's lucky to be alive, let alone start walking again. And to come as far as she has in her recovery."

"Every day above ground is a good day." Pastor Art smiled wide, leaned one elbow on the armrest. "You know . . ."

Alex raised a brow, waited for him to continue.

"We dance on that line a lot with what we do, between life and the afterlife. But we never do talk about death itself. Life is so precious. It's all a great big miracle."

Pastor Art waved a hand in the air as he spoke.

"Like, what's the chances you agreed to help with this in the first place? We never would have met otherwise. Even today, running into each other. One minute could have made all the difference. A single minute within twenty-four hours. That's life."

He nodded, twisted the corner of his lips. "So true."

"Well. Death is a part of life, too. There's so much to say about death. Some people have seen the face of death, in tragedy, in war. Some people have come close to the brink but still live on."

"A-are you afraid of dying?"

"No." The preacher shook his head. "No, my life is in God's hands. So I face death with a smile on. In fact, God has conquered death."

"Like, the hooded figure with a big scythe?"

"C'mon. The real death. People think of 'death' as something like that, a wraith or the grim reaper. But that's not really how it is. I mean, maybe. Again, there's just things we can't and won't know. Not 'til we are on the other side. Even beyond that."

"Right, right."

"I didn't get to say before since our last blessing never happened. I meant to. But there is a certain link between death and water. If you remember, that client mentioned his place was near the water, meaning the lake."

Alex narrowed his eyes, perked his ears up.

"There is sometimes more activity near bodies of water like that. Something about water. Like, water is life. It's essential and nourishing. All life could not exist without water, plain and simple as that. But also, water is death. When you get baptized, for example, you're fully immersed. The old you dies and the new you lives. When they stabbed Jesus in the side on the cross, what came out? Not to mention, Jesus walked on water. Now, all these are symbolic of overcoming death."

"Hmm."

"So, to return to your earlier question. Am I afraid of death? No way. Not a chance. I'm not afraid of dying. There is only one death that I fear. And that's in the midst of the four beasts, at the end of it all. Riding in on a pale horse."

⌘

The second he saw Deidre again, a still image of her wearing the hospital gown and lying in the hospital bed flashed through his mind. He remembered the dried blood, remembered the cuts. Alex blinked, flinched in disbelief, hand still on the door handle. Before him, she was back to her beautiful and elegant self. She faced away to the open window, sat on the edge of the bed wearing a short denim jacket over a flowy dress. When the door closed, she noticed him and turned around. He stood with his jaw hanging, not moving. She hopped off the bed and stepped towards him, only the slightest noticeable limp, using a nearby chair for leverage.

Both wrapped their arms around and hugged tight, swaying as they did so. He could feel a warmth between them.

"You look a little tired there, Alex." She kept her hands on his arms.

He shook his head, smirked. "It is so good to see you. Just, wow."

"Not getting enough sleep at night, huh." Deidre winked. "In more ways than one."

"Yeah, yeah. I'm still getting used to the case schedule."

She shifted, bent to grab a cane that leaned against the drawer. It had a light metallic blue sheen. "This was the coolest one they had in their stash. Believe it or not."

"Actually, kind of matches the ensemble."

"Pastor Art updated me on a few of the cases you guys have worked. Sounds like you went straight to the top. Some pretty hardcore evidence and encounters. Even I haven't experienced some of that."

He nodded, faced to the floor.

"Sorry." Deidre moved to the edge of the bed again. "I fatigue easily still. Trying to get my endurance up."

Alex sat down next to her. He nibbled his bottom lip, twisted on the ball of his foot.

Deidre shifted, stared at him from the side. "You're holding something back. Aren't you? Like, you wanna say, ask, but . . ."

"There's a lot on my mind." He sighed. "It'll be fine, though."

Although she was right, a part of him did want to get it off his chest, did want to ask her for her sound advice, another part just wanted to keep it bottled up. His conflicted feelings about his dad and their recent argument. His lingering guilt for not telling the whole truth to his now unofficial fiancée.

It was easier to keep lying, to himself, to the world, than to tell the truth—kind of breaking a rule for both LIFE101L and LOVE102.

"Ever since I met you, this has been your way."

He lifted his head and tilted towards her.

"You kind of have this . . . wall . . . you try to hide behind."

"I don't know. Pretty sure that wasn't always the case. But somewhere along the way, that changed."

"Well, I can tell you, there is definitely something on the horizon. I can feel it. I can sense it. Remember I told you there was a reason you and only you could help with this?"

Alex narrowed his eyes.

"That particular something you're supposed to find . . . That particular someone you're supposed to run into . . . Any moment now. Very, very soon."

"Is it bad?"

"I'm not sure of that, Alex."

He slouched and took a deep breath.

She nudged at him with a shrugged shoulder.

Alex smirked. "You excited to finally get outta here?"

"I am happy they had an open slot in their special program and all. I am happy to be doing better, but I gladly walk away."

"Literally."

"Yup, literally." Deidre licked her lips then smiled. "I wish I was done-done but no, I'll still be coming for more rehab. I'm good enough to discharge but still not hundred percent."

"That's good."

"Before we know, I'll be back at it and you won't have to help anymore. Unless you want to, of course. I'd be happy to keep you on. You have an undeniable gift."

"I'll think about it, I guess."

She laughed.

"Almost there. Maybe just a few more weeks."

❧

When he took the elevator back down to the first floor, Alex was about to exit through the lobby but noticed a sign for the courtyard. He glanced at the automatic sliding doors and the cushioned seats next to the grand piano where he and Pastor Art talked. Then he turned and glanced in the opposite direction, a short hall with an ATM, a couple of vending machines and another set of sliding doors. For some reason, he felt like meandering a little longer. Alex kicked one foot at the floor and waltzed with his hands in his pockets.

It was peaceful in that area. A few doves hopped on the grass then flew up into a lush tree with long branches. He stood and took it all in. An array of tables and chairs scattered across the right side where he saw co-workers gathered for lunch, venting, joking. To the left, there was a rock wall lined with several metal plaques. There was a single raised stage for special events in the middle. Behind, an angled building and smaller parking lot was still under construction, taped off and walled off.

He plodded forward then sat down at a bench, leaned forward.

This is just what he needed: a little peace and quiet to clear his head.

Oh, man.

How did it come to this?

For a moment, he remembered his plotted scheme to travel abroad and go to grad school. Alex twisted at the promise ring on his finger.

What am I even doing?

He arched his neck, faced up to the overcast skies between buildings. If the main complex was an E-shape, this space was like an accent mark over the E.

On the one hand, Alex loved this girl and loved his new life with this girl. On the other hand, this was not part of his master plan. Maybe that was the reason what his father said left an extra throbbing ache to the already painful sting, like an extremely powerful venom coursing through his veins. And, to top it all off, now he hunted ghosts of all things.

I think I have to tell her. It's time.

Hashing things out with the old man can wait. Fine, sure.

But she deserves to know the truth at least. If we're going to eventually get married, there can be no secrets between us.

No more lying like the piece of shit I am.

6

WHILE THE OTHERS went to take the van like normal, Alex and Pastor Art planned to run a quick errand first. Cameron nodded with his chin. Edward displayed a lazy peace sign. Erin flittered her fingers in a light wave then followed. Alex watched them load in then entered the passenger seat. He heard the preacher rode an old muscle car but never saw it for himself. The engine was loud as the vehicle started up and he could feel the powerful torque. Alex reached across and clicked the seat belt. Before the van pulled away from the back lot past the muscle car parked on the street, he and Erin locked eyes through the glass.

Pastor Art faced ahead, remained quiet. The surface of the road was littered with dry leaves. It was only a short drive.

"Hold on. Just wait right here."

Alex readjusted in his seat when the preacher got out and grabbed a big cardboard box from the trunk. He saw him carry it to the building ahead. A middle-aged woman greeted him, held the door open. With a big smile and a big hug, she thanked him and let him back out.

"Sorry to keep you."

"No prob. Donation?"

"Yeah."

"That's pretty nice."

"Kinda what I do."

Pastor Art glanced in the rearview mirror, rotated the wheel with his palm as he reversed.

"I coulda just dropped it off tomorrow but thought what the heck. Plus, I did want to talk to you."

He felt the gears shift as they made their way again. "Oh, yeah?"

"Deids is about fully recovered, will be back at it. A matter of time. She mentioned inviting you to stay on." Pastor Art shook his head. "I don't know, Alexander."

"I haven't decided anything."

"Right. Guess I would caution against that, in all honesty." The preacher squeezed his hands on the steering wheel, causing the knuckles to whiten. "You still got a whole life ahead of you. You and your girlyfriend. I just . . . I don't want to see anything happen to you."

Alex swallowed a dry lump.

"Like, the truth is, we haven't come across anything super, super dangerous. Anything that is pure evil or pure hatred. With a kind of malicious intent."

He nodded, gazed out the window at the houses and buildings whizzing past.

"Not all cases end with a little treehouse of horror in the yard."

"I hear you, Pastor. Thank you."

"This next one could be a bad one. I want you to know that going in. Be extra on guard, because who knows what might happen."

⸙

It was the second to last house on the corner of 28th and Hartley. The same one he had heard stories about before, and the same one he and April saw on one of their treks. Alex scanned the dull yellow-beige wood panels, the angled roof, the fluffy grass and the light gray fence. There was a small tree to the side, a big tree in back, a few bushes, stones lined and then a paved circle. He remembered the specific window that stood out to him as well as the hollow feeling it gave off. Darkened clouds loomed over the sliver of moon as the five of them stood before the unseeming house. Unbeknownst to them, this place would act as a gate, a doorway, a vortex, a portal.

They all stood together in an upside down pentagonal shape while Pastor Art did his spiel. When the other three walked to the front steps, Alex waited with his hands at his sides, head hanging down. After the preacher checked in and exchanged a few words, Alex glanced up once more.

No goin' back now . . .

Here it is.

The so-called Demon House of Lower Bloom Hill.

Pastor Art went up first, waited for him by the door frame. Alex hesitated then moved forward like a stolid crane.

"Okay, come now. Wake up. Wake up."

He could hear the gentle voice behind the door.

"Look. The good people are here. They're going to help us."

"The . . . The good people, Mommy . . . ?"

"Yes. Let's get ready so we can get out of their way. Time to go to the other house."

"But I don't wanna go."

"I know, I know. Only a little longer, Helena. That's why they're here."

Alex watched the kind exchange between vibrant mother and innocent daughter while passing through the entryway by the kitchen. She appeared way too young to be a mother of two, and still with extraordinary beauty. Her skin and hair were immaculate. Her movement and mannerisms were graceful.

Still sound asleep like an angel on the scatter of comforters and pillows over the spongy trifold futon was her even younger son. Both appeared to be toddler age.

"Ian, Ian. Wake up now."

The young woman tapped his cheek with a light and soft touch, leaning over.

"Hello. I'm Arturo Selga. Just call me Pastor Art."

He reached forward to shake the woman's hand. It happened to be the same hand that touched the toddler on the cheek.

"Nice to meet you. It might take me a little while to get all of your names. Sorry. I am Ayame Moriguchi."

"This is Alexander."

Alex considered shaking her hand but waved instead. Perhaps there was too much on his mind to be sociable.

"Um. We usually give Alexander some space so he can feel any vibrations, any energies within the home."

"That's fine. I have to help the kids get ready."

"I see you're all sleeping together in the living room?"

"Correct. By far, it has been the safest place and it helps if we stay close. We always keep a few lights on."

"Okay. We can chat more 'fore you guys head out."

Edward and Cameron set the equipment down, sat and talked amongst themselves. It was the usual planning out the procedure, considering placement of the equipment.

Erin touched Alex on the wrist as he passed.

"Hey. You all right?"

"Yeah." He paused, narrowed his eyes. "Pastor Art is kind of right, though. Something is different this time. Something is off."

She squeezed his wrist then let go before he continued.

For a brief moment, Alex and the little girl made eye contact. The girl blinked, displayed a smile then turned away, facing her mother again. He glanced down at the little boy now beginning to roll around and reach his arms out. The three huddled together on the mass of sheets.

That scene, the mother and daughter, the son, it brought back memories of the framed photos on the wall of his Aunty Divina and of Lucio and Merced.

I wonder how they're doing . . .

Never did get to meet Merced, but hopefully one day.

Hopefully see you all again. Soon.

Alex panned the living room, noticed the large flat screen in the large entertainment center, a wide sound bar across the front. Behind him was a rectangular dining table where Cameron and Edward sat down. Inside the kitchen, there was a separate counter in the middle of the space lined with marble countertops. The refrigerator, stove and dishwasher were all brand new stainless steel.

He stepped along the back of the burgundy sectional surrounding a glass coffee table and went to the bottom of the stairs. There was a bathroom to the right where he saw the girl help the boy brush his teeth on tiptoe on a sturdy box in front of the sink. The mother reached in a closet beneath the stairs to the left of him, pulled out some luggage.

Each carpeted stair had nice padding to it. It was a comfy, cozy feeling as if it was his own home. It was a few steps, a landing, a few steps left, another landing, and another few steps left. Alex pivoted, touched the rail by the washing machine and dryer. There was a master bedroom with its own bathroom, two smaller bedrooms and a shared bathroom between them. He walked room by room until he found himself on the other side of that one eerie window. From the second floor, he glanced down and envisioned him and April standing on the sidewalk— him still full emo, her still full punk.

God. I've come such a long way.

Funny how much can change.

Alex plodded back down the comfy carpeted stairs.

"Did you sense anything?"

"Not really. When I first came in, there was a tiny something. But as I moved further in the house, it became less and less."

"Hmm." The preacher nodded, thinned his lips. "That's okay."

"Mommy, will the good people make the lady with the melted face go away?"

An icy chill pierced through the air then. Cameron and Edward raised their heads and peeked over. Erin tilted her body at an angle, half-turned in that direction. Alex shifted in place next to her, eyes widened.

Pastor Art folded his arms. "Shall we talk now?"

The woman faced up from the floor, still packing. "Just

about. Ian, Helena. Why don't you two go play? Mommy needs to talk to the good people, tell them all that's been happening."

"But it's scary up there."

It seemed the boy was not yet able to talk. The girl spoke for both of them.

Erin walked over to the two children, knelt down. "You want me to come with you? Show off your toys?"

"Can he guard the stairs? He's big like Superman."

Shaking his head, Cameron went to the bottom of the stairs and leaned against the wall.

"He is big like Superman. See? He can protect us from down here."

Cameron flexed his arm, showing off his bicep.

"Good. Because the lady with the melted face is a bad, bad lady. She likes to stand next to me when I comb in the mirror." The little girl jutted out her lower lip. "She will comb, comb, comb, and then move her hair away from her face. But she has no face. No eyes. No mouth. No nose. Nooothing."

"Oh, no." Erin swallowed, bent down lower. "That is awful."

Alex let out a slow breath then joined them, hunching over.

"Me and her and the rest of these guys, even Superman there, we are going to help you and your mommy. It's going to be just fine. You'll see."

"Promise?"

He smirked with a pinky out. "I promise."

The girl curled her own tiny finger around his.

"Cross my heart and hope to die."

"I'll tell them everything. Okay, Helena? You and Ian go play now. The scary lady can't hurt us if the good people are here."

After the little boy and little girl followed Erin to the second floor, Cameron stuck a crooked thumb out from crossed arms. Edward noticed, nodded back then turned. Pastor Art and Alex circled the space and sat down on one side of the sectional. Ayame sat on the opposite side, closer to the middle of the living room. She glanced left then right at each of their faces, bringing her hands together and dangling them between her thighs. They were all quiet, waited. It was obvious she fought back a wave of tears from overwhelming fear and frustration that had been pent up, blinking her eyes and nibbling her lips in order to do so.

"No rush. Take your time."

The preacher's hushed voice gave the slightest of nudges.

"It's been eighty-four days since my husband deployed. Not even three months." Ayame shook her head. "Things are already tough, even if Patrick was still here."

"Your husband's military?" Edward spoke up from the dining table.

She nodded.

"Go on." Pastor Art cleared his throat.

Alex leaned forward.

"Whenever you relocate, it's always this big scramble. Quit your old job. Find a new job, interview. Pack and move. Find a new place, apply. Move and then unpack." Ayame faced down to the floor. "At least Patrick was able to help us get settled."

Cameron leaned to the side and peeked up the stairs.

"I have to drop off Ian to day care. I have to drop off Helena to preschool. Then, of course, I still gotta pick them up too." Her hands began to tremble. "You know, when we came to view the house, I did have this strange feeling. But I didn't wanna say anything at the time. It was one of the longest days that day and we had already looked at so many places."

Edward ran a hand through his beard.

Pastor Art straightened up.

"Only a day or two after my husband flew out, almost on cue, I saw something . . ."

Alex brushed the bangs out of his eyes.

"When I was holding Ian tight one morning, I stared right into his eyes. He can smile so big it makes his eyeball shimmer, and I just love losing myself in them. But there was a kind of smudge or something, a blur, and it moved in the reflection of his eye . . . That was the very first instance."

"That's pretty damn creepy." Cameron shuddered.

Ayame rubbed the sides of her arms. "I didn't think much of it at the time. I turned and there was nothing there so . . . But I did start to feel like there was a presence here and there. I can't explain it. Like, if I walked from the bottom of the stairs to the kitchen for a glass of water, it felt like something would follow me. If I laid down to sleep, I didn't feel like I was alone in that room. I swear."

"Did the little ones ever encounter anything?"

"Yes, sad to say. And that is when I started to feel really stressed out. My job is to protect them, especially if it's just me here alone. How do you protect them from something like this?"

Edward shook his head.

Pastor Art slumped his shoulders.

"Helena started to see this lady and would scream her head off. If you have a kid, you know how loud they can be. But this was something else. On a whole other level. It was sheer terror." She paused, brought a hand over her mouth. "And then, of course, Ian started to also shout out. He can't talk yet so it's babbling, squealing. I've never seen him like that before."

There was a brief moment of silence.

"It started to happen more frequently. Then, things took a turn when Ian started being scratched at night."

"Oh, God."

"Poor little dude . . ."

"At first, it was one long cut by his knee. I thought maybe he had done it in his sleep. The second was a cut on his back. Same thing, figured it was by accident. Boys will be boys, right. But then it become three parallel cuts, and then four, clearly from fingernails."

Edward stroked his beard again. "Could it be from his sister? Do you have pets? Or maybe he did it to himself?"

"No animals. It would be difficult to scratch between his own shoulders in the pattern I saw that first time. Helena would never do that. She is too kindhearted."

"I see. Hmm."

"The last straw was when he got scratched across his cheek. That's when I looked you guys up and we started spending nights at another military spouse's place. I don't know anyone here and money's tight since we moved not too long ago. Options are limited. She also has a loud dog, and it won't quit barking 'til she's home from work so we have to nap here in the living room in the meantime."

Alex turned around, glanced at the stairs. He visualized a woman in a pink kimono plodding down, slow and steady. Her long black hair obscured her face from view.

He blinked, returned to facing forward. "I don't know why but . . . Have you seen this thing before?"

Before them, Ayame softened to the point she was about to crumble.

"I didn't, no. But I do have a sister. Her name is Akemi. And, when we were little, I remember she also used to cry at night sometimes. She would claim to see all kinds of things actually. My parents never believed her. I wasn't sure if I believed her myself."

So she has a sister . . .

Kinda like Aunty Di and Aunty Sol.

"Once, she saw this lady with a slit mouth. The corners of her lips were cut from ear to ear. Once, she saw a green creature with webbed hands and webbed feet. She spoke many times of different yōkai and of obake, other ghostly beings."

She took a deep breath in and out, as if a great weight lifted from her. There were beads gathered in the corners of her watery eyes.

Pastor Art scooted over, pushed a box of tissues across the table.

"Thank you." She dabbed her cheeks. "I haven't thought about that in years. Back then, me and her grew up in the international school on base. Hard enough fitting in. So, whenever she brought this stuff up, I kind of just played along, played it down. My parents would scold her, tell her she's embarrassing. After a while, she stopped talking about it."

"What about a ghost with no face?"

Ayame blinked, placed both hands on her knees. "You know, Akemi did mention something like that a few times. One of the more common occurrences. She used to call it Kaonashi. I don't know how that could be related, though. It was so long ago."

"There is a chance it's not related. There is a chance it is. We don't know that right now. We don't know anything."

She sniffled, gave a slow nod.

"What is Kaonashi?" Alex interlocked his fingers.

"Kao means 'face.' Nashi is like 'none.' God, that brings me back . . ."

He touched a hand to his chin. "I see."

"Gentlemen. I think we got enough to get started here." Pastor Art turned to Alex then to Edward and Cameron. "Alexander, go and get Erin and the kiddos. Mister Gallo and Mister Berenson, let's get the equipment up and running."

He touched the handrail while going up, peeking down the hall where he saw Erin sitting on the floor. Helena grabbed toy after toy, explaining in great detail their history, traits and personality, showing off their preset capabilities. Ian jumped, rolled around and tumbled in a circle around her.

Alex walked over with a smirk then leaned in the door.

"I'm not sure if I love kids. But they seem to love me." She smiled, pressed the glasses to her face. "At least sometimes, anyway."

"Here." He reached a hand out, helped her up.

They stood face to face as Helena and Ian hugged her around each of her legs.

"I got a new fan club."

"That's cute as hell. Damn."

When they got back downstairs, the others already started setting up. Ayame had the rolling luggage and diaper bag ready.

"Hey. Were you two being good?"

"Yes, Mommy."

"I hope so." Ayame waved to the others who waved back.

"Pastor Art explained how this is gonna work. Thank you all so much."

"Of course."

"Don't mention it."

"And, before we go, I did want to show this . . ." She bent down, lifted up Ian's shirt for them to see. "The latest one."

Down the middle of his soft tummy were four curved lines above the navel. They were flaky dried scabs of dark crimson, pink in some areas where the scabs had come off.

Erin went to the table, grabbed a camera and snapped a picture.

∾

On the multiple screens, Alex and Pastor Art watched as Cameron, Edward and Erin made their way through the house. There were surveillance cameras in the kitchen, the living room, each of the bedrooms, the master bathroom, the hallway in between and then one over the stairs. All of the lights were still on. Cameron pointed the lens back at himself, spinning around and getting a long shot of the living room. Edward took careful and thoughtful photo after photo throughout the kitchen then the entryway and the bottom of the stairs. Erin was already up to the second floor, checked the master bedroom then the master bathroom.

Pastor Art raised the walkie-talkie. "Is there anything?"

"Not yet." She pressed the button which bleeped.

Erin took a deep breath, went to the second bedroom, peeking in. With light footsteps, she scanned the interior. In her other hand was the voice recorder.

Alex watched her on-screen as she walked back into the hall, about to enter the shared bathroom.

"You remember what Helena said?"

"I know."

"Just be careful."

She went into the bathroom just out of sight.

Edward and Cameron turned off the lights in the living room and kitchen then started to head up. When they got to the top, they flicked the switch for the stairs.

"Ready?"

"It was pretty weird standing in front of the mirror after what the little girl described. But nope, nothing."

"All right."

They turned off the remaining lights, blanketing them in complete darkness.

Cameron used night vision on the video camera. "Let's do this thang."

Edward went in the other direction, also changing to night vision on the flipped panel. Erin aimed her flashlight.

"Are you here with us? I heard you scratch innocent children at night. Why don't you come and scratch me then. I'm waiting." Cameron puffed out his chest.

Edward turned around, framing the green and black shot of Cameron. Erin hovered in the background, panning left to right.

The three did their rounds then reconvened back downstairs.

"You guys get any readings?"

"Nothing on EMF, no." Edward shook his head. "Nothing on infrared or ultraviolet. No spikes in temp or drops in temp."

Cameron placed a hand on his hip. "Ain't squat down here either. Laser grids are intact. Motion sensors never went off."

Erin shrugged. "Negatory on any audio anomalies."

"Hmm, so weird."

"Right?"

"This is supposed to be the big, bad house . . ."

Outside the van, they traded off equipment and traded places. Erin sat in front of the split monitors, began to adjust knobs and dials. Cameron and Edward put on their headsets.

Pastor Art led the way and Alex followed.

They did their walk-through, first with the lights on then with the lights off but there was again nothing.

"Well, this is unexpected."

"Sooo bizarre."

The preacher leaned on the handrail at the top of the stairs as Alex flicked the switches. With only a few of the lights back on, it was an interesting scene. Light and shadow created a contrast of black and white.

"You didn't feel anything?"

"No, Pastor."

Both paused for a second.

"In the beginning, I did, but it was pretty minuscule. Later I had that hunch that this might not be entirely new. And nothing since."

Pastor Art shifted in place, rested an elbow on the rail. "Can it be this place isn't haunted?"

"I don't know. It's almost public knowledge."

"You have a point. The others all heard of this old house, mentioned various stories and rumors. But then again, supernatural activity does come and go and rise and fall. It could just be less active right now."

"Have any theories, Pastor?"

"I do got one." The preacher thinned his lips, took a deep breath. "I wonder if this is the power of suggestion at work."

Alex raised an eyebrow.

"What if she was already under such immense levels of stress and then also heard of the place being purportedly haunted? Now, she didn't mention that, but if somebody said an odd comment or asked an odd question, it could have brought back repressed memories."

He listened, nodded.

"Suggestion can affect perception, especially with existing beliefs. In other words, believers are more prone to endorse any occurrence or phenomena. And then add to that the fact children are highly impressionable, of course."

"And the scratches?"

"I mean, she said it herself. Could've happened in the kid's sleep or just been from some roughhousing, perhaps at the day care."

"When I went to get Erin, the boy was pretty hyper."

"See. There you go."

Downstairs, the others came back inside, began to turn the rest of the lights back on.

Pastor Art drummed his fingers on the rail.

Alex scratched his head. "Okay. So now what?"

"I think our true purpose is to help people. And sometimes, helping them is to simply ease their mind. A widow might need some comforting, some closure, for instance. Sometimes a person might just want attention or a distraction. It's almost like a placebo effect."

"Hmm. Kind of like using that same power of suggestion."

"Precisely. Yeah." The preacher faced down to the carpet then faced back up. "We'll do our usual investigation and report, like normal, for show. Do a little house blessing. And that is prob'ly the end of it."

7

IT WAS QUIET throughout the apartment. The only light on was in the kitchen. First, he leaned against the counter and folded his arms, crisscrossed his legs. Next, he peeked inside the refrigerator for a snack, a drink maybe, but realized he didn't have much of an appetite. He went to the dish rack and started putting away glasses, plates and silverware back in the cupboards. For some reason, Alex couldn't sleep. He found himself tossing and turning, lying on the pillow with his thoughts running, then wandered this way. He hunched, placed both hands on the sink and stared out the window.

From the side of him, a dim figure appeared. He darted his eyes, watched as the head of the figure rotated and stared right towards him.

"God. You scared the shit out of me . . ."

"Sorry." April laughed. "My mom and May and June are light sleepers so I got used to walking around in the dark."

"Yeah, you mentioned that before. Still, fuck."

She walked over to him and pecked him on the cheek. "What you doing up? Come back to bed. We can snuggle."

"Ah, I can't sleep. Being my usual emo dramatic self, I guess."

"Ya know, your hair is getting pretty long."

He rearranged his bangs so that it covered one eye. "I know. I got, like, an emo curtain going."

April swept his hair away. "There it is. Your brown eyes, like molasses mixed with honey."

Both stepped closer then embraced. They each hugged their arms tight around one another, swaying.

"Feels like forever since we held each other like this."

"Right. Happy chemicals in the brain."

Alex pressed his cheek against the top of her head, could smell her hair. April rubbed over his shoulder blades.

"I missed you, my precious."

"Ooh. Wait right here."

He watched as she skipped back into the hall.

"You're not gonna turn the lights on?"

"No need, remember!"

Alex smirked, shook his head.

She came back into the kitchen with her Motorola Razr, placed it down. "Okay. What to listen to . . ."

"Playing us a song?"

"Yeah. I feel like we hardly ever get to anymore. So busy all the time."

"We do keep the MP3 player in the car, too. That's our radio."

"Ah, here. This is the one."

The little speaker spewed the slow strumming of acoustic guitar and the heartfelt vocals. It was kind of a soft and sad melody but also happy somehow. Each of them heard the bittersweet lyrics as if for the first time, and the true depth and meaning.

He stepped forward, touched his lips to hers as "The Only Exception" by Paramore built up from the verse to the chorus.

Alex took her hand, placed his other hand on her hip. April let him lead them in a light clockwise rotation. She moved both hands up around his neck, lacing her fingers. He wrapped his arms around her waist, pulled her in close.

"I could do this forever."

She nuzzled into his collar bone then stared up at him.

"The same, love."

"Hold you. Kiss you. Lick you from head to toe. Get old and wrinkly and senile. Just me and you against the world."

With a cocky smirk, Alex gazed at her without hope or agenda.

There was a gleam in her eyes as a wide smile spread across her face.

"I heart you, Nex."

"Heart you times infinity."

∽

Since they shared the car, there was always a bit of coordination that needed to be done day to day. Alex would often drop off April early as needed or sometimes April would have to stay later as well, killing time in the nearby shopping outlet. Every now and then, her sister would help out. It was a good chance for her to catch up on her studies so she liked to keep a textbook with her. However, this time, she messaged to come pick her up which was quite the surprise as it was only halfway through the shift. Alex waited in the parking lot with a hand on the steering wheel and a hand on the shifter knob. He glanced at the back door for the employee entrance.

Time to finally tell her.

Been goin' on long enough.

It started as drizzling on the drive over. But, as he sat in the car, this grew to a steady rain and now a heavy downpour.

Alex reached behind to grab the umbrella from the back seat, was about to bring it outside when April appeared from the entrance. She maneuvered her jacket above her head and shoulders to provide some covering then jogged down to the car. There was a splash from the puddle by the curb.

Next to him, the passenger door flew open and she hopped in.

"I was just about to come meet you with the . . ."

He didn't finish his thought. Right away, he noticed her cheeks were sopping wet, not from the rain but from tears.

"A-April?"

She leaned over the center console, pressed her face into his upper arm and began to sob uncontrollably. He had never seen her cry before.

There were streams trickling down all of the windows in wiggly patterns and beads of water hitting the glass in intermittent splats.

"What's wrong? Is everything okay?"

April pulled away, sniffed.

"It's my . . ." She buried her face in both hands. "It's my mom . . ."

First, living out his solo path, the lesson was always LIFE101 or LIFE101L. Then, as his path began to intertwine and weave with another, his soul mate, it turned into a crash course he called LOVE102. As they made their way, various rules unfolded and revealed themselves, altering their view of the world.

However, a new life lesson was beginning to form for the two of them. Perhaps the harshest and the cruelest of them all—LOSS205. It wasn't a laboratory course. It wasn't an introductory course or secondary course. It was a special class, six credits, two semesters worth of extensive curriculum rolled into one.

&

The gate lagged at first then activated with a sudden thrust. It rolled open backwards in an arc as Alex pulled in and drove to the empty guest stall. April dabbed a tissue to both of her cheeks, taking slow and deep breaths. They each watched as her two sisters waited by the bottom of the stairs. It was a smaller apartment building just off the freeway outside of town, near a dog park and playground which was nice and clean and safe. She held his hand, proceeded to squeeze it. He raised it, kissed the back of it, covering it with his other hand and rubbing over it lovingly with tender affection.

"You sure you don't want me to come with?"

"No, it's okay. Since we heard the news, you have been so patient and thoughtful." April leaned into the cushion. "I can't thank you enough. But go help your friend. Take care of this new client. Leave it to April-May-June today."

He reached around and hugged her.

"Oh. There is one thing . . ."

"Yeah?"

With her hand still on the door handle, she licked her lips. "It might be a good time to try reaching out to your dad. Up to you. But I mean, don't wait 'til it's too late. When he's laid up, sick, hurt, needing help."

Alex paused then spoke. "He did try to call again. Also my mom."

"I know it's not easy, but trust me. I'm not the most family oriented either. Then something like this happens and all that changes. The tables flipped. My mind is wracked with guilt, with regret. I would hate for you to feel that."

Hmm.

"I'll text you later, okay?"

He nodded, already lost in thought.

First, Alex watched her walk away through the side window. Although it was a somber moment, he was able to appreciate the sway of her hips in her tight jeggings. Then, when she joined her two sisters, about to walk up the stairs, he reversed. Alex saw one of the sisters aim the remote and the gate began to roll open again.

When he pulled back onto the road and followed the curve along the freeway, his mind began to wander. This continued past the playground and park.

It was something called malignant multiple sclerosis. A rare, rapid and progressive disease resulting in significant debilitation within a short period of time. According to April, before being officially diagnosed, her mother had been showing signs: odd losses of feeling in limbs, poor balance. After close to a year of unsuccessful tests, all of a sudden, the loss of feeling became weakness and tremors, and poor balance became poor coordination, difficulty with speech. Until then, her mother asked her sisters not to tell April so that she could focus on completing her degree. She was the last of them not to have graduated yet and the last of them to know.

Alex thought about his dad then, beset by the irony. The empty road rolled before him on his way to the SPIRAL head-quarters and the mid-afternoon sun peeked through the clouds.

Fine. I'll talk to that bastard.

But not today.

Internal monologue weaved in and out of daydreaming while he followed the others from the meeting room to the back lot.

Cameron got into the driver's seat. Edward got into the passenger seat. Each of them reached to the side and buckled in. Erin climbed into the back seat and Alex climbed in after her. Pastor Art took up the awkward seat in the middle, sliding the door closed.

Erin nudged at Alex with an elbow. "You all right?"

"Just a little out of it." He forced a smirk.

"The girl?"

He paused, shook his head.

Edward and Cameron talked amongst themselves. Pastor Art rested his eyes, leaned his head back.

Peering out the window, Alex observed his faint reflection stare back at him. Between this imagery and the dwelling thoughts, the drive seemed short.

As they parked in front of the house, he felt a stirring in his chest. The others got out first and started to walk. Alex waited, helped Erin down, then they both followed, lingering behind.

"Can't believe this'll be over so soon."

He nodded without a word, gazing down.

Right when they entered into the door, Ian and Helena ran up to Erin and hugged her around each leg.

"Guess I'm on babysitting duty again."

The two already tugged at her wrists, pulling her away.

"Hey. It's a dirty job but somebody's gotta do it." He watched as the distance grew between them.

Both children ran up the stairs, giggling, waving for her to come follow. She waved back, a big smile on her face.

Erin headed down, turned back toward Alex. "Catch you on the flippity-flip."

Ayame tidied up a last few items as Pastor Art sat down on the side of the sectional. Alex went around, sat closer to the middle.

Cameron pulled a chair out next to Edward by the dining table. They each had a manila folder with printed sheets.

"Would anyone like water, tea?"

"I'm good."

"No, thank you."

Ayame shifted from the dining room to the sectional.

"Uh. I'll have some water, thanks."

"The same. 'Preciate it."

She went to the kitchen then placed the two glasses down as she went to the other side of the sectional.

Alex crinkled his brow, squirmed in place, peeking at the stairs where there was nothing.

Huh. Weird.

"Nice to see you again, Miss Moriguchi." Pastor Art placed both hands on his knees. "I hope it's okay to call you that. I know you're a wife and mother, but you're far too young to go by Misses Moriguchi to me."

She smiled, raised a hand up dismissively.

"Everything okay here?"

"Yes. Since you guys came, there haven't been any disturbances."

Alex again glanced to the stairs then scanned the living

room. He could hear light thuds from upstairs where Erin and the children played. He narrowed his eyes and thinned his lips, unable to pinpoint the slight nagging itch.

"We dug up some history on the house." Edward shuffled the stack of papers. "Actually, there was quite a few newspaper articles, even some police reports."

"Really?"

He nodded. "Police responded to a call once to address a disturbance where a father struggled to console his children who screamed in terror for hours, nonstop."

Ayame perked her ears, inclined her head.

"Police also responded to another call to help a group of friends that got attacked in the night. They were all grad students who found the house for cheap, decided to split the rent together. Almost immediately, the young men reported unexplained movements on the premises, audible mumbling and moaning. One of them even reported being touched."

Edward flipped to the next page with a sharp rustling sound.

"According to the documentation and subsequent interviews, police were called to respond to floating objects and items being hurled at them."

Pastor Art sipped from the glass. Alex crossed his arms.

Cameron waited, chimed in. "There was also apparently a couple murders."

Ayame gasped then covered her mouth.

"In one of them, a jaded and disgruntled employee kidnapped the manager's son and shot him four times. There was also the murder-suicide of a bitter ex. He stalked this poor girl then stabbed her while she did laundry."

Edward scratched at his beard, shook his head.

"There was a whole media circus once around an immigrant house servant who lived in the upstairs bedroom and was allegedly psychic."

She was quiet, continued to hold both hands up over her chin.

"We got tons and tons of info. It's almost too much."

Pastor Art cleared his throat. "So, there is a mountain of evidence to suggest there could be some kind of supernatural activity. I mean, some locations just have a dark past, a negative energy. Bad juju. Like, this black hole that consumes and absorbs."

"I see."

"However, if I can be frank, our actual investigation didn't turn up much. I instead focused on researching the history and the specific entity you described."

The preacher opened his own manila folder.

Alex saw the illustration of a woman but with a blank, smooth sheet of skin where the face should be. Without thinking, he gulped his water.

"Dating all the way back to the 1600s, 1700s, 1800s, it is pretty much contained to ancient Japan. Old travel routes to old Tokyo. Osaka and Kagawa prefectures. Kyoto prefecture. They have been reported by samurai, by geisha. Along bridges, around the capital, near graveyards and by imperial koi ponds. In front of noodle stands."

Pastor Art held up the illustration.

Edward peered into it.

"This is an early depiction of what they refer to as a noppera-bō. Some literature has labeled them mujina, or badger. I guess, in folklore and myth, mujina and kitsune and tanuki are typically mischievous and have the ability to shape-shift, this noppera-bō being a popular disguise of choice, thus the confusion. Kitsune, meaning fox. Tanuki, meaning raccoon dog."

Cameron crossed his arms, leaned back.

"Now, there have been claims of sightings in recent times still, throughout Japan but notably in the United States, areas with large Japanese populations. A renowned historian compiled multiple files, an entire casebook on the subject. There were articles written and radio interviews conducted about a certain drive-in movie theater which had regular hauntings from a woman with no face. But after the place was torn down, it has now been spotted on occasion in the surrounding areas. A public storage facility. A department store. A grocery store."

"I don't understand. All these events in the past, other people experiencing different things, and now a . . . noppera-bō? What's the connection?"

"Sometimes, a location can become a hot spot for activity. It is hard to define, hard to explain. Hard to fathom, quite honestly. It could also be coincidental as well. Like, perhaps these other occurrences are anomalies with their own distinctions and causes. Perhaps this faceless ghost would have appeared no matter which house you lived in, too. I can't say."

Pastor Art placed the manila folder on the coffee table.

Alex nodded a slow nod, blinking.

"If we work on a case, we're not always able to single out the exact cause or source, make complete sense of it. The truth is the supernatural and the paranormal are still very much this nebulous gray area with way more questions than answers."

Ayame lowered her head, appeared sullen.

"What we can do is a blessing. Bless this house. Bring in good energy and good vibes. Hope. New light. I know you may not be a believer but this is almost always successful."

"Um, my family is traditionally Shinto. Patrick grew up non-denominational Christian, but not practicing. I mean, whatever you guys can do. I need to know my family is safe. I can't bear to hear another crying out, see another scratch."

"Oh. Speaking of . . ." Alex adjusted in place. "I was wondering, why do you think Ian was targeted versus Helena? Physically, I mean."

"I'm not sure. Kinda assumed 'cause he was younger hence more vulnerable."

Edward shrugged. "Could be. Or maybe, like your sister, he might be more attuned to the other side."

Alex narrowed his eyes. "H-has he ever had a near-death experience?"

She grew quiet.

"That idea popped into my head for some reason."

Ayame sniffled, fought back a tear. "During labor, he did get tangled in the umbilical cord. He was technically stillborn. More than just blue, the doctors said he was already turning black and feared for the worst. Despite this, they performed CPR for six minutes and were able to revive him. He is our miracle baby."

"God bless that child. He seems fine aside from you-know-what, which we'll take care of here and now. I'll pray for him. For both kids, yourself, and every corner of this house."

"Thank you. Thank you all."

She stood, went to gather the empty glasses.

As she passed by, her calf grazed his shin and the same nagging itch from earlier shot down his spine and then throughout his limbs.

"Wait a minute. Hold on."

Alex got to his feet, stepped closer to Ayame.

"Ned, do we have an EMF detector in the van? You mind getting it?"

"What is it, Alexander?"

Cameron straightened up, scooted forward. Edward went out the front door to the van.

"I don't think we're done after all."

He waved a hand in the air over the space around her then stared at his forearms where each hair stood on end from each pore.

"It's not the house." Alex turned to the others. "No, no. It's her."

"No fucking way."

"Language, Mister Gallo."

"Sorry. Shit."

Edward returned, pointed the device. "Whoa. This thing's off the charts. Cam, come get a pic of this. A vid. Something."

Cameron hurried over, taking out his cell phone. He snapped a couple photos then started recording the EMF detector reading and the goosebumps on Alex's arms.

"Miss Moriguchi, is there anything else that's happened? Or anywhere else this kind of thing has happened? With your friend maybe? The other military spouse."

She stared off, jaw hanging. "I mean, nobody was ever terrified or hurt. It was only talk, a few rumors. I didn't think much of it. That is until now."

"What is that?"

"It might be my workplace."

". . . And, where do you work?"

PART FIVE

A ROSE ON THE GRAVE

1

ALTHOUGH THE SO-CALLED Demon House of Lower Bloom Hill did act as a gateway, a doorway, a portal and a vortex, it was only the opening. Every case leading up until then was mere warm-up, this set of training exercises designed to prepare them for the true horrors that awaited. Pastor Art decided to perform the blessings still for good measure. He sprinkled salt, placed down cloves of garlic, read bible verses, lit the pink candle, and prayed in each room by each window. He also prayed over the mother then the two children. Erin knelt down, scooped the two toddlers in her arms as they prepared to leave. Edward and Cameron nodded, waved. Ayame hugged Pastor Art then hugged Alex.

Before the group departed, they agreed to meet again at headquarters to discuss the new plan going forward. The time would soon come to go beyond the opening well into the tunnel which had been there all along, and that was Saint Florian.

"Thank you for agreeing to meet here. If we're going to meet regularly, I figure away from the kids is better."

"No problem. Our operations center is a little tight, but it'll do."

Ayame sat with her back to the door frame where Cameron leaned. Pastor Art was next to her on one side of the square table. There was a map on the wall behind him. Erin took up the other side and Alex was on top. There were file cabinets behind them. Edward sat on a folding chair off to the corner.

"So, it just so happens that you're living in one of the most haunted houses in the entire pacific northwest, experiencing a major haunting, but it's not the house, it's you." Cameron shook his head, almost flinching at the words. "How crazy."

"The location might be dormant right now. But that doesn't mean it hasn't been haunted in the past or that it won't be haunted again in the future."

"What does it mean?" Erin glanced across the table.

"I guess we need to get to the bottom of whatever's attached to Miss Moriguchi and however it happened. She isn't showing signs of possession, so that's good. Our main lead is that it's the hospital she works in. Right?"

Pastor Art turned to Ayame who affirmed.

"Other than that, we're looking at a big fat question mark."

Alex rested an elbow on the table. "I don't get it. We all been to that hospital before. Why haven't we heard anything, seen anything, *felt* anything in my case?"

"Well, which side?" Ayame lifted a brow.

"Oh . . . Hmm."

Edward crossed his arms. "Maybe could you break down the complex for us?"

"Certainly."

Erin handed her a pencil and a piece of paper.

"This is the general layout of the Saint Florian Healthcare System. Like you said, maybe you've been there. But it is pretty big and with multiple buildings."

She proceeded to draw the E-shape. The top horizontal line and side vertical line were longer than the other two lines. Everybody leaned in to better see.

"Most people probably go to this part." Ayame tapped the top arm of the E with the eraser head of the pencil. "This is the acute care area, the actual hospital. There's telemetry, internal medicine, oncology, neuro, ortho, med surg, respiratory care, ICU, the ER, the OR, all of that. Then there is the subacute area, which is more like stabilization and recovery. There is also a department for rehab but for shorter stays with higher intensity therapy, typically no more than two weeks, except in special cases."

Like Deidre.

Some of the jargon flew over their heads but they followed along for the most part.

"Now, I work in this section here." She tapped the side of the E with the eraser.

Pastor Art leaned forward and tilted his head.

"It is called an S-N-F. Usually pronounced 'sniff.' A skilled nursing facility. This acts as kind of an in-between after the hospital but before the home, a longer stay as in up to three or four weeks, and lower intensity rehab. Geriatric population, mostly."

Cameron pointed with his chin. "What's in the other buildings?"

"These two longer buildings are the main two buildings. The others are mixed, like a cancer center, a pharmacy, diagnostic lab, x-ray, dialysis and a bunch of doctor's offices for private practice."

Alex rubbed the back of his knuckles over his chin. "Can you think of a reason one side would have more paranormal activity and not the other?"

"I know the hospital is new. All these other buildings are newer, built in the last few years. In fact, it's still being built. There are many projects currently in progress." Ayame tapped above the E, the accent mark where Alex sat down that other day. "For example, this will be independent and assisted living, also adult day health, but it's not ready yet."

"So, it looks like they expanded."

"Exactly. Where I work is the site of the original hospital, from long long time ago. They turned that old hospital into a SNF, or 'sniff' as we call it."

"That's interesting." Erin pressed the glasses to her face.

"I could see that being a problem, though. A lot of activity can occur after construction and stuff like that." Edward slouched in his chair.

Ayame took a breath. "I have been working in this field for a while. There is a lot of death. People are sick, are hurt. People are stressed out. Strange things happen. Now, this is generally known, sometimes spoken about, sometimes not, but it is always understood."

Alex stared across the table at her.

"My God. I can only imagine. How many people pass in a given day, week, month. It must be quite a strenuous job. All that grief." Cameron shifted, kept his body half-turned. "Plus, hell, some of 'em may not know they passed."

"I've seen a sink faucet go off by itself once. There was no explanation. And I heard people talk about—"

Pastor Art raised a finger. "Whoa, whoa. Hold on. Remember, it's better for us not to know too much before going in. Especially Alexander."

"Okay. How do we even begin to do an investigation of this kind of huge place???"

"Good question, Miss Woodfeld."

For a brief moment, they all remained silent, reflected.

"We heard of hauntings of abandoned asylums before, run-down and defunct state psychiatric hospitals, old sanatoriums maybe, but never an active working facility." Edward fidgeted with his fingers. "How do we conduct an entire investigation while, I'm assuming, keeping it on the down-low?"

"There is a board of directors to consider, and a president of the board. We can't have a strange group freely roam with strange equipment. The hearsay and potential headlines would be devastating, especially after the multimillions sunk in and the multimillions more in motion planned . . . I have thought a little about this. I can try to pull some strings with HR. I get along well with one of the girls, and she herself has witnessed some of the activity. As the ADON, or Assistant Director of Nursing, I have some leverage."

"What were you thinking?"

"Like you said, we have to keep it hush-hush. But if I can get you on the floors and in the rooms, incognito, we could proceed. Give me a few days and then let's meet up."

"Great. And we will look into the hospital as well in the meantime."

⚜

When they gathered in the meeting room once again, the group found themselves occupying the same spots, like it was completely natural and would be their routine. Ayame sat at the bottom of the square table. Her back was to Cameron who folded his arms and leaned in the door frame. Pastor Art took up the side of the table. The map behind him now had a few pins stuck in and pieces of string connecting them. Edward unfolded the chair and sat down, scooted forward to close the gap. Erin took up the other side and Alex was on top. The file cabinets behind them now had binders laid out that were half-filled up.

"Thank you all again."

"Don't mention it."

Erin smiled. "How are Ian and Helena?"

"They're fine. I'll pick them up after. Things have been a little better at home since the blessing. On the other hand, since our last talk, I have noticed more disturbances on the work front. We must be on the right track. So we really should get started."

Pastor Art lifted a foot and rested it on the opposite knee. "Did everything go okay with your friend in HR? Are we all set?"

"Yes, almost."

"Let's hear it."

"I was able to get 'jobs' for each of you so that we can begin. Alex, you will be helping in our activities department. You will practically have access to every room on every floor, including recreational spaces and dining rooms. Get the chance to interview every patient, patient family, other staff along the way."

Alex fidgeted in place. "Do I have to do other stuff? Run bingo?"

"No, your position will be more one-on-one and in the rooms. I'll make sure of that. You might have to read books, read newspapers and magazines, play cards, print out word finds, that kind of thing."

"Got it."

"Erin. I was thinking since your expertise is AV, we could 'hire' you to do a new advertising and promotional campaign."

She thinned her lips. "I think I can pull that off. That would give me reason to carry still cams, video cams, tripods."

"And speaking of cameras, Ned, it will take a few more days to get your background check for a position in security. They're a little strict about that, but once done, you will get access to the CCTV footage."

"Interesting. Very impressive, Ayame." Edward nodded.

Pastor Art interlocked his fingers over the table. "What about me? Do I get some hip cool undercover role here?"

"Actually, I was going to add you to our list of visiting preachers."

"Oh, okay. That'll be easy enough. You kiddies do all the heavy lifting while I play backup support."

"You can help ask around, interview, be another set of ears." Ayame glanced at each of their faces. "Erin is the eyes on the ground. Ned is the eye in the sky. Alex, you'll be kind of leading this expedition. We're counting on you."

"I see." Alex gulped. "I can do it."

"What about me?"

"For you, Cam, everyone will mostly be covering the day shift. Ned will be rotating. But in order to have more access during the evenings, I got you placed in housekeeping."

Cameron flinched, did a slow blink.

"A-a-are you serious? Pastor Art gets to play himself, be on autopilot. Erin and Ned are badass Double O secret agents. Alex is pretty much a superhero in spandex here. And I'm a god damn overnight janitor!?"

The group held back laughter and smiles.

"I already printed your name tags, except Ned, 'cause of the background check."

"Dude."

"C'mon, Cam."

"Not that big a deal."

Pastor Art turned, faced him. "You'll have to suck it up . . ."

"Fine. Whatever."

Alex shook his head. "Didn't you guys learn more about Saint Florian?"

"Little bit. Take it away, Ned."

Edward stood, grabbed the binder and opened it. "I guess it all started from the early church, back in the plantation days. The influx of cheap labor brought in by ship, the rapid modernization happening, there wasn't much available yet. So they offered up the cathedral to help as an extra tuberculosis ward and to isolate a few cases of leprosy. It eventually developed into a small community clinic then a full-scale hospital which was groundbreaking at the time, cutting edge, innovative."

"That cathedral still there?"

"Yes, right here." Ayame took the drawing before, added an equals sign in front of the E. "The main cathedral and the main quarters. But it's rarely used."

Alex chimed in. "I was also in a courtyard area thing behind the hospital, with another building . . ."

"Oh. The independent and assisted living as I mentioned before." She added the accent mark above the E. "A lot is still under construction so it's really just the SNF and the hospital and other buildings. The back area isn't ready. The cathedral is not in use but open for viewing."

"The guy who started everything had a degree in architecture, which might explain a lot of the building up and expansions. It also looks like there was a circle of doctors who were integral in establishing the joint church-hospital endeavors."

"Has there been any documentation about potential ghosts?"

Edward flipped through. "Plenty. Almost as much as the house. I found reports and articles mentioning apparitions of soldiers marching. There have been incidents of pranksters allegedly messing with the water sprinkler system but it turned out nobody was around. Sounds of the organ were heard playing from the cathedral interior, and specters were seen appearing and disappearing amongst headstones. All in the middle of the night."

"Headstones?"

"It turns out this small cemetery was formed on the property for some of the early members, and a mausoleum as well, which entombs the original founder."

"Are you serious? Jesus Christ."

"Friggin' Catholics. Gotta hand it to 'em." Pastor Art let out a mixed grin and wince.

"One last thing, there's several reports of the shadow of a beast over the steeple. It has been described as canine-like with bright red glowing eyes. People claimed to see this creature crawl along the ceilings, leap from rooftop to rooftop, heard howls and the tapping of claws on the concrete."

"Maybe it's demonic?" Alex shifted in place.

"Could be."

"And that's about it." Edward faced back up. "I suppose we'll continue to learn more as we go along."

"Right. Okay, ladies and gents, we got our work cut out for us. Especially Mister Gallo."

There was a light round of laugher from everyone minus Cameron.

❧

It was already tricky balancing his regular day job, regular boy-friend duties and investigating, but that included helping with a few extra family matters now. The latest turn of events had created kind of an additional part-time job on top of that, some level of volunteering at least, to figure out what was going on. Alex walked by the pillars and cars through the parking garage. He passed the elevator to the stairwell then went around the corner near the entrance with the barrier gate arm. This time, instead of going straight to the hospital building, he took a right to the skilled nursing facility where Ayame worked.

Alex pulled the ID badge out of his pocket and clipped it onto his shirt.

Geez.

Here goes nothing.

On the first floor, there were two small shops. One was a gift shop and one was a snack shop, both with women behind the counter who acknowledged him through the window. Both had glasses, one of them older with a pixie haircut and one of them middle-aged with shoulder length hair that was parted in the middle.

When he got to the HR department, Ayame was waiting out front.

"Hey. You always do the tours like this?"

"No, never." She shook her head with a half-smile. "They noted in your application that you're trying to get into med school and wanted to meet a higher-up, for reference."

"Ah. Doctor Alexander Clark Jacobsen. I do like the sound of that."

"Come on. Let's get going." Ayame started to lead them

through the second floor. "Each floor has a nursing station with its own unit clerk. Feel free to ask them any questions."

"I saw as I came in."

One of the workers waved while they passed.

Alex waved back then put his hands in his pockets.

"You're right, by the way, Ayame."

"Hmm?"

"The vibe here is different. I felt it the minute I got in. Something is weird. I'm not quite comfortable. There is tingling all over my body, running along my skin."

"I know. After you guys pointed it out, I can't seem to relax either."

"Even these paintings on the walls are so eerie, kind of dark and weird. Like, morbid. The outlines of birds and trees. Odd faces. Odd figures in odd positions. Drippy, with strange lines and curves. Very black. Funky shapes and splotchy masses, like from out of a dream."

"The founder was something of a painter and a sculptor."

"I see."

"Much of this floor, about half, is management and other staff. There's the business office, IT, HR as you just saw." Ayame waved her hand while showing these. "On this side, there are the patient rooms. These are all double occupancy, as in room-mates. Here is a recreation area where they have live music, games, art and crafts, maybe a cooking class. This is where the other activity staff will be. They plan, prepare whatever, do paperwork here. You'll probably see one of the other girls in a bit."

"Did . . . Did you hear that?"

"Hear what?"

"I swear I heard someone say, 'Help me.' Like in a hushed whisper."

"Um, I didn't hear anything. Maybe one of the patients pushed the call button?"

Alex and Ayame glanced around, peeked down the hall. None of the call lights were on.

"Phew. This is a lot to take. I'm a bit overwhelmed. Feels like the walls are screaming at me, like this wave of blood could come pouring out at any second."

"Is there anything I can do?"

He shut his eyes, breathed out through pursed lips. "Damn it. Fuck . . ."

She placed a hand on his shoulder.

"I've never felt this before. I feel, like, faint."

"Maybe you should sit down?"

"Nah. Let's keep going. But if this is just the second floor, I am not looking forward to the third and fourth."

"Just tell me if you need to rest, step outside, get a drink of water. Anything."

"Thank you."

Ayame took them up the elevator. Alex stood in the corner, rubbed a hand over his forehead before stepping back out.

"Feeling any better?"

"Little bit. I do got like a slight headache."

"I always have some extra aspirin, when we get to the fourth floor."

"Sure. Thanks."

"Almost all of the rooms on the third and fourth are single occupancy."

"It looks like this floor is bigger than the last, not just a closed loop but also a T-shape to it, in addition to the long rectangle."

"Yeah. The way it's built around the hillside, I guess. The upper floors are a little different. Now, there are two medium sized recreation areas here as you can see." She indicated with an upturned palm. "One here and one at the end, down there. For family visits or more intimate activities. And the social work offices are around the corner."

"I'm not gonna remember half of this."

They both chuckled.

When they got to the next floor, Ayame became more serious.

"Okay, so this is the fourth. If I can be honest, to me, most of the activity happens here. I feel like there's certain specific rooms where patients tend to pass, for example. Is that a coincidence? It has happened quite a few times since I started."

"Hmm."

"Let me get you some medicine before I forget."

"Oh, right."

They walked down to the corner of the T-shape where her office was located. He waited in the hall, scanning a line of abstract paintings.

"Here."

"Appreciate it."

"The two shops downstairs have meds too, if you ever need again. And they're usually open late."

He took the two pills, popped them in his mouth, sipped from the plastic cone cup.

"This is my office. That is medical records over there, and therapy is occupying that other corner space there until the gym is complete. It's still being built upstairs, on the fifth floor which isn't ready."

"Looks like there's no recreation rooms?"

"No, not on the fourth. There is a meeting room, a conference room where we sometimes do in-services and maybe CPR and BLS training. But we do have a large patio if you want to take a patient out for some fresh air."

"I see." He stood next to Ayame by the side of the wall. "Also, I been meaning to ask. Why did your friend in HR decide to help us?"

"You know, one day after work, I caught her in the parking lot and she looked, I don't know, bothered . . . We got to talking and it turned out she was riding the back elevator down and before stepping out, something kind of glided in front of her eyes." She swept a hand in front of her face as a reenactment. "Like this. She heard stories from the night shift. About stools rolling around by themselves, phones ringing and no one on the line, other things, but never believed it until then."

While finishing up the documentation for the day, he was swept up in deep thought. Alex had difficulty maintaining a conversation, following directions, as he continued to brainstorm the different possibilities. It might have been just the one shift but with all the potential reports and possible audiovisual evidence, it was comparable to some of their investigations with the highest activity and the most compelling data. For instance, each painting on the wall appeared to stare at him while he passed, like they were sentient and somehow aware he was an imposter plotting against them with this whole charade. He sat back, waited as his co-worker made sure his daily notes were uploaded correctly.

After a few tweaks and a final thumbs-up, Alex said good-bye and thanks then went on his way. He started walking to the common elevator by the nursing station but stopped and decided to try the back elevator like Ayame mentioned. He saw another worker use it at lunch and another during the shift change.

Huh. There is an odd smell here.

Like a . . .

Like a musk.

It's oddly quiet, too.

Though he didn't see, hear or feel anything, that smell was very distinct. He moved from the back of the building around to the front of it, saw the dialysis center at the foot of the build-ing, the bottom arm of the E-shape. He then pivoted, noticed a pharmacy in the middle arm of the E.

Alex crinkled his brow, jutted out his lower lip, the gears turning in his brain.

"You mad, bro?"

He was caught off guard, turned around.

"That you? Damn, Alex. I haven't seen you in forever."

Standing before him was a familiar face that seemed like a mirage. With a few blinks and tilting of his head, the disbelief was taken over by joy.

"I'd recognize that shit eating grin anywhere." He clapped palms with his old friend, pulled him in for a quick bro hug. "Brad. How in the hell are ya."

"It has been a looong time, my dude."

Alex motioned to a nearby bench and they headed over.

"You 'member I used to ride my moped all the time?"

"That's right."

"Well, I switched to a bicycle. Save on gas. Save the environment. Stay in shape." Bradley counted each pro with his fingers, then counted a con. "Got hit by a car."

"Holy . . ."

"No bullshit. I'm lucky to be alive. I got a settlement out of it. But today was my last day doing out-patient therapy. I was in crutches for the longest time, in this big boot thing."

"Where? In that building?"

"Uh, that one."

"So funny, today is actually my first day."

"First day and last day. What's the odds." Bradley draped an arm over the top of the bench. "I thought you worked somewhere else, though. I saw a post on MySpace."

"We're like the last two idiots still using that thing."

"Hey. I refuse to sign up for any other social media. MySpace ain't going nowhere. I'm telling you."

Alex smirked. "But yeah, I actually work at the credit union."

"That's what I thought. You made some joke about it or something online. So this is a new job, side job?"

"Yeah. More of an extra thing, just temporary."

"Cool, dude." His friend adjusted in place, paused. "Recession got us poor new grads working random jobs. Strugglin' out here."

"Nobody seems to get that. Like, we don't have experience so they won't give us a job, but how the hell are we supposed to get experience if they don't give us a job???"

"Seriously. Things will work out, though. We'll get there. You know, still, we've come a helluva long way from Pine Branch Café."

"Remember? 'Wake Me Up When *Semester* Ends.' Haha."

Both let out a laugh, one slapping at their knee.

"It's good running into you, or you me. Guess I needed this." Alex took a deep breath, arched his neck. "Those were good times. In a way, kinda simpler times."

"We should catch up, hang." Bradley widened his eyes, grinned again. "Talk smack. Go split a cheap pitcher somewhere. Like, one of these days."

"Hells yeah. For sure."

The words were somewhat empty. Alex had a lot on his plate, between helping April out at home and continuing to put off giving his own father a call. There was his regular job, now this other job, and of course the ongoing case—which is the whole reason he perused the grounds like he did, inadvertently leading to this chat.

"And you're still with that girl? What's her name?"

He hunched forward, raised a brow. "April."

"Ah. Right, right. Good for you." His friend let out his signature grin. "Dude, you guys been together for a while. You really like her, huh? The real deal?"

"I do. We live together."

"Nice. All my efforts to help get you laid were not in vain."

"Of course."

"You should lock it down if you're serious. I had a really good girl before but I let 'er slip through my fingers. I kinda messed up, took her for granted. Ya know?"

He was quiet, let Bradley talk.

"I'm sure I'll find another special somebody one day. Plenty of bitches in the sea and all that. But dude, that girl could have been the one. For realsies. So, think it through. When and if you know, you know. Don't let her be the one that got away."

2

HIGH ABOVE, FLOATING in the clouds, towering over the city, the two of them circled around the floor. Even with the overcast skies, it was a beautiful day. Alex held her hand tight, interlacing at the fingers, pulling April close. Both stood in front of the large pane of glass, peering out. They stepped to the side, standing over an area of the floor that was see-through where each stared down into the vertical abyss—at the tops of the pine trees, the lines of parked cars, slow trickling of traffic, and grassy fields. Next, they went upstairs where they walked along the exterior of the steel structure.

April tiptoed close to the edge. "Wow. I've never been to the Cloud Lookout before."

"Yeah, the same. I was trying to think of a way to lift up your spirits."

She squeezed his hand then moved forward to the guard-rail. There was a light gust that blew through her hair.

He smirked at the sight of this, joined her.

The cityscape below sprawled on and on, buildings, streets, on-ramps and off-ramps like a concrete jungle. On one side was the harbor with the ferry gliding through.

"It's so . . . ginormous . . ."

Out in the distance, there was also a rounded mountain with a wave of foggy mist.

He thought about what Bradley said then.

She is the one.

The perfect girl for me.

Alex peeked around them, wondered if anybody else was nearby. He fidgeted on his feet, licked his lips.

This is the chance. Right here.

I don't have a new ring, no.

But I know what's in my heart, without a doubt.

He followed close with her back turned, was about to time the big move, feeling a nervous wave flood his senses. More than the fear, however, his irrevocable affection radiated from within—how he cherished and adored her, everything about her. It was beyond fondness or infatuation. She had become his darling beloved.

Alex was about to bend down but a few tourists appeared. When he waited for another peaceful moment, another couple started walking towards them.

Shit.

C'mon.

This happened several times until April went to sit.

God damn it.

"Nex, I'm sorry if I haven't been myself lately. Guess there is just a lot happening."

"Of course, love." He rubbed at her far shoulder, pecked her on the side of her head above her dazzly ear. "It's no biggie. Totally okay."

"I'm getting a bit cold. Let's call it?"

Alex swallowed, feeling a dry lump lodged in his throat, and breathed out a long sigh.

✺

The next time the group gathered in the meeting room, they occupied the established positions. Pastor Art, Alex, Erin and Ayame sat on the four sides of the square table. Edward took up a folding chair in the corner and Cameron stood in the door frame, hovering towards the back. Each was eager to reconvene and share their different findings, except for Edward who still waited for his background check to clear. Alex scooted closer, his knee accidentally grazing against Erin's thigh beneath the table. He raised a hand in apology to which she shook her head, a faint flush in her cheeks.

Pastor Art cleared his throat. "It's good to see you guys. Guessing we all got a li'l something to say, except Mister Berenson."

"About that, Ned, here is your name tag." Ayame reached back to pass it. "You will be in play starting tomorrow."

"Yes." Edward balled a fist and pulled it to his side. "Finally."

"I don't have too much for myself." Pastor Art shifted in place. "There was a patient that mentioned voices, people whispering in her room late at night. A real nice lady, from Laos."

The others nodded, listened.

"We're probably breaking all kinds of privacy laws here. Whoops." The preacher scratched the back of his neck. "I overheard two aides talk at one point. Apparently one of the patients kept rolling their wheelchair outside the room. This happened again and again so they asked why, and the patient said they saw a ghost. And there was another patient asking how come a doctor woke him up in the middle of the night. Now, pretty sure there was no doctor . . ."

Alex blinked, folded his arms.

"I was expecting maybe a pic or two, some footage. But I got a whole buncha stuff." Erin bent down, took out the laptop.

Cameron stepped closer.

"We got light anomalies. We got the outlines of figures. We got orbs, tons and tons of them. Here are two specific pieces of evidence that stood out."

She clicked, opened the file.

"This was taken outside when I was getting some exterior shots. I don't know about you guys but it looks like a man hanging upside down by his legs from the tree branch."

"Huh. That sounds like an old urban legend I came across. I tried to be less useless by digging around some more." Edward peered at the picture on the screen. "No way."

She scrolled to a separate file.

"And this one, I was doing a time-lapse shot, again outside. Watch and listen."

It was an angle of the corner of the building with a few windows in view. A bright flash went off as well as an echoed boom.

"W-what the hell was that?"

"I don't know. Maybe a spirit passing through, with enough energy it broke a light bulb or something." Erin shook her head, licked her lips. "Like, it's too much going on. It doesn't make sense."

Pastor Art straightened up. "I have to say, it's almost like Sheol, or the realm of the dead, might be closer to our world in that place. As if the veil was thinner, the barrier. The activity happening is kind of on overdrive. It is sort of unnatural to have that much supernatural. Know what I mean?"

Erin lifted a finger, waved it and pointed it in agreement.

"Um, I thought I heard a whisper when Ayame was showing me around. Did you find anything for me, Erin?"

"Oh. Right." She opened a separate folder. "I didn't get anything from that specific recording you went back for. But here is one."

"H h eeee l p p p . . ."

Everybody adjusted, tilted their ears.

"H h eeee l p p p p me, s sso m m eone."

The forlorn, strained whispery voice cut through the air from the tiny speakers.

"Now, that was on the same floor but a different area."

"Maybe it moved?"

"Maybe. That's what I was thinking."

Edward rubbed at his beard. "Hmm."

"Yeah, I heard that voice. Sounds like the same voice, though not a hundred percent sure. A few patients reported a few things, about what you would expect. Lights turning on and off. TV acting up. A drawer closing by itself. Weird scratching. Footsteps. But . . . There was one thing that happened I wanted to ask you about, Ayame."

"Go ahead."

"What are those little bed sensor thingies?"

"Some patients can be restless or have decreased safety awareness, making them a fall risk. For them, we usually will put a bed alarm to notify the nurses when and if they are trying to get up on their own."

Alex narrowed his eyes, leaned back. "Well, I was playing cards with one patient and, on the next bed over, the sensor just went off. Out of nowhere. All of a sudden. Like, the bed was empty. There wasn't anybody laying down. It was pretty damn strange. If I had to guess, it felt like something might have been on the bed and then got up . . . I can't explain it."

Erin stared at him. "That's so weird."

"Speaking of weird, I talked to my friend in HR a little more. She mentioned to a couple others about her experience in the back elevator, and they said that it was used before to carry the dead bodies down to the morgue." Ayame rubbed at her upper arms. "Just thinking about it gives me goosebumps."

"Oh, that might explain the smell. I checked it out for myself." He swallowed. "I was thinking about going down to the basement level one of the staff mentioned. Any ideas on how?"

"You can use either the back elevator or the main elevator but I guess you could help transport a patient to dialysis one of these days. There is an underground tunnel between buildings."

"Thanks. I'll keep that in mind."

Everybody grew quiet while Cameron straightened up.

"Well, I didn't have the pleasure of easy mode or waiting around, or fun detective work like the rest of you. The first night, I had to clean up vomit. One of the patients was nauseated from their meds."

A round of light snickering broke the tension.

"You know, prob'ly Cam would have fit in better with security. I'll be like a twig next to those other guys."

"But anyway, though it may not be fun pushing around a mop and a broom, sweeping rubbish, lugging around a big cart of cleaning supplies . . . I have to say, I got some pretty good access to the insider info."

"What'd you find out?"

"I personally didn't find shit, except in the clogged toilet. However, the night shift has so many damn stories. It's kinda nuts. Like, one guy is something of an enthusiast and compiled all this over time. He said people have mentioned hearing babies cry in what was once the nursery. He said one of his co-workers pulled a double, was of course exhausted, nodded off a bit and then got woken up. Something grabbed 'im and shook 'im." Cameron demonstrated with a violent rattle of his hands. "Maybe the spirit of an old supervisor, or maybe a spirit who perceived him as being lazy ass. I don't know."

Alex rested a cheek in his palm. Erin pressed the glasses to her face.

"This one time, a member of the staff went to clean the room, noticed a patient on the toilet on the way in, apologized, but when they got inside there was a patient lying in each bed so that couldn't have been them. They checked again and the person was gone."

Cameron lifted both palms up in a shrug.

"Now, I'm sure some of these stories are true and some of these not-so-true. It can be like gossip in the high school locker room, a bad game of telephone. Am I right?"

"That's a good point. But I think we can conclude this facility is haunted. Between so many things seen and heard, the evidence already gathered and presented, what a lot of us felt for ourselves, plus enough credible reports. So, Miss Moriguchi, you are not crazy. In fact, you were absolutely correct. There is something going on, without a doubt. Thank you for helping set everything all up where we are able to deeper explore. Let's keep at it, people. We got Mister Berenson there with us now, the last piece of the puzzle. See if we can find the link to this noppera-bō, and whatever other secrets may lie."

∾

It was becoming more and more routine to him, the sneaking around, the probing, prodding, poking, like a scout on a reconnaissance mission. The unit clerk chatted with Alex on the way in, made small talk and niceties. The other activity staff said hi and how are you, exchanged different humorous and light-hearted interactions with the patients. He got his list of patients for the day, grabbed the rolling activities cart then got right to it. Alex glanced around to see if anybody was nearby then waved the EMF detector and pointed the thermometer. He peeked at the readings then put both back under the stack of newspapers and magazines.

Huh.

A little unusual.

The first patient for the day was asleep but he left some printed materials for when they woke up: a crossword, pictures for coloring, other word and math puzzles.

The second patient for the day was getting ready to head out, put on a pair of knit gloves and a knit beanie, wore a thick and poofy jacket.

Oh. Maybe this is my chance.

"E-excuse me. It looks like he has dialysis today?"

The aide nodded, placed the thin lap blanket down and the full shopping bag over the handle, about to leave.

"I'm here a bit early. I could take him for you, if you want."

"You sure? We are understaffed so . . ."

"Of course. Downstairs, yeah?"

"Just go left when you get out of the elevator, walk straight down, and it will be to your right. There will be a big sign."

"Left, straight, right. Got it."

"Thank you. That really helps."

"You're welcome."

He introduced himself then wheeled the patient to the main elevator. When they got down to the basement level, they took a left. Before he turned, Alex noticed two swinging doors to the right, presumably to the laundry and maintenance areas. The area in front of the elevator was flat, and had a pane of glass to the side through which they saw kitchen workers putting together meal trays. After this, the tile floor then slanted downward.

On either side of him, down the long and quiet hallway were framed photographs with printed captions beneath them.

"Do you mind if we take our time? Check these out?"

"Not at all."

"Wow . . . It chronicles the whole history of the church and hospital. The founder was kind of a hero, huh."

As they moved down the incline, more and more of the photos continued on. There was a row of nuns standing together. There were patients sitting outdoors, experimental medical equipment and original schematics of the hospital floor plans.

He had to stop and stare at a group of them. It was the depressing and grotesque images of victims of a smallpox outbreak which grew to a smallpox epidemic. The skin was swollen with reddened bumps and lumps, lips pulled tight, eyelids shut. Each of them appeared to be in such physical agony but also mental and emotional torment. Some were contracted and lay upon their hospital beds, possibly soon to be their death beds— red circles, red dots, like berries, like seeds.

One was only a young child who suffered from the ailment. The angle of the light darkened her eyes as she peered into the lens with a vacant stare. Huge, horrible pus-filled blisters grew over her face, spread to the back, arms and chest, scattered in unforgiving pockmarks.

Alex shuddered to himself then proceeded ahead.

When he got back up to the floors, the next patient was bed bound. He had silver hair combed to the side, wild bushy brows, a big nose and thick glasses. All of the wires ran from the raised machines over the rails of the hospital bed: steady IV drip, tube feedings, oxygen flowing through a nasal cannula, pulse oximeter on his index finger.

"I'll take the paper. Usually I read to him around noon."

"Sure, my last copy." Alex folded it in half then handed it over.

"Great."

The young woman took it and tucked it away by the foot of the bed. He guessed she may have been the granddaughter but didn't get to ask.

Alex rubbed at his arms for a second, feeling a slight chill.

"By the way, I made these for everybody and have been giving them out. Take some, please."

"What is it?" He peeked at the bowl and the cooler, the plate.

"This is a blueberry daiquiri . . ." She churned the mixture using a ladle then filled the plastic cup, dropping a couple ice cubes in. "And these are orange cream scones . . ."

"I'm not really hungry but I could use a pick-me-up."

"You guys all work so hard."

He smirked, raised the cup in a cheers then took a nice long sip, smacking his lips. It gave him enough of a boost to carry on through his usual afternoon slump.

The last patient that day was a heavyset woman. She had a poof of curls over her round head that was propped up on a mound of pillows. Her left leg was spread way out, propped up on another separate pillow.

"Are you physical therapy?"

"No, uh . . . I'm Alex from activities."

"Okay. You can come in."

He could sense the sass and the spunk in her voice, like a fan favorite character from a popular sitcom.

"You look a little younger than the other patients."

"Yeah, I know. These dumb-ass doctors don't know a damn thing."

Alex couldn't help but chuckle then regained his composure. "Is everything okay? Is there anything I could help you with?"

The woman widened then rolled her eyes. "Not unless you could sneak me another coffee, but nooo, I'm on some fluid restriction. Such utter and complete BS, if you ask me."

"Are you . . ." He observed her facial expressions. "Are you kinda tired?"

"I am beyond tired. These fools keep checkin' my blood pressure. If it's not one pill, another pill, another pill, every staff from every department comes by and asks the same stupid questions. There is such thing."

He stared her in the eye. "Aw, I'm sorry. And here I come, bothering you."

With that, she lowered her guard, took a breath. "Nah. I'm the one who's sorry. Just, it is a big pain in the ass being here. All of that isn't even the worst part."

Leaning in, he raised his eyebrows. "I'm here if you wanna vent. All ears."

"I don't know why I'm even telling you this." She shook

her head in an exaggerated movement. "You'll think I'm some insane person. Like, out of my mind."

"Try me."

Her eyes became watery as she forced out the words. "The real reason that I couldn't sleep last night . . . There was this man smiling at me through the window . . ."

Alex was taken aback, shocked.

"Like, he just stood there. Eyes turned up. Lips spread. It was evil incarnate."

"Forgive me, but you're here for . . ." He took the list from his pocket, unfolded it, checked it. "Knee surgery. Right?"

"Correct. I'm not confused. I didn't fall, hit my head or anything. It was elective."

"Are you on strong meds or anything?"

"I'm just taking regular ol' painkillers. I don't want no strong narcotics. Gonna make me loopy. Only thing I need is over-the-counter generic brand, a giant bag of ice, and another effing coffee."

Alex stood, walked to the window, glancing down.

There was no walkway or ledge. And they were all the way up on the fourth floor.

"Crazy, huh?" She narrowed her eyes, bit at her bottom lip. "You know, a lot of these patients cry out at night. Yelling. Swearing. The nurses probably think it's normal pain, confusion, anxiety, blah blah blah. But I wonder if they are also seeing things, hearing things. Like I did. In my honest opinion, there is some kind of demon among us."

∾

As he walked inside of headquarters, he saw Cameron flick on all the lights. They each raised a hand in acknowledgement.

Alex closed the door behind him then passed through the front office to the meeting room. Erin was already there, had a headset on while cycling through different files. She noticed him, smiled, waved, pulled his designated chair out and patted the top of it in a welcoming manner. The map on the wall now had even more pins and strings. The file cabinet now had a whole stack of binders. He glanced at these then joined Erin on the table as she took off the headset and pushed the laptop away.

"Know anything about this?"

"No. Do you?"

"Me neither." She uncrossed then recrossed her legs. "I just got the text, like everyone else. Ned said to come down as quick as possible and that it was urgent."

Alex shrugged. "Well, we'll find out soon enough. I saw Cam. Anyone else here?"

"Pastor Art is out in back. Ayame should be here any minute now. Ned too."

"Ah." He scooted forward, leaned on his elbows.

"You doin' okay, Alex?"

"I kinda been having these headaches on and off since we started this investigation. I don't know why. But this one's a little stronger than usual, even though I took meds."

"I'm sorry . . ."

Her eyelashes fluttered as she blinked. The way the light shined then caused the faintest sparkle. He gazed at her, smirked.

"Simmer down, you two." Pastor Art sat on the other side of the table.

Cameron followed, leaned in the door frame. "Where is Neduardo? That douche is the reason for this last minute impromptu get-together."

"He wouldn't ask us to show if it wasn't important."

Almost on cue, Edward arrived at the same time as Ayame and the two toddlers. They piled into the hallway.

"This is not our usual meeting time so I had to bring the munchkins with me . . ."

Both children ran up and hugged Erin in her chair. Ian had the widest smile. Helena skipped and pranced, excited and hyper.

Edward took off his security cap and security jacket, pointed to the laptop. "Hey, Erin. Do you mind?"

"Oh. C'mon, kiddos. I'll show you guys our nice big van."

"Yaaay!"

Helena hopped up and down while Ian raised up his little arms. The three disappeared down the hall into the back lot.

"Guys, this was a bitch to get hold of, but I wanted you to see for yourselves." Edward took out a flash drive, plugged it into the laptop. "Thanks for coming on such short notice."

"What is it?"

All observed as on the screen the security camera showed a young woman kneeling down and picking a lock.

"Is that your office, Ayame?"

"Yes. It is."

The blurry footage continued, with the woman double checking her surroundings then proceeding inside.

Pastor Art squinted his eyes. "I seen her before. I know her."

Alex stared with his jaw dropped. "The same."

The preacher leaned back, arched his neck. "Her father is the one that's on hospice care, right? In the bigger private room."

"Wait. I thought everybody was short-term stay only." Cameron raised an eyebrow. "How did this chick get the rock star treatment, huh?"

"Not only that but isn't there visiting hours?"

"Her family got a special exception thanks to the CEO, and as such, they get special privileges." Ayame slouched in her chair. "Since they have connections to the original founder."

"Can you think of any reason this person might wanna break in like that?"

"I mean, I'm not her favorite staff member right now. The CEO slipped and hurt their knee pretty bad, has been out a couple months. They might even retire soon because of it. And, above me, the Director of Nursing has been on maternity leave, so I kind of have been unofficially put in charge. It is a major red flag to have this single long-term hospice patient on caseload. We don't want to get dinged come survey time."

"You're trying to push them out?"

"I did mention that we will start discharge planning. Nicely, of course."

Pastor Art folded his arms over his chest. "It looks like we found our smoking gun. Well done, everyone."

"But she seemed so nice in person . . ." Alex gulped, was still in disbelief.

"Very. Always. That's why I never thought anything when I discussed looking into alternative options. She seemed agreeable."

"Um. Who is she?"

Ayame lowered her head, took a slow breath. "Her name is Shalini. Shalini Asaria. She is the adopted daughter of Seymour McGillycuddy, a distant relative of the original founder."

Edward chimed in. "Back when we first looked into the hospital, I did come across that name. I guess it carries a lot of weight since the founder was this great and important man, it sounds like. Very influential. He cared with a passion about his community. Went above and beyond to always help shelter the poor, care for the sick, feed the homeless. The list goes on and on. Sebastian McGillycuddy, or 'Mac' as he liked to be called."

"Hmm. Well, I'll be there tonight. I can check things out for us." Cameron shuffled on his feet. "Pretty sure I have access."

"Also, Cam, text if you need anything." Edward closed the laptop. "These rotating shifts got my sleep cycle all out of whack so chances are I'll be up."

Pastor Art shifted, turned to Cameron. "Yes. Reach out. I'll answer, too. And just be careful. We really don't know what to expect here."

❧

Waiting in the morning traffic allowed his mind to wander. Alex stared ahead in silence, losing himself. He remembered the one bed bound patient with silver hair and glasses, all of the wires and tubes running from machines. He also remembered the angle of the hospital bed and the young woman who sat in the chair right next to him. How she was so kind and so pleasant in that particular moment. With each swish of the windshield wiper, the image of her smile, her face flashed to the forefront of his subconscious vivid yet inconspicuous. He circled around the block and found a parking spot, pulled in.

"Alex! Wait up!"

He turned around, saw Erin carefully jog over to him while balancing a drink carrier.

"Need a hand?"

Erin nodded in appreciation as he took the laptop bag from around her shoulder. "I guess we don't usually meet up this early, huh."

"Yeah. Got all the office workers in this area, regular customers, and looks like some construction guys. Assholes."

"Haha. Pretty much."

They kept the conversation light as they made their way. However, when they stepped into the front office, the mood changed.

Pastor Art, Edward and Cameron apparently had been busy since early on in the dead of night. He placed the laptop bag down on the table next to a thick stack of papers then panned around. There were printed pictures taped along the empty wall of the meeting room.

Cameron hovered over the three coffee cups in coffee sleeves. "Whose are these?"

"Uh, one for me and one for Alex. One for Ayame. I offered to get more for you guys but Ned said you were good."

"Damn it, Edward Scissordick!"

"What? You drank like two pots already."

Each settled down as Ayame entered. Erin handed the coffees out, to which Cameron shot Edward a subtle glare.

"I just dropped off the kids, told the other managers I'll have to miss the morning meeting. Did you find anything?"

"Well . . ." Pastor Art held out an open hand, waved towards the wall. "As you can see, in fact, Mister Gallo came across something. And it is not good."

"Actually, more than one. I was too afraid to even touch it. So I took pictures. There they are, enhanced and enlarged."

The group all lifted their heads up and scanned the wall. Alex had a quick glance earlier but didn't register it. Erin didn't seem to notice until now.

Ayame narrowed her eyes. "What is that?"

"I found them stuck to the underside of your desk."

Cameron moved closer, placed his hands on his hips. "We think . . . We're pretty sure it's a hex bag . . ."

Scattered along the wall were varied angles of the three canvas sacks bound with leather twine.

"How big are these, Cam?" Alex turned, glanced back.

"I did put my hand up near it for comparison. From the wrist to, like, the tip of the finger about."

"We been looking into the lore since like four o'clock. There is so much to go through, black magic, hoodoo and voodoo. Not to mention the different kinds of voodoo. It led us down an unending wormhole." Edward shook his head, raised both eyebrows. "I even came across an alleged concoction for the zombification process using tetrodotoxin extracted from pufferfish, the poisonous and hallucinogenic datura stramonium plant, blue lizards, large toads, and a lot of other weird crap . . ."

Alex faced forward again.

Erin and Ayame were both speechless.

"I mean, there is a whole gamut on witchcraft, from necromancers to folk healers and even shaman."

Everybody paused, waited for the preacher to continue.

"Regarding possible contents, it could be herbs. It could be fur, antlers, claws, snake skin, bird bones or rabbit teeth. It could be stones or pieces of wood with runes carved in. Nails from a coffin. An unbroken spider egg. Devil's claw. Devil's ivy. Devil's apple root."

Cameron titled his neck. "Had no idea so many plants were named 'devil' out there."

"Me neither."

Pastor Art nodded, shrugged. "It doesn't really matter though. What matters is the intent behind it. Hex bags can be for healing, protection, empowerment. Or, it can also be a curse."

Ayame lifted a hand up, covered her open mouth.

Edward rotated on the folding chair. "Is it possible there is any trace of fingernails or strands of hair in your office?"

"I keep my sweater on the chair since it always gets cold. I don't usually cut my nails at work but I have done it before. I'm just so busy . . ."

"It's okay. No shame here."

Erin glanced side to side, crossing her arms. "What do we do? How do we stop it?"

"We gotta burn them. Now, first, we need to make sure those are the only ones. Then coordinate to destroy all at the same time. Also, we need to find an altar, if there is one."

"How long is that going to take?"

"No time to waste. Since there's a new hex bag, we'll do another blessing to be safe. But thoroughly search the premises for a day, two at the most, I say."

Cameron leaned back. "Ned mentioned before that, with the vid and pics, not only can we get her removed from the property, but we can get the authorities involved as well. Maybe get a restraining order."

Edward let out a long yawn. "Pastor Art always has a friend or two in law enforcement. So maybe we can reach out."

Alex rubbed at his jaw. "And what's the plan on the ground?"

"I guess it's all hands on friggin' deck. We need to search every corner of that place."

Erin straightened up. "I can get creative with my shooting, my shots. Help out."

"I'll make some extra security rounds during my shift."

Ayame inclined her head. "Cam, you have the best excuse

to really dig in and be thorough. Maybe I could arrange for you to do some overtime?"

"Oh, man. Always me. . . . That sounds lovely."

Edward nudged at him with an elbow.

"Y'all owe me a beer, dude."

Alex nibbled his lower lip. "There is one area I haven't checked out yet. Been meaning to ever since we started. That's the old cathedral."

"Hmm." Ayame brought a finger to her chin. "You could take a patient out for some fresh air, walk over. Sometimes we take patients out for some sunlight."

"Good idea. Thanks."

"The area is actually open to visitors. It displays some of the old items used and some of the old art pieces. Almost never anybody there, though."

"H-hold on. I just thought of something." Cameron darted his head left then right. "Was it just me or did you guys eat and drink what that bitch made the other day!?"

"Oh, yeah. Same here." Erin touched a palm to her face.

"Shit. Me too." Alex sat still, his mouth agape.

Edward closed his eyes, clenched a fist. "Damn. I thought she was sooo polite, going out of her way to make sure the night shift all had some. I even caught her in the act later but never thought about it. Sneaky."

"Great. I'm at risk now, all for a motherfuckin' virgin daiquiri."

Erin rubbed at her brow. "Stupid scone."

"You all had some, huh . . . Not just you guys but how many other employees. I must've gone in early that day, missed out on the fun." Pastor Art stared each of them in the eye. "Now, it might not mean anything. Maybe she was trying to build up trust and brownie points and all that. Who knows."

Cameron placed both hands on top his head, paced back and forth. "I know. But it's so unnerving to think some psycho who happens to practice witchcraft on the side fed me snacky snacks and a smoothie."

"I guess, we better get to it then. Find any other hex bags. Find an altar."

3

FIRST, THEY STOPPED by the nice quiet courtyard area, the little accent mark above the E. It was calm and peaceful as it had been when Alex went there before. Second, they passed through the buildings that made up the E-shape, enjoying the sight of the pine trees and the flowery bushes. He remembered running into Bradley and having that talk. And then third was his true destination—the equals sign in front of the E where the cathedral and quarters were located. Alex held the push handles tight as the pavement began to slope downward. He took the patient to a cool shady spot between both buildings, locked the brakes, then offered extra birdseed.

"I'll be right back, okay? Have fun."

The patient threw a handful onto the ground where white pigeons and gray doves gathered.

"Just gonna go check something."

Alex noticed the arches, the angles and the design. The walls were painted a rosy peach color. Each window on each door was dim. When he cupped his hands and peeked inside, there was a slight shiver along his skin. It was far too quiet.

He saw old sculptures made by the founder as he pushed

the door open. They were bizarre and morbid, strange structures with strange expressions. Some of them were whimsical, like from an old cartoon. Some of them were otherworldly, like from a renaissance painting. A string of them were on display: a bell, a cat, a fish, limbless torsos, floating heads. A large chunk of hollowed out driftwood was carved in and made metallic in certain parts. Dark abstract artwork lined the walls.

This place gives me the creeps . . .

Before he continued any further, Alex used the EMF detector and the thermometer then checked the readings.

I have to be on guard.

Some of the highest I've seen.

When he headed to the cathedral from the quarters, he peeked over at the patient, made sure they were still all right. Off to the side, Alex saw the small cemetery which had a low rock wall around it and then the mausoleum surrounded by tall pointy gates. He took out the voice recorder and pressed the red button.

As he walked alongside the cemetery and mausoleum, pointing the device, Alex stared up at the cathedral at the same time. There was a set of doors between round columns beneath the steeple and its large analog clock on display. A wide set of stairs led up to it, which was diagonal like the foundation of a mini-pyramid.

His heart thumped inside his chest. He swallowed a dry swallow.

It's broad day yet I'm terrified.

With a sharp inhale through his nostrils, Alex placed a hand on the rail, ascending one step at a time.

However, the church interior was serene and tranquil. He immediately felt relief wash over him as if he had entered the eye of the storm. Empty pews on each side cascaded to the raised pulpit in front. Alex walked between them, touching the cushioned backing and the painted wooden frames.

When he was at the front, he stood in the choir row and turned around, panning in one long sweep. A large fancy organ took up the back corner and each stained glass window had rays of light passing through. Alex noticed the light pouring onto himself, and raised and rotated his forearm to see.

There was a mixture of color on his skin, reds and greens and blues. He felt something he never had before, deep in his bones and in his chest.

A part of him wanted to break right down and cry. A part of him wanted to shout out in bitter anger and despair. And another part wanted to remain in that same position, bathe in that multicolored sunlight forever.

He took his time stepping down from the light and the pulpit, back through the pews and out the door. The minute he stepped outside, there was a vibration in his pocket. It was a voicemail.

Perhaps there was no reception so he missed the call.

Alex again checked the patient then raised the Sony Ericsson to his ear, slid it open, listened as the mumbled message played.

"Hey, boy . . . I know that . . . Listen, about the other day, the other week . . . I just, um, er . . . I've been . . . I been thinking and I guess . . . I'm calling to . . ."

There was the sound of rummaging then a light touch of static.

Alex fought back a watery sheen that formed in his shut eyes. He swept the bangs out of his face, felt his lips begin to quiver.

". . . I'm sorry."

Before the two of them, the penguins waddled on their feet care-free then plunged into the water. From where they both stood, each could see from the side their transition from dry land to the shallow depths. The creatures marched forward single file from the plants and rocky terrain to the edge. Under the sur-face, the wingless birds twirled and spun and zoomed through effortlessly, leaving behind bubbly trails in their wake. Alex turned from the ocean center exhibit to April who rested her chin on both hands interlocked with a half-smile. He wrapped his arm around her from the side, pecked her on the cheek.

"They're so cute. I wanna squeeze one."

He smirked as she spoke those words, sighed.

Ah. Another wonderful moment.

I could try again . . .

Not that many people around . . .

But then, I don't know, maybe I should wait 'til after.

Pretty soon and it will all be over. For good.

Alex didn't realize then but there were always certain forks in the road, defining moments. It was a lesson from LIFE101L which he had forgotten about or perhaps not yet known—and that was to never waste an opportunity and to always seize the moment.

"Have things been better with your dad, Nex?"

"Yeah. I never heard him apologize like that before. So I did call him back. Didn't bring it up or anything, and we were all right."

"That's great."

"It was a weird moment at the time. I guess, with every-thing going on, your mom, my dad, running into Brad as I told you, I don't know, thoughts about life and death were swirling around in my head. And well, at some point, the question of God comes up."

"I feel I'm agnostic, especially now."

"Funny. I used to say with such certainty I was atheist . . ."

He paused, unsure how to expand upon the topic without exposing everything that he did this whole time, in secret, in the dark. The fact there was so much he had seen, heard and felt it was undeniable at this point.

"Come on, my sisters and mom are waiting."

"Oh. Okay."

The two walked hand in hand back to the car. When they got inside, both were quiet but Alex could tell April was about to speak. He turned, faced her, waited.

"Nex . . ."

A single tear rolled down her cheek.

He gulped, blinked.

No, no, no.

"I know I haven't been myself, as I talked about. But the truth is, ever since what happened with my mom, I can't help but feel sorta empty inside."

No. Please.

"And, well, part of that is this. I . . . I don't know if I can be all lovey-dovey, relationship mode right now. I feel like I need some space or something."

"Why, though? I've been trying to be patient, supportive, helpful."

"You have been. As much as you can. You're so wonderful. And that's what's been wrong. I don't think I'm in the right place right now, mentally. 'Cause it doesn't seem to matter. I feel this sadness, this gaping hole. I feel . . . lonely . . ."

There was an extended pause.

Alex sat back against the cushion, his heart sinking beneath his sternum.

"My God. What have I—"

"Nothing, Nex. It's not your fault."

"I know I've been super busy. I'm almost done helping my friend, and then we can work it out. We can make things better again."

"Really, it's not that. It's just . . ." April shook her head, bit at her bottom lip while a second tear rolled down her other cheek. "It's just not the right timing."

A single specific lesson from LOVE102 began to creep in right then and there, and it was one he would have to learn the hard way, that had to hit him like a violent typhoon—the fact that timing is everything.

"So, w-what, are you breaking up with me?"

"I think, let's take a break for a while. I'll go stay with my sisters."

He reached over, touched her thigh then held her hand in her lap.

"Can we just wait, April? Maybe, if we wait, all this will pass."

"I heart you. You heart me. Right?"

Alex brought her hand to his lips, kissed the back of it. He then put his hand to her cheek, his fingers beneath her dazzly ear.

"Of course, love."

"This is something I think I need right now."

Back in the beginning, they were friends, just friends. And then he developed feelings and those feelings overcame him, and he found himself stuck in the friend zone. Then somehow, some way, the stars and even their shroom magically aligned until it was friends with benefits, lots and lots of benefits. Then they officially became In a Relationship status, got more serious as boyfriend/girlfriend, moved in together, and next thing engaged to be engaged with matching promise rings. And here, now, like this, although they didn't change their profiles online, it had turned into It's Complicated.

There was so much conflicting internal thought and emotion that it was overwhelming, almost petrifying. He could feel it radiate throughout each limb to his fingertips and his toes, seeping into each pore on his skin. At the same time, he was numb. During the shift, Alex proceeded without thinking, eyelids low, shoulders low, hunched. The elevator was taking too long for comfort and there were too many other people gathered so he left, went down to the end of the hall into the stairwell instead. He pushed the door open, took out his phone to recheck if perhaps she had texted or called, and then plodded on up with a slow and steady step, step, step.

Alex inhaled deep then released the air through pursed lips. It all came flooding to him, everything and everyone. He thought about April first and foremost. How they rode on the shuttle together, both worked at the shopping center, used to play Nintendo DS. How they kissed and held hands and made love and hugged for extended periods to release all those happy chemicals. How they laughed. How they listened to music. Each emo song and each emo flick of his bangs.

He thought about college and his former plans and goals, hopes and dreams. He thought about his other classmates, about Bradley, about every professor that saw this great potential in him. How he went to the library early in the morning then stayed until late at night, enrolled in more than full-time credits every single semester, even in the summer. How that atmosphere and the whole of academia was so fascinating.

He also thought about his family, dysfunctional though they were. His mother and his father and his little brother. Aunty Divina and Lucio and Merced. His grandfather who passed and even his Aunt Sonsoles.

Each case, each client, each encounter replayed in his subconscious, going all of the way back to the choking ghost and now this faceless woman.

Thoughts of Diedre and of Pastor Art, Edward and Cameron came to mind. His conversations and interactions with each one of them. How they forever changed him. How they forever touched him.

Thoughts of Erin came to mind, and lingered.

Alex placed a hand on the door handle, paused, blinked to himself with a slight crinkled brow. He glanced back then faced forward again.

Wait a second.

Hold on.

By accident and sheer coincidence, he had gone too far. He went past the fourth floor entrance up to the fifth, where the rehab gym was being built and which was closed. Alex felt trepidation as he pulled the handle and somehow it gave way.

No . . .

I don't believe it . . .

How in the . . .

Every single hair on his forearms, his shins and the back of his neck stood up. A deep icy chill ran down his spine, in the pit of his chest and stomach. His eyes were wide. His mouth was open.

The dark and empty space was like an abandoned building. Like an excavation site. Like a rundown parking lot. No tiles. No paint. No walls. No lighting fixtures. All he could see was blank pillars, broken concrete, pieces of rubble, leftover tools and equipment, and pitch black. It was as if time stood still in this forgotten void.

Alex remained frozen until he willed himself forward into the abyss.

He had no idea how but he sensed the exact location. It was this gravitational field out of place, that seemed to pulse like an erratic heartbeat. Behind the first couple pillars was a small wooden table right on the ground. On top, he saw candles with burnt out wicks, a long gray feather and a cracked animal skull with long round horns. He could see a locked box and a book bound in leather, both with strange symbols on them.

Oh, God.

I actually found it.

⌁

Now that they successfully located the altar and concluded there were only those three hex bags, it was time to gather once more, perhaps for the last time. Alex ruminated every twist and turn that led to this moment, each crossroads that could have been different. The way the sun dissolved into the buildings and trees then resembled a solar eclipse. He peered into this, squinting, then got out of the parked car. Before walking down the road, he leaned against the fender. He crossed his legs over and stuck his hands in his pockets with a sigh. From behind him, he felt a presence then shifted to see. Erin had her head tilted, arms at her sides, a half-smile spread across her face. They locked eyes and stood still for a moment.

"Hey. Didn't see you there . . ." He placed his palms on the frame of the car instead, with a subtle squirm.

"Is everything all right?"

"Yeah, I just . . ." Alex shook his head, faced away.

Erin joined him, also sat on the fender.

"The girl again?"

He shook his head, took a breath. "I mean, it's more than that. A lotta things. But yeah."

"It's the big night, Alex. Gotta get your head in the game."

"I know. Still, though, I can't seem to—"

Before he finished the sentence, she pressed her lips to his. It was light and soft, staying close enough for their lips to hover together. She delicately kissed his top lip, changed positions, then delicately kissed his bottom lip. He could feel her take his hand and place it upon her breast, moving her fingers over his.

"There." Erin pulled her head back, paused, covering her mouth with the back of her hand. "See, other women exist. Don't overthink it."

Alex crinkled his brows, smirked, tasting the fresh lipstick.

He gazed at her until there was a faint flush in her cheeks, a flutter in her eyelids.

"Don't tell me. You're overthinking this now, too, aren't you?"

They both let out an awkward laugh.

"Come on." She nudged him at the shoulder. "The others are waiting."

As they waltzed on, their hands dangled close and their fingers grazed, to which they both exchanged a quick glance.

Everybody else was already huddled in the meeting room in

their unofficial assigned seating. They took up the two remaining sides of the square table.

Pastor Art stared each person in the eye, took a long breath. "Okay, so this is it. Have we covered every room, every area?"

"I worked my ass off. And what you see there on the wall, those pics, that's it." Cameron had his arms crossed, pointed with his chin to Alex. "Other than our friend here who walked into the attic from hell."

"Yeah, you mentioned a fifth floor. I even tried pushing the button in the elevator once but it wouldn't go."

Pastor Art nodded along. "Same."

Ayame leaned forward on one elbow. "As far as I knew, it was closed off. Except for planned construction crews, which were on indefinite hiatus last I heard. They are focusing on finishing the independent and assisted living side first."

"That does make sense." Edward scratched at his beard. "I been monitoring her movements, and it's either the patient room or disappearing into the elevator or stairs. Perhaps she picked that lock as well."

"So, the plan is to burn these?" Erin touched her glasses, pressed them up the bridge of her nose.

"Yeah. We'll split up. Me, Mister Berenson and Mister Gallo go to the fourth floor. The rest of you go to the fifth floor. Bring the walkie-talkies so we can sync the burn." Pastor Art snapped his fingers as he explained. "I got my friends in blue all ready to go right after we do the deed."

"Are the kiddos going to be okay?"

"I called a special favor with one of my other military wife friends. Needed a dependable babysitter. This has to end tonight. I am less afraid now, and instead, kind of infuriated. They saw her again, Ian and Helena . . ."

"The faceless woman? The noppera-bō?"

Ayame thinned her lips. "Yes. We have to finish this. I will not allow my child to get hurt ever again."

Cameron rubbed his forehead then his chin. "Maybe, uh, this new hex is more powerful. Or something."

"That could be."

"Either way, it is time. I'll also take my car. Alexander, you ride with me. I got one more pep talk before we wrap up this friggin' case. Finally. Once and for all."

4

IN FRONT OF them, they saw the van go straight as the light changed, heading from the headquarters to Saint Florian. Whatever last rays of sun already disappeared into the horizon, allowing the darkness of night to envelop the city. They pulled up behind the van at the next light, their turn signals rhythmically flashing back and forth with off timing. Pastor Art kept both hands on the steering wheel, tapping his right index finger. Alex could feel the rumble from the engine and the roar from the exhaust pipe. The muscle car idled then revved as they moved forward again, now down a smooth and winding stretch of road.

"Pastor?"

The preacher lifted a brow but kept his eyes fixated.

"I'm glad we get to talk again like this."

"Of course, Alexander. Sorry . . . My mind is . . ."

Alex turned to the side. "Why did you wanna take your ride?"

"I thought it would be a good idea to have that extra firepower, just in case. 'Member what I told you?"

"Right. Always strapped."

"None of us ever encountered a dang witch before. Kinda wanted to have weapons close, cover our rear ends. That's all."

He nodded as Pastor Art spoke, stared out the window. "I never had a chance to say, but the readings were very high in the quarters, like spiking up. It was hella creepy in there."

The preacher breathed in one long breath.

"Now, the old church, though, it had nothing. Nothing at all. It was so peaceful and so calm inside. In fact . . ."

Pastor Art shifted, glanced at him, waiting.

"Although I can't explain it, I swear I felt . . . like, the presence of God . . ."

They took another turn.

While the preacher rotated the wheel with his palm, he smiled. "Fantastic."

"Can you talk to me about that, Pastor? That's so weird. Like, I was never a believer, of anything. And now, well, I don't know anymore."

"I mean, we been dealing with ghosts and spirits. The Lord God is called the Holy Ghost or the Holy Spirit. Right?" Pastor Art paused, narrowed his eyes. "Each and every person on earth has got to make up their mind on the matter for themselves. How this all works. What this all means."

"Hmm."

"You got a gift, Alexander. Many gifts actually. I think God has a very specific and special purpose for you. I'm glad that we met each other. And this is not even me talking right now." Pastor Art let out a raspy chuckle. "My mouth might be moving, sound may be coming out, but I'm just a vessel."

The barrier gate arm raised for the van. They waited their turn at the front of the parking garage.

"Funny. I zoned out at the start of this li'l drive. You shared your epiphany. I had to expand upon it. But still, I did have one thing to say."

"Yes, Pastor?"

After the ramp, they pulled the muscle car into the stall next to the van where the others were already getting out.

"Now, your one gift . . . The same one that makes you a conduit, an antenna, as we discussed. It could also make you vulnerable here. We don't know what's gonna happen. I won't let anything happen to you. But try to watch out. Keep your head up. Seriously. This is unlike all the other cases that we have been involved with so far."

With a slow breath, the preacher paused then continued.

"You remember Miles? Deidre's husband? He was up against a very evil entity in that case. It targeted him, embedded itself, tainting his mind. And he wasn't sensitive like you are. So, again, please, please be on guard. Do you understand what I'm telling you?"

"I . . . I understand."

Alex thinned his lips then undid his seat belt, both of them getting out.

"We're ready, Pastor Art."

The group gathered in front of the van and the muscle car.

"Lighter." Cameron handed one to Alex, kept the other.

He turned it over in his hand. "I guess it's on then . . ."

"Lighter fluid." Cameron handed a yellow squeeze bottle to Edward and to Erin.

The preacher cleared his throat.

"Oh. Also, the three of us will be needing these, right." Erin held a flashlight, gave out two others to Alex and Ayame. "I want to add, before I forget, I been doing tests. It's always a bit cold in and around that patient room, with extremely high levels of EMF. So, be on alert."

"God . . ."

"Um, wait. Is this blowing our cover showing up together like this?"

"Police are on their way soon. It's all gonna be out in the open. No going back now."

Cameron walked in front, taking the lead, followed by Pastor Art and Edward. Ayame stayed close to Erin, appearing stoic. The security guard gave them all a suspicious stare. Alex lingered behind, glancing up at the building as they approached.

"It's windy as hell tonight . . ." Erin glanced back at Alex.

The two locked eyes for a moment, both with worried faces.

❧

Strong gusts rustled every leaf within the branches of the trees, even the bushes and plants and blades of grass. The walls and windows appeared ominous and foreboding against the blackness of the night air. Alex noticed the bright and giant orb of the moon, appearing close enough that he could reach out and touch it. It had a strong deep yellow-orange sheen. The group passed the snack shop and the gift shop which were still open, and squeezed into the elevator. Nobody said a word. Nobody made a sound. Erin huddled close to Alex in back, the sides of their arms touching. Outside of the elevator, Ayame took a fire extinguisher from a case on the wall.

"Pastor Art, there's another one opposite corner from my office."

"Got it."

A nurse noticed them, had a confused expression.

Cameron again took the lead, Pastor Art and Edward

following. Alex led Erin and Ayame into the stairwell and the three went from the fourth floor to the fifth, into the dark and empty space, the void, the abyss.

Beams from their flashlights pierced through the air, hovering and crossing over one another. They carefully stepped around broken concrete and pieces of rubble, some tools and equipment, until the wooden box was on the ground in front of them.

Alex could feel the two girls tense up, their breathing increasing. He took the flashlight from Erin, held it for her, aiming it at the altar as she prepared the squeeze bottle. She dowsed the wooden table, the candles, the skull, the box and the book, sprayed until it was the last remaining drops then tossed the empty container down in front of it.

Erin stepped back. Alex handed her back the flashlight. Ayame put hers away while moving closer, fire extinguisher at the ready.

"This is Erin." There was a loud beep then rolling static.

"Hey, it's Ned. I read you."

"Do it."

Alex flicked the lighter, knelt down and carried the small flame to the edge of the table. In one loud whooshing sound, the altar went up in a ball of fire. The burning and crackling illuminated their cavernous surroundings.

He turned to the two girls, saw the glow reflect in Erin's glasses. Ayame waited, timed it then put out the fire, revealing the scorched items.

Erin brought the walkie-talkie to her mouth. "It's done."

"Same here." There was another loud beep. "Looks like no problems."

With that, Alex could feel Erin relax and breathe a sigh of relief.

Just a split second later, he noticed Ayame was missing. "Wait! Where is she!?"

The two darted their heads around, scanning the area, saw the fire extinguisher on the ground. The door back to the stairs swung on its hinges.

"Oh, shit."

"Where'd she go?"

"She mentioned finally confronting her on the drive here . . . But I thought she meant at the police station or something . . ."

"No. God, no." Alex broke into a sprint. "Follow me! Stay close!"

&

Both of them raced through the pitch black, rushing back out the door and down the stairs. The hollow echo of their panicked footsteps bounced off all of the walls, reverberating from the fifth floor to the fourth floor, all the way to the third, second, first. Alex grabbed the rail and hopped onto the landing, yanking the door open in one swift move. Erin was right behind him as they entered the fourth floor once again. The two glanced at the end of the hall, peeking to the corner of the T-shape then hurried to the other side of the closed loop. A janitor watched as they ran towards and past him, inching away as they did.

"Hurry! Meet us at the patient's room!"

Static cut in and out as Erin pressed then repressed the button.

"It's Ayame!"

"W-what—" There was a loud beep. "I didn't catch—"

"Hurry!!!"

As they turned the corner, Alex and Erin skidded to a halt. There was Ayame and there was Shalini—in the middle of the hallway, squared off, face to face, in between two large paintings up on the wall.

Both paused then walked forward with hesitation.

Off to the side, one of the aides whispered to the other then left, not wanting to get involved.

Tread lightly, Ayame.

We don't know what she's capable of.

"Uhh." Alex raised a hand. "I-i-is everything okay?"

"No. It is not." Ayame shifted, glanced back at him with the corner of her eye. "I am calling her out for all that she has done."

"I have no idea what you're talking about. That is absurd. You sound like you're out of your mind." The young woman appeared so rational, so composed. "I absolutely did no such thing."

"Do you know how many sleepless nights? Do you know how terrible the pain of fearing the worst nightmare could happen to your loved ones at any moment is? Do you know what it feels like to be so powerless to help???"

"Please." The young woman started to back away, raised her hands up in a pleading manner. "You're scaring me. I'm trying to let my father rest."

"No! Tell me what you are really doing, and why."

"I told you. I don't know anything about that. Please. Please."

From the opposite side of the hall, the other three appeared and moved in closer. Now she was surrounded.

The young woman spun around, peering into their faces

with a frightened and nervous demeanor. "What is this? What is going on?"

Edward raised his voice. "We have the footage of you breaking in."

Cameron was next to him, cracked his knuckles.

"We found the hex bags. We found the altar." Pastor Art moved both of his hands in front of him as he spoke. "And police are already on their way. It's over."

"No, no, no. Please. I didn't do anything. This has to be a mistake."

There were shiny shimmery tears welling up in the young woman's eyes. She leaned against the side wall, one arm out in defense. Her lower jaw began to tremble. Her breathing grew erratic.

Alex felt Erin scoot closer to him.

Before them all, the face of the young woman changed. It went from being afraid, playing the victim, pretending to be innocent now to blank, lifeless, joyless.

Shalini at last straightened up with a confident stance, showing her true colors.

"Welp. Looks like you got me." Her lips curled into an almost inhuman smile. "I knew something had to be up. All you guys appearing one after the other, so suspiciously. Asking your questions and snooping and sneaking like good detectives."

The group was silent. The air around them became darker, colder all of a sudden.

Her smile grew as if she knew some great big secret, was about to reveal an amazing surprise, and was fighting off this wave of laughter.

"It doesn't matter now, though. Nope. No, no, no. It's far too late."

Ayame narrowed her eyes. "What do you mean . . . ?"

"This was all just to delay you, can't you see. I only needed to stay a tiny bit longer, enough to last 'til the night of the supermoon."

Alex remembered the huge bright yellow-orange orb of moon outside—like an egg yolk, like amber, mixed with blood orange. He dropped his jaw and widened his eyes.

Holy fuck!

"Which. Is. Tonight."

It was so windy outside that Alex could hear howling come from the nearest patient window. He turned to the side, gazed out the glass pane to the branches and leaves that twisted and bent, about to rip straight off. Somehow, within whatever short period of time, the already strong gusts became borderline gale force.

"And what the heck happens on the night of the supermoon, huh?"

"Welp. I might as well come clean here. Allll cards on table." Shalini licked her lips then smiled again. "I finally get to complete my mass sacrifice."

One of the nurses came from around the corner, a security guard with her, pointing to the mixed group, although this was done in vain.

Shalini upturned her palm and raised her hand.

Her inhuman smile became a wide and evil grin, lips pulled taut and cheeks distorted.

Erin blinked, flinched. "Watch out!"

Alex clenched his fists, stepped forward. Pastor Art and Edward did the same. Cameron crept forward then lunged. But before any of them got near, Shalini closed her fingers into a tight ball.

The fluorescent lights throughout the entire floor flickered on and off, unnatural extremes between black and white like an intermittent strobe effect.

Cameron staggered to the floor, falling down onto his side. Alex held at his abdomen, dropped to one knee. Edward tripped back onto his tailbone. Ayame leaned along the edge of the countertop. Each of them hissed and winced and groaned.

Pastor Art hovered over Cameron and Edward.

Erin checked on Ayame, went to Alex. "Are you okay!? Alex! Alex!"

A sharp guttural cackle echoed through the hallway.

The preacher peeked around amidst the chaos. The young woman had disappeared, vanished as if into thin air.

"I curse you . . . I torment you . . ."

Her voice was audible and crystal clear. It seemed not to be spoken aloud but somehow whispered telepathically into each of their heads.

"By the ghosts of your past . . ."

The flickering lights intensified, becoming even more pronounced to the point they might crack and burst.

"Oh my God!"

From out of nowhere, Alex felt an invisible something pounce on him, knocking him down and pinning him. He couldn't move. He couldn't breathe. He couldn't produce any sound.

"Alex! Alex! Alex!"

He gasped, struggled to keep his eyes open enough to see his surroundings.

"Alex!!!"

Walking slow and steady towards Edward who writhed and gagged was a woman in the nude, stunning, gorgeous, every curve of her body exposed, from her buttocks to her breasts, down to her wisp of pubic hair.

Cameron shouted out in terror, crawled on all fours away from a slender figure that had long limbs and a bony face, big, black and shadowy, with what appeared like tentacles or tendrils flailing.

Ayame backed against the wall, tears streaming down her cheeks, using one hand to cover her open mouth.

He felt something next to him so he adjusted, squirmed.

There was this woman wearing a pink kimono which melted into the floor. She glided her hands with a certain elegance, brushing the hair aside with gangly fingers revealing beneath the strands a pale lumpy mass with no discernible features. No eyes. No mouth. No nose. It was nothing but smooth skin.

Holy fuckin' shit!

Unlike anything he had ever witnessed before, this ungodly presence was a homunculus, an abomination—the results of a lab experiment gone wrong, a horrific accident, a birth defect or a burn victim.

While the choking ghost held him in place, the faceless woman moved forward.

The apparition shifted its head towards Alex, tilting, leaning in. He could sense a sort of malice beneath the blank flesh, at the same time this vindictive pleasure and enjoyment in inflicting fear and pain—a gaze without a face, a smile without lips.

Pastor Art desperately began to pray.

Erin watched in terror as all this occurred.

The preacher then splashed water onto Ayame, Edward, Cameron and Alex. Each breathed a sigh of relief, feeling momentary safety as the entities were gone.

"Dang. Should've brought more blessed water . . ."

Cameron sat up, hung his head between his knees. Edward held a hand over his chest, hyperventilating.

"Is e-everybody okay?" Alex rolled onto his side.

Ayame shut her eyes, shoulders shuddering as she proceeded to break down. "I am so sorry. I couldn't let it go any longer, all that she's done."

Erin stood, put a hand on her shoulder.

"We only got a minute. But any idea why only you four were attacked?"

"Gotta be that random food and drink." Edward moved his hand from his chest to his stomach.

"Right. I didn't have any." Pastor Art turned to Erin. "Didn't you, though?"

"I did, so I don't get it."

Cameron lifted his head between breaths. "Wasn't there something in the lore?"

Edward peeked over, gritted his teeth.

"Like, about ingesting bodily fluids."

Pastor Art searched his memory banks. "Yeah, I remember reading that . . . Shoulda thought about it before."

Alex crinkled his brow, inclined his head.

The lights continued to flicker. Some of the staff became frantic, running about. A few patients called out, cried out. The winds continued to howl on.

"Oh, I got it."

Each of them turned to Alex who staggered to his feet.

"It's the ice cubes."

"Huh?"

"It's the *fucking* ice cubes."

All stared back at him, confused, waiting for an explanation.

"Erin, you don't like ice."

She narrowed her eyes, opened her mouth to say something.

Alex realized then how he knew this minute insignificant detail about her. "You mentioned once how it makes your teeth cold."

"I guess . . . I did insist no ice."

Cameron shook his head, grimaced.

Alex stood firm. "She put her saliva in the ice cubes."

Edward stuck his tongue out in disgust. Ayame gagged, turned away.

"How you know this?" Pastor Art leaned in.

Flashes of Shalini methodically dripping her spittle into the sections of the ice tray played in his mind like clairvoyance.

"I just do." He bit at his bottom lip, pounded a fist on the counter. "That raving lunatic poisoned us."

The staff began to close all the patient doors one by one. Nurses were on the phones, explaining the situation to the operator. Another security guard entered the floor, panicked.

"Like the altar, if you remember, a curse or hex is usually connected to an object. She must be carrying something on her. We have to destroy it." The preacher turned to each of them, staring into their eyes as well as into their souls. "Not just for you guys, but how many other staff and employees in this building are at risk? There's no time to waste."

5

THE ARGUMENT AND confrontation occurred in the middle of the hall, away from the actual patient room. It seemed only logical to conclude Shalini would have gone there. Along the way, more of the havoc and disarray unraveled before them. Ayame held a hand out as she reluctantly followed Pastor Art, making her way half-blind amidst the heavy flickering. Cameron and Edward walked shoulder to shoulder, peeking into the rooms that were still open. Alex was behind Erin, scanned left then right, glancing backwards and facing forward again. In the nearest window, he saw the leaves and branches continue to whip in the wind.

"Are you scared?" Erin waited, let Alex pass, touching at the back of his shirt. "I've never felt so terrified in my whole entire life . . ."

"Take a deep breath. Follow me."

She swallowed, nodded.

Up ahead, in the patient room, a bizarre sight awaited them.

From the ceiling, steady droplets of water fell as if it was raining. Along the walls, water poured out and dripped as if a pipe had burst. The water pooled on the floor and spilled out like a shallow river. It was freezing cold in the area leading up to the room. While the group closed in, they realized the droplets moved down as expected but also moved up along the vertical plane as well. Some of them even floated across sideways on the horizontal axis, defying the laws of physics.

A single raindrop shot out and hit Pastor Art in the shoulder. "What the heck?"

They all turned to one another in disbelief.

In the patient room, the machines beeping slowed. Pastor Art was the first of them to see up close, then Ayame, then Edward and Cameron.

Each of them gathered just outside.

Pastor Art stuck his hand in the pouring water. "It feels weird . . . Like, tears or sweat or something. Not ordinary water."

Reaching a finger in, Ayame dabbed it then rubbed it with her thumb. She wiped it off with her shirt.

Alex and Erin were the last to peek inside, saw the handle of the knife stabbed into the chest.

It was a unique knife, with faces and shapes carved into the handle, part of the wavy uneven sharp metal still visible.

"This must be a ceremonial blade." Edward stared at it. "An elemental tool for rituals. Both weapon and magical object."

"Does this bitch got a cauldron, too?" Cameron placed a hand on his hip.

Just then, the machine sounded a constant and dull tone. "He's gone."

Outside the window, a steady flash of red and blue lights appeared.

"Alexander, come with me." Pastor Art shot him a serious glance. "We'll go and brief the cops. The faster they can get caught up, see this, find her, the better."

"Let's go."

Erin shifted in place. "Be careful."

"I'll be right back."

The two turned to make their way.

"Wait! Wait!" Edward chimed in. "You might wanna take the stairs. I mean, look."

Alex and Pastor gazed at the intermittent flickering that showed no sign of stopping.

"Good thinking, Mister Berenson."

Both raced to the stairwell. Alex shined the flashlight down so they could see. The stairs seemed to go on and on like an infinite, impossible, paradoxical loop until they reached the bottom and exited.

Alex glanced at the two small shops side by side. Both women appeared confused, frightened, frantic. The older one stared up at the lights, one of them beginning to spark. The middle-aged one was on the phone.

Pastor Art rushed out to the driveway, where the police car was pulled over before the incline to the parking garage.

"Oh, no."

Alex was about to ask but saw for himself.

The two officers were slouched, cold, still. It was the same ceremonial blade stuck into each of their chests.

How could she have got here so fast?

"Pastor . . ."

They both turned to the passenger seat.

"Pastor . . ."

Alex watched as the officer grew shaky, sweaty, becoming pale.

"It's okay. I'm here."

"We leave this in, right? The blood loss."

At least he has a chance.

Hold on.

"I don't even know what happened . . . It was all so fast . . ." The eyes rolled into the back of his head, then with effort, returned to facing the preacher. "I called for backup, but they might be a while . . ."

"You hang tight." Pastor Art touched a hand to the man's arm then pivoted.

Should I reach out to April?

No, maybe not.

Maybe leave her out of this.

I don't want to put her at risk.

"This is it, Alexander. It's time we take matters into our own hands. She friggin' killed her adoptive father and now one, possibly two cops."

Both jogged up the hill back to the parking garage, hurried to the muscle car and popped open the trunk.

Pastor Art took a vial and a container of salt, began to unlock two black cases. "Do you know how to shoot?"

"Um, I went like once . . . A long time ago."

"Here. I'll set it up for you. Watch closely."

Alex observed as Pastor Art loaded the five large red shells in. He checked, rechecked then handed the shotgun.

"Okay. That's a pump action. But not rock salt, I put in buckshot. Nine balls of lead a piece. It'll do some major damage."

"Should I get the handgun instead?"

"No, no. Remember?" The preacher stared him dead in the eye. "You're the one at risk. And she already has a hook in you. I want you to have the stronger weapon. If she gets up close, put 'er down. This is life and death."

Alex hesitated then nodded. "I understand."

"First round is already chambered. The second, you'll have to pump it. Five shots and here's an extra five."

He put the shells in his back pocket.

"Now, aim a little low since this thing will pop up once you pull the trigger. Twelve gauge so it's got quite a kick."

"Like this?"

"Hold the butt of it higher up. Firm. To the shoulder." Pastor Art tested the grip of the stock. "Nicely done. C'mon. Let's rock and roll."

❧

By the time the two exited the parking lot and took the right turn toward the building, the yellow moon overhead was obscured. The layer of clouds forming over it glowed with a churning mixture of orange, purple, gray and black. It appeared like molten lava spewing, settling, spreading. Alex stayed close to Pastor Art, off to the side and behind at a slight diagonal. He kept crouched, with the barrel of the weapon pointing down. The strong gusts knocked over a pair of garbage cans which sent random plastic wrappers and crumpled pieces of paper rolling on the ground and then flying in the air, twirling and wafting.

Alex glanced up at the heavy flickering in each window like dots and dashes of Morse code or like an alternating festive sequence of lights on a Christmas tree.

Pastor Art led them back to the stairs past the elevators.

On the way, the two noticed that the shops now appeared empty. He peeked over to both doors that were half open and left ajar. Dark puddles of blood spilled out over the floor.

God damn . . .

It was a bit of a struggle to climb back up, the shotgun

becoming heavier and heavier as they made their way to the fourth floor.

"Stay with me, Alexander." Pastor Art pivoted. "Don't let this old man lap you now."

He felt out of breath, slowed his pace as they made it in.

"Alex! Pastor Art!"

Erin ran and hugged Alex around his shoulders. Edward hurried over and clapped the preacher on the arm.

"So good to see you guys."

The chaos roared around them still.

"You too."

"It's been crazy over here. I gave my walkie to Cam, and then we split into pairs but still no sign of Shalini. What happened to the ECPD?"

"Sadly, she got to them before we did." Pastor Art shook his head. "But backup should be on the—"

Again, her voice was audible and clear, somehow whispered telepathically.

"I curse you . . . I torment you . . ."

The four instinctively stepped backward in unison, turning to each other and huddling closer together.

"Suffer, afflicted and harrowed, all of the ghosts that roam these lands . . ."

Another sharp guttural cackle echoed through the hall, this time higher in pitch and breaking into an almost animalistic squeal.

From the distance, mixed in with the howling winds, Alex heard a growl. He peered through the glass to the steeple. The others noticed him staring, gazed to where his eyes were locked.

"What the hell is that!?"

"Is that the . . . the dog beast thing . . . or whatever???"

Some of the paintings flew off the wall and crashed down, breaking up their huddle. Alex hopped in front of Erin, shielding her from splinters and broken glass as more paintings flew and crashed. On the other side, the space between them widening, Pastor Art and Edward were forced to move away.

There were voices. There were footsteps. There was tapping, scratches. They could see faded outlines weaving in and out. There were orbs and there were fireballs. They heard the organ blare from the cathedral where two glowing red eyes appeared.

All at once, the lights went out. No more flickering, only darkness.

In the pitch black, a single shriek cut through the air.

From every corner of every corridor came unholy apparitions shambling towards the four of them. The ghouls had swollen lumps and bumps up and down their faces, their bare arms and chest and back. Each blister was moist, cherry red, full of pus, and about to burst.

"Move! Move!!!"

Pastor Art splashed water from the vial then poured salt down in a straight horizontal line. Edward shot both arms out while stepping away. Erin held Alex tight around his arm. Alex glanced over his shoulder.

At the far end, he saw Ayame and Cameron also dodging paintings that smashed down while scrambling away from a mob of diseased bodies staggering towards them. The disembodied spirits arched their necks, moaned in agony, flailing their arms with outstretched fingers. One of them walked with a limp. One of them dragged their feet.

The windows slid open, letting in the gusts.

"Uh . . ." Pastor Art switched to a side step, moving alongside the rail on the wall. "That ain't gonna hold."

Some of the staff screamed and ran into the nearest patient room, slamming the door behind them.

Pieces of paper flew up then slid over the floor. Notices and signs posted around the door frame tore off.

"What do we do!?"

Erin held onto Alex, squeezing him. He became rigid and stiff, frozen in place. Next to the two, Edward cowered, his limbs unsteady and wobbly.

Cameron and Ayame were closing in, the gap shrinking.

Up close, the corpses had their eyes shut tight and their lips pulled tight from the swelling, the texture of their drippy skin like moldy cheese full of holes.

"Here!"

Pastor Art opened a bathroom door and let them in before entering himself. He shoved the door closed then poured out salt along the bottom. He also splashed the water onto the panel in a crisscross pattern.

"Dang. Not much left."

Ayame wiped the tears from her cheek.

Edward bent down, his hands on his knees.

"Here, you hang onto this." Pastor Art handed Cameron the container of salt. "We still got plenty of that."

The group then stood together in a circle, not blinking, with shallow breaths.

It was only a minute but it felt like longer.

Erin and Ayame shined their flashlights around, onto a sink then onto the stalls. Alex shined his along the walls and ceiling.

"No windows so I guess that's good."

Half the room went dim as Ayame winced and hunched over, lowering her light. She turned around, reaching behind to her back.

As she lifted up her shirt, exposing her skin, there were fresh parallel scratch marks.

"The fuck?"

With a hiss and a grimace, Ayame touched at them.

Behind, one of the stall doors glided open with a slow squeak, and then another, and then another. While the group searched around the large bathroom, there were glimpses of something—or someone—in the angles of the mirrors over the sinks.

One toilet flushed.

One sink turned on.

"Guys, stick together . . ."

Another toilet flushed.

Another sink turned on.

"Someone's coming . . ."

Each stall door rattled then opened and closed on its hinges, over and over. Every toilet flushed. Every sink turned on.

The group huddled together.

Alex sensed a presence, peeked over his shoulder between them all.

On her knees, in her pink kimono, the faceless woman swept her long black hair aside unveiling her deformed mass of smooth flesh where two eyes, a mouth and a nose should have been. She rose up, hunched, tilted her neck with a cracking noise, outstretched her arms and curled her fingers like an apex predator about to reap its vulnerable prey.

Alex scrambled, held the weapon with his finger off the trigger.

Pastor Art turned around then stepped back.

Erin screamed, leapt away.

Cameron shuddered in place.

Edward pushed Ayame out of the way then hobbled, dropping to one knee. Down his left forearm were scratch marks.

"AH!"

"Ned, are you—"

"AHHH!"

Down his right forearm were a second set of marks, deeper, darker.

Cameron was about to throw the salt but keeled over in pain then and there, dropping it.

Erin saw the container roll towards herself.

Ayame ran to the front door, tried to open it but it wouldn't budge. She pounded on it, kicked at it, pleaded.

The faceless woman was about to follow but Erin sprinkled the salt out in a nice long arc while Pastor Art simultaneously emptied the last of the vial in steady splashes. Before them, it vanished without a trace.

Edward slid down the wall to the floor. "I-it fuckin' stings . . ."

"We got that first aid kit in the van, right?" Alex turned to Erin who nodded.

Erin thought about it more, widened her eyes. "Or maybe, wait, I mean, this is a nursing facility."

"Good point."

"Dang, she got you pretty good." Pastor Art knelt, reached a hand out and shifted. "How about you two?"

"It hurts like shit but I'll manage." Cameron held at his side.

Ayame pounded the door again, took a breath, shifting. "Me too."

Pastor Art narrowed his eyes, glanced around at each member of the group then stood. "Duck down. Cover up."

Bang, bang. Bang.

Pastor Art motioned with his head. "Alexander."

Alex walked forward, carefully pointed the barrel and pulled the trigger.

Boom!

The two opened the busted door, peeked their heads to make sure it was clear, let out a sigh of relief.

"We have to hurry."

❧

Despite the hands of the clock ticking, their first order of business was to patch up those injured. Pastor Art went with Ayame to the nearest medicine cart, got some ointment, gauze and bandage. First, she tended to Edward who was bleeding an excessive amount. It oozed down his forearms to his elbows, dripping onto the tiles with silent splats. Ayame cleaned the wound, placed pieces of gauze but it seeped through with dark crimson. She placed more pieces and wrapped it around starting from the wrist. She did large pieces of gauze with tape for herself and for Cameron. Erin helped Ayame place it on her lower back.

Alex crouched down in front of Edward. "Ned, think you can move?"

"Yeah. I can. But it hurts, and I'm starting to feel lightheaded."

"Just take it easy from here."

"Listen, any more attacks like that could be very dangerous." Pastor Art crinkled his brow. "We find her and we end this. Now."

"S-s-should we wait for the police?"

"I saw the officers downstairs, you guys. This is a dire

situation. On the one hand, we can't sit back and just twiddle our thumbs. On the other, no one would blame you if you chose not to go further with this."

"Alexander is right. You don't have to." Pastor Art hung his head down then straightened up. "However, for me, I'm going to hunt down this evil, despicable wicked wench and send her butt straight to the depths of hell if it comes to that."

The others felt his deep conviction.

"Down there, in that cop car, that is *my* friend. It's my fault. I asked him as a personal favor, and now look. I'm in charge. Four of you are at risk. Three of you are injured. I cannot let this lie with a clear conscience. I must act."

Alex helped Edward up. "I'm with you, Pastor."

Erin thinned her lips but nodded along.

Next to her, Ayame breathed out, paused, then nodded as well.

Cameron stepped forward. "It is on like Donkey Kong's mom in a thong."

Edward raised a brow. "Maybe I won't be front of the line, but I'm in."

"All righty. Let's find this psychopath."

The group spread out, checked the various rooms where some of the staff were hiding and some of the patients were terrified, discombobulated.

Pastor Art and Ayame peeked in her office, her shining the flashlight for them.

Alex and Erin both aimed their lights to check one of the meeting rooms. They noticed odd writing on the wall.

Huh. That's weird.

Edward checked a storage room using the light from his cell phone.

Cameron opened the next patient room then stopped in place. He turned, faced the others with his mouth agape, trembling.

Three strangers stood before him wearing matching spandex unitards that covered their body to the wrists, ankles and nape of the neck—one male and two females, all similar in appearance like triplets.

In the bed, the patient had a ceremonial knife plunged in their chest.

From the hallway, more strangers appeared, standing and staring in silence.

"Um . . ."

Outside the window, another steady flash of blue and red lights glided. Alex saw there was a whole string of them starting to pull in.

"Backup's arrived."

"We'll still have to fend for ourselves in the meantime."

"Alex—"

He turned, saw a stranger about to rush at them with a ceremonial knife, aimed the barrel with his finger on the trigger in a standoff.

Pastor Art held the handgun up with both hands. "I'm warning you . . ."

Cameron swallowed a dry swallow.

Edward breathed out through pursed lips.

"Damn. Shit just got real."

Alex adjusted his grip on the slide, peeked at Erin while still aiming, licking his lips. His fingers were shaky.

"What the hell's going on?"

"Yeah. Why are they standing there like that . . . ?"

Bang. Bang, bang.

Pastor Art let off rounds while moving away.

Bang, bang, bang, bang.

"The shots will let the cops know where to go. Also, it's to keep these freaks back."

"C'mon! Let's head this way!"

Bang.

Cameron pushed the sliding door to the side, let everybody else out onto the patio then followed, shutting the door behind him and locking it.

Each felt the gusts die down, enough to catch their breaths and catch their bearings, although it was still a strong and steady wind.

This time, her voice wasn't whispered telepathically but spoken aloud. By the wall, right next to the group, Shalini stepped forward from the shadows wearing the same black spandex unitard which hugged every curve of her body.

"Welp. Looks like you got me again."

6

EVERY MEMBER OF the group was paralyzed in that moment, watched as Shalini continued to walk out to the outdoor recreation area overlooking the complex. Pastor Art mirrored her movement, raised the handgun and pointed it. Alex did the same, aimed his right eye over the barrel of the weapon. The two made their way to the forefront while the rest stood back but near, no one making a sound. Below, they could hear police cars pull over with a loud screech and officers storm the building entrance, already yelling and opening fire—presumably on the others, the strangers.

"You hear that?" Pastor Art motioned with his head, keeping the gun steady. "Any moment now, and you will be taken into custody. Give it up while you can."

"Ah. But I'm sure they have their hands full. You saw my little friends? My loyal followers?"

The preacher gulped, thinned his lips.

"So you did. The truth is, I, we . . ." Shalini held back laughter. "It's already done. The battle's already over."

Ayame shouted from behind. "What the hell are you doing! Who are you really!?"

Shalini closed her eyes in response, basked in the glorious moment. "My father never lived up to the expectations of his great family name. No, no. Quite the opposite. In fact, on his spare time, he started up an itsy-bitsy cult. It was all about power and control to him, ego . . . I would know . . . That prick. That son of a bitch."

There was a sudden gust of wind that blew through as Shalini reopened her eyes, staring from the patio over the balcony edge.

"As that lonely, pathetic old man got more and more sick, I took over."

Pastor Art and Alex both adjusted in place, listened with trepidation.

"It wasn't about cloaks and daggers for me, or secret passwords. Instead, I took the cult and made it *occult*. And now, well, my master plan is nearly complete. This whole mass sacrifice to appease the beast started with the piece of shit known as my father, as I'm sure you all saw, is devouring souls as we speak, and ends with the cherry on top that is her . . ."

Shalini pointed a firm finger directed at Ayame.

"First, I will break each and every one of you, shatter your bones and scoop out your eyes. Then I disembowel her, crush her beating heart in my hands. And, that's when the true agony begins, preacher man. Work my way through this six-course meal."

Pastor Art moved in closer, gave the trigger a good squeeze.

"Hey. Just you try it, sister. I will not hesitate to put you down. Drop the persona. Quit while you're ahead."

"Oh, Arturo. Look at you and your band of misfits. You really have no idea." A grin spread across her face, unnaturally wide. "You brought a gun to a witch fight."

When she pivoted, the group watched in shock and horror as Shalini walked backwards up the wall with deliberate and precise footing. She remained sideways in place like an insect, a fly with two compound eyes or a spider with eight spindly legs.

"You asked for it . . ."

Pastor Art clenched his fingers tight, rushed forward, aimed and shot at her. Alex followed close.

Bang, bang, bang, bang.

The handgun clicked, apparently out of ammunition.

&

In that strange angle, hair falling to the force of gravity but body like a solid plank jutting out from the wall, none of them saw her face. Shalini was blotted out in shadow. As the sporadic gusts blew, glimpses of her forehead, cheeks and jawline were visible though only for a mere moment in spurts. Cameron moved to the right and Erin moved to the left, both spreading out behind Pastor Art and Alex. Edward stepped in front of Ayame. Pastor Art knelt down, hurried to eject the spent magazine and insert a fresh magazine, darted one eye to Alex who was frozen in place with all of his senses overwhelmed.

He bit down on his lower lip, forcing himself to move.

Boom, shaka, boom!

The blasts left a scatter of holes in the wall but ultimately missed as Shalini lunged onto Pastor Art, wrapping her talons around his throat and squeezing.

"You'll make a fine appetizer . . ."

With a slight twitch of her head, the shotgun and the handgun flung out and slid across the floor.

Alex went to retrieve the shotgun while Erin went to pick up the handgun.

"This little pig-pig went to the supermarket . . ."

Pastor Art yelled as his left pinky somehow snapped at the middle knuckle.

"This little pig-pig stayed at home . . ."

Pastor Art shouted again while his left ring finger cracked and bent back.

Edward cringed at the sight of the invisible torture. Ayame covered her mouth, shut her eyes and faced away.

"This little pig-pig ate quinoa and tofu . . ."

Pastor Art shouted then whimpered as his left middle finger popped to the side.

"Ah, there we go." Her face was still hidden. "One, two, threeee broken fingers to mock your holy trinity."

She let out a sharp cackle that echoed through the entire space.

"You friggin' psychopath." The preacher writhed on the ground, struggled to breathe. "I'll friggin' kill you."

Gusts revealed a glimpse of her wide grin.

"I curse you . . . I torment you . . ."

"AHHH!"

Edward fought through the searing pain in his forearms, swung a chair with all his might over her back.

Cameron tore a crucifix from off the wall and rammed it into the side of her head.

"The power of Christ compels you, bitch!"

With another slight twitch, both Edward and Cameron were hurled in the air.

Ayame shuddered then froze in place.

"Shit! It's jammed—" Erin fidgeted with the handgun.

Pastor Art gasped, face turning red, veins bulging out.

Boom, shaka! Boom, shaka!

The shots were point blank and a direct hit. Alex felt the heat, saw the smoke waft, his right shoulder beginning to ache.

How are you still breathing???

When Shalini turned to him, a burst of wind swept the hair from her face revealing that her eyes were now missing, gone from her skull. There were hollowed out sinkholes where both eyeballs should be, light droplets of blood oozing from the corners like fresh tears. Her wide grin was lined with sharp fangs.

She twitched her head to the side which knocked everybody away like a shockwave. Pastor Art rolled on the floor as if he had been kicked in the ribs. Erin and Ayame fell backwards. Edward and Cameron slid across to the edge of the patio balcony.

Alex glanced down at his two feet, realized he was able to remain in place.

"How did I not see it before, not sense it . . ."

More droplets of blood oozed out as she spoke. Her tongue slithered and her fangs were slick with saliva.

"You're different than the rest. Looks like you might be the real dessert."

"Don't you touch—"

"Shut that hole in your face, preacher man."

Another twitch sent Pastor Art rolling once more. Erin and Ayame were knocked back down. Edward and Cameron crashed through the side railing, about to fall off the fourth floor.

In his subconscious, Alex saw a flash of his late aunty tumbling like a ballerina in her white dress. He felt sadness wash over then resolve as he started reloading the shotgun.

Cameron hung onto a bent pole with one hand, clasped Edward by the ankle in the other, struggling to maintain his grip.

"You let me die here, Cam, I am coming back to haunt your ass for all eternity."

"Dude! Not the time!"

Erin and Ayame staggered up and raced to help.

Before Alex could aim the weapon, he keeled over and held a hand to his stomach. So did Ayame. Cameron and Edward groaned and hissed and winced—the two of them on the edge fighting through the pain and discomfort to hold on and keep from falling. Erin darted her head around, panic stricken.

Shalini relaxed her fingers then lowered her arm. She moved forward, took the shotgun and tossed it aside, pacing in a circle.

With the ball of her foot, from behind, she knocked Alex over with a good hard shove then proceeded to step on him.

"So, preacher man, boss bitch and the pretty boy, boy wonder here." She smacked her lips. "Quite a tasty dish."

"Fuck you!" Alex squirmed on the floor.

She lowered, snatched his head with a strong quick jerk, each tuft of hair about to detach from the scalp from extreme tension. He was helpless as she slammed his face down again and again and again.

"Mmm. Not so pretty anymore."

Blood ran from his nostril, his eyebrow, filled the inside of his mouth from his tongue and his cracked lip.

The heel of her foot twisted into the small of his back.

"Let's see. Ooh. Lookie, lookie, you used to be top honors, huh. This overachiever. And you were supposed to do great and amazing things, make the world a better place. You were meant to be a kind of shining beacon, a hopeful budding example to others. A chosen one. A lucky one. But then you got clobbered by life, beaten, broken, and completely derailed. Off the wagon.

Off track. Off the beaten path. Such a pity. What a giant, giant waste."

"F-fuck you . . . !" Alex fought back hot tears.

"Ah. But there is someone special. The only good thing you got left. The only good thing you ever had. Funny, I thought it was her, your little squeeze."

He peered ahead with narrowed eyes and gritted teeth.

Erin took the lead in yanking Edward up then Cameron, Ayame helping the best that she could.

Pastor Art got to his feet, was about to run at Shalini and Alex, but was flung into a table, breaking it apart.

"This plaything of yours back home. Your partner in crime. Your so-called soulmate. I see the appeal. She's very cute, a cool and groovy chick. And, wowza, the passion and the chemistry. Every little hickey and bite mark. The rug burn. Pull her hair and spank her, huh."

At the edge, the four of them tumbled over to safety with a final heave.

While Erin leaned on an elbow, drained, Cameron shoved up and scrambled to the standing position, limping as he did.

Before he was able to get too close, Shalini twitched again which caused his neck to twist and crack as he fell over with a dull thud.

"CAM!!!!!"

Alex felt his heart drop as he watched Cameron lie there, motionless, eyes closed.

Pastor Art noticed the handgun, crawled over to it. The movement was jerky as his one hand had broken fingers and his other hand was tight at his side.

Both Ayame and Edward gagged on all fours, fought back pain and nausea.

Erin got up and rushed over.

"No, Erin! Wait!!!"

Shalini stood, held an arm out with fingers curled to which Erin floated off the surface, levitating like a lovely assistant in the ultimate illusion.

Her body rotated until she faced up with her back parallel to the floor.

"Ooh. This is too much fun. You obviously have an attachment, a deep connection, though you may try to deny it. I wonder what you would do with this one, hmm? Probably lick her all over, do a little sixty-nine, toss her around and tie her up by the wrists with a belt."

"Please . . . Let her go . . ."

With a swift and hard impact, Erin collided into the floor with brute force.

Bang, bang, bang, bang.

Bang, bang, bang, bang.

Shalini shuddered with each shot, flailing her arms and rotating in place. Enough damage was accumulated that her movements were weaker.

Pastor Art lowered the handgun as Ayame tackled her then Edward.

Alex rushed to Erin, held the sides of her face. She had tears gathered in the corner of her eyes beneath her glasses and fresh blood between her lips and teeth.

"No. Oh, my God."

"A-Alex. My head, i-i-it hurts." Her eyes started glazing over.

His cracked lip quivered as he struggled not to break down.

"You hold on. Okay, Erin?"

"Catch . . . Catch you on the flippity-flip . . ."

Then, with a gentle puff of breath, her eyelids shut and her head fell backwards, limp against his palms. Alex shut his own eyes, half-bawling.

"Got it!" Ayame pulled the necklace from around Shalini, tore it off and threw it.

Shalini shoved Edward and Ayame off, let out an ungodly shriek.

From the two empty holes, streams of blood continued to drip down her cheeks which no longer grinned but scowled.

Pastor Art aimed at the gem shaped like a citrine lozenge and wrapped in intricate silver wiring that resembled veins or roots or weeds.

Bang.

The gusts slowed until there was no wind at all.

Alex rose, moved like a sleepwalker, picking up the shotgun and approaching Shalini whose face returned to normal.

"Please. Please. It wasn't me—"

Without hesitation, Alex pointed the barrel at her torso and pulled the trigger, causing her to crash down. He stepped forward and stood over her thrashing body, aiming at her face which contorted in pain.

The blast left her unrecognizable.

He pumped the slide, about to squeeze the trigger once again but felt Pastor Art touch at his shoulder blade.

"Alexander . . ."

✍

On the ground, in front of Pastor Art and Alex, each limb was splayed out like that of a tattered rag doll. A puddle of blood spilled from the side, beneath the collar bone and above the hips. A messy splatter spread out in a wavy circumference around the head as if it were a macabre halo. The two then turned backwards to face the group. Both moved in closer, got down on their knees in front of Erin on the ground. Pastor Art began to mumble a desperate prayer while Ayame and Edward hovered over Cameron. Ayame had sopping wet cheeks which she wiped at, attempting to regain her composure.

"He's still breathing." She shifted in place, pointed. "Her, too."

"Thank God." Edward placed both hands on top his head.

Pastor Art tucked the handgun away. "What do we do?"

Alex stared at Ayame who paused then spoke.

"Okay, he may have a neck injury so let's secure his head, neck and spine in a neutral position. We will need a few rolled up towels."

"I'm on it." Edward stood, approached the sliding door, was about to go out.

"And get some ice. And tape and scissors."

"Got it."

"She may have a head injury so try to wake her up."

Alex placed the shotgun down, tapped Erin on the cheek. "Hey. Hey."

Pastor Art helped Ayame stabilize Cameron with his good hand.

"Try rubbing at the sternum."

"Erin. Wake up."

"Cops will find us soon." Pastor Art momentarily grimaced in pain. "Once they secure the location, maybe we can straight transport to the hospital side."

Ayame nodded, wiped at her cheeks again.

Edward returned with a roll of tape, scissors, towels and a

plastic bag full of ice. He handed these to Ayame and Alex then joined them on the floor.

There was a long moment of silence, other than a distant gunshot. Alex continued to tap, nudge and rub. Ayame positioned the towels. Whatever tiny sliver of hope began to fall away and diminish.

"A-Alex—?"

When Erin fluttered her eyes open, Alex clasped her hand in his.

"Just hang on, okay? Try to stay awake. We got you ice."

He adjusted the bag that was already melting.

"After they're stabilized, I'll tape your fingers up." Ayame wiped a forearm across her face, this time tears of joy.

Pastor Art nodded, gazed over at Alex and Erin.

His eyes still closed, Cameron then slurred and murmured.

". . . Ding, dong, the motherfuckin' witch is dead."

Edward shook his head with a smile.

Ayame snorted, letting out a contagious laugh.

Pastor Art snickered. "Indeed."

7

SCATTERED ACROSS TWO parallel rows of empty seats in the corner section of the waiting room were the members of the group in various positions. Pastor Art held up his left arm now in a navy blue cast, repositioned then leaned back. Ayame slouched in place, dozed off with her head against the cushion. Edward placed both his elbows on the armrests, laced his fingers in front of him over his stomach. His forearms were wrapped with fresh bandages. Alex was on the other side, facing down to the floor with several bruises and crusted blood. Erin breathed in a long breath while resting her head on his shoulder.

"The doc said you can sleep now. Right, Erin?"

"Yeah. But I'm kinda afraid still. Plus, I won't be able to, not with all we just went through. Maybe in a few hours."

From the door, an aide rolled Cameron in on a wheel-chair. He swiveled and squirmed, had his neck in a soft collar, appeared awkwardly stiff and uncomfortable with his head in a slight tilt. The aide gestured to the group then left.

"Well, what's the verdict?"

"It turns out to be a very bad neck sprain, whiplash basically. And then I guess I hit my head but that's nothing."

Erin raised a finger up. "Mild concussion for me."

Pastor Art pointed to the cast with his good hand. "Three broken fingers. Bastards went and covered my whole dang arm for it."

"Somehow, I'd honestly rather have either of those. I feel so losery, like a god damn poodle in a cone right now."

"I mean, you do look and smell like one." Alex teased with a half-smirk to which Erin chuckled.

Forcing a sarcastic smile, Cameron squinted. "Thank you so much, Alexis. I really needed that kick to the nuts just now."

Ayame reached forward, touched the collar and examined it. "At least it's soft, not hard."

"Yeah, it'll be fine. Though it does hurt and I'll be stuck like this for a bit."

"But seriously, you're very lucky." Alex nodded, shrugged. "I'm glad you're alive, you're awake, not paralyzed or worse. We were freaking out there for a moment, Cam."

"On that note, listen, everyone." Pastor Art cleared his throat and straightened up. "I am so, so sorry. If I had known it would get so vicious, I never would have picked that fight. Please, forgive me. I apologize."

"Pastor, we're okay. We're breathing, aren't we? And it's partially my fault. I am also sorry." Ayame glanced left then right, scanning each of their faces. "I been thinking as we sit here, though, that if things had been different . . . If we weren't there early on to intercept, to intervene and to get the police involved, it would have been way, way worse . . ."

"She could have succeeded."

The preacher skulked. "I know, I know. But I can't help but feel guilty. I feel awful. Look at us. I don't know how I could ever live with myself if anything happened to you. Any of you."

"No. We did the right thing." Erin lifted her head with a smile.

"Plus, it's not like this kinda thing happens every day." Edward raised a brow. "Who woulda knew."

An officer appeared from behind with a clipboard in hand. "Um, I'm looking for a, uh, Mister Arturo Selga?"

"That's me." Pastor Art raised his good hand. "Alexander. Can you help."

∾

Putting the hurt arm around his shoulder, Alex felt Pastor Art shudder to the touch then relax. The cast hung down in front of him. The preacher held his good arm at his side. Both took their time, walked at a slow and steady pace as the officer led them through the short corridor to one of the private offices. First, the officer waited as they entered then closed the door. Then he waited as they made it to the two chairs, sat down, slid closer. Next, he went around and plopped into the swivel chair on the other side of the desk. With a deep breath in and out, the officer blinked and turned to each of them.

"You don't know me, but I'm a friend of your friend. I'm here as a courtesy."

Pastor Art thinned his lips, faced down.

Alex scrunched his brow. "D-did he make it?"

The officer shook his head.

"Fuck."

"Language, Alexander."

"All in all, there were nineteen deaths, thirty-six injured. Several of them police." He paused, tapped the desk with his finger. "I spoke to one of the higher-ups a little while ago. They let me borrow this room to have a private conversation."

Pastor Art swallowed, faced back up.

"Soon, you're all gonna be questioned by local law enforcement. But, within the hour, a division of the FBI will be taking over jurisdiction. These, uh . . . special circumstances . . . need to be handled a certain way. Or so they tell me anyway."

In the window, light pierced the horizon as it changed from dusk to dawn.

"Before I go on, you should know big important people are already doing damage control. They want to bury this as deep as they possibly can. From construction companies to government contracts to the labor union, big bucks are sunk into this place. This goes all the way to the highest level. No media will be running this story. Everybody involved will get fat settlements and nondisclosure agreements, all that legal mumbo jumbo."

"How the heck could they contain this?" Pastor Art adjusted in place.

"Good question. But it seems the lot is very determined. I mean, bad press would kill whatever expansion and investor interest they have planned. Makes sense."

"Do you know more about what happened?" Alex leaned both elbows on the desk, inclined his head. "For instance, everything was going on and I saw writings on the wall. It was like, I don't know, 'B2P' and 'BIIP' or something . . ."

"Yes. Apparently, it turns out this young woman was adopted at a young age by the black sheep of the McGillycuddy family. That man started 'Bridge to Purgatory.' She grew up in a world of luxury and mystique, like royalty. It must have warped her mind because her records indicate a history of bullying, extortion, assault, then depression and also delusions of grandeur later on until she was full-on black magic."

Alex blinked with his mouth agape.

"One of the cultists told us they conjured something, like in a ritual or séance. That whatever it was wanted an ice-cold blood bath on a grand scale." The officer tapped the desk again, swiveled the chair to the side. "You ask me, they're all a bunch of nut bags. Nut balls, simple as that."

"Is that everything?"

The preacher and the officer exchanged a mutual blank stare.

"Yeah. I just wanted you to know, sadly, our friend didn't make it. And I wanted you to know what's about to happen. You did a good thing, to be clear. You all did. However, the world will never know it. Per the cultist, their plan was all one hundred twenty-five beds and every employee in their way. But, there will be no articles, no interviews, no medals, no three-volley salute. Nothing. This never happened, for the record."

Ahead, the light changed from red to green. Now, the first rays of sun began to permeate the atmosphere and blanket the city. Alex saw the outline of Saint Florian fade away in the rearview mirror, caught a glimpse of the van behind them in the side mirror. He signaled, rotated the wheel with his palm then made the turn, glancing at Pastor Art over in the passenger seat. It was quiet out except for the sound of the engine rumbling and the exhaust pipe roaring. As the road before them was less winding, less of a zigzag, more smooth and straight, the two relaxed and opened up. Neither of them wanted to acknowledge it but each could feel this would be one of their last heart-to-heart conversations.

"So, what now, Pastor?"

"I offered for all of us to go get some gyros or kebabs or

something but . . ." The preacher snickered to himself then straightened up. "Nah, but on a serious note, it's been a long friggin' night. Let's go get some shut-eye."

Alex nodded, placing both hands on the steering wheel.

"We're all pretty beat up so pause on investigations, I suppose. I know the list is constant, and it's important to help as many as we can as soon as we can, but look at us. That gives Deids time to take back the helm at least. I'll be packing up and moving home for good. Enough excitement for me to last the rest of my lifetime, I think. Plus, give you guys a break from my quirky ass."

He smirked, glanced to the side.

"Ya know what they say, the show must go on and all of that."

"I guess so. We already covered ghosts and hauntings, a witch. We might as well continue on, huh. Angels and demons next?"

"Heck. We'll find us giants and sea beasts, go to another dimension."

Both laughed as they pulled into the back lot. The van rolled up alongside them.

Pastor Art rested a hand on the handle, paused, turned to Alex. "How 'bout you? What do you think you'll do?"

"Hmm, it might be time to figure out a few things. Life and love, et cetera."

"Never ends. I'm still learning myself. I will say this. Life is messy. It's not a straight line that is black and white. It's this squiggly line and gray area upon gray area, in layers. And love, well, it is just as dang messy if not more so. All is fair. I think the best we can do is take it all in stride and look on the bright side. One day at a time."

As Alex and Pastor Art exited, so did the others.

The six of them came together.

Pastor Art clapped Alex on the shoulder with his good hand. Ayame and Erin embraced and swayed. Edward and Cameron shook hands, closed in for a bro hug.

"I can't say it enough. Thank you all." Ayame scanned their faces one by one. "I can finally rest tonight knowing that it's all over and done, and my children are safe."

"Hey, kinda what we do."

"You're welcome."

Ayame crossed her arms, rocked on her feet. "Maybe I'll invite you guys for dinner sometime. I know Ian and Helena would be happy to see you."

"Of course. Sure. Just let us know."

She went to hug Erin again, Edward, Cameron, Pastor Art and Alex, then walked to her vehicle with a final wave.

"I better head out too. I gotta take another round of antibiotics then pass out." Edward scratched at his beard, twisted on the ball of his foot.

"Ah, man. I wish we could go to a bar, kinda how this started." Cameron grinned, rotated his shoulder and stretched his upper back. "But I am so dead right now. I need to crash."

Pastor Art inclined his head. "What was that one thing again?"

"Jager bomb."

"Right."

"Erin, Alex. Pastor." Edward waved to each of them, started to back away. "You guys take it easy, and we'll talk soon."

"Watch over these two, Alexander the Not So Great." Cameron also turned, lifted a hand up with two fingers showing. "Peace out, y'all."

His pointer and middle finger changed to just the middle finger.

"Oh, what a prick. That's how I know he'll be fine." Pastor Art faced Alex and Erin. "Thanks for driving from the hospital, but I'll manage."

"You sure?"

"Absolutely. I just needed a breather. Miss Woodfeld, are you allowed to drive?"

"No. Pretty sure Cam wasn't supposed to either but just went for it. He said if Batman can do it, why not him."

Pastor Art shook his head. "Of course."

"I can drop her home then help get her car later."

"Sounds like a plan." He patted Alex on the back. "There is one last thing that comes to mind 'fore we call it. And that is Mark 5."

Alex and Erin inclined their heads.

"Jesus helps the man who was plagued, possessed, and He casts out the evil. That man was all alone up until that point, living in the tombs amongst the dead. But after, the man is told to return to family, friends, his people, amongst the living. In other words . . . Loneliness makes people susceptible to darkness. Relationships are the way to keep that darkness at bay."

Pastor Art paused, allowing them all to have an introspective moment.

"Well, it's already way past this old man's bedtime."

The three of them hugged a tight and snug group hug.

"Again, I am so glad you guys are all right."

Erin smiled. Alex smirked. Both watched as the preacher made his way to the muscle car, started it, reversed then drove off.

"Um. You ready to go?"

"I think . . . Let's just stay here awhile. Maybe enjoy the sunrise."

He gazed into her eyes, blinked.

She smiled with a blush.

"Don't overthink it. So emo all the time."

�

It was a long ceremony, with long eulogies and long prayers, then a long viewing. Alex wasn't sure what color to wear but was relieved when he scanned the venue filled with other attendees in mourning. There were rows of fancy wreaths and big banners behind the open casket with an elegant picture frame, which had a vague resemblance to April. The scent of burning incense was soothing despite the somber atmosphere. He placed his white envelope next to the scatter of white envelopes, took a small piece of red thread. During all this, he chose to keep a little distance, out of respect and not burden her further. But there was a moment he noticed her sitting by herself in the corner, dabbing a handkerchief to her eyes.

Alex walked down the aisle and down the row, away from the ongoing, quiet, polite conversation and consolation.

He was wearing all black and she was wearing all white.

April noticed him then broke down, both of her shoulders shuddering as the two embraced and held one another.

"Hey. It's okay. Let it out."

"I'm sorry . . ." She sniffled, dabbed.

While he rubbed at her shoulder blades and the small of her back, he touched his chin to the side of her head. He inhaled the scent of her hair then kissed her on the forehead.

"Thank you for coming."

"Of course, love."

It was an old habit that hadn't faded yet, still came so naturally from his lips. Since it was the two of them sitting alone with a little space between the others, both were able to relax, be open and free like they used to be. Almost like a motor reflex, their hands clasped and their fingers laced.

"We're still wearing our promise rings, huh?"

"Guess I feel sorta naked without it . . ."

"Yeah." Alex swallowed. "About that, I know we already talked about it and this is not the time or place, but are you sure?"

April took a deep breath in, licked her lips. "I think so."

He blinked then nodded. "I never imagined taking a break would have led to us breaking up. I was so sure we were gonna make it."

"Me too."

They gazed at one another, a faint sparkle in their eyes.

"We never did go to Canada." He gave a little half-smirk.

"And I still didn't hear you sing, Nex."

"This is definitely not the time or place for that . . ." Alex widened his eyes, leaned forward. "Unless you wanna hear 'The Reason' by Hoobastank or maybe 'For the First Time' by The Script or something. Death Cab for Cutie."

"I'm game." She winked then raised a brow, appearing as if she forgot where they were for a second. "But pretty sure these people would be like W-T-F."

"You're right, my precious."

He rubbed at her thigh, her knee, took both her hands in his, was so tempted to kiss her right then and there like how he once did.

"So hard to let you go. I don't know if I can." Alex nibbled on his bottom lip. "You were supposed to be the one. You're, like, a part of me . . ."

April squeezed his hands. "Hey, remember our little saying? 'Just be.' Right?"

The two were quiet, scooted closer.

"You know, I always felt like I held you back, Nex."

"What?"

"It was so awesome, our story, our connection. But there was something that always felt a little wrong, almost like it was selfish to keep you. You're more than a mall rat. You're more than an empty nester. In fact, you should have kids. You would make a wonderful father."

"I d-don't need any of that, April. I—"

"See. More than family stuff, personal stuff, I can't keep letting you follow me down this road. I know you were meant for more."

He swallowed, raised a hand and caressed her cheek beneath her dazzly ear. "Do you think we could ever get back together?"

"You never know."

Alex paused, closed his eyes, swept his bangs aside. "What about you? Is everything all right?"

"I'm still working through it. I just wonder, you know, if she is still around somehow in one way, shape or form or another."

He hung his head, lowered his shoulders, realized he never got to tell her everything although he planned to. It was going to be one of the first things he did when they got back together. Now, of course, there would be no point.

"You remember the garlic and the salt when we first moved in?"

She glanced up at him, perplexed.

"I'll tell you. There is a spirit. There is an afterlife. It's as real as the blood pumping in our veins, as real as everything we ever had together. Your mother is not gone. You and your sisters will see her again."

⥼

Each of the deep and dark thoughts floated to the surface, colliding in his skull. Alex stared down at the ground in between his knees, his feet. He adjusted the sleeves of his blazer then hung both hands across his lap and hunched forward. It was nice, quiet, still and empty as he sat on the park bench, watching a single pigeon hop on the grass then along the concrete pavement. While it was so serene and tranquil, he contemplated the harsh lessons about the real world and his place in it, about people and about bonds. The overcast skies spread out above him and covered the afternoon sun.

Just be. Right?

As for LIFE101L, there was always too much to learn and it always seemed too little too late, he realized. In other words, by the time one figures out high school or college, there is already graduation, and by the time one figures a little out about career and health and finance, then there comes all new problems. Next are things like dating and relationships, working on the self, finding the one, settling down, being content, and those stages of development by Freud and by Erikson, as for LOVE102.

Meanwhile, there is also LOSS205 which tends to creep in when one least expects it, hits the hardest and hurts the most. Not just the passing of loved ones, but also healing, and missing someone such as "the one that got away."

In front of him, with a beanie on, a scarf wrapped around

her, with tight jeggings and stylish velvet ankle boots, April stepped on the patches of grass.

Her hair was longer than it had been. His hair was shorter than before.

"Um. Why do you look like the Sad Keanu meme right now?"

Alex smirked, scanned her up and down. "I suppose I could've met you in the dairy aisle, been more like Never Say No to Panda."

She laughed then sat next to him. "Still pretty emo, huh."

"Yeah. I can't help it." He rested an elbow across the top of the bench.

"Listen to any emo music?"

Alex licked his lips, shrugged. "Eh, not as much these days."

"I guess our song is now an emo song. By default." April clasped her hands together, dangled them between her thighs. "Do you remember?"

"Of course. 'Chasing Cars' by Snow Patrol, although I still think 'Open Your Eyes' or 'Signal Fire' would have been fine choices."

"You know, you still never sang for me . . ."

Alex shook his head. "You want some Katy Perry? 'Like a G6' by Far East Movement or 'Dancing on my Own' by Robyn?"

"Hehe. Nah, I'll have to think of something extra embarrassing." Her full lips stretched with her cheeks as she smiled. "Let's take care of that thing then we can chitchat."

"Cool." He handed her the folded paper. "Yeah, our old ride got wrecked while parked on the street. A total loss, the insurance company said. I forgot we're both co-signed on it. I'll give you part of it."

"You don't have to do that. I mean, you've been taking care of it."

"Nah, it's okay. I want to."

"Aww. Such integrity."

She printed, signed and dated, handed it back.

There was a short moment of silence then. Both faced down and forward, peeking over at each other.

"What you been up to these days? Anything new?"

"Not too much. I rekindled my bromance with Brad, if you remember."

"Oh yeah. That's nice."

"Kinda been hanging out, drinking and stuff. Uh, I got into grad school, will be starting that soon. The master's program then maybe doctorate after that. We'll see."

She pointed at her temple above her dazzly ear. "Big brain."

Alex leaned back, shifted, gazed at her.

"Hmm. Doctor Alexander Clark Jacobsen. Very pompous. I love it." April blinked, gazed back at him.

"Your sisters doing all right?"

"Been kind of irking but yeah, more or less." She adjusted her beanie then her scarf. "And you and your dad?"

"I mean, we're okay, mostly ignoring each other in peace."

Crossing her legs, she placed both of her hands together. He straightened up, cleared his throat.

"That time we went up to the Cloud Lookout, I was going to ask you to marry me, you know . . ."

"Really? I had no idea."

"Yeah. Do you think, if I did, things would have been any different?"

April blinked, peered with watery eyes. "Probably."

"Of course." Alex shook his head, slouched. "Such an idiot."

"Don't worry. Plus, still . . . You never know."

While they both said they had somewhere to be and only a short period of time to catch up, the conversation went on and on. It was like when the two were close friends and then more than friends. He watched as she covered her mouth as she leaned back, wiping away the joyous tears.

"Okay, okay. Really, I better go this time, for like the hundredth time."

"I know."

She stood, held her arms out. "Come on. At least forty-five seconds. Remember? It releases the happy chemicals."

As they hugged each other tight, it was if the world disappeared. There was no grass, no trees, no clouds, no birds, nobody else but the two of them. A part of him didn't want to let her go.

"You take care."

He nodded, sat down and stared at her from behind, longing. With each movement, her hips and buttocks were hypnotic. Alex traced the outline of her from that view, trying his best to cease the passage of time and encapsulate that image, every line, every curve.

Each second was like the waning and waxing phases of the moon, full to half to crescent, soon a new moon—a new honeymoon, white, yellow, maybe red, blue.

Despite having seen her eyes flutter and her nose twitch on many occasions, the details were already slipping from his memory. He could remember the taste of her lips and her tongue, the sensation of their palms touching, even her naked body. But, no matter how hard he might try, it became increasingly difficult to recall her face, her smile.

ACKNOWLEDGEMENTS

First of all, I would like to thank my wife, Donna, for all of her ongoing encouragement and support. She helped me to set up a home office and took the lead in caring for the household and our first son, Andrew Nolan Gebhardt. She also carried and delivered our second son as well, Elliott Trent Gebhardt, during the production of this novel. Thank you, babe. We did it again.

Second, I want to thank my little brother, Daniel, who has shaped my taste in all things art. We used to ghost hunt as kids, and were both interested in the unknown. He told me over and over through the years to write horror, and well, here it finally is. I am also frequently featured on his YouTube channel, formerly PandaRoyale and now Pandastic Voyage. Go and check us out.

I want to thank my writing partner, Jeremiah, who writes under JM Payer. We have been working together ever since we met at NaNoWriMo. He helped build my foundation, and kept me coming back when I had fallen off the wagon. This is the third work of mine he's critiqued, and I was so proud when he told me that it broke him. I guess his many notes on adverbs, perspective and scene setting sank in after all. I am the writer I am today, thanks to him.

I want to thank Dr. Laura O'Rourke, a professor of Spanish language and Latin American studies at the University of Hawaii at Manoa who generously offered her expertise in the sections with Mexican Spanish. She helped me to confidently achieve the accuracy I was aiming for.

The professional team under Damon Freeman with their talent and experience working with many established and renowned authors fully realized my vision. Robynne was a treasure, and I appreciate her patience and accommodations. Karis did an outstanding job of piecing together the tones and elements to my liking. This is the second cover of mine that they have produced. Benjamin again worked on the immaculate interior, and I'm grateful for his meticulous work.

SPECIAL THANKS

Ross Allison is a paranormal investigator, lecturer and owner of Spooked in Seattle Ghost Tours. He has written many books on the subject and has done various radio and television appearances from Ghost Hunters to Ghost Adventures, CNN, A&E, The Discovery Channel as well as The Travel Channel, and many more. He was kind enough to spend a solid ninety minutes with me on the phone discussing different topics about the scientific perspective in regards to the paranormal.

Pastor Rodney Wong is a preacher and instructor with master's degrees in religion, divinity and theology. He was awarded by the City and County of Honolulu for his work with the Oahu Community Correctional Center and also volunteers helping youth. We have been acquaintances for a few years now, and talked for a solid ninety minutes on the phone discussing different topics about the spiritual perspective in regards to the supernatural. He also was so helpful with my random questions via text.

Visit my website for more information about myself and about my writing. There are regular news announcements and a blog.

www.tjgiii.com

If you enjoyed this work, please leave a review on Amazon and on Goodreads. Every little bit counts and will help the novel get ranked in the algorithm for others to discover.

To stay up to date with all of the latest posts, follow me on social media. Every like, comment and follow is much appreciated.

www.facebook.com/tjg3words
www.instagram.com/tjg3words
www.x.com/tjg3words

This is the third book in an expanded literary universe. Here is a complete list of the other works available now.

Washington

Everyday Rainbows

www.amazon.com/author/tjgiii

ABOUT THE AUTHOR

Thomas J. Gebhardt III has been seriously writing for eleven years after long days in healthcare, doing occupational therapy in the hospital setting. He lives with his wife and two sons in his hometown of Honolulu, Hawaii. This is his third book, and he did extensive research for authenticity including talking to experts, interviewing a paranormal investigator as well as a preacher, and visiting haunted locations by himself at night with a flashlight. His work is heavily influenced by pop culture including movies, music, shows, video games, comic books, anime and manga.

9 798985 716054